Do You Like Me, Julie Sloan?

A Novel by
Donald Smurthwaite

Bookcraft
Salt Lake City, Utah

All characters in this book are fictitious,
and any resemblance to actual persons,
living or dead, is purely coincidental.

Library of Congress Catalog Card Number: 96-80165
ISBN 1-57008-302-9

First Printing, 1997

Printed in the United States of America

For Mom and Dad,
who reared a Wally Whipple of their own.
With special thanks to
Cory Maxwell, Richard Peterson,
Linda Monson, and Russell Monson.

Contents

CHAPTER 1

September

Today is a day of destiny for Wallace F. Whipple, a time that will rank right up there with the big events of my life—birth, baptism, marriage, and tasting chocolate-covered doughnuts for the first time.

I can see the next life now. My family and friends, every bishop I've ever had, and some other Extremely Important People crowd into a celestial theater, a place where no one in front of you can block your view. The lights go dim, and the polite chatter hushes as the music—I prefer Sinatra singing "I Did It My Way" but am not sure they're into him up there—comes on. Big letters blaze across the screen—*The Wallace Whipple Story*—and soon the major events of my mortal existence come flickering onto the screen, except for the things I've repented of, which have been conveniently edited out, mostly scenes involving Natalie, my maximally obnoxious sister.

My whole life passes by on the giant screen while all my bishops take notes and nod approvingly and I say a silent prayer that I get nothing but thumbs-up reviews. And today, August 31, a warm Saturday in Portland, Oregon, will be right in there with the best, a day that I will rack up some big-time brownie points.

You see, today I got my Eagle Scout award. *Finally.*

What can I say about my Eagle? It only represents years of sweat, worry, toil, tenacity, setting goals, and achieving them all. At least, that's what my mom did. Me? I just kept reacting to her prodding, both gentle ("How are we coming on your communications merit badge, Wally?") and the more direct approach ("If you ever hope to place your hands on a steering wheel and foot on a gas pedal before your 21st birthday, you will earn your Eagle").

Not that this day of note started in any spectacular fashion. I got up at my usual Saturday morning time, about 10:00. After an intense regimen of breakfast, changing clothes, and then briefly lying down for another hour, I decided to get up and do something significant—eat lunch. I wanted to preserve my energy for the big Eagle court of honor in the evening. Then Dad got home from the Aisles of Value store, where he is the incomparable hardware department manager.

"Well, son, I notice that the lawn isn't mowed yet," Dad said, dropping a hint about the size of the Statue of Liberty. "Isn't that your job? And the lawn needs to be edged, too."

I don't like it when parents pose a question that they— and you—know the answer to: "Shouldn't you be doing your homework instead of watching reruns of *Gilligan's Island?*" "Now don't you have a service project with the Young Men scheduled tomorrow morning?" "Isn't that your job, Wally?" We need more parents who simply speak out to their teenagers, who aren't afraid to have open and honest communication.

"Wally, you'd better get moving on the lawn or else you'll be late for the court of honor," Dad zeroed in.

Scratch that last statement about open and honest communication.

"Yeah, Dad. But I figured even more grass would be

there Monday, meaning I'd get more accomplished with the same amount of work. Besides, I sort of wanted to preserve my energy for tonight. Does that make sense?"

"No, Wally. And if you take the third door on the left, you'll be in the garage, where you can find the lawn mower."

"Got it, Dad. But I hope I have some energy left for tonight."

"You will, son. Somehow, you'll rise to the occasion."

Years of experience at dealing with my parents has taught me many things, including knowing when the time comes to give up. So I went to the garage and shoved our lawn mower around to the front of the house. It was warm outside, and I decided in a fit of reckless abandon to rip off my shirt.

No big deal to get a little tannage on a nice summer day, you might say, unless you happen to be 6′4″ and crush the scales at 138 pounds, which I do, and taking off your shirt even in the semiprivate confines of your front yard might provoke a riot. A riot of laughter, that is, as your pea-sized muscles sculpted upon your spaghetti-thin physique ripple in the sun. But, I thought, I gotta be me, so off went the shirt.

I spent the next hour in a Saturday ritual for Whipple males, breathing gaseous fumes and pushing the lawn mower around our fairly huge yard, followed by another hour of grunting as I rolled our lawn edger, a tool so old that it can probably trace its roots back to New England about the time the *Mayflower* landed, along the curb and sidewalk.

By the time I finished, I realized that it had been almost four hours since my last nap, and I decided to put on my shirt and coast a bit. I went upstairs, fluffed a pillow, tossed it on the floor, flopped down on it, and soon was in la-la land.

I truly believe that being able to fall asleep almost anytime, anywhere, and under any conditions is a talent and should be listed in the scriptures as such, so that parents can't get on your case so much.

PARENT #1: "Is Lester asleep again? That's his fourth nap today! Why can't he put his time to better use, like doing the grocery shopping or composing an opera?"

PARENT #2, who is the wiser of the pair: "Dear, we must remember that sleeping is a gift, and our young Lester is immensely talented when it comes to crashing. It says so in the Bible, the Third Book of Malavusians, chapter six, verse one. 'And wo be unto the Hittites, who did not take their naps and now are cursed and waxed sore.' Consider that he is only exercising his gift from above."

PARENT #1: "I suppose you're right. I forgot about the Hittites."

It seems only a short time later—mere minutes, really—when Mom is nudging my shoulder. "Wally, it's time to get up. Your court of honor starts in less than an hour. You need to get cleaned up and into your uniform."

I sit up, groggy. "I gotta shower? Can't I just heavily deodorize myself, Mom?"

"No, Wally. We want you to *be* an Eagle, not smell like one."

Natalie walks by my door. "Saw you outside without your shirt on, Wally. Seriously, I don't see how you could mow the lawn and fight off crazed women at the same time. Unless you turned sideways and they couldn't see you."

"Cute, Nat. At least I don't have withdrawal pains whenever I'm away from a mirror for more than ten minutes."

"That's enough, both of you," Mom warns. "We don't have time to see who can be the most clever. Wally, clean up. *Now!*"

For the second time this afternoon, I recognize the signs of defeat.

I hustle to get myself cleaned up, put on my Scout uniform, and adjust my sash with all of my merit badges on it. I am knotting my neckerchief when Chuck, my six-year-old brother, comes in and stares at me for a few seconds.

"You look nice, Wally," he finally says. "You look like a hero."

Chuck is cool.

"About ready, Wally?" Dad asks.

"Yeah."

"Hmmm. I don't think so. You look a little grungy. Better shave before we head over," Dad says, gazing at the raging crop of peach fuzz sprouting across my upper lip.

"Yeah. Don't want to look raunchy. Doesn't quite go with getting an Eagle," I agree, running my hand across my face.

"Don't scrape your hand, son."

So I shave quickly but carefully, thinking it would not be cool to cause a blood-spurting wound 15 minutes before my hour of glory. I rush down the hall towards the front door when Natalie comes out of her room and we sort of collide in the hallway. Natalie has on a dress, and she looks really nice. Of course, she almost always does, except for early in the morning, which, in her world, means anything before 9:00 A.M.

"Got your stuff memorized, Wally?" she snickers.

"Ha! No problem. I have the Scout Oath down cold. I can say it forward. I can say it backward. I can splice it and dice it, bend, fold, or spindle it. Any way you want it dished up."

"Bet you forget it. Remember Primary advancement?"

"A mere fluke, Nat. And you are probably the only semi-human being on the face of the earth who remembers what happened."

Actually, this is maiming the truth somewhat. Anyone who was awake at sacrament meeting that day will remember. The bishop had me come up to the stand and said all of these cool things about me, you know, basically how wonderful I was and how they'd miss me in Primary where I was a tremendous leader, and by the way, would I mind picking out my favorite article of faith to recite to the congregation?

Naturally, I had planned for this moment and had practiced the thirteenth article about 9,000 times. I began confidently, "We believe . . ."

After that, things sort of went downhill. Like nothing else came out of my mouth as my mind suddenly went off on a deep space mission. The bishop sort of coaxed me through it, while my family slumped lower and lower in the pew.

But that was then and this is now, and there is no way I will blank out on the Scout Oath. I am a more mature and confident Wally, old enough to date and use mouthwash. At the church, an amazing thing happens. We are set to have the court of honor in the Relief Society room, but about five minutes before it is ready to start, the place is already filled with people. Bishop Winegar leans over to Dad and says, "We'd better move to the chapel. Wally is a popular young man, it appears."

So we move and I sit on the front row. I don't dare look behind me. How many people are here? Is all this really happening? I mean, I figured about a dozen, maybe 20 at most, would bother to show up, and that includes my family.

We get through the basics—you know, the welcome, the Pledge of Allegiance, the opening prayer—and suddenly, Brother Hansen, my priests quorum adviser, who is conducting, is asking the honor guard to escort me to the front of the chapel. A couple of the younger Scouts walk with me up to the front and I turn slowly by the podium. And what do I see?

My life. That's what. Basically my whole life. There must be one hundred people down there, all looking at me.

Yeah. My family. Mom, Dad, Chuck, and Natalie, who is turning her head around, checking to see whether any hunks are in the audience and whether they've noticed her.

Bishop Winegar, who got me started on writing a journal last year and who taught me about what it means to be mature.

Sister Lawson, a widow in our ward, whom Dad and I home teach, someone who has become a friend.

Lumpy Felton, my best friend since the time we were in Sunbeams together, a man who would go anywhere and do anything for me, especially if food is involved. And a bunch of other friends—Mel, Rob, Mickey, and more.

Amy Hassett, a friend in the Fourth Ward, who once asked me to dance with her although I was so nervous that I essentially became a quivering mass of blubbering jelly.

Edwina Purvis, math genius who got me through algebra, and the person I will remember throughout the eternities as the first girl I ever went on a real date with.

And get this—*Julie Sloan*, the girl for whom I have had a mad raving case of *like* ever since she walked into my seminary class almost a full year ago, a girl who finally went out with me last May on what turned out to be the world's worst date ever. I mean, we are talking instant relationship amputation with gangrene immediately setting in. It was that bad. But she is here, tonight, and could it mean . . . could it mean . . . that perhaps there is a millionth part of *like* for me somewhere in her soul of souls?

There are others. Brother Pinster, my all-world Scout leader, the man who taught me how to tie a bowline knot and avoid passing out at the sight of blood. Sister Donahue, my Primary president. And literally, almost a hundred more. It is wonderful.

I feel almost like a real human being.

The only people missing from this mass of humanity that makes up my life are Orville Burrell and Joe Vermeer. Orville is a cowboy supremo, a guy who moved to town last year, became a great friend, and then almost got baptized. He is back on his ranch outside of Heppner, buckin' hay bales, ridin' horses, wrasslin' his dawgs and steers, cuttin' a little wheat, and sayin' "dang," "howdy," and "pleased to meetcha" to everyone he meets. But I hope to see him again, too. Joe is simply extremely cool, extremely smart, extremely spiritual, and extremely athletic—the last extreme explaining why he left in early August to begin his collegiate football career at BYU.

The ceremony moves on. Soon, the honor guard is bringing Mom and Dad up to stand beside me. Chuck is all eyes. He thinks I'm a hero. Cute.

And maybe I am, at least to him.

Time to put the Eagle pin on my mother. I fumble with it for a few seconds. I am very careful with it, not wanting to draw blood. Steady, Whipple. Nerves of steel. I snap the pin into place and look into her eyes. Mom, knowing me well, nods slightly, a sign to me that I have not mortally wounded her. I reach for the tie tack for Dad. He has worn one of his old crummy ties, I know, because he hates tie tacks and figures if he's going to ruin a tie, it might as well be an old one. I get the tie tack on, Mom gives me a hug, and I shake hands with Dad. Perfect so far.

Now I'm getting the Eagle charge. Brother Hansen is leading up to my big moment. I glance toward the audience—Julie is here. Awesome. Who told her? I'd only seen her three times this summer, once at the grocery store and twice at stake dances. And after our disastrous date, she

treated me with all the respect and accord I deserved—
which is to say she didn't get any closer to me than an
NBA three pointer and said absolutely nothing to me. But
she is here. Maybe something clicked. Maybe she would
go out with me again. Maybe she decided our date wasn't
that bad after all, that it was fun, in sort of a bizarre way . . .

"Wally, I said, can you recite the Scout Oath now for
us?" Brother Hansen's voice beams me back to reality.

"Oh yeah. Sure." I make the Scout sign. Julie is here.
Julie is here. I thought it was over, but maybe it's not. Is
the future Mrs. Whipple out there watching me at this
proud moment, adoration spilling from her eyes like engine coolant boiling over when your car overheats? I can't
concentrate . . .

"Uh, on my honor . . ." I shoot a look out at the audience. "Let's see. On my honor, I will . . . do my best . . ." Do
my best not to fall in *like* with Julie again . . . but why did
she come? The answer has to be that she still feels a tiny
spark of *like* and is willing to forgive and forget our disastrous date last May.

But the Scout Oath. Oh no. It's happening—again. My
mind is going as blank as a white bedsheet. I look into the
congregation. Natalie slyly moves her right hand up
around her neck and squeezes, the universal sign for chok-
ing. Chuck looks puzzled. Lumpy is trying to mouth the
words to me, but I can't tell what they are.

Brother Hansen whispers, ". . . to do my duty to God
and my country . . ."

"Oh yeah," I mumble and slowly repeat what he says. I
feel dizzy. Every brain cell ever known to have existed
within the confines of my cranium is strapping on a para-
chute, looking at each other, and saying, "The kid's going
under. Time to bail! Geronimo!" I fumble for words, then
start repeating again after Brother Hansen. Every sweat
gland in my body is on red alert. I could make a tremen-

dous contribution to the Great Salt Lake right now. Near the end, I make a slight comeback, coming out of my near comatose state to finish up on my own, " . . . and keep mentally awake [yeah, sure] and morally straight."

Brother Hansen gives me a pained smile, then turns to my closest one hundred friends minus Orville and Joe, and says, "Even the best Scouts can get a case of stage fright. I know that Wally has the Scout Oath memorized, but he just got the jitters tonight."

After the ceremony ends, I spend a little time schmoozing with my friends and the adults who are there. I mentally note, however, that Julie doesn't seem to want to get any closer to me than say, the same zip code, and gives me only a quick "Congratulations" before beating a safe retreat out of the church and into the parking lot with Amy.

Lumpy, on the other hand, is ecstatic about the evening's events. "Great cake, Wally. Do you think your mom would mind if I have thirds?" Loyal Chuck still follows me around and looks extremely proud of his older brother, while Natalie, obviously disappointed in the hunk turnout, spends most of the evening sulking in a corner.

Oh well. What can I say? All those people turning out to honor me and I can't even recite the Scout Oath? Julie is going to think that I'm not just a dork on dates, but that I'm like this all the time.

What does that say about me?

Guess it's simple. For better or worse, good times and bad, long stretches of geekiness interrupted by rare and unexplainable moments of cool, I'm still Wally Whipple.

SUNDAY, SEPTEMBER 1

I started writing in journals about a year ago. Not that it was my idea. It was Bishop Winegar's. He pulled me into his office for the old birthday interview, and then toward the end, after I started to feel pretty good about things, he handed me the 200-page-long diary, and, well, challenged me to write in it for a year.

My reaction was underwhelming. I mean, I greeted this journal business about the way I would if my dentist had said, "Wally, you have a tooth that needs to be pulled today, but all my dental tools are out for cleaning. Mind if I use these hedge trimmers that I brought from home this morning?"

Yeah, you got it. Not exactly brimming with enthusiasm.

But I started writing . . . then I wrote a little more . . . then some more . . . and pretty soon it was a routine part of the day. Looking back, I can see how I changed as I filled those 200 pages right up, all before June rolled around. I felt good about the whole experience, too.

Then came summer, and as quickly as I got into the habit, I got out of the habit.

Oh, I had reasons. Getting my driver's license was a huge priority. Then came finishing my Eagle Scout project. Then . . . then . . . well, it was summer, and the days were warm and I worked . . . and . . . big deep breath, square up, Whipple, face it like a man: I got lazy.

This is where Mom entered. Parents, I think, have a little computer chip implant that lies dormant until their oldest child turns into a teenager. The chip's sole purpose is to make little beeping noises that only a parent can hear whenever a teenager starts to slack off. I truly believe this. Try it. Don't make your bed, for instance, and before you know it, your mom is on your case. (The computer chip in mothers, I am sure, is slightly more sensitive than the one in fathers.) "Wilbur, have you made your bed this morning? No? I hope you don't expect me to. You're 18 years old and I am not your maid."

Anyway, the chip started beeping after about a week of me not writing in the journal. "Wally, have you written in your journal?" Mom began asking.

"I'd really like you to keep up on that journal, son," Dad would gently remind. "Written anything lately?"

"Well, no, like, not exactly, but I plan to. Really soon. Honest. Promise."

That bought me a few days, maybe a week. Then Mom began to turn up the jets a bit. "Wally, you know if Bishop Winegar asks how your journal is coming, you'll have to tell the truth."

"I know, Mom. Not smooth to lie to a bishop. Don't worry."

A few more days went by, and I thought that maybe, just maybe, the chip short-circuited because all was quiet. Then Mom fired another volley at dinner one night. "Wally, you know, I was reading a wonderful book last night about the pioneers. Just think what we'd miss if they'd never kept journals."

"A whole lot, Mom."

"You need to write in your journal again, Wally."

"I know, Mom. And I will. Promise."

She lowered the big guns. "You said that last time, dear."

I was desperate, so I called up my last line of defense. "Mom, I don't have a journal. I've been meaning to get one, but I've been pretty busy this summer."

"I think we can solve that."

And the next night, there was a new journal right on my pillow. And a bill from Mom, indicating I owed her $9.95.

Just then she happened (coincidence, of course) to poke her head into the room, which I share with Chuck. "Good, Wally. I see you found the journal," she said innocently. "Guess you have no excuses now. No need to procrastinate any longer."

Procrastinate. I hate that word. It sounds like a disease. It ranks right in there with other words from the *Parental Dictionary of Words to Make Your Kids Tense*, such as *obstinate, insolent,* and *belligerent.*

I was whipped. Mom knew it. I could almost hear her thinking, "Got you, son. Now, do I have to get a pen for you?" That was Thursday. I managed to squeak out another couple of days, mostly by carefully posing with pen in hand, slouched on my bed, and staring intently into my journal. But with the Eagle court of honor last night, I figured I might as well get on with it again so that my posterity would someday be moved to tears as they read of my struggles to overcome my compulsive nerdiness and the constant trial of being closely related to my sister, Natalie.

Well, maybe it doesn't quite compare to pushing a handcart across the plains in the dead of winter, but it's the best I can do.

At any rate, it looks like I'm back in the journal business again.

MONDAY, SEPTEMBER 2

Labor Day. The last whiff of a dying summer before school once again splashes into the otherwise calm flow of my life.

Yeah, school dead ahead. My junior year. I remember how nervous I was at this time last year, when I was ready to plunge into the mysterious world of high school, where football players, cheerleaders, and other alien life forms lurked in almost every hallway. I remember the night before I started high school last year, and how I had an anxiety attack wondering what I would do if, like, a really gorgeous girl noticed me and maybe even said hello to me. I wondered if it would be okay to say something back to her or if that would break some sort of high school social rule.

Oh, man. What a dork I was a year ago! A mere child. A babe in the woods. And by the same token, it is easy to see how much I have matured in the last year and how my confidence has sprouted like dandelions in the front yard. Yes, Wally Whipple is a much smoother version this year, even with the occasional tilting of the windmills of my mind, such as bombing the Scout Oath Saturday night. But this is the New Wally Whipple, a sturdy oak tree where only an acorn feebly lifted its tentacles skyward at this time last year.

Proof?

Well, let's just say that, you know, your basic super model type does come up to me in the hallway this year, smiles a dazzling smile, and says, "Hi. I'd really like to get to know you better this year. Would you be free on Saturday night?"

Last Year's Wally would have panicked, mumbled something incoherent and utterly unintelligent, then would have attempted to cram himself into his locker until the immediate danger had passed. Wally This Year will know exactly what to do, a man in complete and utter control: he would tilt his head to expose his most ruggedly handsome features, and serenely mumble, "Yo."

Now is that progress or what?

TUESDAY, SEPTEMBER 3

First day of school, and no problems. Smooth sailing from period one through period eight. Hey, I can sleep-walk my way through this year.

Well, maybe. There are a couple of hitches in my giddyup, if you know what I mean.

Take my schedule. I had a big surprise.

First period, math.

Having math the first period of the day should be declared unconstitutional. Math at 7:55 A.M. means you actually have to start thinking about it, say, at breakfast, so that enough of your brain is up and running to handle quadratic equations. It is not natural to be groping for a box of cold cereal and also trying to get a grip on solving conditional inequalities.

Nevertheless, it is the hand dealt to me by the computer that schedules classes.

And that's the easy part of math. Last year, I got a B in math, thanks mostly to Edwina Purvis, who took pity on me and sort of walked me through anything I didn't understand. Although it became almost a full-time job, Ed never complained and always seemed happy to help out. This year, unfortunately, Ed is not in my class, which means I'll be on my own. What's worse, Dick Dickson is in my class.

Dick Dickson is a classic nerd, sort of a toadstool in the great landscape of high school life. I would have hardly noticed him—except for his high-water pants, thick glasses, squeaky voice, fuzzy upper lip, and dazzling array of maximumly grotesque plaid shirts—had I not trounced him in the elections last spring for junior class sergeant at arms. Dick took the election, shall we say, *very* personally. I think he would have won it, except for a severe case of election eve cockiness that inspired him to distribute a flyer bearing my likeness and saying some definitely uncool things about me on it. It blew up on him, and the soon-to-be-junior class, in a moment of extraordinary insight and wisdom, elected me. Anyway, Dick wouldn't even talk to me after the election, other than to snarl, hiss, grumble, and generally act as though he were two years old again. The silent period in our relationship came to a screeching halt today in math, as Dick sidled up next to me.

"So, Whipple. We meet again. I look forward to having you in math class. Perhaps we can put problems on the board together. Perhaps I can prove to you who is better suited to elective office at school."

"Well, Dick, sorry, but I just don't see how being in the same math class can prove anything about the election."

"I wouldn't expect so, given your mental make-up."

"Dick, do us both a favor. Stay calm, and although it may be genetically impossible, try to be cool this year. We have 189 days of school left, and I'd like them to be pleasant."

"Pleasant? Yes, they'll be pleasant. Of that I'm sure."

"Dick, you have really bad breath. Again. Go drink a quart of mouthwash."

He looked startled, then slithered over to a desk an aisle away. That, I hope, will be the extent of our interaction this year, but I'm guessing not.

The last minor problem is that I somehow got placed in the advanced metal shop class for second period instead of the elective I signed up for—advanced boys choir. I'm sure a quick trip to the old counselor's office this week will straighten that out, because I feel somewhat uncomfortable in metal shop, where I am probably the only guy who does not have any of the following:

A. At least one earring.

B. At least one tattoo.

C. At least one conviction. Yes, I mean *that* kind of conviction.

My other classes are normal—English, social studies, biology, journalism, and Spanish. I decided to take Spanish because a foreign language is a must if you want to further your education anywhere beyond truck driving school and I already have a few of the Spanish basics down—*burrito, enchilada, San Francisco,* and *Canada* come to mind, for example.

Enough for one day. Chuck is in Adios City (another handy Spanish phrase) sending sweet Zs to the sky.

I plan to join with him in the snoring serenade in a matter of mere minutes.

Thursday, September 5

Had my visit with the school counselor today, and it looks like I might be in advanced metal shop for a few more days, despite not knowing the difference between an arc welder and an archangel.

I approached Mr. Scleavege, the metal shop teacher, and tried to tell him about my problem. "Uh, Mr. Scleavege, my name is Wally Whipple and I don't think I should be in your class."

He pulled back some sort of face protector mask and set down some kind of welding gizmo. "What's that? Your name is Whiffle?"

"No, Whipple. Anyway, I think the computer made a mistake. I'm not supposed to be in this class—"

"Nonsense. Every boy should take metal shop. Every boy needs a skill. Look around and see the things these boys are making. You can't help but feel the excitement."

I looked around. Most guys, it seemed, were working on motorcycle parts.

"Yeah, I see, Mr. Scleavege, but I still don't think I belong!"

"These are skills that you can enjoy your whole life," droned the king of high school metalworks.

I was beginning to think that Mr. Scleavege had spent a little too much time around the solvent vat. Along with working on their motorcycles, the only other time the guys in this class would use their metal shop skills would probably be when the warden was asleep and they were trying to cut the bars off their cells.

Mr. Scleavege put his welder's mask back on. I was getting a little desperate. "But I haven't taken introduction to metal shop. That's why I don't belong."

Home run, Whipple.

Mr. Scleavege pulled his mask off again. "Oh. Why didn't you say so? Tomorrow morning, you run down to the office and get signed up for beginning metal shop. Then you can take this class next year. Every boy needs to know a trade. Did I mention that?"

I was as close as I was going to get. This was not the time to tell him the truth about my transfer. "Thanks, Mr. Scleavege."

So with any luck at all, I'll be singing my little heart out by the end of the week, in a room where tattoos, earrings, and blossoming criminal records are definitely not the norm. Will I ever be glad!

FRIDAY, SEPTEMBER 6

Upside:

In all my anxiety over advanced metal shop, I neglected to mention several most excellent circumstances regarding the matriculation of Wallace F. Whipple, Jr. I have two of my good buds, Lumpy and Mel Pyne, in biology class. Another friend, Rob Young, is in Spanish, so I can practice my "Como esta is your el taco?" with him. And not that I care, not that I hardly noticed, not that it's any big deal . . . but Julie Sloan is in my English class. It just so happens that English is my best subject and that my English teacher last year, Mrs. English, all but assured me a future Nobel Prize for literature. Not that I care, not that it matters, not that I have any, you know, feelings, for Julie, but if you're going to have a girl in your class that you one time felt intense *like* for, then it might as well be a class where you are a star and not one where you will be subject to intense emotional anxiety.

What I am saying is, English class should give me the chance to do a little basic showing off for Julie, just in case there is the tiniest trace of emotion buried somewhere deep in the ventricles of her heart.

Downside:

I went to the school counselor's office, where I talked with a woman who looked like she had lived on nothing but antacids for the last week of her life. Her basic answer was, "Kid, get in line. The computer messed up big-time, and we're straightening these things out one at a time. Let's see, your name begins with a *W*, so we should get to you by the end of next week. In the meantime, go build an airplane or something in metal shop."

Living life near the end of the alphabet is the pits. But until Miss Antacid can get me into the choir, I guess I'd better try to look busy in advanced metal shop. Maybe I could work on paper clips.

Sunday, September 8

Two challenges lay dead ahead.

One is early-morning seminary. Very early morning seminary, as it so happens in Portland. Our class starts at 6:30 A.M. That's 6:30 in the morning, a time when only bakers, milk truck drivers, criminals, and Mormon youths are bumbling around in the darkness. Last year my dad served as the alarm clock, gently whispering to me, "Wally, it's 5:30, time to get up. Rise and shine!" It's nothing to do with my dad, but I can hardly bear to hear those words now, "Rise and shine!" Once, I heard them on TV while I was about half-asleep on the couch, and—true statement—I pulled myself up off the couch, stumbled down the hallway, and began to brush my teeth before I realized that it was Saturday afternoon and seminary was at least 36 hours away!

This year, I have negotiated to sleep in until 5:53 A.M., which represents the very last minute that I can get up and still make it to seminary on time, fully dressed, clean and without any of my clothes on wrong side out. I did this through my "early-morning back-to-basics approach":

1. Shower the night before.

2. Sleep in my school clothes to the degree possible. This, however, does not include wearing my tennis shoes to bed for obvious reasons. Good thing the wrinkled look is in.

3. Pour my breakfast cereal into a bowl the night before.

4. Do all the little things right, such as knowing exactly where my wallet and schoolbooks are and putting toothpaste on my toothbrush before I go to bed.

5. Shave only on weekends, as long as my hormonal system permits.

6. Bounce out of bed the second the alarm goes off. I can no longer sort of drift back to sleep for even a few pleasurable minutes.

I mentioned all this to Dad, who sounded, shall we say, a little skeptical, especially about my sleeping in my school clothes. However, recognizing the unmistakable signs of genius in his son, he relented, sort of.

"We'll give it a try until you're late for seminary. After your first tardy, then we'll move the clock up ten minutes."

Yes! Twenty-three more minutes of sleep a night. Over the course of the school year, that means slightly more than 3,900 minutes—or 65 hours—more sleep than last year! I'm already feeling better about seminary!

Wish I could say the same thing about challenge #2. Cross-country. I know what everyone says about cross-country: the sport of choice for geeks everywhere. So far, I've managed to avoid Mr. Leonard, the cross-country coach, but I know it's only a matter of time before he catches up with me, casts his eyes on my extraordinarily long (but slow) legs, and gives me some kind of sales pitch that will have me believing I'm a shoo-in for the next three Olympic games and a seven-figure sports shoe company contract. But I'm ready for him. This year, I'll just say, "No!"

I hope it works.

Monday, September 9

A quick check-in tonight:

Number One. My seminary sleep-in plan worked to perfection. Walked into class with at least 45 seconds to spare.

Number Two. My seminary teacher is Sister Habben, who is from Chicago and talks cool. (Although I have a hard time imagining her saying, "Da Bears.") I think it is going to be a good year.

And yes, Julie is in my class, although I hardly even noticed her in her jeans, tan top, and white sweater, with a white ribbon in her hair, as she sat on the second row, fourth chair, in between Amy Hassett and Jill McDonough.

Number Three. Still no word on my transfer out of advanced metal shop, where most of the guys are now into building heavily armored tanks.

Number Four. Overheard Natalie on the phone with one of her friends, worried sick about her tan, or more to the point, her lack of one. "I feel like everyone is watching me, and when I walk by, they go, 'Wow, Natalie Whipple didn't do any tannage this summer.' It makes me really self-conscious, and that's not like me, because I hardly ever think about myself, except for how good I look. Seriously."

After she hung up, I couldn't help walking by her a few minutes later and sweetly saying, "Natalie, are you feeling okay? You look a little pale." This produced a fast trip to the bathroom, where she stood in front of the mirror for 15 minutes looking for her tan line and mumbling about the rotten weather we had in Portland this summer.

It was mean, I know, but I couldn't help it. I'll begin repenting soon, perhaps as early as next week—sometime.

Number Five. I do not want to foolishly fritter away my extra 23 minutes of life a day, so I am going to Z-land right now. Wally Whipple, signing off, or as we say in Spanish class, "El Waldo es una into siesta muy bueno."

WEDNESDAY, SEPTEMBER 11

Okay, it happened today. Mr. Leonard, part bloodhound that he is, hunted me down and caught up with me just as I was heading into the cafeteria. Brace yourself, Whipple, I said to myself. Think of him as temptation—show ultimate resistance. Repeat slowly, "I will not be a cross-country nerd this year."

I was ready for his best shot—and ready to dish it right back.

"Wally. Good to see you again," he said cheerily.

"Uh, thanks. Nice to see you, too, Mr. Leonard."

"Have a good lunch." Then he continued walking right on toward the teachers' cafeteria. Not a word about cross-country. Hmmmm. Does he think I'm unworthy? Nothing to offer the team? *Not good enough for his crummy old team?* What is going on here?

Still no progress on the "Free Whipple from Metal Shop" front. Mr. Scleavege did ask me what I was planning for a project, and on a whim I blurted out that I wanted to build an Indy car. Some of the budding criminals in class sort of nodded approvingly, although I realistically have as much chance of building an Indy car as they do of understanding the time-space continuum. Anyway, Mr. Scleavege, once again probably wandering too close to the heavy metal vat, just mumbled, "Good, good, Whiffle. Let me see your plans when the time comes."

Am I ever going to get out of this class?

FRIDAY, SEPTEMBER 13

Not that I'm dwelling on metal shop, but I guess I'm dwelling on metal shop. Because math and metal shop are so far from my locker, I usually take my books, coat, lunch, and all my other junk to the closet in the classroom, leave them there, then dump them in my locker after second period when I have to walk right by it. But today someone stole cupcakes out of my lunch sack.

I sort of like to think of Mom as the Einstein of baking. She is a genius with a cup of flour and a little baking soda and salt. She could bake dirt clods and somehow make them taste good. For this reason I enjoy it when I have a sample of her labors in my lunch sack.

But when I opened my lunch bag today, no cupcakes. Snatched clean out of the sack.

Who's responsible? I have a suspect: Evan Trant.

Evan, also known as "Spider," "Gorilla," and several other names derived from the animal kingdom, is the star of metal shop class. He has tattoos. He has a ponytail. He has earrings. He has biceps the size of a culvert and a personality to match. Since his locker is right above mine (thanks to "Trant" immediately preceding "Whipple" in the alphabetical order of our class), rummaging through my lunch bag would be a piece of, well, cake. Evan has so far ignored my existence, other than to once look at me and sneer, "Wimp Pole. Bad name, dude." I think he is building an aircraft carrier in metal shop.

So what should I do about my cupcakes? Evan is not the kind of guy you accuse of stealing your cupcakes, at least unless you want to undergo a series of surgical procedures to repair your face. I can see it now:

ME: (dressed in white, pushing my way through the saloon doors) "I'm a here to settle a score. Trant, you're a sidewindin', low-life, cupcake-stealin' varmint."

HIM: (dressed in black, slowly sipping a root beer) "You callin' me a cupcake thief? Them's fightin' words and you better be smilin' when you say that, pardner."

ME: "Yep. You heard me right. I ain't smilin', neither. And I think yer yallow, too."

And what follows is not a pretty sight.

So for now, I guess, I won't do anything. Yeah, I know, chicken way out. But I once heard (I think on TV, maybe a *Brady Bunch* rerun) that it takes as much courage to walk away from a fight as to get into one. (I think Alice the maid said it.) And if the Very Tense Woman in the counselor's office finally gets me into choir, then I won't have anything to worry about anyway. Evan Trant will become a small, albeit ugly, clause in the book of my life.

Monday, September 16

First cross-country meet this week, and Coach Leonard has not yet come begging me to join the team. After school today, I saw the varsity working out, and it looked like they only had seven or eight guys. That's not enough to have much of a chance. But why hasn't he even mentioned it to me? A little attention and who knows? Maybe I would have joined up. Has Mr. Leonard lost his touch? This is a guy who could sell blue shirts to missionaries. He's that good. But a polite wish for a good lunch is all he's said to me since school started.

I don't get it.

WEDNESDAY, SEPTEMBER 18

Something has been nagging me about school, and I don't mean the missing cupcakes (for the record, two more were lifted yesterday and Evan Trant was all smiles during class), and I don't mean waiting until the next decade to get into boys choir, where I belong. I figured out today what didn't seem right to me in the hallowed halls of Benjamin Franklin High School this year.

There is no Orville Burrell.

Orville came clomping into my life last year during English class. At first, I didn't know what to make of someone who had spent more time on a horse than I had on a bicycle, but we started hanging out together and purtinear (a word that Orv taught me—means sort of close) became best friends.

How do I describe Orv? Well, from his own cowboy talk, *steady.* Always there. Solid. Dependable. Loyal. Smart. Sensitive. Orville is a guy you can count on. We almost had him baptized, but then he and his dad packed up four weeks earlier than anyone thought and headed back to the family ranch near Heppner.

Sure, he did write once, and we talked on the phone about how maybe I could take the bus to Heppner and spend a week, during which he would take the city starch right out of me and have me walkin', talkin', eatin', dressin', and even thinkin' like a cowboy within 48 hours, but it never worked out.

With Orville at the center, a bunch of us used to eat lunch together every day. We called ourselves "the Posse" and talked about everything from cafeteria food to the women in our lives. (Note: the last item was usually a very brief discussion.) But the Posse no longer exists for one obvious reason: you can't have a posse without the sheriff. Orville was our sheriff. And Orville is gone.

FRIDAY, SEPTEMBER 20

Cross-country took on a new urgency today. Two reasons:

One, I saw the team's first meet yesterday. I sort of hung around and watched it after school. The following statement makes no sense whatsoever: Yeah, I know those guys were in pain, I know half of them felt like tossing their cookies, I know that their muscles will make them wish that they had a switch to temporarily shut down the part of the brain that registers pain, BUT I kind of missed being with them.

Two, at seminary today, Julie and I sort of bumped into each other in the mad rush toward the door after Sister Habben dismissed class. "Oh, hi, Wally," she said, a very insightful and clever statement at that hour of the morning, I thought.

"Oh, hi, Julie," I replied, choosing something that, while losing points for originality, was at least safe. I held the door open for her.

"Thanks, Wally."

"You're welcome, Julie," I said, again playing things safe.

She seemed to want to say something else but wasn't sure what. Then she smiled.

"Are you on the cross-country team again this year? I really admire cross-country runners. They are so dedicated."

Horrors! Entering Perturb City! What do I say? I mean, here is Julie, a girl that I at one time sort of liked (although now I have hardly a trace of feeling for her), and she is asking me if I am on the cross-country team—*practically asking me out*, for Pete's sake, if I give her the right answer.

"Well . . . uh, no. That is, not now. But I will. Very soon. I am . . ." think quick, Whipple, try not to lie, but think fast ". . . injured. Yeah, an injury."

She looked concerned. I love it when Julie looks concerned. It has only happened one other time in my life, in a hallway at church during a stake dance; I loved it then and I love it now. My heart was pounding. "That's too bad. What is your injury?"

"It's internal," I said, sort of bagging my previous attempt at not telling a tiny white lie. "It's my elbow. Like the inside part."

"Is it hard to run with an injured elbow?"

"Oh, definitely. Your legs can only move as fast as your elbows swing." Mr. Leonard had said that once. And the part about my elbow wasn't a complete lie. Three weeks ago, I scraped it after falling down on our driveway while shooting baskets with Chuck.

"Well, I hope your elbow feels better and you begin cross-country soon."

"It will. I'll probably start next week." Then we were in the parking lot and split up. I took one long look at her getting into her car. Good thing I no longer really *like* her. Well, maybe only just a little.

So I've done it. Committed to cross-country, without Mr. Leonard sending a word of guilt my way. Second year in a row that I turned out for the sport of geeks because of a girl.

And I don't even like Julie as much this year as last. I think.

SUNDAY, SEPTEMBER 22

I need an ally in cross-country, someone to share the glory, the joy, the recognition, the feeling that you are about to throw up. I called Lumpy tonight.

ME: "Lumpy, we've been through a lot together, haven't we?"

HIM: "You got it, pard. Miss Orthcutt's third grade class—"

ME: "The chicken pox—"

HIM: "Our 50-mile hike when it rained the whole week—"

ME: "We even shared the same zit medicine—"

HIM: "Doesn't get much deeper than that!"

ME: "Lump, there is nothing I wouldn't do for you."

HIM: "Same here, Wally."

ME: "Can always count on the Lumpster. A veritable Gibraltar. A great constant in my otherwise life of turmoil."

HIM: "Yep. That's me."

ME: "Then I hardly even need to ask, but since I'm going out for cross-country tomorrow, why don't you join up, too?"

HIM:: "No way, Wally."

ME: "But you just said—"

HIM: "Correct that. I'd do anything except go out for cross-country. Does this have anything to do with trying to impress Julie?"

ME: (trying to sound vaguely wounded) "No! I am totally surprised that you would even think that! I just want to get in better shape."

HIM: "Sure, Wally."

ME: (going for Lumpy's Achilles' heel, namely his stomach) "I thought you'd want to start up again because, well, haven't you put on a few pounds?"

HIM: "Me? No. I'm doing a lot better on my eating habits. I even ordered a salad the last time we went out to eat."

ME: "And then you had a big meal to go along with your salad, right Lump?"

HIM: "Only sort of . . . the salad made up for the triple-decker cheeseburger."

ME: (sensing it was time to move in for the kill) "I guess if you don't have much pride in your appearance . . ."

HIM: "Pride? I've got pride. When's practice? No pride, huh? You win, Wally."

ME: "No, you're the winner. I'm only doing this for your health and because I care about your well-being."

HIM: "Wally, I hate you."

ME: "And someday you will thank me when your capillaries and blood vessels are clean and everything is flowing clearly instead of pumping industrial waste sludge around your circulatory system."

Chalk one up for Wallace Whipple. Misery *does* love company, and Lumpy will be there every miserable step of the way.

Monday, September 23

Mr. Leonard was very pleased to see me show up with running shoes on today, ready to run my legs into the ground.

"Glad you finally decided to come out, Wally."

"Yeah, me too," I said, altering the truth somewhat. "But, uh, I mean, how come you never really got on my case about not coming out?"

He sat back in his chair in the coaches' office.

"It's like this, Wally. You and Larry ran cross-country last year. You know the benefits. You know what it is like to wake up and say, 'I'm in the best shape of my life.' I could walk from here to San Francisco and never break a sweat. Once an athlete has tasted that kind of success, I expect him to want more. I seldom ask someone to turn out for cross-country once he's tasted of its fruit. They'll return on their own almost every time. By the way, we're running up Mt. Tabor twice today for our workout. It will be a good one for you to start with."

I got into my practice gear and started to jog up to the tennis courts, where the team met before practice. I was out of breath by the time I got to the top stair.

It's going to be awhile before I'm ready to hoof it to San Francisco.

WEDNESDAY, SEPTEMBER 25

Mr. Scleavege has warned us many times this year about some nuclear-powered gizmo machine in the corner of metal shop that can make, break, or shape steel. He says that if it is left on for too long a time, it will overheat, and the least that will happen is that the school will burn down, and the worst case scenario is something akin to a nuclear meltdown, taking most of Portland with it and perhaps wiping out a portion of southwestern Washington.

Evan Trant, naturally, uses the white-hot, steel-spitting gizmo a lot, probably because of the sense of power that he must feel, knowing he holds the fate of about 1.8 million people in his hands.

Anyway, today the unthinkable happened, and the gizmo was left on as class broke up. Right at the bell, Mr. Scleavege noticed it and immediately let loose with an ear-piercing shriek. "Who left that on?!!" he screeched, looking up and down the class for any signs of guilt among our suddenly ashen faces.

Every guy in the class knew it was Evan who walked away from the doomsday machine. And every guy in the class would have rather faced the possibility of a nuclear winter than have Evan mad at him. So there was a long, cold, dead silence as Mr. Scleavege fumed and fussed.

Call it some kind of instinct kicking in, but after a few seconds of watching Mr. Scleavege sputtering and drooling, I raised my hand. "Sorry, Mr. Scleavege, but I must have been the one who left it on. I was welding a lot today." Since I hope to be in boys choir by this time next week and never have to deal with metal shop again, I thought I might as well take the bullet for Evan, even though he's the guy raiding my lunch.

Mr. Scleavege stared at me, then loosened up. "Well, I guess you can be forgiven, since you are in this class by mistake. But anyone else, and there would have been severe repercussions. Okay, clear out!"

I walked over to the little pegboard locker. Evan was right behind me. When I turned, we were face-to-face, and I got this creepy feeling similar to what it must be like waking up in the jungle with a tiger staring at you.

"Walter Wimp Pole," he half-sneered, then whirled away.

Funny thing is, I think that was his way of saying thanks. That's probably the way lower life forms communicate, I reminded myself. Simple. Heartfelt. Not a lot of brain behind it. But both of my cupcakes, I noticed later, were still in my lunch bag.

Thursday, September 26

My first cross-country meet today brought back a lot of memories from last season—like how it feels to finish near the end (46th out of 59 runners), trying not to toss up my lunch, and wondering where my next breath of air is coming from.

I was also reminded of the tremendous pain that comes from running three miles up and down hills when you are out of shape. All of the cells in my body got together after the race and said, "Dudes, he shouldn't do that to us. Let's all charge up our pain batteries and bombard the kid's brain with them. That'll teach him."

And for the record, yeah, I did sort of look around at the finish line for Julie, just in case she decided to stick around and watch the meet after school. I was thinking I could hold my elbow or limp or something like that to sort of get her thinking that there may be a reason for me finishing so far in back of the pack, other than I am not a fast runner, which is the real truth. But she wasn't there.

Of course, I did make out better than Lumpy, who did not achieve his goal of going the whole season without getting nauseous. He had to drop out after about a mile.

I have just one question, as I lie on my bed, my weakened fingers hardly able to hold my pen as I feebly scribble these sad, pathetic lines in my journal.

Why do I do these things to myself?

SATURDAY, SEPTEMBER 28

Natalie continues to have major stress about her lack of tannage. Today, she and her friend Lindy Hightower were lying on the trampoline in the backyard, catching the last few rays of Oregon sunshine. Any day now, it could cloud over here and start drizzling until next May.

Anyway, Natalie and Lindy have a unique relationship. It is based on sharing the same priorities—clothes, guys, and looking in mirrors, in exactly that order—and the fact that each of them thinks she is slightly cuter than the other. I was out chipping away at the yard work this afternoon and heard their conversation.

Natalie: "Seriously, do you think I have a bad tan?"

Lindy: "Well, your tan is not wholly bad, but it's not wholly good, which makes it somewhere in the middle."

Natalie: "That totally depresses me, because you know, like I laid out as much as you did, but nobody at school stops and looks at you and goes, 'Wow, she has a bad tan.'"

Lindy: "I don't think your tan is totally bad. Seriously. But maybe you should go to a bake shop."

Natalie: (panic in her voice) "Like I should go get a fake bake? Seriously? Is it that bad?"

Lindy: "No, I don't think so. But maybe. Of course, it could be something else, like you have a disease."

Natalie: "Serious? A disease?"

Lindy: "Maybe. You know, like something that won't kill you, but at least you could tell people at school that the reason your tan isn't good is because you have a disease. You'd get, you know, like sympathy. And then the kids who said you have a crummy tan would feel bad because they made fun of you because you had a disease."

Natalie: "Yeah. That would be cool, as long as it wasn't one of those diseases like where your arm falls off."

Lindy: "If I were you, I'd go for the disease. Seriously."

Natalie: "Okay. You can tell some people that I have a disease, you know, like the measles, but more complicated. Start with Ashley Wilkins, because she will tell everyone. But don't tell anyone I have a gross disease, because then the guys won't want to be around me. I'll tell my Mom tonight that I don't feel good."

Later on, I saw Natalie with a thermometer in her mouth. It seems that the mysterious tannage disease is about to descend on the Whipple household.

CHAPTER 2

October

Joy! Ecstasy! Relief.

Yes, the Very Tense Woman finally got into the Ws, and Wallace Whipple is now free from metal shop. No more acrid smell of molten metal. No more worrying about what I will do when grade time rolls around and all I have to show for my work is a long strand of metal that looks something like a miniature brass hoola hoop, an object which I took out of the scrap bin in desperation when Mr. Scleavege said our first project would be due in a week. (I got a C+ on it.) No more worrying about Mom's cupcakes getting swiped from my locker.

Today, I eagerly showed the transfer slip to Mr. Scleavege, who for one final time told me every boy needs a skill in case our economy gets out of whack and all the freeloaders of society—such as lawyers, accountants, engineers, and talk show hosts—suddenly were out of work, in which case they'd wish they'd learned a trade like metal work. I nodded and told him that I agreed, then almost skipped over to my class locker to gather my stuff.

I turned around to make my final exit, and there was Evan Trant.

"Wimp Pole, you leaving?"

"Yeah, Evan. Transferring." I didn't want to tell him I was trading advanced metal shop for boys choir. It would be sort of like telling Arnold Schwarzenegger you were giving up body building for crocheting.

"I don't like that, Wimp Pole. You're okay for someone who don't ride a bike."

"Thanks, Evan. You're okay for someone who does ride motorcycles. See you around."

He grunted, which I took as a sign of mutual acceptance and friendship—sort of a male-bonding thing meaning that we had successfully bridged the huge physical, mental, moral, and spiritual gaps between us.

Anyway, I gleefully walked away toward the choir room and entered when the group was just about ready to launch into a bit of Sinatra in preparation for the fall concert.

Mr. Ashbury, the choir director, nodded happily as I flashed my transfer slip to him, and I knowingly took my place among the tenors, which is where the guys with the higher voices sing. Tenors, I guess, are sort of a necessary evil.

Ah, life is good. No more metal shop. Back in choir. And singing Sinatra. It just doesn't get much better than that.

THURSDAY, OCTOBER 3

Cross-country today was brutal. There were about 50 guys in the race, and I finished 46th. Just didn't have it. How bad was I? Put it this way: Lumpy finished 47th.

In the back of my mind, I sometimes envision myself running across a snowy landscape with a pack of raving mad dogs nipping at my heels. But thanks to my cross-country training and superior physical condition, I am able to outrun them and find refuge in a mountain cabin, which happens to be inhabited by a beautiful girl and her family, all of whom are immediately taken by the unexpected young stranger, who, though slightly out of breath, is still very ruggedly handsome and very wealthy.

Well, that's the vision, but if the mad dogs were on my tail today, I think I'd be lunch.

About two-thirds of the way into the race, I found myself jogging slowly with Lumpy. This is not a good sign, because Lumpy has earned the nickname "Limpy" among our cross-country teammates, a nickname *not* designed to call attention to his high rate of travel. So if that's Lumpy, and I'm running right next to him, I'm probably next in line for the kind of nickname that you won't want to have spread around on your next date.

ME: "I run cross-country, you know, and all the guys have a special name for me."

DATE: (with surprise in her voice, thinking for a brief moment that while she is out with a cross-country runner, at least maybe he's a good cross-country runner) "Oh! And what might your nickname be? Flash? Swifty? Lightning?"

ME: "No. All the guys call me 'Waddle.' Waddle Whipple."

HER: (the magic of the moment rapidly evaporating) "Oh. How charming."

At times such as these, when I am discouraged, tired, sore, and questioning my own mental capacity for having signed on to run cross-country, I need to remember that my real purpose is not to win races but to get buff and to hammer the old bod into shape for basketball season. Plus, now that I've turned out, I also need to remember how deliriously happy my parents are that I am too tired to get into any trouble so I generally wander off toward bed, only slightly whimpering, by 10:00 P.M. on Friday nights.

Yes, I know it's all a conspiracy on the part of my parents and billions of parents around the world: get your kid exhausted and he'll be a whole lot easier to handle.

I hope my parents appreciate what a good kid I am.

Note: I heard Natalie on the phone tonight saying, "Well, yeah, you know, it could be serious, but it's not catchy or anything. Like about all it really does is not make me able to tan and it gives me a sore throat, too. It is a little painful, but I'm not trying to like, let it show. The mall on Saturday? Oh sure. Yeah, my disease doesn't stop me from going to the mall. Seriously."

SATURDAY, OCTOBER 5

Today was sort of gloomy. It started to rain about nine and only got darker and wetter as the day wore on. Dad had to work, Natalie was at the mall, and Chuck was at Marshall Phelps's house, one of his neighborhood buddies.

I was spread out on the couch, sort of halfway browsing through the New Testament, hoping to keep up on my seminary reading for Sister Habben. I have to admit, though, that the eyelids were fairly droopy, the sentences were regularly running together, and I wasn't really catching the thread of Matthew 17 when my mom popped in.

"Reading for seminary?" she asked.

"Yeah, Mom. Sister Habben is a good teacher, and if I don't keep up I'm going to get behind." Given my mental state, this sentence made perfect sense.

"Wally, I've been thinking."

Little bells started ringing in my head. The phrase is a universal parental cue that something is coming that you're not going to like. Frankly, I think parents have too much time to think. Face it, they have made all the difficult choices in life, like who to marry, where to live, where to work, how many kids to have, and what color to paint the house. This leaves them too much time to think, and much to the dismay of their offspring, particularly teenaged offspring, much of their free time is spent thinking about their children. At least this time my theory was totally correct. Mom had been thinking of new ways to gum up my already complicated life.

"I was talking with Sister Smisore this morning, and she told me that Nancy isn't dating much."

Uh-oh. Mom was making a run at improving my social life. She thinks of me as, shall we say, socially challenged. She thinks I should show more interest in girls, totally unaware of my once-smoldering like for Julie Sloan (which has since cooled to the approximate surface temperature of Pluto, I should mention). Every so often, she takes it on herself to try to line me up with a girl. And while Mom has wonderful taste in most areas, she has yet to get a girl who appeals to me in the cross hairs of my love scope.

"I think Nancy is a darling girl," Mom said, as if telling me a state secret.

"Yeah, Mom, Nancy is nice all right. Really nice," I said, desperately searching for neutral territory.

"I think she's cute and, from what I understand, very spiritual."

Spiritual isn't the word for Nancy. I mean, the guy who marries her has his ticket punched for exaltation. He could be a slob, a total slacker, but a few months with old Nancy would clean up his act. He'd be a stake president for sure. I mean, Nancy is perfect. She is always alert in seminary class, always has the right answer, always gets 100% on her tests. She visits the sick, sends out birthday cards, listens to Church tapes in the car, and makes her own clothes. Every once in a while, she'll throw a breakfast before seminary, just to get everyone in tune for the lesson that day. She must get up at 4:00 A.M. to get things ready. Adults everywhere love her. Every mom in the stake, if not the entire Church, wants her son to marry Nancy.

It's because she's one of their own.

"Anyway, Sister Smisore said that Nancy doesn't date very much . . ."

No doubt. Who wants to study the book of Leviticus on their date?

". . . and I told her you didn't go out very much and maybe you two could get together and go out sometime."

The thought of going out with Nancy chills every male hormone in my body.

I needed to wriggle out of this delicate situation. "Yeah, Mom. I'll go out with Nancy sometime, but I'm so busy with athletics right now that I don't think I'd be very much fun on a date. And first dates are everything. I'll go out with Nancy when I know I'll be fun."

Like in the year 2018, provided we are both still single.

"Good, Wally. I'm glad to hear that." With that, Mom drifted away and I was left to feel good about dodging another disastrous chapter in my crinkly social life.

WEDNESDAY, OCTOBER 9

Today, we had our second meeting of the junior class cabinet. At the first meeting, we all sat down and carefully outlined our agendas for the year and drew up the responsibilities that each of us needed to perform to ensure that our stewardship of the junior class would be well accounted for and that our goals and objectives would be achieved. My contribution, as it turned out, is to lead the flag salute at the beginning of any formal sessions. That's about all that's in the sergeant-at-arms position description, along with being on the clean-up crew for every major student council function. The class president, Alex Cole, also told me to keep an eye out for people who may want to disrupt our orderly proceedings, and in the case such a rabble-rouser infiltrated our meeting it was my duty to throw the bum out. "Can't sit idly by as the fabric of 11th grade civilization is torn in two," Alex said, and I don't think he was trying to be funny.

Sure thing, Alex.

The cross-country meet was almost a repeat of last week, although I finished three places in front of Lumpy. Progress, I guess.

Before I cave in to the Sleep Fairy, who is throwing dust by the handful at me on this cool October eve, I noticed Natalie got some get well cards in the mail today. On the phone with Lindy tonight, she discussed new symptoms that she could develop. Natalie's criteria for symptoms is that they can't be gross, they can't stop her from shopping, and that they can disappear on command if they might interfere with her social life.

Being Natalie's brother, I've decided, has one big advantage: our family never lacks for entertainment.

Saturday, October 12

As part of my journalism class, I had to cover our football game last night. It was everything I've come to expect from a football game in Oregon—22 players out slogging around on a field of mud, looking for someone to run into. Good old Benjamin Franklin High played to its usual standard for this season. We lost 27-6. I started my story off with, "Neither sleet nor mud nor the Franklin defense failed to slow Grant High, as the Generals pounded out a 27-6 win over the Fightin' Quakers." My journalism teacher said it was a good story and that I had a flair for writing. Obviously, he is a keen judge of literary talent.

What I really think is that our team misses Joe Vermeer and a few other seniors who graduated. We were more than respectable last year, winning seven games and just missing the state playoffs. But with Joe gone, we are reverting to the fine, long-standing tradition of our football team, that of rolling over dead almost every Friday night. Maybe we should start with our nickname—the Fightin' Quakers? What's wrong with this picture?

Oh well.

Sunday, October 13

List of people who miss the one and only Orville Burrell, famed cowboy, poet, philosopher, friend, and good guy, who left life in Portland to return to his beloved ranch near Heppner.

1. Coach Waymon

Yes, the wrestling coach has pinned me down in the hallway no less than a half dozen times, with a note of desperation in his voice. "Are you sure that Orv isn't coming back? Any chance at all? He was my ticket to the state meet this year. Please let me know if you hear anything from him, Wally."

As a 10th grader last year, Orv wrestled on the varsity and did super. He always said that tossin' around little city fellers warn't nothin' like wrasslin' a steer or ridin' a bull. "Now that's *real* work," he would say.

2. Natalie Whipple

Call them the odd couple, but Natalie, the mall princess, a young woman who will soon have her own name stenciled in a reserved parking space right near the main entrance, has a mad raving crush on Orville, the cowboy hunk, whose idea of shopping is to buy a new pair of cowboy boots through the mail order catalog every five years. Somehow, though, it's a little tough for me to see her clanging the iron triangle and hollering, "Supper's on! Little Chester and little Rex, go on out and fetch your Pappy for vittles!" But she remains head-over-heels about him. "Do you think Orville is coming back?" she echoes Coach Waymon. "Does he ever tell you what the girls are like wherever it is he's from? Do they, like, tan a whole lot there? If I wore more leather would that impress him? Seriously."

3. My Mom

Orville and his dad came over to our house for Thanksgiving last year and made a big hit with the whole family. Eating dinner with the Whipples once sort of entitles you to a lifetime membership in the household, and we got used to seeing Orv—and occasionally his dad— hang out with us. Mom really took to Orv, and whenever I'd hear from him, she was full of questions: "How is Orv? Is he coming back? I really wish he could have stayed."

4. Mr. Leonard

Mr. Leonard misses Orv for basically the same reason that Coach Waymon does. Orv also happened to be the sophomore city champion in the shot put, and I know Mr. Leonard was counting on him to help out on the track team next spring.

5. Various and Sundry Young Women

Yeah, I get questions all the time from girls about Orv. Edwina Purvis. Amy Hassett. Even Julie Sloan. They all want to know what he is up to and if they will ever see him again. Two weeks ago, a couple of complete strangers came up to me after school and wanted to know if Orv was at Benjamin Franklin this year. "You sort of hung out with him. We thought you'd know," one of them said. After telling them, no, he was back at the ranch in eastern Oregon, they both got a really disappointed look. My first experience at heartbreaking, even though I was only the messenger and not the cause of a split ticker.

Note: If I were to move, would females everywhere in southeast Portland inquire of my whereabouts? Five seconds to answer . . . tick, tick, tick, tick, tick . . . And the answer is: naw, probably no one would ever give it a second thought.

6. Wallace F. Whipple, Jr.

Yeah, I miss the old sidewinder. His company. His humor. The weird way he talked, although I was beginning to understand cowboyese better by the time he left. And there is one other thing, a piece of unfinished business with Orville. After a tidal wave's worth of spiritual sweating, I finally got him to take the missionary lessons. Then he moved, and it was so sudden that we never finished. Something is still hanging, not seen to the end. I do not want to go through eternity feeling that I moved too slow.

"If we'd only had another week or two, I think we could have baptized Orville," laments Dad, who is a stake missionary. "He was a member who just didn't know it."

Yeah. But I do know it. Somehow, I've got to find a way of finishing the job.

TUESDAY, OCTOBER 15

Six weeks into school and time to evaluate my scholastic progress.

Math. I'm holding my own, but barely. We got a test back today, and I got a C–. Dick Dickson, of course, leaned over and eyed my grade as the teacher, Mrs. Simmons, handed it back. "Nice going, Whipple. Run out of fingers and toes on the test?" He came very close to having my calculator for an early lunch.

Choir. Sweet, heavenly choir. Mr. Ashbury has already

exchanged a couple of tapes with me. He is still deeply moved whenever we talk about our kind of music. "Wally, I don't want to make too much of this, but it gives me hope for your generation when I realize that someone like you appreciates Bennett, Sinatra, and Torme. It makes my job seem so much more worthwhile."

"Well, let's just face it, some people are born with superior taste," I say humbly.

English. Okay. I need to put a little bit more into my reading, but I like the teacher, Mrs. Garrison. We've had to write a couple of papers, and I got an A on both of them. I also answer tons of questions, and firmly sort of believe that Julie's presence has only a tiny bit of influence on my performance. Maybe.

Social studies. Ditto. Good start, good teacher in Mr. Donati.

Biology. Lost in space. I understand the material so far, but I don't understand the teacher. With Mr. Flagg, there's no feedback. He's an ex-Marine and sort of runs his class that way. He barks an order, we follow it. Or else. He's not a teacher that I'd like to cross. He'd have me doing one-handed push-ups if I ever contaminated my petri dish. A different dude, for sure.

Journalism. Yes, the kid is a natural in this. Writing has always been easy, and I'm enjoying the class, other than covering football games or pumping out profiles of new teachers. ("In his spare time, Mr. Gurkle raises dahlias and collects china figurines of military heroes.")

Spanish. My teacher is Miss Richardson, who a year ago at this time was student teaching. She is unlike any other teacher I've ever had, which is to say that she has no gray hair and a complexion that doesn't resemble a raisin. Well, that's an exaggeration, but not much of one. Seriously, they are all at least middle-aged, and some of them are in their 40s or 50s. But not Miss Richardson, who is young, sort of like us, and yeah, kind of pretty. And I love the way she trills her Rs.

Oh yeah. Physical ed, which I naturally excel at and am sure to bring home nothing but a long string of As this year.

So far, so good in school this year. Now it is time to say buenos notches or buenos burritos or buenos garbanzo, all of which mean "good night" in Spanish.

WEDNESDAY, OCTOBER 16

Went to our Young Men's activity tonight and played broom hockey. (Priesthood purpose: to build brotherhood by whacking each other with various and assorted sizes of brooms.) My good friend Michael "Mickey" Winn at one point wound up and took a huge swat at the puck, but instead connected with my shinbone.

Now I can hardly walk, much less run, and we have another cross-country meet tomorrow. I may plead lameness and see if Coach Leonard will let me skip out.

News Flash From Natalie, as told by her brother, who was only slightly eavesdropping on a phone conversation with one of her friends tonight:

"So, like I was really worried, totally, when Mrs. Neff called me up after English because, seriously, I thought that maybe I had messed up on an assignment. Well, I get up there and she looks, you know, like, concerned, and she goes, 'Natalie, I understand you have some health problems.'

"Like, I didn't know what to say, so I decided to tell her the truth, and I go, 'Yeah, Mrs. Neff, but they aren't as serious as you probably heard.' She smiles, then she goes, 'Well, I just want you to know that if you are not feeling well and it causes you to be a little tardy on an assignment, then I will understand. Getting better is what really is most important here.' And I go, 'Okay. Thanks, Mrs. Neff. You are really cool.' Then I coughed a little, and she looked, you know, worried, but I told her it was okay. But can you believe it? My disease is going so good, I can't wholly believe it. Seriously."

So Natalie's lie now seems like the truth to her. I have this huge urge to rat on Natalie and watch as my parents go ballistic. It would be great entertainment. But something tells me that even without my help the other shoe is going to thud squarely on her too-smooth life.

In the meantime, I'll just sit back and see how far her disease progresses until Mom and Dad find a cure for it.

THURSDAY, OCTOBER 17

My conversation with Coach Leonard:

ME: "Coach, I hurt my leg last night playing, uh, working out. I think it's broken, and I wanted to know if I could skip the meet."

MR. LEONARD: "No. If you run hurt, you'll prove to yourself something that you will never otherwise learn if you only ran healthy."

ME: (thinking that the only thing I'll prove is that not only am I a geek but not even a smart enough geek to stop inflicting pain on myself) "What?"

MR. LEONARD: "All the great ones run hurt. Once you learn you can perform hurt, when you're not hurt, you will be all the better."

ME: (thinking that I'm not a great one, never was, never will be, and may not want to be) "Huh?"

MR. LEONARD: "You will learn more about the inner Whipple, what makes him tick, what he feels, how mentally tough he is. You will be more at ease with yourself, more confident, more dedicated, and more tough. In athletics, what is, is."

ME: (thinking, I already know a lot about the inner feelings of Whipple, and they can be summarized in one word—*pain*) "Oh."

MR. LEONARD: "Good. Then we'll see you at the bus at 3:00 P.M."

ME: (thinking, I don't want any more of this combination of Zen, pain, and Jock 101): "Okay."

So I ran hurt. And it showed in the results. Finished 35th out of 38 runners. Even Lumpy broke across the line before I did. And while I'm not sure exactly what Mr. Leonard was trying to tell me, I do know one thing more clearly than ever: my shin hurts.

SATURDAY, OCTOBER 19

The roof caved in on Natalie today. Her bubble burst. Her pretty world stopped spinning. The Big Lie caught up with her. Mom and Dad found out about her serious illness, and they weren't happy. Nat might have been better off having an incurable disease.

We were all doing our best imitations of limp sweat socks this evening just before dinner. Dad worked today and he was tired and a little grumpy. I'd spent a lot of time in the yard, trying to get it ready for winter. Natalie had done her usual "Saturday Tour of Malls" with friends, which is becoming a regular feature of our weekends, right in there with breathing, eating, and sleeping. When she got home, Mom sort of cracked down on her about her room, basically because if you took a photo of it and compared it to a photo of a house that had been devastated by a tornado, you probably couldn't tell which was which, at first glance.

"But Mom, I like having everything out where I can see it," Natalie whined. "Seriously. I know you probably don't understand this, but I know exactly where everything is in here. I can go right to it."

"Everything in here is on the floor. I have two words, Natalie. *Clean* and *now*."

So she sulked off to her room and actually got most of her stuff off the floor and onto her bed. Progress, I suppose.

So we're all doing nothing for the first time today and the phone rings. The call is for Mom. We hear only her end of the conversation, of course, which goes something like this:

"Oh . . . how interesting, Bonnie. We appreciate your offer of help. But I'm sure Natalie is going to be feeling better soon. [At this point, Natalie sits up on the couch, stands, and begins to slowly slink from the room.] No, that's not necessary. You see, Natalie's illness is not nearly as serious as it sounds. Actually, it's nothing. Nothing at all. [Natalie is now moving quickly—rounding the corner and charging up the stairs. I hear sounds from her room. She may be packing. This could be the end of the affiliation between the Whipple Family and Natalie.] I need to talk with Natalie and tell her not to worry people as much as she has. Yes, she is a sweet girl, and I'll let Natalie know about your call. I know she'll be interested in what you have to say. And thanks again."

Mom hangs up the phone and stands there thoughtfully and purposefully for half a minute. She taps the receiver with her finger and calls out, "Nat, we need to talk."

At this point in my life, I would not trade places with Natalie for a bazillion dollars, front row seats and a backstage pass at a Sinatra concert, or a date with Marie Osmond in her prime.

Natalie meekly comes down the stairs. The thumping

around I heard was not the sound of packing but of her changing her clothes from her definitely with-it mall attire to a more subdued church dress that Mom and Dad gave her last Christmas. Only Natalie would think of clothes as a defense against mounting parental hostility.

"Natalie, that was Sister Knight, your Mia Maid adviser. She was calling me to ask how she could help out since your illness was causing such a strain on our family, and there was some question about your long-term health. She wanted to bring a casserole. Now, would you like to explain what illness it is that you contracted and why we didn't know about it?"

Dad's attention meter was suddenly pegged at the top too. Natalie sat down at the dining room table, while both my parents hovered nearby. This is not going to be pretty, I judge. Should I take Chuck out for a walk and spare him the ugly scene sure to follow? Naw, I decide. This might be kind of fun. And I do need quality entertainment. This is going to be more of a kick than Lumpy's wolfing down that green hot dog yesterday.

"Well, Mom and Dad, it's like, you know, that story they tell at church all the time, about how, like, when you cut open your pillow and the feathers blow all over and then if you want to get the feathers back, it's like, too late." Natalie's strategy was clear: she was going to go megaspiritual on them, hoping for a little mercy and compassion. "So seriously, I just told a couple of friends at school one day that I, like, didn't feel good, and the next thing I knew they had me, like, with some huge big disease, and I guess some people thought, you know, like, I was dying or something."

"Did you ever try to correct the false information that was going around about you?" Dad asked, and I wondered if Nat was going to pull victory out from the jaws of defeat.

"Oh, yes!"

"Tell me who, then."

"Lindy. She was the one I told, when I was talking about my tan."

"Tan?"

Mom zeroed right in on the word. Big mistake by Natalie.

"Well, someone mentioned that I sort of looked pale, that I didn't have a good summer doing tanning, so that's where the story really got started—"

Natalie had just tied the noose and now was throwing the rope over the tree.

"Let me get this straight," Dad cut in. "Someone at school said you didn't have a good tan, and you told her that it was because you had a disease?"

Bingo, Dad. Can't fool a Whipple male for long, that's for sure.

"Well—"

Mom jumped back in. "And you purposely let this rumor grow so that you could gain sympathy and also have an excuse for not being as tan as some of the other girls?"

"Well, no. It wasn't like that . . ." Her voice trailed off as she hoped for a miracle.

"Then what was it like?"

"It was, like, different. Seriously."

Mom and Dad had her on the run. It doesn't happen often. I should have sold tickets for this. Was it too late to call Lumpy and invite him over?

"In what way?"

"Well, Lindy did a lot of the talking, not me . . ." Natalie stuttered. She was a broken woman.

"Natalie, what you've done is wrong. You let people believe something about you that wasn't true," Dad said, huffiness in his voice.

"I'm sorry! I'm really sorry; I didn't mean to hurt anyone. Seriously," Natalie whined, throwing herself on the mercy, scant as it was, of the court.

"For starters, you will call your friends, Church leaders, and, for all I know, teachers and tell them you are not sick," Mom stated.

"But Mom! That's like, you know, telling them I lied!" Natalie protested.

Mom put her hands on her hip and bounced her head from side to side, a perfect imitation of Nat. "That's because, seriously, you did lie, Nat."

Dad waded back in. "And you will be grounded for a month, other than church activities. No dances, no hanging with friends, no trips to the mall—"

At that Natalie screeched a sound very much akin to what I imagine a wildebeest makes as the lion pounces. "AWWRGHHZZWEELK!" is about as close as I can come to it. "You can't keep me away from the mall! Seriously! That's no fair!" she shrieked. Now the tears gushed, fast-flowing rivers cascading down her cheeks. Her worst nightmare had just come true. It was a blow to her self-image, a piece of her foundation yanked away. Shopping is what Natalie is all about. Her natural habitat is the mall.

"Please . . . anything! But I want to shop," she begged. "I'll go on a mission."

Dad held firm. "No, Nat. No mall for a month. When you cross the line, you pay the price. Whipples don't lie. That's a family rule. But you did, and that affects all of us."

Natalie, doomed, slowly stood up. She walked toward the stairway. She looked back at my parents once, sniffed, then made the melancholy march up to her room. The door clicked softly and there was complete silence.

The fireworks were over. Chuck was impressed. "I think Natalie is in big trouble," he whispered.

"I think you're right. But she'll recover," I predicted, "probably by Monday."

My parents were both talking near the table.

"Can you imagine?" Dad said, shaking his head. "That bit about the feathers."

"All because of a tan. I wonder how many people think Natalie is on her deathbed because of this," Mom said. Then they both turned away.

And I'm not sure, but I think Mom was trying to suppress a giggle.

Sunday, October 20

Kind of a blue day around the Whipple household. Natalie is brooding over the lecture she took yesterday, not to mention being in a near state of shock about being denied mall access for a month.

"This could change me forever, Wally. Like, I'm not going to be the same person. They'll go, 'What happened to our old Natalie?' You know, like, they feel guilty about the way they treated me, and maybe they'll apologize, but it won't be any different because, seriously, I will have changed and it will be their fault," she earnestly explained to me.

"And then Mom, when she moved her head around and said I was sort of, like, lying, and she put her hands on her hips. She looked so totally weird and she talked funny, too. I don't get what she was trying to prove," she fussed, not ever catching on to the fact that Mom was mimicking her. So Natalie spent the day quietly staring into outer space and generally feeling sorry for herself.

I indulged in a bit of that, too. I started to think about my social life, or more precisely, the lack thereof.

I mean, here I am, 17 years old, with all of these hormones running around in my body, thinking a little companionship of the female type would be nice and reaching the point where I honestly and legitimately need to shave a minimum of once a week, and what do I have to show for it all? No dates for five months. That's what I have to show for it.

Maybe I should just get bold and ask out Julie again. "Julie, I know our first date was miserable, and in your universe I am something along the lines of old orange peels, but can we go out just once more so that I can prove to you that I am a fairly normal human being who can act in a somewhat civilized manner in a social situation? Please?"

And how about Edwina Purvis, a girl with whom I have gone out more than any other female in the universe? (Twice). She's not in any of my classes this year, so it's hard to keep up any kind of relationship. I mean, I can't just call her up out of the blue and start talking to her. Last year, we had math class and Mr. Herk in common. This year, zippo. "Ed, Wally Whipple here. Say, I was reminiscing last night about the good times we shared last year—solving quadratic equations, making fun of Mr. Herk's ties, sharing a few special moments as we put math problems on the blackboard—what do you say we rekindle the fire of algebra and get together for a little root beer and burritos? Fine with you? Good. Friday, eightish, your vehicle. See you then, babe. And Ed, did I ever tell you how much I admire your ability to deal with determinants of the third order? I really mean it! There was something very special in the way you handled those problems, and I'm not just saying so. There's something very appealing about a woman who knows math."

Never work. So here I sit, a bystander in the weekend of life. Again. Mix in with that my horrible cross-country finish, no Orville to lean on for advice and counsel, and the facts that it's raining, my shin still hurts, and even Brother Hansen's lesson today was a little on the boring side.

What's going on here? My life, that's what. Plain, boring, and loaded with many artificial flavors.

I feel a slump coming on.

MONDAY, OCTOBER 21

Today was the one cross-country workout I look forward to every year. It's the workout where Coach Leonard gathers us all around and gives a speech something like this: "Men, I firmly believe that each of you has the ability to be a champion. Yet, I do not think we are performing like champions. It is not lack of ability. It is not lack of talent that is keeping us from being the best we can be. I think, gentlemen, it is the lack of heart.

"Today, I will not give you a workout. You may run wherever you like. As you do so, though, I ask that you think about your personal commitment to our team and answer two questions: Am I giving my best? Am I giving my all? After today, I expect we will be a better, more united team, firm in our purpose. That is all, gentleman."

And just like last year, he turned and walked toward his car, hopped in, and drove away.

The other guys on the team milled about for a few minutes. Some grouped up and laid out really tough workouts, harder I'm sure than anything Coach Leonard would have put us through. Then they took off. Lumpy and I followed the same pattern. We talked a little bit, decided to pair up with each other for the run, then immediately went to the locker room to grab a few bucks and headed straight to Hamburger Bob's.

"If cross-country were like this every day, I would be

all universe," Lumpy sighed contentedly while mashing down a Bob's Red Hot Nuclear Turbo Taco.

"Definitely. I could get used to this," I agreed, making a kamikaze-like dive into my pile of french fries. "And for the first time, my shin isn't bothering me at cross-country practice. This is the life, totally."

We sat there in a pleasant stupor for another ten minutes, picking over the remains of our most excellent workout. Then Lumpy sat up and his eyes bulged out a bit. I thought it was merely a delayed reaction to the nuclear taco, but he frantically gestured toward the parking lot.

Uh oh. Coach Leonard was headed toward the door.

This was one of those defining moments. We could stay and face Coach Leonard, meet his gaze firmly, square up to the situation, and tell him that we didn't feel like running much that day, and we were sorry if we had let him or the team down. That would be the manly, mature thing to do. We are, after all, human beings who have driver's licenses and will be able to vote for the president of the United States in another year.

"Quick! Let's get to the rest room!" I whispered hoarsely, temporarily deciding to put off full-blown maturity for a while. And with speed seldom seen from Lumpy, we were out of the booth and hiding behind the john door, almost praying that Coach Leonard was there for a quick burger and nothing else.

"He's going to think we're slackers if he sees us," I mumbled.

"Wally, we are slackers. How long do we wait in here?"

"I don't know."

I could see the headline in the school newspapers. "Juniors Suspended from Cross-Country Team!" it would scream. The writer—one of *my* journalism peers—would quote Coach Leonard, who would simply say, "They broke team rules." What does that mean? Drugs? Alcohol? Skipping practices? My reputation, skimpy as it is, would be ruined. Maybe I'd have to give up being sergeant-at-arms—my political career in ashes. Maybe it would show up on my college application. Maybe Bishop Winegar would place his hand on my shoulder Sunday and suggest, "Wally, we need to talk." And all this because I craved an onion burger and double order of fries.

"I think he's gone," Lumpy said, peering out of a crack in the doorway. We tiptoed out, looking around nervously, like soldiers creeping across a mine field.

And around the corner came Coach Leonard.

Please let me die. Just die. Or at least be buried deep in a six-month coma.

"Hello, Larry, Wally. I didn't expect to see you two here."

"Neither did we, Mr. Leonard," I rasped.

"See you at practice tomorrow then, gentlemen. And enjoy the food."

"Yeah. Practice tomorrow."

Then he turned and left. I was glad that my wish about a quick end to mortality didn't come true.

Or was I?

Adults are sneaky. I mean, if Coach Leonard had just yelled at us and told us how disappointed he was, we would have felt better. But he was almost nice about it. Is it because he is just a benevolent kind of guy? No. It's because he knows that we'll punish ourselves the rest of our lives for porking out when we should have been running our hearts out. It's a guilt trip supreme. There should be a rule, passed by every nation on the face of the earth. When a kid messes up, one adult (and one adult only) should yell at the kid.Then the incident should be declared over. Forever. Never brought again to memory.

The slump drags on. And I have learned one valuable lesson out of the infamous Scandal at Hamburger Bob's:

sometimes you dig yourself in deeper. Suddenly I had just the slightest hint of empathy for Nat and her feathers in the wind.

THURSDAY, OCTOBER 24

A brief look into the life of Wallace F. Whipple, Jr.

1. I did a little better in cross-country today. At least I beat Lumpy. But my shin still hurts.

2. Alex Cole came up to me after the junior class council meeting and said, "Wally, I like your style. You have something about you that not many people have. You do a great job on the Pledge of Allegiance. I hope we can work together on many other projects." This confuses me. On one hand, is Alex, the king of hair mousse and designer jeans, setting me up for something? On the other hand, is he an exceptionally good judge of human character?

3. Natalie is still in a daze. She's been dropping all sorts of hints about going to the mall ("I need to go to the mall as part of a homework assignment, Mom. Honest. Really. No, you don't need to call the teacher."), but my parents are hanging tough, although it's a little like digging in against the U.S. Marine Corps. I've heard her apologize to a couple of friends. Basically, it went like this: "I'm really a lot better now and my health wasn't, you know, like, as bad as we first thought, so you don't need to worry a lot about me anymore, just a little, but only if you want to. My parents were really surprised about how good I'm feeling, and so they go, 'Why don't you tell your friends?' so that they'll all know, too."

4. Chuck is manhandling the first grade. Mom and Dad went to a parent-teacher conference tonight, and the big guy got glowing reports. Takes after his older brother, no doubt.

5. Saw Evan Trant today at school. He sneered at me and grunted, "Hey, Wimp Pole. Still singing with all those pretty boys?" Yep, ol' Evan and me are getting to be pretty tight buddies, I'd say.

That's all for today, folks. Say good night, Wally.

Good night, Wally.

SUNDAY, OCTOBER 27

In an attempt to reverse the sliding fortunes of my entire life, in a feeble effort to take control, be my own man, and chart my own course, I went to the stake dance tonight.

Looking back at the experience now, I've decided that a stake dance is not the best place to set a new direction in one's life journey.

My basic problem at stake dances is that I don't dance. I don't dance for several reasons.

First, and most basic, I can't dance. I have tried to remedy this by watching others dance and copying moves (didn't work); by taking lessons from my sister, who can dance (a complete and abysmal failure—even Chuck told me as much); and by dancing ultra slow, with almost no perceptible movement, in an effort to look very cool, like I was listening to some inner music that only I could hear (this also proved to be a monumental failure; in the words of Natalie, in hearing range of no fewer than 50 or 60 of my peers, "Wally, are you alive?"). A number of fine, outstanding young women in our stake, sporting a variety of bruised toes and feet, give stark testimony to my lack of dancing skills.

Two, there aren't enough girls to ask to dance. Not that there aren't girls in wads at the dances, but most of them are Mia Maids. It's really not too cool for a guy of my advanced age (17) to be asking a Mia Maid to dance. And what if I ask one of the really young Mia Maids to dance? Boom—there's Wally Whipple out on the floor dancing with a 14-year-old, and my reputation as a cradle robber is firmly established. I know Joseph Smith had some amazing experiences at 14, but I don't think many (or any) Mia Maids are in that league, and I wasn't either.

I know age shouldn't mean anything. In fact, Brother Hansen is always telling us that we should be nice to the Mia Maids because when we get back from our missions, the only girls left are going to be the ones who are now Mia Maids. "Get a head start, brethren," he is prone to say. "You're going to marry a Mia Maid," he tells us, and although he's probably right, it still sends a chill from my toes to my teeth.

But even if you wanted to dance with a Mia Maid, it's hard to break in. Literally. Mia Maids attend stake dances in swarms. All this mass of arms, legs, and faces, moving as one throughout the night as though somehow magically affixed to one another. They even swarm together as they go to the rest room. I can't figure out why a trip to the rest room is considered a social event, but with the Mia Maids it is.

If you approach one Mia Maid to ask her to dance, you are within earshot of at least a dozen. You can hear them whispering as you approach. "Here he comes," they hiss excitedly. "He's going to ask you to dance," they buzz. "He's such a hunk, go for it," they murmur breathlessly. (Well, I hope that's what they whisper when I'm getting near.) Anyway, you ask one Mia Maid to dance, and it's like you're asking the whole class. They almost have to hold a presidency meeting to decide if you're worth dancing with. Then, if you do manage to pry one away from the group, as soon as the dance is over, she makes like a bullet for the rest of her group. She starts talking, occasionally looking over her shoulder at you, and you know that you're getting critiqued. I mean, add it all up, and it's just easier to hang out at the refreshment table, which is where Lumpy spends all of his time anyway.

Three. The music. I know my credibility is zilch on this, since I like singers that were middle-aged when my parents were born, and it's a cinch we're never going to hear Torme or Sinatra at a stake dance, *but . . .* the music just doesn't have it. I'm not sure who is asked to do the music, but it might be one of those calls that a tad bit more fasting and praying would help out on.

Well, as I said, the stake dance didn't exactly rocket my social life into the stratosphere. Lumpy and I were out of there by ten, right after the refreshments were served but seconds before all the Mia Maids began moving in a huge mass moving toward the refreshment table, sort of like locusts in Africa bearing down on the corn crop.

Natalie, of course, is a Mia Maid. Natalie, of course, is the exception. She does quite well on her own at stake dances, although being grounded kept her at home last night.

Life sort of trudges on. Someone at church today was giving a talk about how life is an empty canvas and it is up to us to determine what kind of picture we'll paint. For me, that's an easy choice right now.

Color my canvas blue.

MONDAY, OCTOBER 28

A first in the life of Wally Whipple. I got sick at school today and actually was sent home. By third period, I felt woozy. Beads of sweat broke out on my forehead, and I started to feel as though the Chicago Bears were using my body as a tackling dummy. Mrs. Garrison noticed and suggested that I check in with the school nurse. I went to the nurse's office, and she stuck the thermometer in my mouth. She gave one long, "Hmmmmm," when it popped out, then called Dad at work. Fifteen minutes later, I was pushing through the back door of the Casa de Whipple, looking forward to the love, sympathy, and attention that Mom would shower on me for being truly ill.

I walked into the family room and was ready to flop on the couch when I noticed something stirring under a bright blue wool blanket: Natalie.

"What are you doing here?" I demanded.

"I'm sick. Got sent home from school. What are you doing here?" she demanded.

"I'm sick, too."

This foiled my vision of being waited on and moaning to my heart's delight. When you are sick, you do not want to share the limelight. You want all attention focused on you. It is one of the few times you can be wholly immersed in yourself and not worry about all the Sunday School lessons you've had about selfishness. There is something sort of peaceful about being sick, as long as you're not too sick. Most of the rules are suspended—temporarily. You can whine, pout, not do your homework, and eat almost whatever you want to, provided your stomach is holding up its end of the bargain.

But there was Nat, sick. And when Nat is sick, she gets all the attention. Let me emphasize the word *all* once again. In fact, she had just started a moan when I arrived in the room, a moan which she now commenced again.

"OOOOHHHHHHHHHH, Mom," she groaned, then turning to me and quickly whispering, "I'm sicker than you are, so don't get any ideas about getting all the attention. Mom . . . AAAHHHHHHHHH . . . I need pop to make me feel better . . ."

Wisely, I marched upstairs to my room, grabbed my

headphones, and climbed into bed. This was one battle with Natalie that I wasn't going to fight. She would win, hands down, and besides, I didn't feel up to it.

By late this afternoon, nothing had changed: still sick. No interaction with any human being, except Natalie. Hmmm. I stand by my original statement on second thought. My one encounter went like this, after I stumbled downstairs to watch some television while Mom was out. Nat wanted to watch a talk show; I wanted to watch a rerun of "I Love Lucy."

ME: "I want to watch Lucy."

HER: "I don't. I want to watch Oprah."

ME: "I'm sicker. I should get my way. You've had the TV all to yourself."

HER: "You're not sicker. I'm sicker."

ME: "No way. I'm sicker."

HER: "Big way. I'm totally sicker than you."

After about two minutes more of meaningful and insightful dialogue similar to what I have just written, we decided to find out who was sickest by dueling with thermometers. The winner (the sickest) was who had the highest temperature. If I won, it was Lucy on the TV. If she won, we stuck with Oprah, who was interviewing a woman who had lost 237 pounds in six months and transformed her life from that of an aimless housewife who watched soaps and ate chocolate bon-bons into a new and successful career as a motivational speaker and weight loss consultant.

But I digress. Nat stuck the thermo into her mouth and I watched her like a hawk for three minutes. Honestly, I wouldn't have put it past her to run a little hot water on the thermometer to jack up her temp a bit. Anyway, when her time was up, she pulled it out and handed it to me. (One of the ground rules—the other one got to read the temperature.)

"Well?" she demanded.

"Looks like 100.7. Deathbed to me, Nat. My turn."

After washing off the thermo, in it went. I concentrated as hard as I could. I imagined myself sick, lost, and wandering in the searing Sahara Desert. I tried to guide all the little hot and achy feelings of my body toward my tongue. I felt good, which is to say, I felt bad. Had this one in the bag, and Lucy would be mine.

"Your time's up," Natalie announced. "Let's see how you did, Wimpus." She took the thermo. "You may leave now, Wallace. Ninety-nine point four. Not even a real fever. You lose," she flouted, curling up on the couch, glorying in her triumph. I grabbed the thermometer, and she was right. I lost, 100.7 to 99.4. I slid away, figuring that I had better not press the issue. But too late. Nat noticed.

"Oh, and Wally, would you mind bringing me some orange juice?" she asked sweetly.

I got her the orange juice, all right, and I think even Natalie would have been startled to know how close she came to getting it poured on her head.

TUESDAY, OCTOBER 29

Another day with the flu. How can it get any lower?

By the doctor saying that you have a broken leg, that's how.

Mom took both Natalie and me into the doctor today. After examining both of us, sticking the stick down our throats, doing a little of the poking and prodding that must be a very important part of the curriculum of any med school, Dr. Pratt announced that we both had a virus and should be feeling better in a couple of days. He prescribed some pills, told us to get lots of rest, and drink lots of fluids, advice that he could have very well picked up off an aspirin commercial.

I put my shirt back on and was heading out to the waiting room where Natalie was softly groaning in an effort to milk a little more sympathy out of Mom. (Actual conversation: "Mom, like I think I'd feel a lot better sooner if I only had something to look forward to . . . like maybe new clothes or going to a mall. I really think it would help my recovery. Seriously." To which Mom replied, "Nice try, Natalie.")

Anyway, Dr. Pratt noticed I had a little limp from where I got whacked playing broom hockey. "Where did you get that limp, Wally?"

"Playing broom hockey, three weeks ago."

"Three weeks ago? Is it improving any?"

I thought hard. "No, it really isn't, Dr. Pratt."

"Maybe we should take an X ray. You shouldn't be limping after three weeks."

So we did. And surprise! I have a stress fracture in my lower leg. Nothing too serious; should heal okay with rest. No cast, no crutches even.

What it does mean is no more cross-country. (I will have to put on a really long face when I break the news to Coach Leonard. Lumpy will be really upset that he doesn't have a broken leg, too, and has to finish out the season.) Perhaps I should buy a small token of appreciation for Mickey, who is the guy who struck the mighty blow that fateful evening three weeks ago.

This development may also have a positive effect on my love life.

JULIE: "Does it hurt much, Wally?"

ME: "Well, not too much. I keep a piece of wood nearby and when the pain gets too intense, I put it between my teeth and bite on it. As you can see, I have chewed through several two-by-fours, but the pain is easing somewhat, I believe."

JULIE: "Oh, Wally, you're the bravest man I've ever known! Can we date lots and perhaps get married after your mission?"

And my parents feel awful, of course. It is the maximum guilt trip.

"How did we miss it? Why didn't we see it before?" Dad will ask Mom. "The kid has been walking around for weeks on a broken leg and we hardly noticed."

Note: I'm going to keep this in my mental file and use it at just the right time, say, when I am in huge trouble for wrecking the car or signing the papers to have Natalie institutionalized or some other major family crisis. "Yeah, maybe I messed up," I'll say with a certain amount of self-righteousness. "But at least I didn't overlook a certain someone when he had a broken leg and was hobbling around for three weeks, *like some other people I know, whose names I won't mention.*"

Now I'm home, it's raining hard, I'm missing more school, I have the flu, and my leg is kind of broken. I haven't had a date in months, I have no prospects, my grade in math is hovering between a C and a D (much to Dick Dickson's delight), and I have only one question to ask:

Is this what life is really like?

WEDNESDAY, OCTOBER 30

The blahs continue to roll unchecked in the Whipple family. Yes, Natalie and I stayed at home once again, spending our daytime hours alternately snarling at and ignoring each other. We both feel better but weren't up for going to school today.

Tomorrow is when we will assume our normal orbits again. Natalie is especially cranky today. She hasn't received much attention from her friends while she's been sick, and it's been a blow to her ego, which is roughly the size of the Pacific Ocean. Worse (at least to her way of thinking), she can't call anyone and tell them she's sick.

"They'll go, 'Well, didn't you just tell us you were sick, and then you go you weren't sick, and now you're going you are sick?' And like they'll think I'm totally lying or something or that I'm looking for attention, which I'm not. It's just, like, if one of my friends was sick, then I'd want to know, seriously. Then, like, I could include them in my prayers or something," she told me in one of our rare moments when we spoke civilly to each other. "This is totally gross."

Dad is a little down, too. There's a job vacancy coming up at the Aisles of Value store, and I think he wants to apply, but he doesn't believe he'll be selected. I'm not sure, but he acts like he doesn't want to go through the whole process of applying and interviewing and then get rejected. In this sense, being a parent is a lot like dating.

Even Chuck is dragging. Tomorrow is Halloween, one of his favorite holidays of the year. But he's been having trouble figuring out a costume and now he's running out of time. Halloween costumes are a big deal with Chuck. Last year, he went as a box of corn flakes and all the adults who answered the door went bonkers and were dishing out the candy to him by the handful.

So here we are, the Miserable Family. It's raining hard outside, has been all day. We need a ray of sunshine, a little hope that life is going to get better soon.

Tonight Dad is working late and Mom is at the store loading up on my medicine. Natalie is lying on the couch in the living room, dressed in a dingy plaid shirt, her hair tangled and twisted. Chuck is spread-eagled on the floor staring at the ceiling.

I'm at the kitchen table, writing these few meaningless

lines in my journal, fighting off my sore throat, and listening to the wind and rain slam into our dark, brown house.

I hear footsteps on the porch. Clomp, clomp, clomp. The doorbell rings.

Who on earth is out on a night like this?

I walk over and open the door.

There, framed in the light of the doorway, is a tall, square-built man, dressed in a full-length rain slicker and a big-brimmed cowboy hat, water cascading down to the porch. He lifts his head slightly. Natalie dives under her blanket, covering her head.

Chuck pipes up, "I want to be a cowboy for Halloween!"

The man at the door smiles.

Yippie-yo-kai-yay!

"Howdy, Wallace. You folks got a spot where a stranger can come in and wait out the storm?"

Suddenly, my day—naw, my whole life—gets a lot brighter.

Orville Burrell is back.

CHAPTER 3

November

A knock at the door, a smile, the voice of a friend. That's all it took to get life back on track for Wallace F. Whipple, Jr. For a few hours, and maybe a few days, nothing else—broken bones, the flu, a social life that exists only in the wildest stretches of my overactive imagination—is going to matter. Orville is back! I repeat, Orville Burrell, Cowboy Extraordinaire, is back in my life. And things are definitely looking up.

Didn't write anything more in the journal on Friday, skipped Saturday completely. Too much catching up to do with Orv. He could only stay a little while on Friday night, "Me and Dad ain't finished movin' in yet. Got to wrassle in a little more furniture," he explained, but he promised to come back Saturday evening.

"You can go out trick-or-treating with Chuck. I walk him around the neighborhood."

"I'd like that," Orville said. "That cub brother has grown the length of an ax handle since last summer, Wallace. He may outplay you yet in basketball."

"Hope so, Orv. Chuck is a monster on the court now."

"And see you purty soon, Miss Natalie," Orv called over his shoulder as he left. Nat was still under her blanket, mortified that Orville, the object of her crush for almost a year now, would see her with greasy, stringy hair and dressed in one of Dad's old plaid shirts and a pair of yellow sweat pants that even I wouldn't be caught wearing.

Anyway, a hand appeared from under the blanket and sort of flip-flopped a wave in the general direction of Orv. "Natalie's sick," I charitably explained to Orv. "She doesn't want you to catch any of her germs."

"Mighty considerate. But I wouldn't expect nothin' different from Natalie. Then I'll mosey on by 'bout six and we'll do some city trick or treatin', Wally. See you then."

From under the blanket, I heard a muffled, "Good-bye, Orville. Wallace, Charles, and I will so look forward to you returning to our home tomorrow evening."

The next night, Orv appeared at our doorstep right on time.

"Great to see you again, Orville," Dad greeted, stepping up to pump hands with him. "Oh, Orville, we've missed you so much since last spring," Mom welcomed. "Are you at all hungry, Orville?"

And Natalie, of course, was at her best. "We are so charmed, you know, to seriously see you in the walls of our home," she said in her best honey-coated voice. She'd been in her room for almost two hours, getting every hair in the right place, selecting just the right outfit, and rehearsing her greeting no less than 20 times.

Then Chuck came down the hallway, dressed in his cowboy outfit. Big tall hat, huge belt buckle, chaps, a penciled-on mustache, and a cowboy shirt that would have done the Lone Ranger proud. He set a new standard for kids dressed as cowboys on Halloween.

"And looky here. Chuckwagon, you are one real hand with them duds on. You look as if you could ride a bronc trick-or-treatin' tonight."

"Speaking of trick-or-treating, I view it as somewhat gauche, you know," Natalie jumped back in, vying for Orville's attention. "I personally have not participated in the event for quite some time, seriously."

"Quite some time" in this case meant all the way to last Halloween, and I had the hunch she'd be making the rounds of the neighborhood again as soon as we took off, but I kept my lips tight.

"Can we go now, Wally?"

"Yeah. Let's clear out. There's a ton of candy out there waiting for you, Chuck."

Mom took a few pictures of Chuck, then we were out the door, watching Chuck from the sidewalk.

"You know how to surprise a guy, Orv," I said as we walked slowly down the street. "Hardly hear from you for four months, then, boom, you're on our front doorstep."

"Guess I did show like a mustang bustin' from the chute," he said.

"So why are you back? You told me that your ranch was home and that's where you and your dad belonged."

"Yep, I reckon I did. But things can change. You remember my Uncle Jess? He's the one who runs the feed store. When my dad was feeling pretty sorry the year after Mama passed away, it was Uncle Jess who came ridin' in to the rescue. He told me and dad to come on over to Portland and work in the store for a bit. That's what brought me here last year. Turned out to be real good for my dad. Took his mind off things a bunch. Everything around the house and ranch reminded him too much of Mama. So it all worked out more than okay for us, but we did miss our ranch and wanted to get back. That's why we up and left last summer faster than spooked grouse."

"But here you are again. And you said you were moving furniture in. Are you staying for a while, Orv?"

"We are. The way we figure it, my Uncle Jess put my

dad back on his feet. So when Uncle Jess got sick this fall—"

"You and your dad came back to Portland to help him out. Is that why you're here, Orv?"

He stopped walking and looked at me square in the face. "Seemed the decent thing to do. Never felt that I lost something by doin' things for others."

"Yeah. The decent thing," I repeated. "How is your uncle?"

"It'll be six months or so before he can whip up a cloud of dust. You got to take it slow and easy when your heart ain't hittin' right."

"I hope he feels better soon."

"Thanks, Wally. I got to admit this, too. When I was thinkin' about headin' back to Portland, I knew I'd miss my friends, my animals, and the other things about my home. But when I recall you and Chuck, Lumpy, your folks, and even that little sprite of a sister you got, the thought of stormin' back this way wasn't none too bitter."

"Good deal for us."

"Say, Wally, you ever done anything more with that gal you was so sweet on, Julie Sloan?"

"Well, Orv, let's just say that my relationship with Julie is about where it was when you left. You know, right after you and I took her out in your truck and she spent most of the night picking dog hair off her white dress."

"Sorry to hear that. My truck's clean now, though. Ain't a hound hair on it."

"Maybe that's a good omen. Heck, we're in English class together and I hardly even notice her, even though she is only two rows to my left and one seat up."

Chuck was knocking them dead at the doorway. Once again, he was raking the candy in by the handful. We were out about an hour, and Orv and I got caught up on a lot.

He joined us for the ceremonial dividing of the candy

back at our house. That's where Chuck divides all his candy into three piles—the stuff he really likes and shares with us, the stuff he shares with his friends, and the gross candy, which he gives to Lumpy, who is so moved at being remembered each Halloween by the gesture that he has vowed to name his firstborn son Charles.

It's been a good weekend. And even though I'm faced with about a dump truck's worth of homework tomorrow, and I'll have to face Coach Leonard and let him know that my cross-country season is over, I'm looking forward to school for one simple reason:

Orville's back and the Posse is gettin' ready to saddle up again!

MONDAY, NOVEMBER 4

Today got off to a most excellent start. I walked into seminary, and Julie Sloan, the girl for whom I felt intense like only a mere few months ago, looked at me and said, "Wally, are you feeling better?"

Now, do I exaggerate or do I merely follow the normal flow of human logic:

One, since she asked me about how I was feeling, it means she knew I was sick.

Two, since she knew I was sick, it means she missed me at seminary or English class.

Three, since she missed me, it means I am more than just another blip on her radar screen. It means I am *someone*. It means that in some small way, at least, and maybe some big way, I am out of the ordinary in her universe.

Yes!

I was very glad that I wore deodorant and changed into clean socks this morning. Maybe it was inspiration, kind of.

Other news:

Orville made a triumphant return to the school, the cafeteria, and his circle of friends. "Dang nice to see my ol' saddle pals." Plus, he is in two of my classes—English and P.E.

I limped down to the coaches' office after school today and broke the news to Coach Leonard, who seemed very disappointed.

"Wally, I am truly sorry about your leg. Now I understand better why you and Larry were at the restaurant [Note: referring to Hamburger Bob's as a restaurant is like calling the wristwatch Chuck received in a box of cereal a fine timepiece] when you should have been out running."

Mr. Leonard looked at me sympathetically. "You must have been experiencing great pain. But I admire someone who does not complain but continues to compete no matter how great his discomfort. You are a champion, Wally. I mean that."

"Yes, Mr. Leonard. And thank you. And I feel bad, too, about not finishing the season and perhaps letting down all my teammates. But be assured that I will be there on the sidelines cheering them for the rest of the season."

"Will this affect your basketball?"

"Well, I haven't thought that much about it." Okay, so I lied. Actually, tryouts for the junior varsity are in four weeks, a date that has been circled on my calendar since June. But I didn't want to seem too eager in front of Mr. Leonard, so that he wouldn't think that cross-country wasn't my favorite sport, even though it isn't. Does this make sense?

"Best of luck to you, Wally. And you take care of that leg so that you can compete in the high jump this spring. You have the potential to be a city champion, you know."

So my day went pretty well. I hitched a ride home with Orv in his cowboy truck, which indeed was remarkably free of dog hair. The only downer—and it came as no surprise—is that I have about 16,000 pages to read for homework, not to mention two tests and a paper due this week.

But other than that, I'm fine. Just fine. And I wonder, only a little bit, what Julie would say if I asked her out again?

WEDNESDAY, NOVEMBER 6

Natalie is facing a big moral decision. Her best friend is Lindy Hightower, who, until last spring, was her biggest rival at school. Then Natalie started to say hello to Lindy in the hallway, a gesture that she felt deserved Nobel Peace Prize recognition.

So Lindy and Nat began to talk, found out they had much in common (boys, clothes and doing cute extremely well), and a true and fast friendship was formed, at least until they both decide they like the same guy or wear the same outfit to school.

To me, it's a scary relationship, simply based on the fact that there is someone else in the world who is a lot like Natalie. I will not comment further on their strange relationship for fear of sending the stock market into a panic and upsetting delicate world relationships everywhere.

Nat's dilemma is this: she is trying out for cheerleader in a few weeks and is thinking that she'd like Lindy to try out also. Should Lindy make cheerleader, it would give Nat a close confidante with whom she could compare notes about the guys playing basketball, which, in Natalie's perspective, is the main object of being a cheerleader. If all this sounds somewhat twisted, I remind myself, it is because it is.

"So, if I go, 'Lindy, you should try out for cheerleader,' and she goes, 'Yeah, I should,' then that would mean more competition for me," Natalie said tonight as we were all winding down. "Like, I'm cuter than Lindy, but maybe not everyone would think so, and so some people might vote for her instead of me. Do you see what I'm saying, Wally?"

"Yes, Natalie, I understand what you are saying. You are worried that Lindy might ace you out of being a cheerleader."

"Yeah. I guess that's it."

"What makes a good cheerleader?"

"Mostly how you look and how popular you are."

"Is that all?"

"Well, I guess it, like, you know, helps if you can yell and jump around and do those things where you bounce off your hands and stuff."

"Cartwheels and flips?"

"Yeah. That's what I mean."

"So it comes down to if you think you're cuter than Lindy and more popular, right?"

"For sure."

"Well, are you?"

She thought hard and long, which for Natalie meant about a full second. Her chin grew firm. "Yeah. I am."

"Then maybe you should invite her to try out. It will help you to look good, you know, like you're not afraid of the competition."

"I get it. And like if I win and she loses, then I could, like, feel really bad for her and say that I wish she had won and not me, even though I don't really mean it. Seriously."

"There's a cooler way to handle it, but I don't want to get into it now."

"I think I'll talk with her then. Maybe she was going to try out anyway, but if I mention it before she says anything, then it will be like I'm really concerned about her, and she'll think I'm way nice."

"I suppose, Nat."

I hope my advice, such as it was, is good. If by some long chance Natalie doesn't make cheerleader and Lindy does, I know who will take the full brunt of the blame in her eyes.

Yep, you got it. Wallace F. Whipple, Jr.

FRIDAY, NOVEMBER 8

From the Whipple Chronicles:

First up, Mr. Waymon, the wrestling coach. With an unusual amount of emotion for a man who earns part of his livelihood by teaching guys how to grab and push other sweaty-smelling guys, he stopped me in the hallway. "Wally, I don't know if you had anything to do with getting Burrell back in school, but if you did, thank you. Thank you very much."

I should have told him that I had absolutely nothing to do with the Miraculous Return of Orville Burrell to Portland, but it is so seldom that you get the upper hand on a teacher that I merely lowered my eyes slightly, put on my most humble face, and softly said, "It's okay, Mr. Waymon." Is that a repentable sin?

Next, Natalie. She asked Lindy about cheerleading, and apparently that was all the convincing Lindy needed. She'd been thinking about trying out, she told Nat, and now, she felt like, you know, seriously, she should go for it. For Natalie, it was something akin to a significant emotional experience, too. "I felt like I was really doing something for someone else. I'm starting to get what they mean at church about serving other people. It makes you feel good inside, not at all like a dork, which is what I always thought you'd feel, seriously, when you did that kind of stuff. You know, like the teachers were only making it all up about feeling good."

Natalie is not exactly a spiritual giant, but she may at least be a quarter-inch taller than she was yesterday. Progress, I guess, comes in minute measurements for most of us.

SATURDAY, NOVEMBER 9

History replayed itself last night—me, Orv and Lumpy in the pickup truck, cruising around, hoping to make eye contact with three females of similar age, goals, and ambitions, although it's doubtful that pizza will be as high a priority on their lists as it is on ours.

History replayed itself in more than our reunion in the truck. We batted zero in the game of boy-meets-girl. Part of the problem may have been that when we got to the place where a lot of kids hang, Palacio del Pizza, Lumpy discovered that he had dribbled toothpaste down his shirt and pants. It's hard to be suave when you're with someone who has toothpaste slobbered down his front.

"That boy might be crampin' our style a bit," Orville said, as Lumpy went to pick up our pizza from the counter. "Sort of like ridin' a swayback horse in the Fourth of July parade."

"Yes, but he's Lumpy and we need to love him," I said.

"S'pose so."

So on a big Friday night, when teenagers dominate most of the planet, I am unable to contribute to the movement. I am home and writing in my journal by a few minutes past ten.

Do I have the picture all wrong here? I sit at home and assume that most normal 17-year-olds are out socializing somewhere, having more fun than I am, and making rapid strides toward maturity while I sit on my bed, write in my journal, and listen to my younger brother snore away across the room from me.

Yeah, I know a lot of my friends aren't exactly dating machines. Lumpy, for instance, is pretty sneaky about how many dates he's gone on. (The answer, I suspect, is zero, although he has mentioned the great time he and Christy Michaels had inner tubing at a stake priest and Laurel activity last summer. Still, I don't think you can count that as a real date.) But I'd like to feel more a part of . . . of life. Why am I on the sidelines so much when the big game is being played? Why in the great interstate of life do I always seem to have a flat tire?

Suck it up, Whipple. Tough it out. There's always another weekend coming. Things will change. They will get better. You may be more normal than you think you are.

I need to convince myself of that.

MONDAY, NOVEMBER 11

Okay, okay, I can take a hint. In seminary class this morning, the lesson was about missionary work. In priesthood meeting yesterday, the theme was about missionary work. One of the speakers in sacrament meeting spoke on—think hard, look at the evidence, don't rush too quickly and draw a hasty conclusion . . . yes, missionary work.

I've been tiptoeing around the subject of the Church with Orville. Mentioned seminary to him, and he said he'd like to come again after he got a tad bit more settled. But I know I need to get more direct.

ME: "Orv, Saturday, 5:00 P.M., at the church—bring a towel and prepare to get wet."

ORV: "Gotcha, pard. Need to dress down in white?"

My goal, pure and simple, is to soon approach Orville about the Church, *again!* It was great to hear him agree to take the lessons last year, even though I was in a high jump pit when I asked him. Now, he's come riding back into my life, and I have to believe it is more than mere coincidence. No waffling. No dodging. Nothing but straight-ahead talk, man-to-man, Whipple to Burrell. In fact, I could call him right now, drive over to his house, and lay it all out. Yeah, I *could* do that. Now.

But I think I'll sleep on it instead.

Wednesday, November 13

Conversation between Natalie and one of her cheer-leading friends, Stacey, as they prepared (namely, stared at themselves in front of the mirror in the bathroom) for cheerleading tryouts next week.

STACEY: "So, like, are you going to do a new routine?"

NAT: "Are you kidding? Seriously? No way. I'm just going to do, you know, like, something I did last year."

STACEY: "Oh, wow. Shouldn't you do something new? I was going to. Seriously."

NAT: "Well, I thought about it, but if what I did last year was good enough to win, then, you know, why mess with success? Do you see what I'm saying?"

STACEY: "So you're saying, like, you're going to do what you did last year because it worked and because it worked you think, seriously, it will work again?"

NAT: "Yeah. Like I said, why mess with success?"

STACEY: "Oh, I get it. Did you just make that up— 'Why mess with success'?"

NAT: "Yeah."

I wonder if Nat's not overconfident. She's relying on her reputation and the fact she was a cheerleader last year.

But I have my own troubles. I went back to Dr. Pratt today, and he said I should rest another week or two before putting much stress on my leg. Since basketball tryouts start next week, I need to seek out the coach and explain my situation, then hope for mercy. I am confident, however, that he will see my 6′4″ frame and immediately start drooling. "Sure, Whipple, take all the time you need. Why don't you just sit around and watch the first two weeks? Then we can break you in slowly. We'll have you peak right about the start of the season, just in time for you to trot onto the court and take your rightful and deserving spot as a starter, and score 30 points. We're counting on you this year, Whipple. I expect nothing less than greatness from you. By the way, has anyone told you that you walk exactly like Michael Jordan?"

That's what I *hope* he will say. I'll track him down tomorrow and take care of it.

Thursday, November 14

Basketball is important to me. I mean, you list all of the big basics in life—family, home, church, friends, Mexican food—and the first temporal thing I'd put down on my list of essentials is basketball. (I realize some may argue about the eternal significance of Mexican food, but they have never tasted Hamburger Bob's deep-fried, double-dipped-in-guacamole chimichanga, a new addition to his ever-expanding menu.) Put it this way: Basketball is me. The essence of Whipple. The only real purpose for air, other than to breathe, is to fill basketballs. I have a firm testimony of this. So I will do almost anything in the name of basketball, even approaching the junior varsity coach and asking for a couple of weeks of down time due to my bad wheel.

Big break for Whipple: I feared the JV coach would be Mr. Ackley, who coached the sophomore team last year.

Mr. Ackley, as a basketball coach, was a fine physics

teacher. I think he knew enough about the game, okay, but he didn't know the guys. You have to understand your players, and I don't think Mr. Ackley ever tuned in to us. He seems like the kind of guy who would be more at home playing chess with his wife on a Friday night than leading his troops to hoops glory.

The JV coach is a guy named Mr. Tim "The Torch" Rourke. He came by his nickname honestly. Played basketball for a major college, where he was the sixth man for three seasons. The guy could put it up. I mean, he came in sometimes and was unconscious, couldn't miss a shot. I remember a game against Washington State in which he hit twelve shots in a row, four of them from three-point range. Finished the game with something like 37 points. He was almost good enough to play pro—but here he is, coaching our team. This guy is going to be good. Heck, he's not that much older than us. He knows basketball and he understands players.

Mr. Rourke is a P.E. teacher, so after school today, I went down to the P.E. teachers' office. He was there, doing what all P.E. teachers do so well—hanging out, feet on his desk, looking cool. I began to get pumped. This is a guy I could play for, be a star for.

"Uh, Mr. Rourke?"

"That would be me. You look like a player."

"Well, yes, I am. A player, that is. In basketball."

"You going to give the JV team a shot next week?"

"I'd like to. But see, I have this sort of broken leg—"

He quickly looked down at my legs, no doubt expecting to see a huge cast clinging to one of them. Then he looked back at me, puzzled.

"Okay, I give. Which one is it?"

"It's the left one. Just a hairline fracture. Should be better in about two weeks."

"Oh. Tough."

"Well, I was wondering, uh, hoping, if maybe I could try out for the team, but closer to December when my leg is good enough."

There. That was it. My whole basketball career on the line. Somewhere, Michael Jordan, Shaquille O'Neal, and Shawn Bradley were holding their breath. Mr. Rourke shifted his feet on the desk and peered at my very long and lanky frame, no doubt calculating my height and weighing other factors. "What's your name?"

"Wally Whipple. Maybe you've heard about me from Mr. Ackley—"

"Whipple? No, I haven't heard of you. But . . ."

Here it comes. Judgment Day. I can't imagine being more nervous about anything, not even when the real judgment time comes and I'm about to be sent to whatever mansion in wherever place for numberless eternities. Well, maybe I exaggerate, but only a bit.

". . . that would be cool. No problem, Wally."

YES!!! Michael, Shaq, and Shawn, you may all breathe again.

"If you're going to be laid up a bit, though, why don't you hit the weights some? You could spend an hour lifting, then come up to the gym and watch the workouts. Need a little beef on you. You're on the scrawny side, Wally."

"Yes sir, that's me. I am scrawny, very scrawny, but I like to think of myself as being stronger than I look, sort of wiry, if you know what I mean."

"You ever lifted before?"

"Yes," I said, hoping that helping my Mom bring in groceries counted as lifting.

"Go on down to the weight room tomorrow after school. Mr. Podnorsky supervises down there. If you want to play basketball these days, you've got to buff up, Wally."

"Okay, Mr. Rourke. Will do. I'll be pumping that old chrome tomorrow," I enthused.

"You mean iron. Pumping iron, Wally."

"Right. Iron. I knew that."

A new chapter unfolds in the life of Wallace F. Whipple, Jr. Hitting the weights. No matter that my spaghetti-thin body is capable of pumping, oh, maybe 34 pounds. If it helps me to get a spot on the JV team, I'll do it. Like I said before, basketball is me. And me and The Torch are going to be one sweet team this season.

Friday, November 14

All day I am highly apprehensive about hitting the weight room. I mean, I'll be as out of place as a fly in jello. My biceps measure about 3.5 inches and my chest is the width of a dozen straws tied together. In the third grade, my nickname was "ostrich neck." The guys who hit the weights are all buffed up, and my grand entrance will either cause them to break out in hysterical laughter or start weeping from the sheer pity of seeing me in a tank top.

But I told Mr. Rourke I would, and in case he ever asks I don't want to have to square up, look him in the face, lock gazes, and lie through my teeth. And there is the added possible benefit that a little more muscle on my beanpole-like frame will help me to become a better bas-ketball player. So, as a semi-adult capable of making wise and correct decisions with maturity beyond his years, I show up at the weight room after class.

I fool around a few minutes at my locker, waiting for the traffic to quiet down. I pull on my tank top and head toward the weight room. I can hear clanking and grunting and get a whiff of pure raw sweat as I near.

I step inside.

Every person in the room immediately ceases all activ-ity and stares at me. I feel as though I've just gone into the world's best steak house and asked to see the vegetarian menu. I look in vain for Mr. Podnorsky, who may be able to shield me from the looks of disbelief and contempt.

I think maybe it's a total error, that I'll just sort of back out of the room slowly, like I took a wrong turn and accidentally ended up in the weight room by mistake. I take my first step backward, then hear a grating, deep voice from one of the benches.

"Wimp Pole!"

It is Evan Trant, he of the bulging biceps and tattoos.

I am so nervous that I may throw up.

"Wimp Pole, you gonna be a lifter?"

I nod my head and lower my voice about two octaves. "Like to try, Evan," I squeaked.

"Great. Wimp Pole, you need the work. You gotta be tough to sing in boys choir, right? Never should have transferred out of metal shop."

Evan looks around the room and barks, "This here is my pal Wimp Pole. Whatever he wants, he gets. Wimp Pole here is okay, even though he's a pansy and couldn't press a bag of peanuts. We got to put some muscle on this boy. Anyone got a problem with that?"

No one does, thank heaven. As quickly as the noise stopped, it starts up again, the clanking and clinking, the squeaking and grunting, the sound of good honest sweat being manufactured by the gallon.

"Wimp Pole, we're gonna work on your pecs. You're pitiful. Come over to this here machine, and what you do is grab these bars and pull them down. You repeat it about a hunnert times and then you'll be just a little stronger. That's the way it works. You tear down muscle to build it up."

"Thanks, Evan," I say, still speaking in my low voice. "You're cool."

He looks at me funny. "I know I'm cool, Wimp Pole. I owe you one for what you did in shop class with

Scleavege, but now we're even. And don't talk funny."

Happily, I start to work pulling on the contraption. After about six tugs, my arms feel like they are going to fall off, but it doesn't bother me. I am being left alone in the weight room, feeling a little bit comfortable, and doing my first real lifting.

Sure it hurts, but like Evan said, you've got to tear it down to build it up.

SUNDAY, NOVEMBER 17

Yesterday it was cold and windy; one big cloud after another blew across, dropping enough rain to drown toads. In other words, it was a typical fall day in western Oregon.

I was restless. Something was churning inside, something was bothering me, but I couldn't put my finger on it. I played like Nephi and took off, not sure of where I was going but knowing that something needed to be done.

I got in the car and started driving. I stopped by Sister Lawson's, the lady my dad and I home teach, to see if her yard was ready for the winter. Maybe another bagful of leaves, I decided. Something to take care of when the weather wasn't so disagreeable. Next, I found myself on the porch of a small, white house on Woodward Street, the place that Orv and his dad had rented. No one was at home. On a hunch, I drove out Foster Avenue to the feed store where Mr. Burrell worked.

"Well, I'll be! It's young Mr. Whipple," Mr. Burrell greeted me from behind a counter. "How ye be, Wally?"

"Really good, Mr. Burrell. It's great to see you again."

"And how's the family? Your dad, your mother?"

"They're all fine, too."

"And that younger brother of yours and your sister, Natalie?"

"They're doing great. Chuck is some basketball player now. And Nat hasn't changed much. Just about the same."

"As it should be. You've a mighty fine family, Wally. Are you lookin' for Orville? He's in the back, puttin' away some of our summer stock. He'll be pleased to see ya," Mr. Burrell said in his cowboy twang, motioning toward the back of the store.

"See you around, Mr. Burrell. I'm sure my Mom is getting ready to invite you over for Thanksgiving, if you don't have plans of your own."

"That'd be a pleasure for the Burrells. Your mother is a fine, fine cook. I look forward to hearin' from her."

I walked to the back of the store, through swinging doors. Orv was hefting fertilizer bags onto a storage rack.

"Hey, Orv."

He turned and looked surprised, pleasantly surprised. "Howdy. Caught me buckin' bags. I been helpin' out a bit. What we didn't sell this fall needs puttin' back now. I'm comin' to find out that weekends get a mite too long if you just sit around."

"Yeah. I guess that's what I was thinking. Got a big-time case of boredom today."

"You can always heft a few bags."

"Okay."

Although my body was sore from my first day of lifting (proving, however, that I do have a few upper body muscles), I grabbed a bag and sort of wrestled it up on the pile that Orv was building. Then another, and another, and another, all the while wondering why I'd driven all the way out to the store.

"Orv," I said, between several variations of the basic grunt. "I've got to ask you . . . something."

"Shoot, pardner. You don't need to fuss about breakin' your eggs with me."

"Remember . . . last spring, when you said you'd

(aarrgghh!). . . take the missionary lessons . . .?" As soon as
I said it, I knew what had been nagging at me. "Well, would
you (ooofff!) like to start them off again . . . (urrrfff!) or
maybe even . . . throw in with us at church? It'd be like
teaming up, you know, like a rider and his horse."

Well, I had wanted to ask Orv about the Church in the
worst possible way and had succeeded. *"Throw in with
us at church"?* In the history of the world, nobody has
ever come up with such a crummy way of inviting someone to begin the missionary lessons.

Somewhere among the angels, at this very moment, a
guy dressed in white is walking into the huge videotape
room where everyone is having their lives recorded. "Hey,"
he motions to his supervisor, "come here and catch this.
You won't believe what Whipple just did."

"Oh yeah?" says the supervisor. "Let's have a look."
They rewind the celestialized VCR (one that never breaks
down, never eats a tape, and doesn't require a Ph.D. in
electrical engineering to program it) and gaze at my pitiful
approach.

"Yeah, it's awful, all right."

"You think that I should edit it out?"

"Naw. A little repentance might even be needed for
that one. Better send it up to the Big Mansion and see
what they have to say there."

Back to the moment at hand, though. Orville stopped
hefting. "Wally, I've felt like I hadn't quite squared the knot
on that. Always felt that I had left behind a bit of unfinished business."

"Really, Orv?" I was beginning to feel a tiny bit of hope
that I hadn't completely biffed it. Maybe I hadn't quite
communicated spirit to spirit but at least had conveyed
something cowboy to cowboy.

"Yep. Got a taste for what you believe in last year, and
I kind of guess now I believe the same way. I got to wire all

the bundles together now and take the next step. Besides, I like that Mormon dude. Let folks know right square where he stood."

Having known Orv for a year now, I was able to instantly translate his cowboyese: "Wally, I want to learn a little more, then join up."

I'd thought about this moment for five months. I figured that if it came, when it came, I would let out a shriek, give Orv a hug, and pound him on the back. Now it was here, the moment I'd waited for so long, and instead all I had was a strong sense of peacefulness. No jumping with joy, no big talk. Just a good, serene feeling. Maybe the other would come later, and I'd pump my fist high in the air and hiss one good long *YES!* but now wasn't the time. Instead, I looked at Orv—plaid shirt, bib overalls, and pointy toed boots—and only said, "I'll take care of it, Orville."

And I will. Wally Whipple hasn't had an exactly astounding life to this point. I've said and done my fair share— maybe more than my fair share—of dumb things. But what happened yesterday was right, so right, and felt so good, that nobody will ever be able to take it away from me.

What I feel now must be a little bit like what heaven is all about.

After the videotape has been edited.

MONDAY, NOVEMBER 18

Reality beckons. Let me count the ways.

1. Grades. They are due out tomorrow. I am not at all nervous about them. I do not care about what glad or sad tidings my report card brings. Grades are a mere judgment passed on by another person who may or may not realize my eternal value as a human being. They are not a true in-

dication of what I am learning, my intelligence, my ability, or my potential.

However, all this being said, and feeling at peace with myself, I also realize grades can instantaneously ruin my life if I mess up on them.

2. Natalie. She is feeling immensely wonderful these days for two reasons. One, cheerleading tryouts are only a week away, and she feels confident. How confident? "Like, Wally, I think they shouldn't even make us try out if we've been one already because, seriously, it's like we have no competition. I hope Lindy makes it, but if she doesn't, and I don't think she will, then I hope she doesn't, like, cry in the hallway or something."

The other reason she is running on maximum wonderful is that her month's banishment from the mall is over tomorrow. "It was like a trial for me, Wally, but I got through it. I think, like, I'm a stronger person now because I had, you know, this adversity, and I did okay on it. It's kind of like that guy in the Bible who had all his stuff taken away from him, but then he got it back again."

"You mean Job?"

"Yeah. Either him or Moses, but I think it was Job. Anyway, I can relate to Job better now. I think Job was cool. He's not the guy who did the ark, is he?"

3. Edwina Purvis. I need to call, talk, or do something for Ed. If my social life is to ever pick up, I think it will begin with another date with Ed. Trouble is, she's not in any of my classes, and when that happens, it's hard to keep a relationship going. (Note: Next time you're stuck on a math problem, Whipple, call Ed for help. Math is not the usual channel for improving one's social life, but it just might work with Edwina.)

4. Dad. He told us tonight that he's going to apply to be the manager of the whole Aisles of Value store. I know he's been worrying about this for a long time, but I don't

know why. Changing jobs shouldn't be a big deal. Heck, I have friends who have changed jobs every couple of months. Adults, I think, worry too much.

TUESDAY, NOVEMBER 19

Grades arrived in the mail today. As a sign of the new, less maturity-impaired Wally Whipple, I calmly opened them up right after dinner, in full view of my parents, who were both in the kitchen trying not to look too interested and failing miserably in the attempt.

I scanned the column quickly. It looked like this:

Math: C. C for curses, crud, crummy. Somewhere, Dick Dickson is smiling at my grief. Ed Purvis, where are you when I need you?

Choir: A. Good old Mr. Ashbury. As long as you show up, sing loud (and not necessarily on key), look earnest and sincere, you've got an ace in this class. It also didn't hurt, I think, to let him borrow my Tony Bennett CD.

English: B. This is one of my best subjects, but Mrs. Garrison must be a tough grader. I did pretty well on my tests, wrote a couple of decent papers. May have to talk with her and see what it takes to bump up the grade a bit.

Social studies: another B. Need to work on raising this one, too. I started off well but then went into the glide mode. Can't be too far away from an A. Our main course of study is American History. The teacher, Mr. Donati, is good but from the old school. Very old school. Like when he talks about the Civil War, I think he may be speaking firsthand. He's a tough grader, gives tough tests, and dishes out tough reading assignments. I need to roll out the old Whipple charm a bit more and see if I can't earn (read that "brown nose") a better grade out of him.

Biology: C. This is the most disappointing grade of all.

Mr. Flagg, are you there? Are the lights on? We've had one test and a bunch of homework that he never has handed back. His favorite saying is, "When I'm done with you, you'll know biology better and be tougher, too." Funny, but I never thought of biology as a way of becoming more macho. Even Mel Pyne, who is assured of getting accepted by any college he applies to, was worried that he might get a B.

Journalism: A. Whew! Notify the Pulitzer Prize committee. Mom and Dad were looking at me with great curiosity. I nodded confidently to ease their concerns. Maybe a sly smile helped, one that fairly screamed, "Harvard will soon be calling, Pamela and Wallace." Covering those football games in the rain helped me run up the grade in this class.

Spanish: Miss Richardson is wonderful. Miss Richardson knows how to inspire her students. Miss Richardson's ability to trill her Rs alone is enough to start me burbling Spanish. I also happen to believe that all of the Mexican food I've eaten in my life sort of prepared me to learn Spanish. Just a theory. Did I mention I got an A in the class?

Let's see. Two Cs, two Bs, and three As. An okay start.

Mom could no longer stand the mounting tension. "How did you do, Wally?"

"Very well, Mother. Always room for improvement, and I'm not completely satisfied with my academic performance, but I believe this year has tremendous scholastic potential."

"Sounds to me," piped up Natalie, "like he got at least two Cs."

Thursday, November 21

One week to go until Thanksgiving. I need a break; can I tough it out? Do I have any other choice?

Got home late tonight because I had to walk. I only get

the car a couple of times a week, and that's on the good weeks. The rest of the time, I am sort of left to rely on animal instincts for a ride home. This entails sensing who has a car, who is in a good mood, and, most of all, who is in my same relative social caste in school. There is not a quicker social death than to ask someone a league or two higher than you for a ride home.

ME: "Say, Lance, even though you are a student body officer, on the honor roll, could date a super model, got early acceptance into Stanford, and drive a $30,000 sports car, would you mind giving me a ride home?"

HIM: "Who are you?"

Next scene: Wally trying to fade into the cold gray walls of the Benjamin Franklin High School locker room, mumbling incoherent apologies for interrupting the otherwise smooth flow of a high school superstar.

When my animal cunning fails and I do not catch a ride, I walk. Tonight, I walked.

Got home just about the time Dad was driving in. He was putting in a few extra hours, too, I guess, maybe to get an edge for the job he's applying for. We met at the garage door. He got out of the car and seemed a little tired.

"How was practice, son?"

"Didn't do much except lift. I think I'm up to pressing 86 pounds now, though."

"Good. Still don't think you'll be able to take me for a few years though."

"Guess not, Dad."

"Did I ever tell you that I used to lift?"

"Only a couple of hundred times or so."

"Sorry, Wally."

"Why did you stop? You've never told me that."

He paused a second. "Well, I got married. Guess that's the short answer."

"Didn't Mom want you to lift?"

"No, that wasn't it. You see, when you get married, Wally, your life changes in a lot of ways. You don't have time for everything you once did. All of a sudden, you're responsible for more than just yourself. In our case, you came along a year later, and not only wasn't there much time for lifting but it didn't seem as important."

"You used to play basketball, too, didn't you Dad? And go to college? Once Grandma told me that you were taking some night classes in writing—"

"All true, Wally," he broke in. "And I didn't give up all those things at once. Just decisions. You don't often come to a fork in the road as much as you choose to walk on another part of the same path."

You can tell when dads are trying to teach you something. They talk in a little different way; they seem a little more mellow; they seem to be choosing their words carefully. Dad was hitting on all three tonight.

What I think he was telling me is this: you can't always hold on to the things you like to do, and maybe the things you love, forever.

You've got to make choices about what is most important, then sort of let that determine what your course is. Then because of your decisions, some things drop out of your life. I know that tonight we were talking about more than pumping iron. We were talking about growing up.

About two more bends around the road and I'm going to be there: an adult. Less than two years of high school now, only one year of college, and I could be on a mission in about 800 days. It all seems to be coming too fast.

"But, Wally—your mom, you, Natalie, and Chuck, I wouldn't trade a day in my life now for something that might have been. Do you understand?"

"Yeah, Dad. I think I do."

And I meant it.

SATURDAY, NOVEMBER 23

Today was the day of Natalie's release from her bitter prison.

She went to the mall.

The official reason was to look at a few new outfits as she heads down the stretch run toward cheerleading try-outs.

Actually, she could have gone a couple of days ago, and I was impressed that she somehow resisted what must have been an overwhelming urge to shop. "I've got, you know, like, some self-control," she sniffed when I asked her about it.

In my role as the family taxi driver, I was selected to drive her to the mall, the prospect of which was not too thrilling to the Princess of Prices. "Like, could you just sort of drop me off and I'll walk the last little way?" she pleaded.

"Well, I can drop you off, but I know Mom will want me to make sure you're okay."

"This is the mall, remember? This is, like, My Place, seriously," Nat huffed.

And she's right. Most of the salespeople in the mall know Natalie. I mean, we're even talking the toy store and the computer store. The only store where she's a stranger is the bookstore. "I feel, you know, like I'm at home there," Natalie once told me. "When I get there I go, 'Wow, people here really like me,' and that makes me feel good." We've actually had three calls from mall merchants in the last month asking why they hadn't seen her out there. "Is she sick?" one of the salespersons asked.

"In a manner of speaking, yes," Dad coolly replied.

So I drove Natalie to the mall and dropped her off a discreet distance from her favorite store, right near the main entrance, so she wouldn't be seen with her nerdy brother by any of her friends who happened to be there. She almost leaped out of the car before it came to a stop, uttered a quick thanks, and was off at a sprinter's pace for the entrance. But luck was with me and I found a parking space close to the door. Wanting to have solid answers to Mom's questions upon my return, I followed Natalie toward the mall.

Having Natalie for a sister is a constant source of wonder. I will credit her with keeping life around the Whipples almost always fairly amazing. She is a source of surprises, someone who does not stroll through life but rushes through in a string of slightly out-of-control cartwheels. So I have come to expect the unexpected from my sister.

But what she did today sort of pushed the limits of surprise to new heights.

She arranged her own Welcome Back party at the mall!

I pushed through the door just in time to catch the blitz of camera flashes as Natalie stepped ahead. There were a dozen friends and a couple of mall employees, all greeting her with open arms and huge hugs. I saw a computer-generated banner strung between two pillars that read, "Welcome Home, Nat! We Missed You!" Natalie was cute, very cute. She talked to each of her friends. "Seriously? You missed me? Like wow, that means so much to me, Heather."

She got misty-eyed when someone handed her a giant cookie with icing on it that read, "We Love You, Natalie." Barely containing her emotions, she stood back for a minute and gave a speech. "This is really great, you guys, and I'm so happy to be here. Like, whenever I was sick, I thought about all of you, and how bad I wanted to, you know, get back to the mall again and see my friends. Without you guys, I would have not, like, been here, and instead been somewhere else. And this cookie is so special,

I'll always keep it, even when it gets moldy and stuff. You're the best, I really mean it. Now, can we go shopping? I have my mom's credit cards!"

True Statement: You would have thought she had been held prisoner by terrorists and this was her homecoming after being released.

The crowd all did sort of a general hug again and then began to drift away. I called to Natalie. "See you at two o'-clock, right?" She smiled and said something to her friends, which I suspect was along the lines of, "No, I really don't know who he is, but I will go find out since he knows my name," then came over to me.

"Nat, did you call your friends and arrange all this? And do they still think you've been deathly ill?"

She gave me her look of supreme indifference, an expression that she has mastered. "No, Wally. I got a phone call from Heather and Lindy, and they go, 'Would you mind if we met you at the mall?' and I go, 'No, that's cool.' And they go, 'Would it be okay if we did something special?' and I go, 'You guys!' So I didn't, like, encourage them, but I didn't exactly discourage them either."

"I'll be back at two, unless the mall management arranges to have you chauffeured home."

"Okay, Wally. Like, you don't have to tell Mom and Dad about this, do you?"

"No, I guess I don't have to tell them." I was feeling benevolent.

"Here. Take this." She thrust the cookie into my hands. "I hate these cookies. They give me zits, like, overnight. You can eat it, because you already have zits, so you might as well enjoy getting a few more."

"Thanks, Nat. All heart."

I turned and left, and wondering how Natalie and I could be brother and sister, a common origin from the same basic gene pool, and yet be so different. After giving it deep and considerable thought all the way home, I have come to one conclusion:

There is no explanation.

Tuesday, November 26

Check in:

1. Bad Basketball Vibrations

Yeah, I make my appearance every day at practice, hang around long enough to get the idea of what's going on, then sort of fade off to lift. I'm doing what the coach and I agreed to, so why do I feel nonexistent?

Today I stopped by to talk with Coach Rourke before practice.

"Hey, coach. Just wanted to let you know I'm still lifting and the leg feels better, so maybe after Thanksgiving I can get on the floor."

"Good, good. That's great. Nice goin', Williams."

I didn't feel like telling him my name is Whipple.

2. The Tryouts

Natalie tried out today for cheerleading. This is a great blessing to our family. It means that we will no longer have to endure endless telephone calls on the subject of cheerleading; endless chatter in the car, at mealtimes, during family prayer, during family home evening, during, well, basically, our waking hours; constantly hearing about cheerleading.

I asked Nat how she did. "I did great, of course. Why are you even asking?"

3. Encounter with Evan Trant

Saw Evan in the cafeteria today, which is something out of the ordinary, because most of the guys of his, shall we say, "ilk" usually go off campus for lunch, meaning that they go steal something to eat at a convenience store.

Evan spotted me, slugged me on the arm (yes, it hurt, but crying in his presence is not a good idea), and said, "Wimp Pole, my bud. You dress bad. And you're ugly."

"Gee, thanks, Evan. I needed a little pick-me-up."

"That's what I like about you, Wimp Pole. You say funny stuff."

Yep, we're definitely on the road to a long and lasting friendship.

4. Dad's Big Interview

Dad's interview for the store manager's job is on Friday. He went out tonight with Mom and came back with sort of a with-it tie and a new shirt. "This will go well with my suit," he told me.

Even Natalie had faint praise for his wardrobe additions. "Nice, Pops. Not quite kickin' gear, but okay. Beats that grody brown tie that you like."

5. Missionary Lessons for Orville

This was so easy. I just mentioned Orv, his background, what had taken place over the last few months, to Elder Milne and Elder Roberts. They got pumped. "Can we meet at your house with him? When? Tomorrow?" Everything is set up for next week at our house. I'm getting this big ol' blue-skied feeling that we're going to be calling him "Brother Orv" before much longer.

THURSDAY, NOVEMBER 28

Yes, Thanksgiving.

The sights, the aroma, the feeling of a day on which nothing can go wrong. Let's take the vote right here. Yes, I like Christmas. Yes, I like birthdays. Yes, I like the Fourth of July. But in a way, Thanksgiving smokes them all. A day just to give thanks—not to mention football, awesome food, more football, and even more food.

Mom invited the Burrells. Natalie, sensing the opportunity to impress Orv with her highly developed culinary and homemaking skills (she can warm up chili in the microwave), stunned the entire family last night by saying, "Mom, is there something I could do to help with dinner tomorrow? Seriously."

"Well, Nat . . ." stammered my clearly shaken mother. "What, uh, did you have in mind?"

"Oh, I don't know. Maybe the turkey. And I like your rolls, too."

"If you want to help with the turkey, I'm going to start at six in the morning—"

"I think I'll do the rolls, Mom."

And Natalie did try to make the rolls, but it didn't work out so well. She biffed them by mixing the yeast with water that was boiling.

"I think you killed the yeast," Mom said, after the dough failed to rise after an hour. "You have to have the water temperature just right. If it's too hot, it does in the yeast. Did you boil the water first, Natalie?"

"You mean, like were little bubbles sort of floating all over?"

"Yes, that's what boiling water looks like."

"Yeah," she said triumphantly. "I, you know, wanted to make sure there were no germs in the water."

"You wanted to sterilize the water?"

"Yeah. I didn't want anyone to get sick from, like, polluted water."

"No one would've got sick from the water. The yeast is dead, though."

"Well, gross, Mom. It's not like yeast is alive or anything. I mean, what are they, little animals or something?"

"As a matter of fact, they are."

"You mean little animals are what make your rolls taste so good?"

"Pretty much, Natalie."

"That's the grossest thing I've ever heard of. No lie. I'll do something else, like open the can of cranberries." And with that, she left for her room while Mom started digging through her recipes for quick-rising breads.

As it turned out, we didn't need the rolls anyway. Right on time, an hour before dinner, the doorbell rings and Chuck runs over and opens it.

"It's Orville and his dad!" he shouts.

In walk the Burrells. Both of them are dressed in corduroy sport jackets, nice blue jeans, white shirts, and string ties. Shiny cowboy boots poke out from beneath their long-cut pants, and they both hold their cowboy hats in their hands.

"Stan, Orville, come in. It's good to see you," Dad greets.

"Pleasure is all ours. Thank ye for the hospitality," Mr. Burrell says. "It feels almost like home to us here." He hesitates a second, looking around our house, his eyes pausing on a family portrait. I notice a sad look flicker across his face. Then Mom comes in from the kitchen, and Mr. Burrell smiles. "I brought ye some flowers, Mrs. Whipple. We're hopin' you find them to your likin'."

"Oh, I will. Mums are so beautiful! Thank you so much. And both of you look so handsome."

"Thank you, ma'am," both of the Burrells say in unison, bowing their heads slightly.

"These here are what we call our Montana tuxedos," Orville says, and everyone laughs.

"And we brought ye these," Mr. Burrell says, reaching down to the doorstep and grabbing a big flat pan. "Sourdough biscuits. I was considered a good hand at cookin' when I was tendin' sheep in the summers up along the Big Belt Mountains. That was long ago, but I reckon I never lost the feel for sourdough."

"Coyotes from four counties around came to camp hopin' one of Dad's sourdoughs would get dropped in the dirt," Orville says. "But they never did. They was too good."

"And where's the purty little gal?" asks Mr. Burrell.

Before I could answer, "Probably in front of a mirror somewhere," Natalie, with her usual wonderful feel for the dramatic, comes around the corner and into the living room.

"Hello, everyone. So wonderful to see you, Mr. Burrell and Orville." She walks over to Mr. Burrell and gives him a warm handshake. "May you have the happiest of Thanks-givings with us today, seriously."

Mom and Dad just sort of stand there with frozen smiles. Chuck starts to ask something like, "Why is Natalie talking so funny?" but Mom slides her hand over his mouth before the incriminating words tumble out.

"You look awful nice, Natalie," Mr. Burrell compliments.

I was just beginning to notice Natalie's outfit myself. I guess you could call it contemporary cowgirl. She has on a denim skirt, with a white blouse, a red scarf around her neck, and a leather vest. And as the final dash of flair, she has on brand-new cowgirl boots.

Dad speaks very softly in the general direction of Mom, without moving his lips. "How much did that cost me?"

"Thank you very much. I so adore the western style of dress, you know."

"Where did you get those clothes? You never wear cowboy stuff," Chuck blurts, after Mom's hand drops from his mouth.

"Oh, Charles. Sweet, Charles," gushes Natalie, who must have been figuring that she'd blast Chuck into an-other orbit after the Burrells left. "Seriously, out of the mouth of babes. I think it was Shakespeare who uttered those lines first, for sure. He was a writer, as you know. They called him the Bard of Avon, because he also invented perfumes."

Dad tries to salvage things. "Come on in and let's sit down. There's a little bit of time before the turkey's ready, and the Dallas game is still going on."

"That'd be nice," Mr. Burrell says. And before you know it, Mr. Burrell and Dad are talking about fertilizer, nuts, bolts, screwdrivers, and hammers, which I guess could be expected given their respective livelihoods. Orville and I wander out to the driveway to watch Chuck shoot a few baskets. Natalie is on the verge of fluttering back to her room, when Mom says, "Nat, how about a hand in the kitchen?" After one quick, dark look, Natalie says, "But of course, Mother," smiles once and waltzes toward the oven.

The rest of the day is simply perfect. Natalie arranges to sit by Orville, who holds out her chair and helps her get seated. Natalie turns almost the same consistency as the brown gravy as Orv gently pushes her chair to the table; she hardly takes her eyes off Orv the rest of the evening.

"Seriously, it is so nice to have a gentleman in the house," she titters to no one in general and to me specifically. "It will be good to now enjoy the fruits of our labors."

Mom, in what must be a prearranged deal, says, "And thanks, Natalie, for all your help. I'm not sure I could have pulled this all together without you."

Natalie beams. Chuck says something about how Natalie opened the can of cranberries all by herself. Natalie no longer beams.

Dad offers the prayer. He gives thanks for our family, our health, our friends, special guests, the Burrells, who have joined us this day. He gives thanks for where we live, what we do, and for the blessings of the Church and the Savior. He asks for a blessing on the food, and we all say amen. Mr. Burrell gives an appreciative nod to my Dad at the end of the prayer.

Then our Thanksgiving feast begins.

An hour and a few minutes pass. Without a word, Mr. Burrell and Orville begin clearing the dishes as the meal winds down. Surprisingly, Natalie pitches in, too. I am soon feeling the sudsy warm water in the sink, and between the conversation, the chatter, and the good feeling of having friends nearby, the dishes get done.

The Burrells say thanks one more time right at eight o'clock. Mom packs a hefty plate of leftovers and shoves them in Orville's hands, over polite protests. "Well, at least ye keep the sourdoughs," Mr. Burrell suggests, and Mom says fine. They don their hats, then head into the night.

"I feel like I've known them all my life," Dad says.

"Good people. Just plain good, decent people," Mom says.

"Orv showed me how to twirl a rope," Chuck says.

"I'm going to go change my clothes now," Natalie says.

It won't be long before we're all back into it—Dad and his job interview; me and basketball, school, seminary, and whatever else; Natalie into cheerleading, cute, and clothes; Chuck into cruising through the first grade; Mom holding it all together for the rest of us. But right now, it feels good to have taken a time out and given thanks this day for everything—the good we see and experience all around us.

Right now, I wouldn't trade places with anyone.

Friday, November 29

Dad didn't say much about how his interview went

today. He was up early and left before any of us were out of the sack. When he got home, he was still dressed in his suit, new shirt, and tie. "Went pretty well," he said. "I was interviewed by three people, Fred Chandler, Ray Petrow, and Janice Clendenon. Now I guess we wait."

Late last night, I heard him talking to Mom. "I don't know. They seemed friendly, fairly positive about everything. But the interview was, well, I guess superficial. I wonder if they don't have someone else in mind. I know I could do the job—"

"We just need to figure that whatever happens, we'll make the best of it," Mom said.

"I just want a change. I need a change."

A change. You think of your parents as the anchor, steady as a rock, always there.

Yet my dad wants change. Needs change.

He's an adult, though. His course is charted—he knows who he is, what he's good at, what his children are like (practically perfect). He loves my mom. He's a great guy. What's there to change?

Is being an adult more complicated than I thought?

SATURDAY, NOVEMBER 30

First missionary lesson with Orv tonight. I know Saturdays spent with missionaries may not exactly ring the chimes of most people, but, how do I say this, everything went great. I felt the Spirit. Orv did too. The elders were awesome. Even Natalie sat in on the discussion, and for once didn't try to be the center of attention. When Elder Milne asked Dad to select someone to close with prayer, he looked at Nat. She said a nice prayer, even asking that Orv would be blessed to know the truth, and once he found it, that he would have the desire to follow it.

I was impressed. About the time you think Natalie has, say, limited vision, she comes through with something that surprises you, totally. I think Dad was inspired tonight when he asked her to pray.

"Do you think Orv will be a Mormon someday?" Chuck asked me as we got ready to call it a night.

"Yeah. And I don't think we're going to have to wait long," I told the Chuckster.

No later than Christmas. That's my guess.

Go Orv!

CHAPTER 4

December

I walked in from basketball today a little after five and immediately sensed that something was not right. Not that it took a Ph.D in psychology to figure out that not all was well in the Whipple household. In the middle of the living room floor, Natalie was stretched out on her back, staring directly at the ceiling. Her arms were flung wide and her feet spread out. She was motionless, which only happens when she is asleep, ill, or exhausted from ten hours of shopping.

But the biggest clue was that Natalie was listening to classical music. Natalie never listens to classical music. I mean, this is a young woman whose tastes in music can only be described as "primitive," with groups such as Brink of Extinction, the Dead Earthworms, and the Rolled Hard Oats among her favorites. Certainly, she has little taste in music and probably thinks Sinatra is a pasta dish and Como an Italian dessert. But there she was, lying on the floor, still as a word in a dictionary, eyes wide open.

"Natalie, are you okay?"

No movement. No reply.

"Uh, Nat, are you feeling all right? Do I need to call 911?"

Almost imperceptibly, she slightly tilted her head in my direction. "Is that you, Wallace?" she whispered hoarsely, against a backdrop of solemn orchestral music.

"Yeah. What's wrong?"

"Nothing," she murmured. "Except that my life is over. That's all. Seriously." Then she resumed her staring into space routine.

"Where's Mom?"

No response.

"Nat?"

Nothing, except a vacant look, the sense of a mind wandering a million miles away.

I walked to the back of the house looking for Mom. I didn't find her, but Chuck was upstairs in our room. "What's up with Natalie?"

Chuck looked up from his basketball cards. "I'm not sure. She is acting a lot different, though. I think Mom said something about cheerleading."

Cheerleading! That was it. Natalie didn't make cheerleader! No wonder she was acting as though there had been a death in the family. She would be less upset if, say, the evening news announced that a comet was on a collision course with the earth or that the Soviet Union had revived itself and was mobilizing an army.

Problems, I guess, are all relative.

Now, although I am a caring, sensitive man of the '90s, my next thought was: what does this mean for me?

1. Natalie will undergo some intense brooding, followed by long stretches of pouting and thinking only of herself, although the argument could be made that her behavior is that way almost any day.

2. She will get loads of sympathy and probably con at least one new outfit from my parents.

3. The phone will be tied up for hours on end as Nat

explains to all her friends why she should have been chosen but wasn't.

4. Next year, she will conduct a killer campaign to get elected. She will, after all, be in high school, a 10th grader, and will stop at nothing to make sure she does not go through the embarrassment of losing. She will begin by spring, practice hard, lobby faithfully, and go into her all-time cute mode the week before tryouts. She might even learn how to do a cartwheel, although the splits are still too much for her. Her effort will be as calculated and cunning as a coup in a moderate-sized nation, and I will spend much of my senior year right in the middle of it. Oh goody.

In the short term, I decided to avoid Nat. I got through a little biology, fiddled around with journalism, read a few pages for English.

Downstairs, everything remained still, except for the somber music. I got the feeling that I should go down and try to talk with Natalie. I crept downstairs quietly, where everything was dark. I saw the outline of a lumpy mass in the middle of the floor, though, so Nat had not moved a muscle in the last hour. Not a good sign.

"Nat . . . sorry about the cheerleading. I thought you had it in the bag."

No answer. The air in the room seemed chilly. Outside, the rain pattered against our window, and shadows caused by the streetlight and tree in our front yard swayed against the walls. Natalie remained motionless.

"Well, if I can help, let me know," I offered.

I was about to leave when I heard a long, sad sigh, followed by a voice in the dark.

"I thought I had it too. Like seriously. I thought, 'These other guys, you know, bzzz, no way.' But they made it and I didn't. It's not fair."

"I guess not."

"And what bugs me is, you know, like, Lindy made it.

And I didn't think she would and I was the one who told her, 'Seriously, you should try out,' thinking she wouldn't, but it would, like, be way cool of me to ask, then she'd really know I was her friend. I even planned to, like, cry when she told me she didn't make it, but when she did and I didn't and we saw each other in the hallway, she, like, didn't even cry and she was really happy, but I did cry and all for the wrong reason. It's not fair, Wally," rambled the voice in the dark.

"She probably didn't cry in the hallway because she was happy, Nat. She'll think of you later and do something nice, like cry for you."

"I hope so. She owes me sort of."

"I know you feel really bad, Nat, and this won't make a lot of sense, but the world is still going to be okay. I mean, I know this is important, but you still have a lot to look forward to in life. The after Christmas sales. Dating. Getting your driver's license. Callings to the homemaking committee."

She stirred a bit. "Yeah, I know. But it's like this, Wally. I don't feel like I'm any good at anything, really, except clothes. Cheerleading meant a lot to me. And I did the right thing by being nice to a friend, but it, like, goes backwards and she makes it and I don't. I didn't think that's the way it is supposed to work. You know, like, what they teach you at church. Do what is right and let the consequence be awesome."

I began to glimpse how upset she really was. Not being a cheerleader was causing Nat to question her self-worth. Nat's image of herself, I always figured, was like a brick wall. Now I was seeing that even the Mall Princess's confidence could sag. What fragile people stare back at us in the mirror! It doesn't happen often, but I actually felt sympathy for her.

"Nat, sometimes doing the right thing is about all you

can hope for. If people did the right thing and always got an instant award, there would be, like, no challenge. It would be too easy." Then for added emphasis, I spoke in her native tongue. "Seriously."

"I don't get it."

"Trust me on this one. Someday you will. Someday it will make more sense."

"But I feel like such a loser."

Losing is something I am intimately familiar with. It's become part of my emotional makeup. Natalie—maximum popular, ultra cute, best dresser in her whole school and maybe in the Top Ten of Young Females Everywhere, someone who has success stamped all over her—and *she's* feeling like a loser. She ought to trade places with me if she wants more of a real life experience at feeling like a loser. But I digress.

"You're not a loser, Nat. You know that. You have lots of talents."

"Yeah? Name one."

"You . . . you . . ."

"See, you can't."

"You . . . are a good person. Not everyone would have even thought of asking Lindy to try out. See? There's one. And you want to see Orv baptized. You have, uh, like, con-cern for others." Borderline lie, I know, but maybe they'd go easier on me on the Other Side because it was a fib for a good purpose.

"Yeah. And look what it got me."

"Nat, you can't base your self-image on being a cheer-leader. There's so much more in life than jumping around and yelling things to athletes who aren't even listening."

"They do listen. Last year, the guys on our team said we were the reason they won so many games."

"Nat, your team only won one game."

"Well, cheerleading is not stupid."

"Okay, cheerleading is not stupid. But it's not the most important thing in life. You've got a lot of other stuff you do well, and you know things about life and what you want out of it. You know why you're here, and that puts you way ahead of most other people. Those are the things you should be thinking about. Not cheerleading."

I realized I was beginning to sound like a parent, a chilling thought.

Nat grew quiet. I could tell she was thinking, which isn't hard, since she so seldom does it. It was almost as if she'd called all her brain cells together for a quick meeting. "Cool," they say. "We haven't all been together since 1989!" Finally, I heard a weak little mumble, followed by a more discernible "Okay."

"I'm going back to my room now. I've got more studying. Things will be okay. I really feel that, Nat." And as I left, I heard one other small voice in the dark.

"Thanks, Wally."

For some reason, I enjoyed hearing those two little words. They made me feel a lot like an older brother.

Friday, December 4

The classical music has stopped. Natalie made a phone call tonight to a friend and mentioned the "M" word. (Mall.) And the sure sign that there is life after cheerleading is that she mentioned Christmas being three weeks away. "Seriously, I feel like so unprepared for it," which in Natalie's lingo translates to "I haven't cleared enough space in my closet yet to fit all the new clothes I'm going to get." She's climbing back into her natural orbit an inch at a time.

Which is more than can be said of her older brother. My life seems on a steady, relentless trip to the pits, a downward spiral into a very dark vortex. Specifically, I speak of basketball, roundball, hoops, leather in the peach basket. I've been staying for the entire workout this week, yet I haven't exactly set the court on fire. Coach Rourke hardly even notices me. I'm beginning to think this is going to be a replay of last year, when I spent most of the time polishing the pines with the backside of my sweat pants. I think I'll make the team—being 6′4″ has a lot to do with that—but I want to do more than be the tall geek who sits on the end of the bench.

"You look about as down as a grasshopper after a heavy frost," Orville told me tonight after practice. "Can't show your stuff yet?"

"You got it, Orv. I may be playing in Pine City this year. How's wrestling?"

"Purty good. Not much to it. Jes' toss them boys around the mat a bit before I sit on 'em. Don't want to hurt nobody, so I go kind of easy most of the time. Drives Coach Waymon nuts, but I believe he'll get used to my style after a piece."

So that's about it from Wallace Whipple's Mission Control tonight. School's kind of dragging, I'm not even on the basketball coach's list of recognized human beings, and it's cold, rainy, and dark outside. About the only thing going for me is that Orv is taking the missionary lessons and Christmas is just around the corner.

SUNDAY, DECEMBER 8

Church today. Christmas carols. It felt nice to belt out a few of my favorites. That's one thing about being in boys choir. A year ago, I didn't have the confidence to do much more than sort of lip the words in a whisper, but now I can confidently sing out with no bizarre fears of being several octaves off key.

When we got home, Dad started talking about his new maybe-possible-potential job. He thinks this is the week that they'll break the news. Dad's up for it, I can tell. He's been a little jittery, more hyper than usual. Again, all this reinforces that maybe even parents have a few goals and aspirations in life, even though they've got the biggest part of things all settled; namely, marriage, professions, the cars they drive, children, and the fact that they will never again be as skinny as when they first met.

I was trying to do the right thing this afternoon, catching up on some reading for seminary, cruising through Romans to the degree it is possible to cruise through most anything that Paul wrote. Dad had his jets turned down and seemed to be dozing in the living room, Chuck was messing around with his coin collection, and Natalie had sneaked off to make some phone calls. Mom came into the family room and looked over my shoulder.

"Studying a little, Wally?"

"Yeah. You know, Sunday and all, it seemed like a good time to catch up for Sister Habben's class."

"Well, that's good. You need to be well rounded, Wally."

The term *well rounded* got my attention. It is a shot fired across the bow by mothers everywhere that some part of your life is out of balance, at least from their perspective. "Randolph, have you noticed that Billy Bub hasn't gone out on a date since the last solar eclipse? He's 33 years old and been watching videotapes of football for the last three days, and when the games are finally over, he's going bowling. Something may be wrong. Should we call a doctor? He needs a more well-rounded life."

When the oldest son is, shall we say, socially challenged (in my case, the possessor of a social life without any vital signs), it is always the mother who is most worried. Dads, if they are even aware of the fact that their oldest son has not dated since the last solar eclipse, will shrug their shoulders and say something like, "The kid's gonna be fine, Thelma Sue. He just happens to like football more than girls right now. I was the same way until I met you down to the bowlin' alley. Cut the boy some slack. Why, I bet he meets some pretty little thing down there tonight. It's league night and those gals sure look nice in their bowling shirts." Moms, though, are the ones who worry. It has something to do with the tiny DNA strand that controls grandmotherhood. Because it is in their genetic code, they all want to be grandmothers, and they start worrying if their oldest sons don't show much interest in the female of the species, even if it is several years yet before they want the actual grandchildren to start showing up at their front doors. I knew I was in for a lecture when Mom mentioned that I needed to be well rounded.

"Well, Mom, I think I'm pretty well rounded. I'm a student athlete, Honor Roll material, an Eagle Scout—"

"You are well rounded. But I'd like to see you have some more fun in your life."

Fun. Shrewd, Mom. What 17-year-old guy is going to say his fun quotient is filled?

"Sure. I guess I could use a little more fun."

"Well, I was talking at church today with Sister Simpkins, and she said that Barbara is really a fun girl to be around."

Ah-hah! Barbara Simpkins. One statement about her, guaranteed absolutely to be true: Barbara is not fun. Not that I'm making a harsh and quick judgment about Barbara, it's just that we've been in the same ward for six years and she hasn't said anything to me during that whole time. I mean, *not a single word*. This is a sure sign that her heart doesn't go into overdrive every time she thinks about me. Maybe if a meteor should come crashing into the earth and life as we know it is wiped out, and by some very long chance only Barbara and I are left alive, and in the rubble of civilization we happen to stumble into each other while scavenging through the ruins for food scraps, then we might have to talk with each other.

ME: "Oh. Hi, Barbara."

HER: "Oh, it's you. Hello."

ME: "Loud noise, wasn't it?"

HER: "Yes."

ME: "You lose everyone?"

HER: "Yes."

ME: "Sorry. Me, too. Guess that just leaves the two of us."

HER: "Yes."

ME: "Well . . ."

HER: "Be seeing you around."

ME: "Yeah. Okay. Hope you find something to eat."

HER: "Why don't you just stay on this side of the river, and I'll stay on the other side? Just so there's no confusion about anything."

ME: "Sure. Sounds good to me."

My point is, Barbara, through sheer lack of good sense or some warp in her personality, does not like me. Not now, never will. And it's okay with me. Sure, you want everyone to like you and be your friend, but it will never happen with some people. One of them is Barbara Simpkins. Now, how do I convey this distasteful message to my mother? Hmmm. Tact and diplomacy, Whipple.

"Yeah, Mom, Barbara is a nice girl (lie #1). But I was talking with her the other day (lie #2), and she said (lie #3) that she really wanted to go to work for the State Department and live in foreign countries for several decades."

That was smooth, if I do say so myself. Mom immediately went through a thought process like this: If Wally and Barbara ever marry, they would move to some distant third-world nation and I would see my grandchildren on the average of about every seven years. Barbara is not the one for Wally, and now I must stop this dead in its tracks."

Mom began a full retreat. "Well, just a thought, Wally. But there are many other nice girls around. And Barbara never really talks much. Maybe she needs someone more outgoing than you."

"Yeah. Like Lumpy. There's a good match."

"Yes, like Lumpy. I'll mention it to his mom the next time we talk."

Well, I felt a little bit like a toad for setting up the Lumpster that way, my best friend, a guy with whom I trust my most valuable possession, such as my Ken Griffey Jr. rookie baseball card. But one thought eases the pain and guilt of doing the Benedict Arnold on Lumpy: given the same circumstances, he would have done it to me.

Hey, what are best friends for if they can't take an occasional bullet for you?

MONDAY, DECEMBER 9

Update time:

Item #1: Good second missionary discussion with Orv tonight. The elders are a little worried about getting a commitment from him. In two weeks, Orv will be back in eastern Oregon for the Christmas break, and I know the missionaries don't want him to make the trip without a baptism date set.

Item #2: I need to finish up my Christmas shopping. So far, I've selected a basketball shirt for Chuck, two pairs of really nice socks for Dad (both of which I can borrow on important occasions), a small bracelet for Mom, and for

Nat . . . well, I haven't got that far yet, but I'm thinking of a baseball hat for her.

Item #3: I did get into a scrimmage today at basketball practice and did absolutely nothing. Coach Rourke called me "Williams" again, and my friend Andy Salisbury piped up and said, "Coach, his name is Whipple, not Williams." Mr. Rourke sort of apologized, then sent me in to play center against John Craddock, who is my height but outweighs me by about 60 pounds and who spent the next ten minutes pushing my hapless body from one baseline to the other. Weight lifting hasn't quite paid the big dividends yet.

Item #4: Seminary Christmas activity coming up next week, a service project where we select someone who needs a little yuletide cheer and do something nice. We're meeting on Sunday to work out the details.

Item #5: Got an A on tests in journalism and social studies; my enthusiasm for academia was somewhat tempered (shall we say doused with a fire truck load of water) by a C+ in biology and a C– in math. Dick Dickson, in his snide way, commented on my grade, "Still don't get it, do you, Whipple? Never will, either. You don't have enough fingers and toes for this kind of math!"

"Dick, I read a story in the paper the other day about an impending cure for viruses. You should be worried."

Item #6: Saw Julie in the hallway today, at the end of school. She walked right up to me (a very good sign), smiled (another very good sign), and spoke to me (a most excellent sign). "I hear Orville is taking the lessons, Wally. I think that is so cool. If there is anything I can do to help, let me know."

I successfully fought off the impulse to invite her to our house for the lesson that covers temple marriage and only said, "Thanks, Julie," which is probably the most coherent sentence I've spoken to her in four months.

Things may be looking up!

WEDNESDAY, DECEMBER 11

Okay, December is a month of traditions, and I started one last year—The Great Tradition of Wally Whipple Sending Christmas Cards.

Yeah, I know it sounds dumb for a guy my age to be sending Christmas cards, but last year I was filled with the joy and peace of the season, good will toward all, a willingness to share my good fortune, plus the teeny weeny hint of a desire to impress Julie.

To make a long story very short, it worked. Every person I sent a Christmas card to thanked me for it. And Julie? She was blown away by it. I honestly thought she was misty-eyed and on the verge of throwing her arms around me when she mentioned the card. Her exact words were, I think, "That was sweet, Wally."

So, since it's the season to be jolly, and since my shipwrecked social life could use a boost, I asked Mom tonight after I finished my homework if she could dig into her stockpile of Christmas cards and maybe pull out a dozen or so for me to use. Mom said that was cool, and about an hour ago I started in on them.

First up, the easy ones. Sister Lawson. A simple "Merry Christmas" and I'm out. Orv gets one, too. On his I write, "Have a Very Merry Christmas and I hope you get baptized soon. Your saddle pal, Wally." Nice touch. Direct. Good message. Next up, Lumpy. "You are a good friend and so cool that wherever you go, it will be a white Christmas." Hmmm. Not exactly my best piece of writing, but Lumpy won't mind. Next, a new addition to the Christmas list, Edwina Purvis. I haven't spoken to her in a few weeks and hardly ever see her in the hall anymore. However, she was the first girl I ever went out on a date with, and since that is an important eternal event (just slightly behind a mission and marriage, and maybe ahead of being an Eagle

Scout and a star athlete), Ed deserves a card. Plus, she represents my only realistic chance of another date in the foreseeable future (about six years). "Ed," my card to her reads, "although we've not been close to each other the way we were last year, I think of you often and hope your math class is going okay for you. We must get together soon. Merry Christmas, Your Admirer, Wally." Just call me Silk. I especially like the part about thinking of her often and getting together soon, both of which sound very mature.

Another card for Joe Vermeer, down at BYU. "Stay cool, and have a great Holiday Season." One for Sister Habben, my seminary teacher, another for Brother Hansen, my priests quorum adviser, and I'm about there. One person left. The Big J: Julie.

Let's see. Every word has to count, every word has to have meaning, deep, hidden meaning. The kind of meaning that will cause her to spring up from her pillow at 3:30 A.M. and think to herself, "What did he mean by that?" Yes, that kind of meaning. I want depth and sensitivity, even if I have to work on it for ten or fifteen minutes.

I concentrate hard and long, at least five minutes. Writing, I've decided, can be difficult work. Let me think this through . . . "Julie," . . . good start.

"We've been friends for many years (two) and from the depths of my heart, I want to wish you and yours a very Merry Yuletide." Great, so far. The part about friends for many years is loaded with symbolism. "What did he mean by that? Two years is not a very long time, unless . . . unless . . . Wally and I knew each other in our premortal life!" she thinks. "Yes! I'm sure that's it! *And he knows!* Maybe we, well, made certain promises to each other there. Oh, Wally, now I understand what you've been trying to tell me in your sweet, bumbling, and moronic way! But you wanted me to discover it on my own. I respect that and like you all the more for the way you've handled all this. You knew all along, didn't you? How could I have been so blind . . . and so foolish?"

Hit the brakes, Whipple. Don't get too carried away. There goes your hyperactive imagination. Bring it in, pal.

Back to the card. I like the word "Yuletide." Christmas is a great word, but everyone uses it. "Yuletide" suggests a quiet, intellectual depth, plus a better than so-so vocab. Yeah, Whipple. Just right. The part about "you and yours" I'm less certain of, but what the heck, there it is in ink, so let 'er rip. Now, the closing. This is critical. "Your friend." Naw. "Affectionately." No way. "Like." Get serious, Wally. Get, you know, poetic. "With the joy of the season in our hearts." YES! A monster ending. Notice how carefully the heart motif is worked in again. And I have to believe that after reading this card and its giant message full of symbolism, somewhere between Julie's sternum and collarbone, just a little to the left of her esophagus and a bit north of her gallbladder, Julie's heart will want to hit the highway of love driven by the engine of sweet thoughts about Wally Whipple. This is going to work, I just know it.

Yes, they will say, Wally Whipple may have slight complexion problems, he may never be suave, he may not be the star of the junior varsity basketball team, he may not exactly talk the language of *like*, but one thing can be said of him: He puts together a heck of a good Christmas card when he sets his mind to it.

I can hardly wait to get this in the mail, then sit back and watch for the adulation to come springing forth from Julie's eyes, her mouth, her arms, her . . . *yes, her heart!*

Sometimes, I amaze myself by these rare and unusual bursts of cool.

SATURDAY, DECEMBER 14

Dad didn't hear anything about the job this week and I think he's getting tense. He seems restless, too. There was a great basketball game on TV today but ten minutes into it, he was up and pacing. Finally, he told me that he was going on a drive and would be back in an hour or so.

"I know Dad's worried about the job, but it's not that big of a deal," I said to Mom after he'd left. "You either get it or you don't. The interview is over, so all he has to do is wait."

"Waiting is the toughest part, Wally. He wants the job not just for him, but for the whole family. It could mean some big changes. We'd breathe a little easier about college expenses, that's for sure," she said. "You and Natalie aren't that far away."

"Is beauty college that expensive? Six months and you're done."

"Don't be funny, Wally. Natalie has a good mind. We've also been thinking of moving. We like this house, but . . ."

Moving! The old brown house on Craig Street is the only home I've known. We moved here when I was a baby. Moving! I'm too old to move. I can't adjust. Now I know why Mom and Dad had been taking long drives late in the summer. Scouting out new neighborhoods, no doubt. It would mean a new ward, a new school, leaving behind friends—Lumpy, Orville, Mickey, Rob, and Mel. And Julie. A move across town and pffftt! A temple marriage in the making slipping right through my fingers. I can't do this! I have this huge fluttery feeling right in the gut. No way, Mom! I can't move. This is home!

"We've been looking at a nice neighborhood in Sandy and another near West Linn. We could afford a much bigger house. You'd have your own room, Wally."

My own room? Let's put a hold on my runaway emotions expressed a paragraph ago. A room of my own? No Chuck to keep me awake by snoring? My own private getaway?

And me in the suburbs—streets that wind gracefully up and down gentle hills, with little weed-free lawns and flowers always in bloom; where all the adults are cool, wear shorts in the summer, and let you call them by their first names; where the parents make you take off your shoes so that you can't soil their white carpets; where there is a community club with a swimming pool and maybe tennis courts. Where there are restrictions about parking your car on your front lawn and not having any houses painted green—and my own room. Did I say that before?

I can see it now. "Hello, Orville, Lawrence. So good of you to visit us. Welcome to our new home. Come in to the Great Room. May I take your coats? Thanks. As you can see, our formal dining room is to the left, a perfect place for entertaining. Notice the massive kitchen with plenty of storage. Mother adores it! Of course, the huge family room is the heartbeat of our home, gentlemen.

"Upstairs is the master chamber, and you will note, my own room, as well as other rooms for Natalie, Charles, and our guests. Notice the oversized closets in Natalie's room. Please, come in, gentlemen, and relax."

And with more money, maybe we can even squeeze a car out of the family budget for me. Too sweet! I could drive to the old neighborhood anytime I wanted. I could take Julie out on more dates. I could face her square in the eye and never feel inferior to anyone, because now *the Whipples have money!* Everything would be smoother. Everything would be right. People at church would whisper, "The Whipples are moving. I hear their new house is gorgeous! Brother Whipple really landed a good job, I heard." Dad could buy some new clothes. Mom could buy expensive furniture. Natalie could get charge cards with a higher limit! We could have trips to Hawaii, spring break jaunts to Florida, expensive gifts at Christmas. If money is a plague, let our family be cursed! We're strong, we can handle the temptation! I'm ready for this. I truly am. I stood up and started pacing.

"What's wrong, Wally?"

"I hope Dad gets this job, Mom." Man, I really do.

SUNDAY, DECEMBER 15

Had the planning meeting for our Christmas activity. We put the final touches on everything tonight. What we're doing is dividing into groups Tuesday night and going to the homes of people who need a little Christmas cheer. We've been baking goodies and making small gifts, and we're going to deliver them next week.

Since I was one of the activity's ringleaders, I was free to select who would be in my group. Surprise! Orv, Lumpy, Nancy Smisore (who will make a ton of gifts and baked goods), a girl named Vanessa Peterson, and a girl named Julie Sloan are in my group.

Did I say Julie Sloan? Well, well, well. How about that. Not that I would purposely try to hang out with only people I knew well and liked. Nothing like that at all. For example, I hardly know Vanessa Peterson. And I'd be shocked and appalled if anyone suggested that I was using a church activity, an errand of mercy and kindness, to perhaps boost my sagging chances of going out with Julie ever again. Only a nerd of the highest order would dare suggest a thing like that.

ME: (on the phone tonight with Lumpy) "Yeah, you, me, Orv, Vanessa, Nancy, and Julie are in our group."

LUMPY: (with a definite snicker, which shows an absolute lack of maturity, in my opinion) "Julie, huh? What did you do, draw straws, Wally? What a coincidence!"

ME: "Ha! It was a pure coincidence. Sort of."

LUMPY: "Yeah. Right."

Today at church I heard that we need to create our own opportunities for growth. The way I look at it, all I was doing tonight was heeding some very wise counsel.

MONDAY, DECEMBER 16

This is the sweaty palms week for me in basketball. I'm right back where I was last year, on the bubble. I thought making the team this year would be no big deal, but missing the first two weeks of practice is costing me. Although Coach Rourke called me by the right name today, it came as, "Whipple, can you get that ball behind the bleachers?" We scrimmaged today, and by the time I got in, the coach was hardly paying attention to what was going on. Three minutes later, he blew the whistle and we hit the showers. Did Shawn Bradley ever have to go through this? Michael Jordan? Danny Ainge? Did they ever have to go shag basketballs that had rolled underneath the bleachers?

I doubt it.

TUESDAY, DECEMBER 17

Tonight was the big seminary Christmas service activity. For me, it was the best of times and the worst of times, which is something I think is in an old Elvis Presley song.

The beginning was sweet. I was the driver, since our old family station wagon was the only car available that could hold everyone. Before starting, I said a little prayer to the effect of 'please bless the alternator, the generator, the carburetor, the little gadgets that go up and down in the engine really fast that make the car run when you step on the gas pedal, that the brakes would brake, the transmission would transmiss, the horn would honk, and the steering wheel wouldn't fall off.' Sort of your basic bless-the-whole-car prayer. I figured it was okay to pray for the car, since we were out doing something nice, and given the history of our family car, which in a nutshell is that it breaks down about every three weeks and almost certainly at the worst possible moments.

So I took off. First to Orv's. ("Evenin', Wallace.") Then to Lumpy's. ("You did say there were refreshments, right, Wally?") And on to the females of the species, first Nancy's, then Julie's.

The last home we got to was the Petersons'. Since I was in charge of our group, and therefore was sort of like the patriarch, and since I already had laid a prayer on the car, I thought maybe a prayer was in order so that we could travel in safety. Naturally, being a spiritual guy and the leader of our group, I offered to say the prayer. It started off okay; in fact, I was really getting into it, mentioning the safety aspect, that we would have a good time, return home after doing much good, and so on, when I decided to really take it up another notch. "And bless Orville, Lawrence, Julie, Nancy, and, uh . . ."

BIG TROUBLE. I couldn't remember the other girl's name. Being a spiritual giant has a downside. I cleared my throat. I coughed. I hoped everyone standing in the circle would think that I was, you know, overcome, and that the prayer was so meaningful and heartfelt that it was, well, getting to me. I cleared my throat again. One eye opened, as I searched desperately for a scrap of paper, a homework assignment, a magazine subscription label—*any-thing*—that would have her name on it. Now, it was getting awkward. With my one eye, I could see Julie and Nancy sort of shifting from one foot to another. So much for being overcome by the Spirit. Orville was still. Lumpy was extremely red in the face, his stomach shaking. I figured about three more seconds before he would burst out laughing and it would be all over. HELP!!!

Just as I was about to slip out the back door while everyone's eyes were still closed, Julie opened one of her eyes. She quietly mouthed the word *Vanessa* to me. For the sake of show, I coughed one more time, sniffed slightly, then said, "and Vanessa."

Never in the history of humankind was anyone more grateful to quickly tag on the amen to a prayer.

Before anyone could begin to discuss the prayer, I cheerily said, "Okay, out to the car!" and everyone seemed relieved to have something to do besides critique my prayer.

Although shaken, I coolly got behind the wheel of the car, trying to begin my comeback. "Buckle up, everyone," I said with a certain amount of authority, hoping to strike the delicate balance between concern for my peers and sounding like a cranky adult. Then we were off.

The person we visited lives in a nursing home off of Division Street, beyond 82nd Avenue. Sister Habben got all the names of the people who needed a little holiday cheering up from a community group. All we had was an address, and a name, Mrs. Galvin.

We found the nursing home without much of a problem, which was good, because it was really dark outside and not many streetlights. After parallel parking the car on the first attempt (Ha!), I gallantly jumped out of the other side, as Orville hopped out, too.

"It's as dark as a cow's stomach out here," Orville drawled. "You all be careful steppin' on the curb." With that, he offered his hand to Vanessa and helped her out of the car. Lumpy was by the car now and he helped out Nancy.

It was then that I realized that the gentlemanly thing to do was offer my hand to Julie and help her out.

I want to report that I did not mess up, that I did not say anything silly, that I did not make a big deal out of holding Julie's hand. I would like to say that I did not break into an instant sweat, nor did I get a sore throat and turn into jelly at the thought of holding Julie's hand.

Remember, that's what I want to report. But I can't. Instantly, my brain turned to overcooked oatmeal and my legs acquired the relative strength of tapioca pudding. Slowly, mechanically, with intense effort, I held my hand out to Julie.

"Hee muh hand, Julie."

In the darkness, I detected a smile. "Thanks, Wally."

"Ith okay."

Then, heaven, for all of 2.4 seconds or so. Her hand in mine. How many times had I wished for a moment like this? It was soft. It was small. I fought off the impulse to throw down my coat or call the temple.

"Leth go in," I mumbled.

"Sure, Wally."

Deep inside of what passes for my brain, the more rational gray cells began to send out little messages to my hand. "You've got to let go of her now, bud. She's going to think you're a dork if you don't. Got it? Okay, on the count of three, let go. One, two, three! Now!"

Reluctantly, I let her hand slide from mine. In the dim night, she looked at me.

Ahhh. I felt like I had just hit a home run in the World Series. Our relationship had taken on new meaning. We'd held hands, at a wholesome seminary activity, on December 17th. Someday, I would tell our children of this moment. Sinatra was singing "Dream Girl." It was wonderful. I floated into the nursing home.

A nurse met us inside. Her name tag said "Martha."

"So you're here to see Mrs. Galvin? That's great because she could use some company, I'm sure," Martha said. "She is 87 years old and has no family in the area. Mrs. Galvin has some good days and some that aren't so good. We'll see how she is doing tonight."

We followed Martha down the hallway and turned to the left. We came to room 136 and walked in quietly. A white-haired woman in a wheelchair had her back to us.

"Mrs. Galvin? These young people are here to see you," Martha said, turning her around to face us. I'm not sure what I expected, but maybe twinkling eyes, a warm smile, and some kind words come close.

Instead, there was nothing. A vacant stare. Uncomprehending. No sign of recognition or understanding.

"These young people are from a local church. They're here to see you," Martha explained slowly.

Nancy stepped forward and placed our gifts on the table near the wheelchair. "We want you to have these," she said.

Orville put a box of cookies on the same table. "Ma'am, here's some treats for you. We're hopin' you enjoy them."

Vanessa handed her a card. Mrs. Galvin looked at it for a brief second, then back into Vanessa's face. "It's a Christmas card. We want you to have a Merry Christmas."

Lumpy and I chimed in. "Yeah, please. Have a good Christmas." Mrs. Galvin blinked, but said nothing. Then she ran her fingers over the face of the card, and looked again straight into Vanessa's eyes. It was awkward for a moment. We thought we should do something, but we didn't know what.

Then Julie bent down, close to Mrs. Galvin and gave her a hug, saying nothing.

"She's pretty quiet tonight. But I'm sure she understands what you are doing here," Martha said. Mrs. Galvin stared out of the window.

And then, I don't know why, I'm not sure how, and before I could even think about it, I started singing "Silent Night." Thank heaven for boys choir. By the third word, everyone else was singing too. Even Martha. Mrs. Galvin turned and looked at us, one at a time. She closed her eyes and the slightest trace of a smile flickered across her face. Did she think of a Christmas long past? Perhaps when she was a girl, or a young mother. I felt that for a brief moment we had reached her, a ray of light piercing her confusion, the darkness of her December night.

We finished singing. "Guess it's time to go now. Merry Christmas, Mrs. Galvin." Everyone wished her a Merry Christmas, too, before we quietly filed out the door. Orville was last. He stopped, turned back to the slight figure in the wheelchair, and whispered, "You ain't alone, Mrs. Galvin." Nancy stood by him and said, "We love you." Then they quickly turned away and headed into the hallway and joined the rest of us.

"Thanks so much. You just gave her about the only Christmas she'll have this year," Martha said. "You'll never know . . ."

It was a quiet group on the trip home. This time, I didn't notice holding hands with anyone.

"Guess I expected something else," Julie said softly. "I'm not sure what, but she seemed so, I don't know, by herself." One by one, I dropped everyone off. We were all home within an hour of when we left.

And tonight, sitting here on my bed, while Chuck snores away the night, I can't get the face of Mrs. Galvin out of my mind. Yeah, maybe we expected the kind of elderly lady who would have had cookies and cocoa for us, and we would have had a good time visiting her, and she would have thanked us for the gifts and goodies, and we would have gone home thinking we had a great experience.

But we *did* have a great experience. We learned something. Maybe it would have been too easy if we had experienced a cookies-and-cocoa kind of night. Does that make sense? Is Mrs. Galvin the kind of woman the Savior would have visited first?

The answer isn't too tough to figure out.

Wednesday, December 18

Let us build upon the experience of last night: I had a pretty good day. The best part was basketball practice. After doing a bunch of drills, Coach Rourke called out some names for a scrimmage. I was already looking for my customary seat on the slats, but then he surprised me by calling my name. Playing time for Whipple? My cynical side burped up immediately. "Probably just going to give you one long look before cutting you," said the whiny little voice. The counterattack came from the sunny side of my disposition. "Look, the coach isn't stupid. You're 6'4" and he wants to give you a little more time in preparation for the starring role on this year's team. You've earned this, Wallace. Now make the best of it."

With confidence fairly oozing out of my high-topped basketball shoes, I took the court and huddled with the guys on my team. Our ball out. I dropped to the low post, spun around the guy guarding me, and, to my utter disbelief, there was the ball being lobbed to me. I grabbed it, faked one way, went straight up, and the ball tore the twine for two. "Good look, Whipple," said one of the guys on my team, and I pointed to the player who had tossed the pass inside to me.

That's the way it went for the next 20 minutes. I'm sure I had a dozen points or so, half that many rebounds. Yeah, I did a couple of things that would get me recognition on the all-geek team, but it was by far my best practice. Coach Rourke didn't say much to me, but I'm sure he was taking some heavy mental dictation. "That kid's better than I thought. Good touch from in close. Runs the court decently, too, other than when he dribbled the ball off his foot. Could be someone special."

I drove to school today, and on the way home stopped at a supermarket not far from my house. I was after something to drink but noticed a rack with a bunch of pins on them, in the aisle that had lots of other stuff that you don't expect to find in a grocery store, such as motor oil, little plastic golf balls and posters of soap opera stars. The pins were shaped in the letters of the alphabet and were all sparkly because of some diamondlike gems glued to them. They caught my eye immediately. Heck, if Julie and I were on better terms, I could pick up a *J* for her. I looked at the price, $14.99 . . . and then noticed a thin red line drawn through it. The next figure was $7.99, but it also was crossed out. The numbers at the bottom of the tag now read $4.99. It was then I realized what I had. *A bargain!*

I searched through the rack and fortunately found an *N*. Yes! Natalie was set. My last Christmas present done, with more than a week to go. I felt pretty good about it.

Anyway, then it was home, homework, a little reading, and then time to call it quits for the day. Orville's next missionary lesson is on Friday, so all I have to do is avoid disaster tomorrow, survive Friday, then cruise full blast into the weekend.

At this moment, I am feeling faint but steady impulses that life is going to turn out okay.

THURSDAY, DECEMBER 19

I don't have to write in my journal today. I don't really

have to. Years from now, when I read this entry, I want the record to show that I didn't have to write in my journal. But I chose to write, which I hope shows something about my character, not to mention my basketball ability.

Or in the eyes of Coach Rourke, the lack of it.

I got cut today.

Yeah, cut.

I will not play on the J.V. basketball team for Franklin High School this year.

In fact, I may have played in my last organized game of high school basketball. Can this part of my life really be over? I'm only 17 . . .

Cut. Can't they find a better word? Turned loose? Allowed to pursue other interests? Eased off the team? Allowed to resign? Nope. Cut. Just plain old cut. Like what happens when someone takes out a sharp knife.

What will my friends think? My family? The other guys who are still on the team?

And what does this tell me about myself? Whipple, you are a loser—that's what it says about me. Can't even make a crummy basketball team. Second tallest guy on the team and I still can't even make it. Not even as a third stringer.

And how about the way I got cut? We're all sitting in the locker room, I mean the whole team, getting ready for practice, and Coach Rourke comes in with a clipboard. "Whipple, can I see you in my office?" he says. Complete and utter silence washes through the room. It's like you just found out someone has flesh-eating bacteria. The guys on either side of me slide away. I've got one shoe on and the other off. "Uh, coach, do I need to put on my other shoe?"

He gives me a blank look. "Whatever you want, Whipple."

Not a good sign. I really want him to tell me I need both shoes on.

I take off my one shoe and follow him into the coaches' office. He sits down and clears his throat. He doesn't make eye contact. "Well, Wally, this isn't easy for me to do," he says smoothly. (Yeah, right. Like it's a picnic for me.) "But I'm going to have to cut you. You have some ability, Wally, and you are tall." (Duh, coach.) "But you got a late start, and I feel like the guys who have been here from day one deserve to be on the team. I can't carry 15 players. Some of you would only sit on the bench. That wouldn't be fair. This way, you can go out and play on some other team and get more experience."

Sure thing, coach. Like the Jazz and the Trailblazers are both bidding for my services. And I wouldn't mind playing for the Knicks to get the media exposure.

"Put on some weight and try out for the varsity next year. Maybe you'll make it," he says unconvincingly. Then he stands up, the cue for me to leave. He shakes my hand, a wormy soft little grip. "Nice getting to know you, Williams."

I am so numb I can't think of anything to say or do. I just stand there until he motions toward the door with his head and gives me a whistle. Stunned, I sort of shuffle out of the office and head back to the locker area. All my teammates—my ex-teammates—look up at me.

Okay, Whipple. This isn't fun, but try to handle it with some poise and humor. "Looks like you'll have to get along without my muscle on the boards," I manage to say. Then I flex my right bicep, which is roughly the size of a garden pea. A few guys giggle nervously, but they also act like I'm some kind of ghost.

"Dude, you should be startin'. You are good, man," says Curtis Nickleby.

Andy Salisbury puts a hand on my shoulder. He has been my sit-on-the-bench soul mate since we rode the pines together last year. "Sorry, Wally. Rourke is making a mistake, big time. Maybe I'll be next."

Just then, the door opens again, and the Grim Reaper, Coach Rourke, enters. "Holloway, can you come into my office?" Brad Holloway turns to a sheet of white and stiffly gets up and heads out through the door.

I have to get out of here. I'm not on this team. I don't want to be in its locker room. I'm not a part of these guys anymore. *I don't belong.* I'll come back later for my stuff. The air seems thick, heavy. It almost feels like I'm suffocating. I quickly put on my shoes, throw on my sweat pants, and head out into the slate gray afternoon and the steady rain.

I walk. I walk for a long time. I don't even know where. Way out past 82nd Street, I guess. Past all the cars on their way home. I am soaking wet. Still I walk. It gets dark. *Basketball is me.* And now I don't have it.

An hour passes. Then another. I'm cold and I ache. Finally, I find myself back in the locker room. I spin the combination on my lock and pull the door open. I grab all my things and wad them into my duffel bag. I throw on my coat, then slam the door shut.

Once more, one more time, I decide, I'll go back up to the gym floor. I climb the steps. Only one bank of lights is on. Near one wall is a solitary basketball. I walk over and pick it up, squeeze it, then bounce it. I notice someone in the shadows.

It is Coach Rourke.

I put down my bag, take off my coat and slowly dribble the basketball to the top of the key. I know . . . don't ask me how, but I know . . . Coach Rourke is watching me. I charge toward the hoop. Five feet out I jump, shifting the ball to my right hand. Then I slam it through, a perfect tomahawk, in-your-face, out-of-my-way, the-train-is-here dunk.

The backboard rattles and sways. No one else on the J.V. team can dunk like that.

I turn around and in the darkness say only one word in Coach Rourke's direction.

"There."

Then I leave the gym.

Outside, the rain has stopped, but it is pitch dark. I can make out the form of someone else, standing alongside the wall of the gym. I move closer.

It is Evan Trant, my pal from metal shop, leaning against his motorcycle.

"Yo, Wimp Pole."

"Yo, Evan."

"You okay?"

"Yeah. Well, not actually."

"What's wrong, Wimp Pole?"

"Just got cut from the basketball team."

"Huh. You want me to beat up someone?"

"Don't tempt me."

"I could do it."

"I know."

"You need a ride? Room for two on my hog."

"No, thanks. The walk will give me time to sort a few things out."

"Okay. Like when I go for a ride. Gets me away from troubles."

"Yeah. We all have troubles."

"One good thing, Wimp Pole. You can lift now. No prissy basketball practice to get in your way. You can be a man, Wimp Pole."

"Yeah. Got to go now, Evan."

"Okay."

I watch as he feels around in his jacket and pulls out some cigarettes.

"Evan, don't smoke," I say. "It's stupid. You're smarter than that."

My life may be over, I realize. Calling Evan Trant stupid is pretty darn close to a death wish, but without hoops, what does it matter? In the dimness of the evening, he looks at me with a mixture of anger and awe. If he punches me, I reason, at least I will be out of my misery. He grunts, then puts the cigarettes back. "Yeah. I know. Work hard lifting, then burn my lungs out. You think I'm smart?"

"Smarter than you probably even know."

"Wimp Pole, you are one of the only people in the world I'd let call me stupid. Like I said, you don't back down from me. You got guts."

And in a bizarre, strange, nothing-seems-right-in-the-world-kind-of-way, I need to hear that. I've got guts.

"See you, Evan."

"Pumping?"

"Maybe."

I trudge home, thinking about how I'd break the news to my family. Evan says I have guts; I've got to handle this. Get solid, Whipple. Do it now. I have to avoid showing much emotion, no matter how much I hurt. It won't be easy, but I will try.

I push through the door and walk toward the kitchen. For a second, it seems that everyone has already heard about me getting cut. It doesn't take much to feel that things were pretty somber around the Whipple household. Everyone is in the kitchen, heads almost at the table level, glassy-eyed. Even Chuck seems down. Mom looks at me and says, "Oh, hi, honey."

"What's wrong?" I blurt out.

Mom sighs. Dad gets a funny expression on his face.

"Your father found out today that someone else got the job."

Friday, December 20

Natalie didn't get to be a cheerleader. Strike one.

Dad didn't get the job. Strike two.

I got cut from the basketball team. Strike three.

Merry Christmas, right?

I told my family about basketball last night after I wrote in my journal. Dad was upset. He knows I'm a good player and should be on the team. "I'd like to talk with that coach and let him know what I'm thinking." Mom put her arm around me. "Hasn't been a good day for the Whipple men. Something good may come out of all this, something we haven't an idea about yet. Hang in there, Wally." Natalie looked at me sympathetically and said, "That's too bad, Wally. Seriously." Maybe not being elected a cheerleader has bumped her empathy needle up a point or two. Chuck, who thinks I'm ready for the NBA right now, just couldn't understand it. "The coach is wrong, Wally. You are awesome. You can even dunk," he said.

Still, I feel like some of those guys in the New Testament who asked if they or their forefathers committed the sin for which they were being punished.

Did we do something wrong? Are we cursed or just being tested? Why is nothing going right? It's bad enough when something bad happens to me, but Dad . . . he's the best worker Aisles of Value has. Fifty hours a week, sometimes more. Knows where every thumb tack and screw is in the store. He deserved the job. And Natalie . . . for all the teasing, all the rivalry, I do wish she was a cheerleader. Yeah, I know jumping around in front of hundreds of people and yelling things in nursery-rhyme-like cadence isn't my idea of fun in life, but it does mean a lot to Nat.

And me. Basketball. I was *born* to play hoops. When I think of myself, when I picture myself in my mind, I see a semiruggedly handsome guy *with a basketball in his hand.* Does that tell you something?

This is a big deal to me. And what if . . . if since I can't play basketball, like I don't get the other basic things in life down? True, I am only 17 years old, but I have a few of the basics down about what I want before checking out of Hotel Earth. I mean mission, marriage, family, active in the Church, good friends, sports in there somewhere, a near endless supply of pizza. I want these things to happen, but I wanted playing basketball to be a part of my life this year . . . and I muffed it.

How will I do at the other things in life?

I hope everything will be okay.

But I hoped to be on the basketball team, too.

Is there a chance that when I'm getting old, like in my 40s, 1 might wake up and say, "Wait a minute! This isn't how I wanted things to turn out? Can we try it over?" I can't go back—just like I can't go back and play basketball now.

Am I getting too carried away by all this? It's only a game, Wallace.

Is life just a game though?

I looked back in my journal, and it was only a few pages ago that I was telling Nat not to base her whole self-image on being a cheerleader. Base it on the things that count, right? Good advice, but hard to take, especially right now. Maybe it's too easy to define your life on the big, shocking, negative moments, like getting cut from the basketball team, getting brain lock when you talk with a girl, or forgetting the Scout Oath at your Eagle court of honor. Maybe you've got to define who you are on what you do well, day in and day out.

Okay, Whipple, so you're not on the basketball team, but Evan Trant says you have guts. Chalk up one point. Orville is coming over tomorrow for the next missionary lesson before he goes back to Heppner for Christmas. That's two. You can start singing "Silent Night" to an elderly lady who might not even be able to hear you. That's three.

Look in the mirror. Tell yourself, "I know who I am. I am a good person. I'm going to get life right. I can do this."

I repeat, I CAN DO THIS!

Saturday, December 21

Orville came over tonight for a discussion. The elders feel like things are going well with him, but it's been such a busy time of the year that they are a little worried that not everything is soaking in with Orville.

My opinion: Orville is not missing a thing. The guy is a sponge.

I told him about basketball yesterday at school: no whining, no whimpering, just a simple, "I got cut on Thursday."

"That so. Sorry, pard. Know how that must hurt."

"Yeah. But maybe this is a wake-up call, you know, like Wally, there is more to life than shooting round leather spheres through round metal spheres while dressed in underwear-like clothing." I was being *a lot* more stoic about it than I felt.

"Sometimes things don't work out, sometimes they do. Can't always be the tallest hog at the trough."

Orville arrived a few minutes before the missionaries did. My whole family was there in the family room. It wasn't long before Elder Milne and Elder Roberts came and the discussion began. Everything was going along well, and then we branched out a little bit about the eternal nature of families. Some of that we discussed before, but Orville seemed more interested in it now. Being good missionaries, the elders shifted the lesson a bit and followed Orv's lead.

"So you're sayin' that families on earth can be families up there?" Orv asks.

"Yes, that's it."

Orville's face seems to cloud over a bit. Suddenly, it hits me what he is thinking . . . and probably what he is going to ask next. *He wants to know about his mom.*

"So, if I got this down pat, even though a family might be separated a bit here, they all can be together there?"

"Yes. They need to be what we called 'sealed,' which takes place in the temple, Orville," Elder Roberts answers.

"And if someone passes on, then things down here can still be fixed up so that everyone is all together?"

"Yes," both of the missionaries chime. Dad looks really intense. Natalie senses something big is happening. Chuck is very still. Mom softly says, "You know what that means, don't you, Orville?"

Orville hangs his head for a moment. We can't see his face. Not that I'm expecting exaltation right away (yes, I still have a few rough edges, I realize), but the Spirit is so strong at this moment.

Orville looks up. Big guy. Tough as a winter wind on the prairie. Proud, in a way, in that he doesn't often let you in on exactly what he's thinking. And there he is, sitting in the Whipple home, eyes leaking and his voice a little dry.

"Yes, ma'am, I do. It means me and my mama can be together again. I miss her so much." There is a long silence, everyone sitting and letting the moment soak in, trying to understand the meaning and feeling of what is happening. Momentarily, the disappointments of jobs, cheerleading, and basketball teams fade. Use this as a defining moment, Whipple. "Guess that means I need to be baptized," Orville says, "although it's gonna be hard gettin' used to callin' all of you brother and sister."

"Oh, you don't have to think of me as your sister," Natalie bursts out.

The date is set. January 10th.

Yes! Orville is going to be a Mormon—no, Orville is going to be a Latter-day Saint!

There may be a Christmas in the Whipple home after all.

SUNDAY, DECEMBER 22

The Whipple household is on your basic roller coaster right now. In the great toy store of life, an apt analogy given that Christmas is four days away, we are yo-yos. Look at the evidence:

1. Orville getting baptized soon. (Up.)
2. Dad not getting the promotion. (Down.)
3. Christmas is here. (Up.)
4. Natalie not making cheerleader. (Down.)
5. No school for two weeks. (Up.)
6. Cut from the basketball team. (Down.)
7. Lots of nice comments on my Christmas cards, although Julie didn't say anything. Maybe the heart motif was a little too subtle. (Up.)
8. No dates since last summer. (Down.)
9. The strange compliment from Evan and how it made me feel good when I needed to hear something positive about myself. (Up.)
10. No pizza in our household tonight, not even the frozen kind that tastes like cardboard dipped in a combination of ketchup and brake fluid. (Down.)
11. Nice church service today, with lots of music, and a great talk by Bishop Winegar. That we only had sacrament meeting might have helped my outlook, too. (Up.)
12. The bleak realization that even though I have had

no dates in six months, and the law of averages should be catching up with me such that very soon the percentages would indicate I should go on a date, I have no prospects of a social life throughout the long, dreary, and bleak winter months. (Down.)

13. Christmas shopping is done, so all I do now is veg out for most of two weeks. (Definitely an up.)

So that's it for the yo-yo people. The "Perry Como Christmas Special" is on tonight, so I am going to tune it in. Although it is Sunday, I have to believe that I'm not going to get graded down too much by the Guys-Upstairs-in-Charge-of-Taking-Notes. I mean, it is Perry Como we're talking about.

WEDNESDAY, DECEMBER 25

Christmas is a time of tradition and custom in the Whipple household, when we all enjoy the presence of one another, the spirit of the season, and the spectacle of Natalie opening up her presents at near warp speed.

Natalie is a master on Christmas morning. Last year, she faked being sick and started coughing hard enough to shake the foundations of the house. After her hacking went on for about 20 minutes, we were all wide awake; in her own words, "Well, hey, like since everybody's already up, let's, you know, like, go open our presents!" Although it was barely past five in the morning, that's exactly what we did. Her cough, by the way, miraculously disappeared during the Opening of the Presents Pageant. Call it a Christmas miracle.

So I was curious about what she would come up with this year to get at the Christmas loot early. It's sort of an annual tradition, one that Nat has been carrying on since she was old enough to become clothes conscious, which for her was at the age of two. Natalie never repeats herself on Christmas morning; every year it's something original and fresh. But I have to believe that even her vivid imagination is being taxed.

Or so I thought. Once again, Natalie handled it with grace and aplomb, and we were up hours before any sane rooster would even think of crowing.

Chuck was her unknowing partner, her easy mark, this year. Chuck is just in first grade, and is still a, well, believer in the jolly old guy who wears a red suit and jumps down chimneys, even though in this day and age it sounds like a good way to end up in jail. Natalie knows that Chuck is pumped about Christmas, and about two weeks ago seemed to be taking special care to talk with Chuck about Santa, something she has been doing continually since.

"So, Chuck, what will Santa be bringing you this year? Any ideas? Seriously."

"I wonder how Santa can do it all, Chuck. I mean, he must be one great guy."

"You know what I think? It would be absolutely way cool to see Santa, like, in person, not, like, at a mall, but, like, in our house. Don't you think so, Chuck?"

"If I saw Santa, I'd go whacko. Absolutely nuts! It would be like, 'Wow, here he is, bzzzt, right in our own house!' What do you think, Chuck?"

What Natalie is doing, of course, is getting Chuck into a full-blown frenzy about seeing Santa Claus. For what purpose, I'm unsure.

At least I was unsure until this morning. It's early, about ten after five—the skies still dark, the house cold, everything silent. But I get the feeling that someone is in our room. I open my eyes, let them adjust to the dim rays coming from the streetlight, and see what appears to be Natalie crawling slowly into our room. My first impulse is to say something to her, but I decide not to, wanting instead to see what evil plot she is hatching. She inches her way to Chuck's bed and cups her hand close to his ear. Now, I wouldn't bet my baseball card collection on it, but I'm pretty sure she says, "Chuck, I think Santa's here!" Then she bolts toward the door on her hands and knees and shakes these tiny little bells that we have as part of our Christmas decorations. Chuck, though groggy, jerks up in bed. "He's here! I heard him, Wally! It's Santa Claus! Did you hear the bells!" Then he is down the hallway, tearing into Mom and Dad's room, telling them all about what he has heard. Mom and Dad think it's cute and of course believe that he was dreaming. I stumble out of bed and follow Chuck down the hall and into my parents' room. I was just about to say something that would indict Natalie, when in she stumbles, rubbing her eyes, yawning, acting as though she had just awakened.

"What's going on?" she asks innocently.

"I heard Santa!" shouts Chuck.

"You did? How cool! Wow, I mean, he was probably right here, Chuck! Do you think he left anything? Bet he did! Especially toys!"

"Maybe he was just dream—" Dad starts.

"Chuck, this just makes Christmas like, so special. I'm so excited, I couldn't go back to sleep now if I wanted to!" says Natalie, successfully blunting Dad's comment.

"Can we go see if he's been here?" Chuck pleads.

Natalie shrugs her shoulders, holds her hands out wide to Chuck, and turns to Mom and Dad. "We can't disappoint him, seriously. Come on, little brother. We should all, you know, open our presents now. I mean, we're all up and it *is* Christmas." She picks up Chuck and heads out of the door.

Mom and Dad sense a rat, but what can they do? Their youngest child is so wound up that they're going to have to pull him down from the ceiling in another two minutes.

This is definitely not the time for Dad to clear his throat and say, "Chuck, there is something I need to tell you about Santa Claus. He died 300 years ago. Merry Christmas, son."

"Let's go," sighs Dad. "We'll be right down."

Five minutes later, Natalie is poised in front of the Christmas tree, ready to hand out gifts. She is bouncy; she is bright; she is radiant—even though it still feels like the dead of night. Understand, greed is powerful, even to the point of transforming Natalie into a beaming brilliant being at this awful hour. Dad reminds us of our tradition of reading about the birth of the Savior from Luke. Natalie, who already has three presents in front of her, gives a small gasp, as if to say, "Silly me! I forgot!"

But she rallies from this temporary setback. "Dad, may I read from the Bible?" This stuns Dad, because Natalie heretofore in life has shown about as much interest in the scriptures as she has heavy earth-moving equipment. So he hands the Bible over to her.

Natalie clears her throat and begins reading, "And it came to pass in those days, that there went out a decree from Caesar Augustus, that all the world should be taxed."

She pauses. She smiles. Then starts again, "And the angel said unto them—"

"Natalie, you skipped about ten verses," Mom says.

"I did? Oh, I'm sorry. Really." And on she goes, hitting about every third verse, until she gets to ". . . for all the things that they had heard and seen, as it was told unto them." Then she sits back and looks very pleased with herself. "That, you know, really makes me understand a lot better about why we have all these presents. Seriously. I feel super spiritual right now, like my testimony is all swollen up like glands when I'm sick. Let's open up the gifts."

And so it goes. Natalie gloms onto every gift she can

find with her name on it, leaving the rest for Chuck to hand out. She tears through wrapping paper and slices open boxes at a pace that makes the rest of us dizzy. I mentally note that if circumstances should ever come to it, and we entered a huge war where only the fittest survive, Natalie would be a formidable foe in hand-to-hand combat if she uses the same energy and determination as she does when opening presents. She has two piles, one for keepers, the other for returns. She gets to my diamond-like piece of jewelry that I bought in the grocery store and says, "That's really sweet, Wally," just before she tosses it over her shoulder into a small third pile, which I assume is the "no hope, not worth taking back" stack. I am mildly disappointed, but I guess even Natalie has lapses in good taste, and perhaps Mom will rescue it from the reject pile.

Natalie finishes about 30 minutes before anyone else. While we're still picking through gifts and slowly opening them, she clearly is done for the morning.

She yawns, says something about not feeling so well, and a few minutes later is gone, leaving the rest of us in the rubble of wrapping paper and cardboard boxes, heading in the general direction of her room. We don't see Natalie again until almost noon. Catching up on her sleep, I suppose. Not a word more has been said about Santa on the premises all morning. Once Natalie achieved her objective—get to the tree and open the gifts fast—any thoughts about old Saint Nick disappeared faster than cheesy chicken casserole at the ward Christmas potluck dinner.

We all sit back and listen to the Christmas music that Mom slipped on the tape deck. A nice, warm, kind of good-hearted gauziness overtakes the members of the Whipple family who are still awake. I think about the CDs Mom and Dad gave me and the old Dale Murphy baseball card that Chuck so carefully wrapped up and handed to me. Life is good. Mom begins to pick through the wrapping paper. Dad leans back in his favorite chair, with a new church book in hand. Chuck plays with the big road grader that Santa brought him.

"Do you really think Santa was here?" Chuck asks.

"No doubt, bud. No doubt."

And I think that of anywhere in the world I might ever be on Christmas morning, it will never be sweeter than here at the old brown house on Craig Street.

SATURDAY, DECEMBER 28

Not much going on right now, mostly just kicking back, sleeping in, and pigging out. We had a visitor today, one who came to talk with Nat. The visit was from Lindy Hightower, the friend who beat out Natalie for cheerleading. Their relationship has always been up and down, but probably reached a new low when Lindy was selected and Natalie was not. I'm not sure they've even spoken to each other since the tryouts. Anyway, when Nat opened the door, I think she was surprised to see Lindy, but her animal instincts kicked in, the instincts that say something about showing no weakness.

NATALIE: "Oh. It's you. Hi, Lindy."

LINDY: "Yes. It's me. Hi, Natalie."

NATALIE: "Well, did you just come by to go hi or something?"

LINDY: "Yeah. I wanted to go hi."

NATALIE: "Well, hi."

LINDY: "Yeah. Hi."

NATALIE: "So."

LINDY: "Okay."

NATALIE: "You, like, want to come in?"

LINDY: "I don't know."

NATALIE: "So."

LINDY: (bursting into tears) "I'm so sorry, Natalie. Seriously. Like, about me getting selected and you not. And it was kind of, like, your whole idea because you were so sweet and wanted to share, like, something really important with me, your best friend, and then it all got messed up when you didn't get picked and I did. Seriously, I've even thought of quitting because, you know, it didn't feel right for me to be out there at the games and not you. Do you see what I'm saying?"

NATALIE: (somewhat warmer now that she has been assured a moral victory) "Yeah, Lindy, I see what you are saying. And you don't have to quit, unless you really want to. (Deep breath, long pause.) And it's okay. Like my brother says, you shouldn't let something like cheerleading tell you what kind of person you are; it should be based on, like, if you're good to everyone and if you dress well, stuff like that. Wally's sort of a dork, but I think he's right about that."

LINDY: (now down to an occasional sob) "Wow, Natalie. That's really neat. I feel better. And I have something for you." (She reaches into a bag she's carrying and pulls out a neatly wrapped package and hands it to Natalie, who is delighted.)

NATALIE: "I have something for you." (Nat runs upstairs and returns with a small neat package and hands it to Lindy.) "I hope you like it. Do you want to come in?"

LINDY: "Yeah. We can talk about what we got for Christmas. This is great. I'm glad we're still friends."

NATALIE: "Me, too. But we always were friends, and I really like exchanging Christmas gifts with you. Party on, Christmas! Let's do it again next year."

Later that day, after Lindy had gone, I asked Natalie about the gift she gave Lindy. "That was really thinking ahead," I said. "And Nat, I've got to say it, way to go for getting Lindy a present when you weren't getting along so well. That shows me something."

"Well, every Christmas I get a couple of extra presents in case, like, someone surprises me, so I can hand them something in return. I think about who might surprise me, then I make out the tag, so like all I have to do is slap the right tag on and then they think I was going to give them something all along. It's sort of like being prepared. And if I don't give them away, then I just keep the presents for myself," she told me.

Not much takes Natalie by surprise. Give her credit for that.

The vacation is starting to wind down. Other than the New Year's Eve dance, not much else to do except veg out for a few more days. (Yes!) I've done a little homework, listened to a couple of new CDs that I picked up at Christmas. One of them is Sinatra, and I like the title of the first song on it, "The Best Is Yet to Come."

I hope Ol' Blue Eyes knows of what he sings.

CHAPTER 5

January

Starting out the new year by going to a stake dance might not be the ideal way to begin the next chapter in your life. I mean, it's a jungle out there. All your social survival skills have to be at their best or you feel like you're going to be gobbled up by some large and powerful beast. You get an instant printout on where you stack up in life, and in many cases—specifically mine—the news isn't much fun. A couple hundred kids were at the dance last night, and about a third of them (the group I shall loosely call "The Natalie Crowd") danced a lot and had a good time. The rest of us were all on the sidelines, in the shadows for most of the evening, fearing that we'd make some kind of mistake. You know, say something dumb, kick the shins of someone you are dancing with, have a glob of strawberry topping drip down your shirt, or start the evening with a perfectly clear complexion only to have a case of the rampant galloping zits develop midway through the dance. For people like us, that's the whole purpose of a dance. Not to have fun. Not to meet someone we'd like to get to know a little better. Not to let the hormones flow freely within our systems for a couple of hours away from the scrutiny of parents and siblings. Our purpose is to not make any social blunders. We live in fear. With that in mind, how can you really have much fun? So we go home a little bit discouraged and thinking, "Uh oh. Another year of life as a mold spore." I speak the truth. Unfortunately, I have a personal testimony of it.

There are a few rare exceptions to what I am writing about. Take Lumpy, who judges the success of a dance (or for that matter, almost any of life's events) by the quality and quantity of the refreshments. Last night, it was pizza, chips, salsa, and root beer floats, so Lumpy was a very happy guy. But I digress. Let me painfully recall the events of last night.

Lumpy and I drove over to the dance. It was church dress, based on some adult's theory that if we are all decked out in Sunday clothes, we'll be less inclined to get into food fights or grind refreshments into the carpet, and the chaperons wouldn't be there until 4:00 A.M. cleaning up. We figured on meeting Mel, Rob, and Mickey there. Orville had said he might be back from eastern Oregon in time for the dance, but he wasn't sure and told us before he left that he'd show up if he could.

We pulled into the parking lot about 10:00 and parked toward the outer limits. Last year, my dad drove us because we were both licenseless. He dropped us off a block away from church because it is definitely uncool to have your parents drive you to a dance. This year I drove, which should have made a big difference in our whole attitude, but really didn't. The reason is that I've discovered having your license helps but is only the first step toward social respectability. *What* you drive is even more important. Lumpy's family has a van, like about 96% of all other American LDS families with more than two children at home. (This is the stage before all the kids leave and your parents suddenly have the urge to buy a big, American-made car.) My family is a throwback—we have a station wagon as our main set of wheels. Given the choice between me driving the wagon and Lumpy driving the van, we decided to go with the Whipple Cruisemobile, on the slim hope that if anyone (specifically, girls) asked about the station wagon, we could say, "Best car around for our surf-boards," even though the closest to surfing Lumpy and I have ever been was watching those ancient Annette—what's her name?—Funicello (I think) movies from the 1960s.

We arrive, and I pull out the bottle of aftershave that Santa left in my stocking. (A significant gift for me, I'd say. My own aftershave. I will no longer need to steal my Dad's.) I splash some on in the car, while Lumpy watches in total awe. "Good thinking. Aftershave in the car. If you'd put it on at home, most of it would have worn off by now. You're going to smell really strong."

I think he is on the verge of asking me for a handful but probably decided that two males with the exact same animal scent might be too much for the girls to handle, es-pecially the Mia Maids.

After a quick trip to the rest room to make sure my hair looks good, that I have no new facial blemishes, and I don't have any ketchup on my tie from the three hot dogs we ate as hors d'oeuvres at a convenience store on the way to the church, I feel ready. I look into the mirror once more, grin my most rakish grin, and tilt my head just right so that my most ruggedly handsome features are at the right angle of exposure. Maybe this will be the night when the old Wally finally is cast aside and the new, more ma-ture and confident Wally emerges, like a handsome and virile butterfly evolving from a dormant cocoon stage. I walk down the hallway, guided by the steady impulse of a throbbing rock band beat. I check in with the chaperons and stride confidently into the cultural hall where . . .

where . . . I can't see a thing. It is dark and my eyes have not adjusted.

At this point, I decide to do the safe thing, namely, find Lumpy, although the thought of Lumpy as your anchor in choppy social waters is a little scary. I head toward a table on the kitchen side of the cultural hall, where he is keeping a hawklike eye on the preparation of the refreshments. "Man, Wally, the food here is awesome. Glad we came," he says, joy shining from his puffy face. "I forget how good the food is at these big dances. They're really putting on the dog tonight."

"Good, Lump. You checked out the girls yet?"

"Girls?"

"Yeah. Girls. You know what they are."

"Sure. And yeah, I checked out the girls while you were in the bathroom staring at yourself. Wally, I am pleased to report that there definitely are girls here tonight."

"Well, duh, Lumpy. But are there any, you know, good-looking girls here?"

"Yeah. But what difference does it make to you?"

"Hello—anyone in there? Remember, this is a dance. I have come to dance. With girls. Tonight. This should not come as a huge surprise to you, Lump."

Just then Mel, Rob, and Mickey find us. The Posse, minus Orville. The timing couldn't be better—for Lumpy. "Gentlemen," he says, with a touch of cynicism in his voice. "The well-known social animal here, the party guy supremo, none other than Wallace F. Whipple, has just stated that he is going to dance tonight." Lumpy's announcement is greeted with a general reaction of what could be termed, "Yeah, sure." Seeing that my personal credibility, my integrity, my good name, if you will, is at stake, I have to say something in a hurry to salvage my sinking image among my peers.

"Ha!" I say, firmly, decisively. "Ha to each of you!"

Sure told them.

"You only say that when you're nervous," Lumpy says. Then he makes a really obnoxious chicken noise. "Bocka, bocka!" he clucks at this critical moment. "You're chicken, Wally."

Now, this is not the first time I have got myself into what Orville would call a box canyon. Rather than shake my head, smile coolly, and turn the tables and challenge Lumpy to put down his pepperoni pizza and dance, I always choose to stumble through these situations the hard way. "Bocka, bocka!" Lumpy again chides.

I can't stand his chicken noise. I hope he outgrows it soon.

"Okay, okay. You guys do this. You guys pick out a girl right now, and the next dance, fast or slow, whatever, I will go and ask her to dance. Then I will escort her to the center of the floor and I will dance like you have never seen me dance before."

"We've never seen you dance before," Mel reminds, "except for the hokey-pokey."

Lumpy and Mickey, on the other hand, eagerly accept my manly challenge. "You got it, Wally. No backing down," Mickey says.

I immediately realize the vulnerability of my position. I know these guys. They will not select Julie, even if she is here. My guess is that they will select a girl who is, shall we say, mooselike in size, personality, and appearance, one who can twist steel in her bare hands, or who can install a diesel engine with one hand tied behind her back. Not that I'm afraid of strong women, I just don't want to dance with one right now. I trust these guys with my life, but not to choose someone to dance with. It doesn't look good for Wally at the moment. My friends—four men with whom I have spent some of the most memorable experiences of my life, from totally bad campouts in driving rain to sharing pizza crusts with absolutely no fear of spreading germs, are huddled and looking over the crowd. They motion and gesture. There seems to be some disagreement, perhaps discord. I await nervously. Finally, they break huddle and step toward me. "We show you great mercy," Lumpy says. The others nod. I think I am in huge trouble. Their idea of mercy may not exactly mesh with mine in this circumstance.

"See the girl over there? Red dress, white trim on whatever you call that?"

"Her collar," Rob says.

"Yeah. Her collar. She's the one for you, Wally. She is tall, like unto a dish," Lumpy says. "You will make a lovely pair. Your children will be over seven feet."

"Tight like unto a dish, not tall like unto a dish," I say. Then I squint into the gloom. I see the girl. Hmmm. She is not the size of a modest house, at least. In fact, she looks sort of cute. Tall, for sure. Blonde hair. Skinny like me. But hey, we can't all have the perfect build, right?

"Okay. You have spoken. Next dance, I will do the honorable thing," I say, feeling lucky that my friends actually did show some mercy instead of picking someone like unto a moose. One song ends and the lead singer starts to babble an introduction to the next. I turn and look at the grinning mob of friends behind me. "Farewell."

I walk across to where the girl in the red dress is standing. She is talking with a friend and sort of looking around.

I close in . . . ten feet, five feet, we have it, mission control, eye contact! She looks at me with the obvious question splashed across her features. "Who are you?"

Quickly, I try to think of some clever, inspiring line, that will melt her heart and affirm in her mind that she is about to get her New Year off to the right start. I'm right here, she's right here, I open my mouth. Speak, Wallace!

"Yo!" I say.

"Huh?" she says.

"Yo."

"Oh. Do you want to dance?"

"Uh-huh."

"Now?"

"Uh-huh."

"What's your name?"

"Wally. Wally Whipple."

Somewhat feebly, I reach out and take her by the hand. My brain begins to thaw slightly, and I decide to get right down to it. "Do you have a name?" Really dumb, Whipple. What do you expect her to say? "No, I'm just known as Girl."

"Yes. My name is Molly Davis."

"What ward are you in?"

"Fourth Ward."

We're near the middle of the floor. The band plays a fast song. I start to sort of jerk my arms around a bit and shuffle my feet.

I kind of pretend I'm playing basketball and move my feet from side to side, like I do when I play defense, only not as fast and not in as big of steps. I shoot a glance over my shoulder to where the other members of the Posse are standing, a look of supreme triumph spreading across my rugged yet boyish features.

No luck, though. More refreshments are being put out, and the Posse has descended on them like when you see those nature films showing piranhas attacking a goat that accidentally falls in the river. So I'm left with Molly, although, I mentally note, my honor is intact.

The dance ends, but the band breaks right into a slow number. The natural thing to do, I figure, is just to stay and dance some more, although slow dances bother me because it is much easier to step on your partner's feet and you do have to sort of actually touch her, but Whipple is nothing if not courageous. "Do you want to dance again?"

"Sure."

I hold out my left hand. She takes it. I sort of sneak my right hand around to her back and lightly place it down somewhere, although I'm not sure, except it was in the general vicinity of the shoulder blades.

"It might be more comfortable if you put your hand under my arm, not over it," she suggests politely.

"Yeah. Right. I will."

Now the time has come to actually dance. I move cautiously, trying to avoid her feet. Molly, I note, is not much better at dancing than I am, which makes me feel better. "I'm not too good at slow dancing," I blurt out. "Can we go two steps ahead and one back?" This is my standard line for slow dances, sort of like setting the ground rules.

"That's fine," Molly says, and my confidence soars. "I'll let you lead," she adds, and my confidence plunges.

She sort of tilts her head toward my shoulder. Slow dancing has potential, I decide.

The music stops. I think I've done my share to make good on my word, so I start off the floor with her.

"Are you a Laurel?" I ask, trying to fill in the last few seconds with conversation before I plop Molly back on the sidelines and then go hide out somewhere and try to recover from the fact that I've danced two in a row with the same girl, which establishes a new world record for Wallace Whipple.

"No. I'm a Mia Maid. I'm tall, so most guys think I'm older."

Horrors! A Mia Maid. I'm a cradle robber! I danced with someone who is my sister's age! Fortunately, I hide my severe angst at learning that I've been seen in public with someone much younger with a few insightful, wise, and well-chosen words.

"Are you woofin' me?"

"No. Is that okay?"

"Yeah. Fine. A Mia Maid. I guess we're all Mia Maids at one time in our lives."

She gives me a look that implies, "Has your brain taken the night off?" Then she says, "Thanks for dancing with me, Wally. I don't get asked very much. I think it's because guys don't like to dance with someone taller than they are."

"It's okay, Molly. Tall people are cool. Everyone looks up to us. See you around."

I head back to the refreshment table. Rob looks up. "Saw you out there, Wally. Food's good. Better grab some."

You mean that's it? My honor on trial and I do the noble thing, and all I get is a simple, "Saw you out there" followed by a quick food review? I am crushed. I am not going to let them get away with it.

"Her name is Molly, and she's a Laurel and really nice," I say in a loud voice, loud enough that not only do all the Posse members stop grazing and look up at me, but another dozen or so people nearby do also.

"We're really happy for you, Wally," Lumpy says, diving in for more chips and salsa.

That was about it for last night. I spent the rest of the evening between refreshments and the foyer, plus a couple of trips to the rest room to check the hair and facial condition. I made sure to avoid my sister Natalie, because we have this deal that if I don't say anything to her all night long, she pays me two bucks. So that was the story of my gala New Year's Eve dance. Two dances, two bucks, lots of food, and still left wondering if things are going to ever get easier before I slip into adulthood and wonder why I never had many of those good teenaged memories that everyone else seems to have.

I grabbed Lumpy and dragged him out to the car ("But

Wally, there were still some chips left!") as soon as the balloons came down from the ceiling at midnight.

The one good thing about tonight, I guess, is that it will be another 365 days before I have to go to a New Year's Eve dance again.

Saturday, January 4

It has been a long Christmas break this year, and I've used the opportunity to think about the meaning of life on a couple of occasions for a minute or two. It has been a time of quiet reflection and introspection, a period of setting goals and evaluating my life's course. It has also been a time when I have twice, out of my own pocket, ordered pizza, delivered right to the door of Casa Whipple

The results of this up-close and personal look are my New Year's Resolutions, the road map to a new and improved version of Wally Whipple. Roll the drums, please. It is now time to reveal the fruit of my labors.

1. Oil Up the Old Social Life.

Once upon a time, I had a social life. Not a great one, but it did exist. A dance, a concert, a movie, all the things that lead up to the big stuff, like serious dating, engagement, marriage, and death. But that was then and this is now, and my social life has evaporated like spit on a hot frying pan. (Credit Orville for that phrase.) I am going to be, how shall I say it, more aggressive in the next few months. My first goal is admittedly modest. I plan to actually start talking to girls again, even when I don't have to.

2. Bulk Up.

Evan Trant is the guy behind this. Since I have no basketball to look forward to, I might as well kill some time and build a few muscles by lifting. Evan has been encouraging of late. "Hey, Wimp Pole," he growled yesterday.

"You got a pea under your shirtsleeve or are you getting buff?" I will grunt, groan, lift, and push in the weight room at least three days a week after school.

3. Eat Better.

At least twice a year, I will eat salads.

4. Do Good unto All People Everywhere, Even My Sister Natalie.

The drift here isn't too hard to get. I came up with it soon after getting cut from the basketball team, during a period of intense self-doubt. If I'm going to build up my confidence, this seems like one good way to do it. Then, when something tragic happens, such as not making the basketball team, having my brain cramp up during a test, or talking with a female-type person, or getting a pimple the size of a hubcap on the end of my nose, I will be able to think of something good I have done lately, such as helping little old ladies across the street; cheering the homeless, sick, hungry, and downtrodden; offering Dad the use of any of my socks; and so on. Instead of letting the bad experience tell me who I am, I will have something good to fall back on. Make sense? Do unto others as you would have them do unto you, so that you can feel more awesome about yourself. That might not be quite the way they teach it in church, but I think it will work.

That's about it for this year. A pretty ambitious lineup. Now, all I need to do is make it happen.

MONDAY, JANUARY 6

Orville arrived home late Saturday. I saw him at church yesterday, and he asked if we could eat lunch by ourselves today. I wasn't sure why. Maybe he'd had some second thoughts about being baptized. Or maybe he wanted to go over all the details. (My Dad, having served three stake missions, was already on top of organizing the service.) I had a mild case of nerves when we sat down in the overflow cafeteria, where only the biggest nerds in the school eat. After spotting Dick Dickson and making sure to get in a corner far away from him, Orv and I pulled up to a table and started in on our sandwiches.

"Everything still okay for Saturday?" I asked after we had gone through all the chit chat about our Christmas breaks.

"You betcha. I'm a bit jumpy about Saturday, but it'll all be fine," he said. "There is one biddy favor I'd like to ask for a hand with."

"Shoot and you got it," I said, eyeing my next bite of tuna fish.

"I'd like you to baptize me, Wally."

I choked on my tuna fish and not because of a bone. My face got red and I started to cough. Orville smiled, reached over, and pounded me on the back. My eyes filled with water and my breath finally started to come in choppy, wheezy little gasps, like when I finished a cross-country race. "Didn't spook you, did I?" Orville asked innocently.

"Orv . . . you sure? You want me to baptize you?"

"Yep. The way I understand it, you can take care of it."

"But I thought you'd want one of the missionaries to do it."

"You thought wrong, Wally. You're the man. If you're willin'."

Willing? Definitely. I don't think I'd ever been so . . . so honored in my whole life.

"Yeah. Sure. I'd really like that, Orv."

"Then it's done. Shake on it?"

"Yeah." He reached a big meaty hand over to me, and we shook each other's hand— brother to brother.

Mom and Dad were ecstatic about the news. "What a

great experience, Wally! This is something that will help you on your mission," Dad said.

"Maybe in a couple of years, Chuck will want you to baptize him," Mom added.

"Does it really count if Wally baptizes Orv?" Natalie interrupted.

"Yes. It counts," Mom told her.

Natalie also had a spiritual experience of sorts. Bishop Winegar had an appointment with her and he asked her to be the Mia Maid class president.

"At first, I thought, like, no way, Bishop," Natalie told me while we were both finishing up the dishes tonight. "I'm going, 'So where do I have the time for this?' And I thought, if I had made cheerleading, then, like, I'd feel maybe I'd owed one, but seriously, then I thought, wow, like I can plan all of our activities almost, and we won't do anything dorky like baking stuff or doing quilts for poor people. We could instead like visit some clothing stores or have some models come in and talk with us about make-up and how to look really good. So then I told Bishop Winegar that yeah, it was okay with me."

I think the Mia Maids are in for some interesting times in the next few months.

WEDNESDAY, JANUARY 8

The weight of baptizing Orville is hitting me.

It's like I want to have a great week, so that when we get into the font on Saturday, I'll feel really spiritual, sort of be in tune in a major way, a true testimony guy. To accomplish this, I must show kindness, compassion, wish for everyone everywhere to succeed, obey the commandments like crazy, and get speedy repentance down to an art.

Not that I'm putting pressure on myself. I just want to be almost perfect in 72 hours.

It's not easy. Tonight at Young Men's, we were shooting hoops before our activity, and one of the teachers banged into me as I was soaring high in the air. Hit me in the back in midflight, causing me to crumple in a heap on the floor. Normally, I would have jumped up, glared, and grumbled. But the new, more perfect Wally Whipple, merely got up, brushed himself off, and said, "I'm sure that was an accident. Nice hustle."

Grrr. It wasn't easy, but I guess perfection wasn't meant to be.

Natalie knows what is going on. Her first clue came last night when I did her part of the dishes without being asked, bribed, or coerced. She just stood there with her mouth open, her brain on overload. Really shook her up.

Of course, she sees an advantage in this. It dawned on her that she could probably say or do almost anything to me and I wouldn't react. In her mind, I became easy prey.

"So, Wally, like, you have to say a prayer when you baptize Orville?"

"That would be correct, Nat. You know I do."

"Oh. You're not, like, nervous are you? I mean, like, you don't think you'll flub it all up or anything."

"No, Nat. I will not."

"You sure?"

"I am sure."

"Well, okay. Good luck, though."

"I don't need luck. I can do this, Natalie."

"Whatever you say, Wally. Seriously."

My only ace is that she wants to see Orville baptized even more so than I do. In her mind, a temple marriage may be at stake.

I wonder if Orv has any inkling of Natalie's long-range plans.

Friday, January 10

Orville and I both had interviews with Bishop Winegar last night. He took about a half-hour with Orv, and mine was much shorter.

"You should feel very good about your missionary efforts, Wally. Orv is an outstanding young man and going to be a great addition to our ward," he told me. "Orville has many things to achieve in life, things that he doesn't even realize yet but will in time."

Orv came home with me and we went over the service. Dad showed us what to do when we got in the font and gave us a few tips.

"You want to bend your knees, Orville, as though you're sitting down, then allow Wally to guide you back. That way, Wally doesn't have to worry about lifting you out of the water." I'm glad Dad filled us in on that, because I was fretting about how I was going to lift Orv out of the water. He outweighs me by about 60 pounds. I know the Spirit will be strong tomorrow, but maybe not *that* kind of strong.

Lumpy and Mel are going to offer the prayers, and Dad will confirm Orv. A special musical number is going to be performed by some of the girls in seminary class, plus Natalie. I'm not sure how she wormed—oops, for a moment I forgot the near-perfect edition of Wally—not sure how she managed to get in on the music, but she did, no doubt because of her kind and compassionate nature. Mr. Burrell is coming, too.

Only one slight hitch has popped up in all the preparations: Orville's middle name. I need to say his entire name for the baptismal prayer, but Orv is not exactly eager to tell me his middle name. I've asked him twice and he put me off. I tried again tonight, on our way back from the interviews.

"Orv, I really do need to know your middle name."

"You have to know?"

"Yeah, I have to. Can't get around it. It's right in there with death, repentance, and taxes as things we've got to do."

"I ain't told many people my middle name. Don't reckon I like it much."

"Well, I reckon not, too. But I need to know," I said as we drove in his pickup back to my house. "I mean, what is it? Shirley? Patricia? Dinwoodle?"

"No, but it ain't much better. Wally, this ain't easy." He leaned over, red-faced, as if 10,000 people were in the truck and he were about to reveal a state secret. "It's . . ." he glanced nervously over his shoulder, swallowed, then hoarsely said, "Julius."

"You're kidding! Julius? You are a Julius? I don't believe it," I squealed. Orv pulled back and gripped the steering wheel tighter.

"See, I knew you'd think it was a real knee-slapper. Yeah, Julius. And the only time I ever want you to say it aloud is tomorrow, pard." He bit his lower lip.

"You got it, Orv. Tomorrow. Once." We drove on for a little bit. But I couldn't help it. "Julius," I said softly, then started shaking with laughter once more. "I can't believe it."

"Old family name," he grumbled. "But it's gonna disappear like a three-legged mouse in front of a calico cat with this here generation."

"Whatever you say, Orville J."

He dropped me off at our house and I climbed out of the truck.

"G'night, Wally."

"G'night, Julius."

Never realized how fast Orv's old rusty truck could get down our street until then.

SATURDAY, JANUARY 11

Orv is a member.

His ticket has been punched for the celestial kingdom.

Does this guy really know all that he's gotten into?

Missions, temple marriage, callings, early-morning meetings, talks, high council Sundays, and blue-and-gold dinners.

Maybe he does, maybe not. But there is a lot of time for him to break into it. And there's no doubt in my mind that he has a testimony. Orville was the calmest and happiest person at the baptism, no small statement considering that everyone's joy meters were over the top tonight.

And the service was flawless, el perfecto. Our whole seminary class was there. Brother Hansen and his family. Bishop Winegar, Brother McNair, our seminary teacher last year, and dozens more people, some of whom I didn't think even knew Orville.

We marched right through it: the prayer, the talks by my very own awesome mom and Sister Habben. The musical number was great. Natalie, Julie, Nancy, Amy, Vanessa, and a few other girls from class. Then it came time for the ordinance itself. I stood and led the way through the door. I walked into the font. The warm water felt good, comforting. I beckoned for Orville to follow me in. I took his right wrist in my left hand and had him hold my left forearm with his left hand. I looked up at the witnesses, Elder Milne and Elder Roberts; they nodded, and I held my right arm up to the square.

"Okay, the moment is here," I said to myself. "Maybe the most important thing I've done in my entire life, and it is happening now." The funny thing is, although I've experienced my share of humiliating moments while standing at the front of a group at an important moment, this time I felt completely calm and knew that Wallace F. Whipple, Jr., was going to come through. It was such a cool feeling to *know* that.

I started the prayer. "Orville Julius Burrell . . ." My voice was clear. The words came easily, right through the "amen." The curse of the wayward tongue was lifted.

Then, Orv bent his knees just as Dad had told him. I guided him back, my right arm slipping behind him. He was immersed. I pushed on his back and Orville came up, wet and smiling. The elders were all grins and nodded, meaning that everything was okay. Orville looked at me and said softly, "Thanks, Wally. This here was meant to happen." And although neither of us are what you'd call the hugging type, we embraced in the font. Fifteen minutes later, Dad, Bishop Winegar, Brother Hansen, Brother McNair, and the missionaries stood in the circle and confirmed him.

That's about all I'm going to write for today. Yeah, there was a little get together back at the Whipple Estate, and we had a nice time with Orville, his dad, and all our friends. Mr. Burrell seemed at ease about the whole idea of Orv joining the Church. "I haven't seen anything but good from you people, and if Orville's happy about it, I'm pleased that he's joined with you," I heard him tell Mom. "He's a mighty fine son, and a good friend, too."

This is a part of real life. Two years ago, I didn't even know Orville Burrell. Now, I feel like he is my brother. Somehow, I feel like I've been an important part of something that, as Orv put it, was meant to happen. And I can't imagine that even hitting a three-pointer at the buzzer in the seventh game of the NBA championship would be more of a thrill.

Let me finish this entry where I started, with one simple phrase that means everything to me and my family right now: Orville Julius Burrell is a member of The Church of Jesus Christ of Latter-day Saints!

Monday, January 13

Orv stopped by after school today and handed me an envelope. Mom saw him and tried to get him to stay for dinner, but he politely refused. "Jes' somethin' I scratched out on paper, Wallace. Wanted you to read it. Wanted you to have it." Then he was off the porch like a polecat with its tail on fire. I opened the letter after closing the front door. Inside was a poem. I'm copying it into my journal because, well, it fits in here.

From the Mountain
by Orville J. Burrell

In the valley
the night shifts to shadows,
only now is it letting go.

On the mountain
a thin yellow line creeps along the crags and swales
tracing its shape with fingers of gold.

Sunrise
soon will creep my way.

From the mountain,
you first can see
the wheat fields, rippling in the wind,
the river, with a red-tailed hawk gliding high,
the day, with all its promise,
and you understand where you might go, where you might go.

Daybreak, and I want to be
on top of the mountain,
so I can see,
so I can see.

Friend,
You took me to the mountain,
and light glows from the east.

My eyes are awake,
My eyes can see.

Need I say anything more?

TUESDAY, JANUARY 14

Life came back to me with a jolt today as I walked by
the gym near the end of school with Orville. He was getting ready for wrestling practice (Orv is on the varsity and
won his first four matches, three by pins), and I had decided to start lifting today. I walked by the locker room
just as the guys on the junior varsity started charging upstairs in their nice white and maroon uniforms, getting
ready for a game. It shook me up to see them with their
game faces, pumped. Everyone except Andy ignored me.
He gave me a quick exchange of the palms and said, "Wish
you were with us, Whipple." But the others, well, they
acted as though I was invisible. No way around it, I miss
basketball. A lot.

Orville noticed. "Two kinds of people in this world,
that's 'bout the way I got it figured," he drawled, pulling off
his cowboy boots a couple of minutes later.

"Tell me."

"Some folks are dirt clods and some are rocks, Wally."

"How's that?"

"Well, you look at the side of the road when you're
goin' down it, and you can't really tell what's a dirt clod
and what's a rock. You got to get out and grab 'em in your

hand. The dirt clod, when he's in a little bit of a squeeze, why he just crumbles and goes blowing away. He ain't steady a'tall. But the rock, he ain't like that. You put the pressure on and he's steady and firm. Sometimes when you get the grip put on you, you find out if you're a dirt clod or a rock."

He yanked off the other boot and didn't say anything else. He didn't need to. I got the message. I've got to be a rock. Got to.

THURSDAY, JANUARY 16

Big week. I've got an oral test in Spanish tomorrow, where I will have to habla my el hearto out for Senorita Richardson, she of the wonderfully trilled Rs and beautiful dark eyes. Lots of math homework, and we're getting a load in biology, too. A paper is due for English on *The Red Badge of Courage.* After that, Mrs. Garrison told us that we're going to start *Romeo and Juliet,* a real big thrill, since not only do people fall in love but they also die in it. Why do love and death seem to show up in pairs all the time? One of the great questions of literature that has yet to be answered.

Seems like all the teachers decided to dump a lot of work on us to make up for the slack time at Christmas.

Around the family, not much has changed. Dad is still really down about not getting the promotion at work. "They gave the job to Susan Dellinger, from the store in Salem," he told Mom the other night. "Bright woman, degree in business management, but only with us for five years. I don't know. Maybe my future isn't in retail."

Natalie got a call from school today, but she wasn't at home in time to take it. She has been busy trying to think of who her counselors should be, and I know the first counselor in the bishopric, Brother McCausland, would really like to know.

"It's like I don't know if I should call people I really like and I know I'll get along with and who will tell me everything I do is really great, or if I should, like, call someone spiritual so that I can like delegate everything that I don't want to do," Natalie confessed to me tonight. "Seriously, it's hard to be spiritual."

"Why don't you call one of each? Someone you like and someone who's really spiritual? You sort of get the best of both worlds that way."

Natalie looked thunderstruck. "That's a massively good idea, Wally."

So she's solved that problem, and I heard her talking on the phone to Brother McCausland later in the evening.

It was a pretty good solution, if I don't say so myself. I only wish it were as easy for me to solve my own problems.

Friday, January 17

Natalie is pumped. She is not on Cloud Nine, more like Cloud Ninety-Nine. This may be the happiest I've ever seen her, including (1) when she returned to the mall after being grounded, (2) Christmas morning, and (3) the time she was told by one of her friends' mothers that she should consider a career in modeling. "Jan's mom was a model herself, so, like, I think she's really serious about it, like, I totally have a future in it," she solemnly told our family.

When Nat got to school today, she found out that one of the cheerleaders had to drop off the squad because of poor grades, and since the season is less than one-third finished, the adviser asked her if she would mind filling in for the rest of the season.

Natalie, I'm proud to say, apparently demonstrated the well-known Whipple family trait of keeping your cool no matter what the circumstance. According to several eye-witnesses, she started screaming "Yes!" before the adviser finished the sentence. Then came hugs to everyone nearby for the next ten minutes, followed by the ritualistic gushing of the tears.

Natalie is one happy woman tonight. She even offered to take out the garbage, which, according to Mom and Dad, has only happened one other time in her life—the night she was trying to repent for wearing some of Dad's clothes without his permission to her school's "Nerd Days" contest a couple of years ago. "But your yellow tie helped me win, Dad," she later pleaded. "You don't want me to, like, fail, do you?"

But there is more to my sister. She sees the day's events as a spiritual experience.

"I feel, you know, like I'm blessed because I accepted to be the Mia Maid class president," she told our family at dinner tonight. "This has helped my testimony, seriously. It's like that song about not knowing beforehand what to do, then doing it, and then everything turns out super," she rambled.

Dad looked at her, an eyebrow raised. "I think you're talking about a scripture in the Book of Mormon, Natalie, not a song."

"Song, scripture, TV talk show, as long as it's truth, it doesn't really matter, for sure," she said blithely. "I think it just means that if you do good, good things happen to you, and you can overcome adversity and become a cheer-leader. I'm really thankful that other girl got rotten grades and got kicked off. Seriously. I bet she's not a Mia Maid class president."

"Is she even a Church member?" Mom asked.

"No. That, like, proves my point. Like I said, she's not a Mia Maid class president."

Mom and Dad held their forks still for a moment and just stared at Nat, who, without a clue, just kept eating and smiling and telling us all of the other newly discovered truths in her life, such as the power of prayer and fasting. "I like fasted and prayed that a way would, you know, be opened for me to be a cheerleader, even though I thought, 'Bzzt, too bad for the other girl.'" The sound of Natalie's milk-of-human-kindness sloshing around tonight was almost enough to cause the rest of us to go deaf.

Oh well. I'm certainly not going to rain on her parade tonight. At least one of the Whipples has some good news. Let's hope it's the start of a trend.

TUESDAY, JANUARY 21

Been super bogged down with homework and haven't had time to do much. Broke away to shoot a few hoops with Chuck on Saturday, but other than that, pretty much kept my nose in the books. Getting close to grades again, and I want to see if I can't elevate the old GPA from the terrestrial to the celestial kingdom.

I did go to watch Orville wrestle tonight. Lumpy was there, too. Orville is a good wrestler. He's strong enough to lift a barn and he's very quick. He drives Coach Waymon absolutely bonkers because Orv doesn't seem to take it all very seriously and could care less about technique. To him, it's a game, and when you think about it, he's right.

Tonight, Orv went through his usual routine. When it was time to come out and meet his opponent, Orv extends his big old paw and says, "Pleased to meetcha." The other guy, of course, is trying to play the head game with Orv and is grunting, growling, drooling, and putting on the ugly face, hoping it will convince Orv how tough he is. Orv doesn't buy it. Remember, this is a guy who has ridden bulls and roped steers since about the time most guys our age were learning to ride a two-wheeler. As he has said to us on numerous occasions, "These ol' city boys don't throw much of a scare into me."

So the other guy goes out and gets after Orv pretty hard in the first round. The crowd loves Orv, and they go nuts with every move he makes. Orv lets the other guy try a few moves. Once he actually flips Orville over and gets a couple of points. Orv sort of looks at Lumpy and me from underneath and smiles, his way of saying, "No worries, I just don't want to crush this little feller's feelings right yet."

He even says to the other guy, "Nice move, pardner. You're a tough little flea." This gets his opponent really steamed, and he tries a couple more fancy moves on Orv, hoping for the pin. Coach Waymon is on the edge of the mat, getting really red in the face and yelling for Orv to do something.

Orv decides things have gone on about long enough, so he basically stands up with the guy on his back, then pulls him around to the front, throws him on the mat, grins once at us in the stand, flops on him, then pins the guy late in the first round.

He shakes hands with his vanquished and slightly dazed opponent, tells him, "You're a feisty little guy," then heads back to the bench where he is pounded on the back by his teammates, and Coach Waymon finally relaxes a bit.

Orv amazes me. Great wrestler. Honor roll student. Cowboy. Philosopher. Poet. Super friend. He could play the game and be one of the most popular guys in the junior class. But he just takes it all in stride, doesn't let much phase him—other than his middle name. Tonight when I got home Mom asked me how it went. "Franklin won. Orv pinned his guy in the first round."

"Is that like a touchdown or a home run?"

"Yeah. A lot like a touchdown and a home run, Mom."

Natalie flitted around the corner from the family room, dressed in her cheerleading outfit, obviously after an intense workout session in front of the mirror. Nat, who tends to be more open about her social life than her older brother, pops a question.

"Do you know if Orville, like, likes anyone?" she asked.

"You're still his number one woman, Nat."

"Funny, Wally." And then she pranced off, with visions of white dresses and cowboys dancing in her head.

WEDNESDAY, JANUARY 22

Got a call tonight from Brother Owens, who is new in our ward and the basketball coach for the Young Mens team. He said that our season starts on Saturday, and he'd heard I was a good player. He asked me if I'd like to be on the team and mentioned that we didn't have that many guys in our ward, a subtle message to the effect of, "Even if you are a warm body, we need you out there."

Church basketball. An experience like no other. A time where middle-aged men who don't know the difference between technical fouls and water fowls are given a whistle and a black-and-white shirt and told to go referee. A time where the prevailing rule seems to be, "No autopsy, no foul." A time where everyone seems to think every game is for the national championship and that they are playing in front of 20,000 screaming people. A time when guys try to be cool by wearing baseball hats backwards while they run up and down the floor in high-topped black shoes that leave big ugly streaks all over the floor. A time when each game opens with a prayer that always includes the phrase, "And help us to be good sports and not get injured" just before you take the court and try to beat the brains out of the other team's players.

All of these thoughts and more flashed through my mind. Church basketball. Ugh.

"We have a couple of guys from the teachers quorum, plus Larry Felton, Mel Pyne, you—I hope—and a kid who was just baptized, Orville Burrell," Brother Owens said. "I'd really like to field a team."

Should I encourage Orville to play? He's so new to the Church. This might be more than his testimony can handle. We'll find out if he's a rock in a hurry. "What time?" I caved in.

"Ten o'clock at the stake center," a definitely more chipper voice answered. "And if you have any friends who like to play, bring them along, too. We'll need them."

Church basketball. I know exactly what sports will be like in the telestial kingdom. A league where Laman and Lemuel are stars and the Sons of Sceva have their own team.

And now I'm about to join in. Did Danny Ainge ever have to play church hoops?

THURSDAY, JANUARY 23

Crazy thought for the day: Should I ask Evan to play on our church basketball team?

Yeah, the refs might give us a technical foul just because of his appearance, but I'm getting this strange feeling that I should at least invite him to play. While we were lifting today, Evan swaggered on over. Come to think of it, Evan swaggers wherever he goes.

"Wimp Pole, glad you don't have no hoops."

"Yeah, Evan. I'll be lifting at least until track season. But I might play in a church league."

Evan looked faintly thoughtful, probably the way a

caveman did when he took his first bite of animal flesh that had been seared by fire. His bushy eyebrows sank a bit, and he pushed back his long hair. "I like hoops, Wimp Pole. Don't tell no one here, though."

That's all he said before swaggering over to one of the benches where he had someone spot him while he lifted about 6,000 pounds in each hand.

But would Evan fit in our church league? If things got, shall we say, rough, it would be nice to call a time-out, point out the offending player, and simply say, "Evan, kill." But what if Evan did something really out of hand?

I told my Dad about Evan and the unmistakable push I was feeling to ask him to play on our team. "Is there anything wrong with it, Dad? I mean, the guy doesn't live church standards, exactly. He's got tattoos on his arms and wears an earring. Hey, not that I mind, but I mean this is a guy I don't expect to see gathering fast offerings soon. Beating one of the deacons over the head and ripping off fast offerings, maybe."

"Why do you want him to play on the team? Is it because he'll help you win more games, or is there something that you think is deeper?"

"I don't even know how good he is, Dad. Maybe he's a klutz. But in his own primitive way, he's been nice to me and I think he figures I'm his friend. Funny thing is, I don't think he has many friends, even though every kid in the school knows who he is. But Dad, I think that way underneath, and we're talking miles down, there is a real human being there."

"Do what you think is right, Wally. But I've seldom if ever regretted doing something for good reasons. If your motives are right, then the outcome will be right."

I was hoping that Dad would say, "Yeah, go for it," or "No way! He sounds like a flake to me." But in my advancing years, I know that Mom and Dad are turning more decisions over to me. All preparation for adulthood, I'm sure. Sometimes I miss those days when my biggest challenge was tying my shoes and not losing my lunch pail on the way to school.

As of this moment, 10:09 P.M. on January 23rd, I think my decision is to ask Evan to play on the ward team. Hope it's not a mistake.

FRIDAY, JANUARY 24

So I slithered into the weight room today a little early. Evan was there, working on his upper back muscles.

"Hey, Evan."

He didn't look up at me, just recognized my voice.

"Wimp Pole."

"You want to play on our church team? First game is tomorrow." I learned long ago that with Evan it's best to take the direct approach.

Now he stopped lifting and looked at me. Sweat streamed down his face. "Maybe."

"We could use another big guy. You look like you can rebound."

"Yeah, I can. I like pushing people around."

"We've got rules, Evan. You can't smoke and you can't drink or use drugs. And during the game, you can't cuss and you can't hit anyone, even though someone might try to hit you."

"You guys take all the fun out of it, Wimp Pole."

"It only seems that way."

"When and where?" I told him. "Anybody else I know on the team?"

"Maybe. Orville Burrell. Lumpy Felton. Mel Pyne."

"Know 'em all. Burrell's a good guy. Felton's that fat little guy I had in English. Pyne's a smart guy, but he's okay. He helped me in social studies last year. But this is in a church. Too much."

"It's a nice gym, Evan."

"Well, maybe I'll surprise you."

"Hope so. And one other thing. Everyone calls everyone else Brother or Sister."

"All the old guys have beards in your church?"

"No."

"Do the women?"

"No. Well, maybe a couple."

"Good. I don't like big hair on guys, except for me."

He grabbed the bar again and was ready to start lifting. I turned and was about halfway out of the weight room when I heard his voice.

"Brother Wimp Pole. Haven't smoked since you said it was stupid," he shouted, before grunting and pushing the bar from behind his shoulders and over his head. "You was right."

I walked out of the gym slowly. "Never doubt me, Evan," I hollered back. "Never."

Saturday, January 25

The great social experiment involving basketball as an alternative to a probable career as a major crime figure got off to a start today. A bit rocky, but it turned out okay.

I got to the church a half-hour before the game. Brother Owens was there, and I tried to prepare him for the appearance of Evan. "He's got hair—lots of it. In fact, he'll probably be wearing a ponytail today."

"Ponytail? That's okay. I can handle that," Brother Owens said.

"And he has, well, you know, tattoos."

"Tattoos? Oh. Huh. Like what?"

"Motorcycles, mostly."

"Does he ride a motorcycle?"

"Yeah. But really, Brother Owens, he's a good guy."

I walked on the court. We warmed up. Quarter till ten. No Evan, although everyone else was there. I watched the other team go through a lay-up drill. Sure enough, about half of them had on baseball hats, and at least a couple had on black-soled shoes. They had a lot of players. None as tall as me, but a couple of guys who could double as a gorilla stand-in on a movie set. It was going to be muscle against muscle. I flexed, just to scare them. No one noticed. Ten minutes to game time. No Evan. Maybe he'd stand me up. Like he said, basketball in a church? Too much. I walked to the door and looked outside.

Then I heard the roar of a Harley-Davidson in the distance, and a minute later in walked Evan, impeccably coiffed in his ponytail and earring. "That's him!" I pointed out to Brother Owens, who gulped hard. Evan, the monster of understatement, came over to me. "Wimp Pole. I'm here."

"Great, Evan. Better get a shirt on and sign in at the scorer's desk. And I'll introduce you to Brother Owens"—at this point Evan gave a definite snicker—"our coach."

The cultural hall almost came to a stop when Evan pulled off his shirt to put on our uniform. The guy definitely had muscles. And he definitely had tattoos.

"What now, Wimp Pole?"

"Warm up. Then we pray, then we play the game."

Evan winced. "You didn't say nothin' about prayin.' I don't do prayin'."

"I know. But they're short and you don't have to say anything except amen at the end, and since it's your first time, you can even skip the amen part," I said. New Church doctrine, I guess, but it made a lot of sense under the circumstances, and if I'd done something horribly wrong that knocked me down a few kingdoms, I could always repent.

So we prayed. Evan, I noticed, just looked around the whole time. Then Brother Owens called us together and gave us our starting lineup: Pyne, Burrell, Felton, Brewer, and Whipple. Sure, it was only a church game, but it felt good to be starting. Evan took his place at the end of the bench, slouched in a chair, and yawned.

The game started. I will not go into too many details of the first quarter, other than to say that the score was about even, proving that miracles still do happen, since it more resembled hand-to-hand combat. The strategy of our opponents seemed to be summarized in the words *grab*, *pull*, *push*, *trip*. These guys were brutal. They must have been in training for the Marine Corps' special guerilla warfare unit. Every time I shot the ball, I had one guy hanging on my arm, another hacking my wrist, and a third pushing me in the back. I had a few buckets, Orville had a pair, and Mel hit a bomb from the outside. But the refs weren't calling anything. They looked like a couple of nice older men on loan from the high priests quorum who probably had their choice of officiating or a shift at the cannery and decided being elbow deep in pears wasn't much fun.

At the quarter break, Brother Owens told us to keep our cool, don't worry about the lack of calls, and take good shots.

"Them guys are an ornery bunch," puffed Orville. "I thought you said this was a basketball game, not a wrasslin' match."

Brother Owens looked down the bench. Maybe it was Evan's rippling muscles or the general sneer on his face. Maybe it was the tattoos. Maybe it was desperation; maybe inspiration. We needed someone with an attitude. Whatever, Brother Owens barked Evan's name and sent him in for Lumpy, who was only too happy to come out.

It was a decision that probably saved the game for us.

"Let 'em know you're in there, Evan. They're getting

physical, so we need to do a little bit of that ourselves. Can you handle that, Trant?"

Evan smiled cherubically. "Yeah."

"And you'll have to take off your earring."

Evan frowned, but he pulled out his earring.

The other team took the ball out and one of their guards put up a long jumper. Evan was standing near the foul line, but as soon as the ball went up, he crashed toward the basket. *Crash* is the operative word here. Evan went up and over two of the other team's players and came down on a third. When the pile of limp bodies was untangled, the three victims had a look of terror in their eyes, Evan had a foul, and it was the last time any of them tried to push a guy on our team around. Evan's reputation was set. We had an enforcer.

"So, I guess you'd call yourself a finesse player, right, Evan?" I asked at our next time out.

He grinned wickedly. "Basketball ain't for pansies."

Soon we got into a rhythm. Now that Orville had some help on the boards, we cranked up our fast break. Danny Brewer and I were getting easy buckets off the break, and we pulled into the lead. Five points. Eight points. At half we were up 12, and when the fourth quarter ended, we had the game won by 23 points. A breeze.

Since winning hasn't been a regular part of my life, I enjoyed trotting off the court near the end of the game and taking my place on the bench while the subs finished things up. Brother Owens looked over at me. "Twenty-six points, Wally. Nice game."

Evan scored our last basket. Orville got a rebound and threw a nice outlet to one of our guards. He flipped the ball to Evan, who put his head down and barreled toward the basket. The two players on the other team between Evan and the basket wisely chose to get out of the way rather than risk mayhem by staying in his path. Evan jumped high and softly laid the ball in off the glass.

"Nice game, Evan," I congratulated after it was over. "We turned it around when you came in."

Evan let a small smile briefly curl at the corners of his mouth. "You expected less, Brother Wimp Pole?"

"Glad we were dogs together in this fight," Orville said.

"Yeah, Burrell. You're not bad on the boards either," Evan praised.

"Can you play next week?"

"Think so. But don't call me no Brother Trant."

"Deal," I agreed.

We split up and went our own ways. It was cool and clear outside, and the east wind was gusting, making the air feel just right. As I was ready to climb in the family station wagon, Brother Owens caught up with me.

"Wally. Is that big guy, Trant, is he a member?"

I thought about it for a second. "Not yet, Brother Owens. Not yet."

MONDAY, JANUARY 27

Certain things lead you to realize that your life is in a rut, such as when you wear the same socks three days in a row, or you haven't changed your toothbrush in over a year.

Another way to determine if your life is into deep, well-grooved channels is if your grades remain exactly the same as the previous quarter, which is the case with me: two Cs, two Bs, and three As. That's it. Boring. Monotonous. Bland. In the great ice cream cone of life, I am low-fat vanilla. Truth.

I had hoped for a better grade in English and biology, but no luck. Mr. Flagg, my biology teacher, said he only gave one A in our class, because we weren't mentally tough enough yet. "Your brains are still mush in here," he growled. "No wonder our national test scores are falling in this country, while we let foreign nations pass us by." Yeah, I'm sure he's right that our inability to understand semipermeable membranes and nitrogen-fixing lichens is the reason behind the decline of America.

Not much more I can say on the subject. Not much more I want to say, except that we'll give it the try once more and hope for some improvement next time around.

February, the month of red hearts and little angels barely clothed and shooting arrows of love, is just around the corner. Perhaps it will be the month when my (pick the proper adjective: 1. dismal; 2. nonexistent; 3. pathetic; 4. miserable) social life picks up a bit.

You gotta have faith, Whipple. You gotta believe.

THURSDAY, JANUARY 30

Good intelligence today. The source: my very own Mom.

Mom talked me into driving her to the grocery store, a request I gladly accommodated, thus exhibiting my willingness to use my license for the betterment of humankind.

On the way back, Mom said, "Wally, I ran into Joyce Smisore today when I was getting some copies made for my lesson."

Uh-oh. Alarms and bells go off in my head. Sister Smisore is the mother of spiritual giantess Nancy Smisore, the girl whom every mother in the stake wants to line up with their son. As previously recounted in my journal, as well as in countless conversations and perhaps a bad dream or two, Nancy is ready to step into a Relief Society presidency right now. And I'm not talking about being an individual counselor or even the president herself, Nancy is ready and able to fulfill all three callings at once. Mom drops big hints every so often that she wouldn't object to Nancy Smisore someday being Nancy Whipple. While Nancy is a nice girl, cute in her own way, and a far better human being than I will ever be, I don't want to marry her. Is that fair?

"Joyce said that Nancy seems to like someone. Joyce said it's her first real crush."

Oh no! Nancy is in *like* with me! How will I get out of this?

"I guess she's absolutely flipped for this guy."

Well, credit Nancy for good taste. I must escape, though. A mission. Tell Mom I need all my spare time to concentrate on preparing for a mission. Might work. Tell her I'm not worthy of Nancy, that I'd feel inferior to her in every way and it could cause possible permanent warping of my personality.

Tell her I just don't think Nancy would be a fun date.

"And since you know this person so well, I thought it would be okay to let you in on Nancy's little secret."

Okay, okay. Defeat. So I have to take Nancy out. How do I let her down easy? Maybe I could burp really loud, then wipe my mouth with my sleeve. Maybe I could not brush my teeth for a couple of days before I go out with her. Yes, gross is good.

"In fact, maybe you could diplomatically let Lumpy know that Nancy likes him."

Lumpy? Lumpy Felton? Nancy Smisore likes Lumpy Felton?

This is great! I can't believe it! It proves two things beyond a shadow of a doubt: Love is strange, and humor is alive and well in heaven.

This is an unbelievable combination! It is matching a Ferrari and a dump truck. It is a pizza supreme and tofu! It is a princess and a warty green frog!

Nancy has the hots for Lumpy! Incredible!

"Mom, I will only be too happy to tell Lumpy that Nancy is madly in love with him. As his friend, it is my duty."

Mom's radar is functioning well. "Wally, I don't want you to make fun of Lumpy or be insensitive in any way. I think it's all very sweet, and I don't want you to hurt anyone's feelings. Do you understand?"

"Sure, Mom. Honest, I wouldn't have hurt anyone's feelings," I said, instantly shelving my plan to sneak the news into the daily announcements that are read to the entire student body each morning. "Give me a little credit."

But this is almost too good to be true. Nancy and Lumpy. They make a lovely pair!

CHAPTER 6

February

SUNDAY, FEBRUARY 2

Church was good. It meant something for me to look down the end of the Whipple pew and see Orville next to Chuck. This is a fairly amazing sight since Natalie almost bent herself into the shape of a pretzel trying to make sure she got to sit next to Orv, but was aced out by my little brother, who displayed some pretty nifty moves to squeeze in ahead of her. It was fast Sunday, and I got this funny, excited feeling deep down, which I'm beginning to recognize as promptings from the Spirit. So I made the long walk to the podium and shared my testimony. I'm not exactly sure what I said, but it was something along the lines of how thankful I am for my family, my friends, and especially Orville.

Later in the day, I was vegging out, thinking about life in general. I remembered my number one resolution for this year and made a historic decision: I decided to talk to more girls. Let's be honest about it. I've depended on the powers of my natural charm and raw animal magnetism long enough and the results are zero. Now, I have to be a man of action, a guy who is in control, one who plots his moves carefully and defines the future on his own terms. These kinds of experiences will, I believe, help me in my professional life.

ME: (20 years from now, entering the corporate board room) "Good afternoon, gentlemen and gentle ladies. As you know, Whipple Smidget Amalgamated has had a record sales year. And the future looks even brighter, especially based on our decision last meeting to diversify from our main product lines of skyscraper construction and state-of-the-art smidget manufacturing into our new line of pizzas and zip-up socks."

VICE PRESIDENT # 1: (who may be Lumpy, if things work out) "Here, Here! W.F.! We couldn't have done it without your inspired leadership and tremendous foresight!"

ME: "Thank you, very much. Your point is well taken, and you've always had the knack for sucking up at the right time, L.T. Now, on to today's business. P.F., I believe you're first up today."

VICE PRESIDENT #2: "Well, about those french fry futures —"

ME: "Dump 'em. Idaho had good weather this year. The market will be flooded. Next."

VICE PRESIDENT #3: "The stock purchase of Clodney and Sons, supposed to be on line to make a breakthrough to cure acne—"

ME: "Buy. Ten thousand shares. Get me some samples. Good work, A.J."

VICE PRESIDENT #4: "How does the old man do it? What a guy!"

ME: (overhearing the comment) "I'll tell you how I do it, G.S. When but a lad, I decided to take control of my life—be firm, fair, and decisive. The moment came when I decided to talk to girls and take my social life into my own hands. The same principle holds true in the business world. Pursue what you want. Pursue what you like. Pursue what you need. Pursue or be pursued; be the pursuer or the pursuee. You get my drift."

Well, maybe that's a bit of an exaggeration, but the point is that I am going to call Edwina Purvis soon, maybe stop by her house. I'll talk to Julie—a nice, normal conversation on the way out of the door to seminary or before English class. I may even go up to a girl I don't even know and tell her something like, "Has anyone ever told you you're gorgeous, and would you like to go out Friday?" My future is in my own hands. I will take control. The time is now for the emergence of Wallace F. Whipple from his lowly oysterlike bearing to a noble being capable of spitting up pearls.

Fair warning, world: Wallace Whipple is coming at you!

TUESDAY, FEBRUARY 4

Lumpy has a cold and wasn't at church on Sunday. This caused me considerable torment because I wanted to tell him all about his secret admirer, but I thought as sort of a guy thing that I should do it in person. I also considered what Mom had said, and decided that, yeah, she was right; I needed to be sensitive and understanding about it.

To show my sensitivity and maturity, I asked Lumpy if he'd like to go to Hamburger Bob's after school. "I'll even buy," I humbly offered.

"Sure, great, super," Lumpy wheezed through his stuffy nose.

So there we sat. Lumpy was working on Bob's renowned Gutto Blaster hamburger, a creation that almost defies words, other than to say it contains about a side of beef, two eggs, sausage, wads of smooshy cheese, triple onions, and tabasco sauce. Those are the only ingredients we've been able to identify so far. Bob himself says we've only got about half of them down.

Lumpy looked so happy, wolfing down enough cholesterol and grams of fat to last him about two decades. He
looked calm, serene, in his element. I wanted to remember
him just like this, other than perhaps the trickle of tabasco
that was dribbling down his chin. All in the world was
good for Lumpy—lots of food that someone else bought,
disposing of it in the company of a friend. Nevertheless, I
had a mission to perform.

"Lump, I've got news."

"Hmmm. Ymmmm. Good. Slrrp. Hmmmm."

"It's fairly big news, Lumpy. It might change your life."

"This is great," he said, temporarily clearing his mouth.

"Lumpy, I know someone who likes you. Someone
who wants to go out with you."

"Pass the ketchup?"

"Yeah. Sure. Here it is."

"Thanks, Wally."

In my new man of action attitude, I decided to compete with the Gutto Blaster and drive home the point immediately.

"Lumpy. Nancy Smisore has the hots for you. She
wants to go out with you."

It worked. After 17 years, I found a way to get Lumpy's
mind off food. Love can work wonders, I mentally noted.

Lumpy stared blankly at me, then put down his Gutto
Blaster. He started to cough. He turned flannel-red and for
a brief instant I thought his eyes rolled back in his head.
He wheezed again, coughed again, and madly groped for
water. I wondered if he needed the Heimlich maneuver.

"Nancy wants to . . . go out . . . with me?" he said in absolutely the most hoarse voice I've heard in my life.

He was in a near state of shock. I felt bad. Me, his best
friend, springing this unexpected news to him. Love is like
death in this respect. You shouldn't just slap on the news
about either without taking some precautions. His system

wasn't ready for the news that a female on the planet somehow deemed him desirable. It was beyond his comprehension.

Gradually, he caught his breath. Color came back to his face. "Wally . . . Nancy? Wally, I've had a crush on her for the last two years! Cool! This is awesome!" Then he took another bite of the Gutto Blaster. So much for the first blush of true love.

Now it was my turn. I coughed. I sputtered. The milkshake that I had in my hand slipped to the floor with a thud. The brain cells all flickered and went poof! I was instantly turned into a jellyfish.

"You okay, Wally?"

"Huh?"

"Are you okay?"

"Yeah. Maybe. Why didn't you ever tell me you liked Nancy?"

"You never asked. We were always too busy talking about your love life."

"Oh."

"So what do I do with Nancy? What's my next move?"

Wallace F. Whipple Jr., the Mentor of Love, the Advisor to the Lowly and Lonely. I wasn't ready for it.

"I don't know, Lump," I mumbled, feeling slightly dizzy. "Can we talk about this later? I need time to think."

"Sure. This is great. Maybe Nancy likes Gutto Blasters, too."

"I don't think so, Lump."

We really didn't say much after that. Lumpy dropped me off a half hour later, and I am only now getting over the shock. How could I have missed that one? It's a little like sitting on the top of an erupting volcano and not noticing the temperature rising and the noise level going up a few hundred decibels. Lumpy's in *like* with someone who is in *like* with him. Amazing.

And a little spooky. For the first time in history, his social life is about to jump out ahead of mine. If this were a race, and sometimes it sure seems like it is, I just dropped into dead last place. Will I date again before my mission? Will I date after my mission? Am I going to be a social outcast forever? Is it time I move to Wyoming and become a cowboy?

Life is complicated. *Like* is complicated. It can make your brain fuzzy and clear at the same time.

I don't understand it.

WEDNESDAY, FEBRUARY 5

I talked it all over with Orv the next day as we hung out before English class—my conversation with Lumpy, my complete and utter shock that he had admired Nancy from afar for so long, my total mental checkout at the news. Orville was a whole lot more solid with the idea.

"Don't surprise me none," he said. "You remember when we visited that nursin' home in December?"

"Yeah. What about it?"

"Well, he'd like to have busted my leg gettin' out of the way when Vanessa got out of the car, jes' so's he could grab Nancy's hand. At the time, I thought there might be a little somethin' goin' on. Then, I seen him peekin' at Nancy durin' seminary. Dead giveaway was last week, when we read them lines in Corinthians about "neither ain't the man without the woman" and all. Lumpy was spyin' at Nancy like a dog lookin' over a stewbone. And I think she knew purtinear everything that was goin' on, and not mindin' a tad."

Maybe it's because Orville grew up on a ranch in eastern Oregon and always had to be watching for coyotes that might devour him, his sheep, and his dog, or maybe it's just that he is extraordinarily observant, but he doesn't miss much. Lumpy could have been dropping clues for a year, and I probably wouldn't have picked up on anything. Earth to Whipple; come in, Whipple.

"Bet they get together for the Anything Goes Dance in a couple of weeks."

"Yep. I 'spect they will."

The Anything Goes Dance is just that. A few years back, the student body got rid of the mushy, gooshy, squeezy, stars-in-your-eyes, Cupid's-on-the-loose Valentine's Dance and substituted the Anything Goes Dance. Girls can ask guys. You can wear bib overalls or your P.E. uniform. You can come in a formal and a tux, eat at an expensive restaurant, or down a box of macaroni at home. Unless it will get you in trouble with the law or our vice principal for discipline, Mr. McCloud, you can stretch the bounds of normalcy any way you want.

My first date in my entire existence was an appearance at the Anything Goes Dance last February with Edwina Purvis. Now, the dance is coming around again, and I have this feeling that the social slump might be ending.

Face it—I'm available, semiruggedly handsome, and available, and, if nobody has noticed, *available*, and some girl is bound to seize the opportunity. Maybe even Julie, though I wouldn't exactly bet anything really valuable, such as my Steve Young football card, on it.

"Yeah. The old Lumpster. It will be his first date. Have you been asked?"

"Nope. Thought Viola might ask again, but she hasn't so far. If nothin' happens, then I might ask her."

Viola is, of course, Viola Barkle, the famed high school shot-putter, she of well-muscled arms and masterful physique. Viola could beat up about half the guys at Benjamin Franklin—all at once. Fortunately, she has a sunny disposition and is not inclined toward violence. Orv went with her to Anything Goes last year, and they had a great time.

"How 'bout you?"

"Haven't been asked yet, which is fairly amazing."

The bell rang and the class ahead of us barged out of the door.

"Guess it's time for us to hit it. What are we doing in English today?"

"More of that *Romeo and Juliet*. Danged funny book. Can't figure out why them people spent so much time fussin' and feudin', when a little marryin' probably would've drove 'em all together in no time. They didn't have 'nuff sense to pour water out of a boot."

With that, we went in and opened up our books, prepared to read and discuss romance, death, intrigue, and Shakespeare, subjects that 17-year-olds everywhere are experts on.

THURSDAY, FEBRUARY 6

I need to catch up on a few of the loose strings in the yarn ball of my life.

1. Alex Cole stopped me after our class meeting today and said that he wanted to get together with me and several other friends "to discuss the future and where we all fit in." I'm not sure what he means, but he might be plotting his next political move. This guy is ambitious. I once heard him tell a girl that his goal was to be elected to congress by his 34th birthday, "which only gives me 17 more years." Be all you can be.

2. Natalie is settling right into her new role as a leader of youth and a leader of cheers. "I'm doing so many awesome things right now, Wally, seriously," she told me tonight. "I'll bet I'm mentioned in someone's testimony

soon." She did get with her counselors and went to the home of a girl who is new to the ward, which I thought was nice. "I think she'll fit right in, and she has some good clothes, too. We looked in her closet," Natalie reported.

3. Dad. The Rock. The Steady One. The Man upon Whom We All Count. I can tell he's still bummed out about not getting the promotion at work. I've heard him say a few times something like, "I'm not sure this is what I want to do for 20 more years." This worries me some. I don't like midlife crises or anything like unto them when it involves one of my parents.

4. Journalism class. My star is rising here. Mr. Turner, the teacher, talked with me after class today and said that my writing was good to start with and getting better all the time. I bowed my head slightly and said, "Thank you," doing humble very well. "You might keep in mind that we'll have some openings on the editorial staff next year, Wally."

5. Evan greeted me with a hearty "Yo, Brother Wimp Pole" in the weight room today. It caught on. Before I left an hour later, everyone was calling me Brother Wimp Pole.

Evan played in our second game last week. It was a laugher. We won 67-33. Evan and Orville muscled their way through the other team the whole game. I ran the fast break, hit a few outside jump shots, and had 22 points before Brother Owens sat me down for the entire fourth quarter.

And another good sign: Evan didn't flinch when we prayed. He might have even mumbled an amen. That's progress.

6. No hints that I'm going to get asked to the Anything Goes. I managed to track down Edwina Purvis at school today, tilted my head to a rakish angle, and very suavely said, "Hi, Ed. What's happenin'?", which was almost a blatant statement of, "Hey, Ed, if you want to go to the dance

with me, all you have to do is ask. I'll say yes without even consulting my parents." But she didn't take the hint. All she said was, "Hi, Wally. Not much. Miss you in math class." Maybe she's just playing hard to get. I wonder if I should ask Ed? Or Julie? Or Vanessa?

7. Chuck. We are spending lots of quality time on the driveway shooting hoops, reading before bedtime, and doing all other things that role models do with those who worship the ground they walk on. Chuck also commented on my lack of social activity. "How come you don't go out with girls anymore, Wally? Don't you like them? You should be nicer and maybe they'll want to go out with you again."

You know your love life is bad when your six-year-old brother is giving you tips. Worse, he's probably right.

Lights out. Tomorrow is the most excellent Friday, my favorite day of the week, even if it is slightly hampered by school. Maybe something good will happen.

FRIDAY, FEBRUARY 7

Mrs. Garrison is calling our English class to order and we reluctantly obey. We are deep into *Romeo and Juliet* now, all the way into act 2, and we're going to do some reading today in class.

This is one of the extremely mushy parts of the book, which makes me feel queasy yet definitely interested, sort of a classic case of mixed emotions. I think it has something to do with hormones, although Shakespeare probably didn't have the endocrine system in mind when he wrote it.

"Let's start with scene 2, in the Capulets' garden. Let's see. We need some players to take the parts of Romeo and Juliet," Mrs. Garrison says. "Julie, would you take the part of Juliet? That seems natural."

Whoa! Julie is Juliet. Instantly, I take a keen interest in Shakespeare. What I would give to have Mrs. Garrison call on me to do Romeo. The chance to read sloppy lines to Julie, to show my maturity and sensitivity, not to mention my appreciation for plays, even if it is a seminauseating love story. The chance to show her beyond a shadow of a doubt that I have an appreciation for something in this world besides pizza and basketball. Please, Mrs. Garrison, call on me! Let me be your Romeo!

I make direct eye contact with her. I sit up straight in my chair. I smile and give the slightest of nods. She knows I want this part. She knows I need this part.

"Wally. Would you take the part of Romeo?"

"Be glad to, Mrs. Garrison. I can do Romeo."

A few snickers erupt from behind me. Orv raises an eyebrow. Ha! Doubters. All doubters! I clear my throat in a masculine sort of way. Shakespeare, here I come! Ready to blast away!

I begin very sensitively. " 'He jests at scars that never felt a wound—' " Good line. Rugged. Very manly. A lot like me. The stage is set.

" 'But, soft! what light through yonder window breaks? It is the east, and Julie is the sun!—' " I boom. More giggles from around the classroom. Horrors! I said Julie, not Juliet! I clear my throat again.

Sure am glad that I wore deodorant today. My stomach is churning like a cement mixer. I read a few more lines, even managing to get through the one about being sick and green, which is not a bad description of how I'm feeling.

" 'It is my lady; O, it is my—' " The next word is *love.* Oh man! Maybe I'm not ready to do Romeo. I start to pronounce it, " 'lo . . . lo . . .' um, *like!*" I finally burst out. Now the whole class is laughing, and Mrs. Garrison is fighting back a smile, too, without much success.

"Go on, Wally," she says.

And I do. Fortunately, I get all the way to Julie's first line, giving me a brief but needed rest.

"'Ah me!'" says Juliet. I am up at the plate again. Why does Romeo do all the talking?

"'She speaks:—O, speak again, bright angle!'"

"The word is *angel*, not *angle*," Mrs. Garrison corrects.

"Uh, thanks, Mrs. Garrison." Bright angle? Whipple! I push ahead, though I can feel my brain cramping up. I do fairly okay, until I get to the line, "'And sails upon the—'" oh no! "'Bos . . . bos . . .'" I gulp. I hope for an earthquake, the bell, the end of the world. No luck! "'Bos . . . buzz of the air!'"

The whole class goes bonkers. I'm funny, but I don't want to be. Even Julie is shaking with laughter. Orville, true-blue friend, is rolling. Mrs. Garrison can barely contain herself.

"The word is *bosom*, Wally," Mrs. Garrison interjects between deep bursts of laughter. "It's a fine word. Don't be embarrassed."

"Uh, I'm not." Huge lie. "I, uh, know it's a fine word. I just thought *buzz* sounded better. Like at night when the crickets buzz. And it's night in a garden where Romeo is, and I'm sure the crickets are buzzing, not bosoming. See what I'm saying?"

"You're a good writer, Wally, but not good enough yet to edit Shakespeare."

When the laughter finally dies down, Juliet begins, "'O Romeo, Romeo! wherefore art thou Romeo?'"

I sit at my desk with what must be a simple look of contentment on my face. Julie is reading some of the most famous lines in literature *to me!* This is nice. Extremely nice. ("Wally-o, Oh Wally-o, wherefore art thou Wally-o?")

She finishes her lines. My turn again. "'I take thee at thy word: Call me but—'" Uh-oh. The *L* word dead ahead. I back up to get a running start.

"'Call me but . . .'" Long breath, deep sigh. Once more, this time with feeling, Whipple!

"'Call me but LOVE!!!'" I shout and the whole class goes into a fit of laughter again. Mrs. Garrison even caves in and is laughing so hard that she has to sit down at her desk and grab at some tissues to dry her eyes off. Who says *Romeo and Juliet* is a tragedy? I'm singlehandedly turning it into a comedy, if not a farce!

When order is restored five minutes later, I am still a deep beet red in color and looking for a crevice in the earth to magically open up so that I can slip right in.

"Wally, you make a wonderful Romeo," Mrs. Garrison gasps, apparently out of energy from laughing so hard. "But we'll never get through this scene with you at the helm. Orville, will you take over?"

"Yes, ma'am, but I don't think I can hardly touch the way Wally here performed."

Julie looks at her new Romeo. At least Orv will be able to get through his lines, although I'm not sure how Shakespeare will sound with a cowboy twang. Julie begins, "'What man art thou . . .'" while I slump in my chair and lock in on the linoleum.

The funny thing is, Julie and Orville really click. We went from comedy (me) to high drama (Orv). As they read, there almost seems to be a rhythm, a feel, to what they are doing. Maybe even a bit of electricity.

When Orv looks right at Julie and reads, "Love goes toward love, as schoolboys from their books . . .'" I wish I hadn't biffed it. *Those could have been my words to Julie.*

The class ends. Mrs. Garrison thanks all of the players for "the most memorable 45 minutes in my career."

"You had us in tatters. You could've coaxed a grin from a fencepost," Orv says.

"You and Julie were the stars," I say. "You guys are good together."

Orville shrugs a little. "She's a nice girl. Purty, too."

And for some reason, I wonder if Orville is sort of in *like* with Julie.

Sunday, February 9

Another church league game yesterday, another easy win. I enjoy winning, especially after last year when my school team took a whole one (1) game. But if the question is asked, "Wally, would you rather be playing church ball and winning or be on the high school team and sitting on the bench?" the answer is, "Polish up the pines, I want to play school ball."

Orville and Evan are so tough inside. Pity the fool who drives down the lane and runs into them. We're starting to click really well. When either Evan or Orv grab the rebound, he instinctively heaves the ball toward Danny Brewer or me, and away we go. Brother Owens mostly sits on the bench and smiles.

"Brother Wimp Pole, when we gonna play someone tough? This is too easy," Evan told me.

"Don't know, Evan. It's not like we exactly scout out all the teams. I heard Sixth Ward has a good team, but we don't play them for a while. They've got a guy who's about 6'6", and he's supposed to be tough."

"Tough? Yeah, and I bet they call him Brother, too. Brother Stick, maybe."

So, hoops is going okay, school is fine, church is good. That leaves only one basic component toward achieving a well-rounded life—I've gotta date. My social life stinks.

How bad is it? May I make an analogy: In the great swimming pool of life, someone forgot to put in the algae control.

I botched up Romeo big time. But maybe, just maybe,

Julie thought I was trying to be funny, in which case I have succeeded wildly. I can almost predict her thoughts.

"A sense of humor is important to me. I want to be with someone who can make me laugh. So what if a man is strong, handsome, and a future neurosurgeon who will make zillions of dollars? If he has no sense of humor, he's not my guy. That Wally Whipple has the best sense of humor—pure comic genius. Who would have turned Romeo into a comic figure? Could it be that I judged him a little too fast, a little too harshly?"

Maybe I should get bold and ask Julie out to the Anything Goes. So what if she says no? That's where I am now. Julie's the one. What's there to lose?

My ego, that's what. What if I ask Julie, her face clouds over in panic, and she mumbles something along the lines of, "No! Definitely, no. Not in your dreams. Not in this life or the life to come." Then I am in shambles, pure wood putty.

Next, Edwina. I had a great time with her last year at the Anything Goes. And I sort of owe her one. True, I took her out later on, but the date she rigged up and pulled off was far superior to what I slapped together. And the most crucial element of all, if I asked Ed, I think she'd say yes. In a heartbeat. Ego remains intact, I break my social slump, have a good time, and we maybe talk about ways to improve my math grade. Can hardly lose with old Ed.

That's it. Ed. Ed is the choice. I look at it as a conservative, steady investment, sort of like U.S. savings bonds. Not like Julie, who may be thought of as an investment bank located on a small Caribbean island.

Of course, I could go off the wall. Ask Vanessa Peterson or someone else I hardly know. Good chance to expand my horizons. And maybe someone who would be lots of fun on a date. Adds an air of mystery, excitement. Plus, I come into the date an unknown quantity. She wouldn't have any preconceived notions about Wallace

Whipple, the dork, the king of klutz. And if she says no, not a big deal. The ego is not shattered into millions of pieces. I'd probably only brood about getting rejected for two or three days. Yeah, that's it. Gamble a little bit, Wallace. Ask out Vanessa.

Yep, that's it. Vanessa. Unless it's Ed. Or unless I go for the home run, the half-court shot, the 90-yard touchdown pass, and ask Julie.

Ah, life. Filled with choices. It's a great comfort to know that I'm a man not afraid of making decisions . . . most of the time. Well, some of the time. Occasionally, anyway.

MONDAY, FEBRUARY 10

Oh no.

Ugh.

Not now.

I wake up this morning feeling puffy about the face. Mumps? No. Not that lucky. Abscessed tooth? Huh-uh. I lightly run my hand over my face. There it is—a humongous, mountainous, extraordinarily large zit roughly the size of an aircraft carrier.

I'm closing in on ending my horrible social slide and I grow a county fair–sized tomato on my face overnight.

It's not fair. Usually, you get a little warning with these things. You sort of feel the swelling, see the redness, and can go into your pimple prevention mode. Not this time. Overnight, the volcano appeared. And on a Monday, too.

I know how kids operate. I mean, they almost graph and chart the progress of your pimple. "Hmmm. Looks bigger today than Tuesday. Whipple's got a whopper. Let's see, we think it will crest about 9:00 A.M. on Friday. Best to stay clear of him about then."

Yeah, sure, it's only a little bit of bacteria mixed in

with goop compressed into a little inflamed pustule that is of a temporary nature, but, trust me on this one, *it can ruin your whole life.*

I can tell Dad I'm sick, can't go to school. "And what are you sick with, Wally?"

"A pimple," I whimper.

"Not good enough, Wally. Pimples don't count. Out of the sack and face life like a man. Pimples never ruined anyone's life."

Yes, they have! Many is the romance, I'm sure, that has been ruined by something less, such as prospective mothers-in-law or different political affiliations, religions, or views on the origin of matter.

I stagger out of bed and to the mirror. Ooofff! Just like a punch to the stomach. Vesuvius! This one's name is definitely Vesuvius, after the famous Italian volcano. He looks like a Vesuvius—red, angry, almost ready to boil over. He's bigger than Everest and Rainier, two of my other hall of fame facial landmarks of days gone by.

Am I the only person in the world who gives names to his major zits?

What will I do?

For a brief, insane moment, I consider waking up Natalie and asking her to grab her makeup and help out. No. Even in my moment of crisis, I shall not stoop that low. How about a bandage? Naw. Everyone would ask, "Hey, Whipple, got a new zit?" A stocking cap? No. Too obvious. And I'd have to pull it down over one eye. I could try to pass it off as a fashion statement, but it would never work. Do I perform surgery on myself this morning? Not. Too risky. With my luck it would look even worse.

I'm stuck. I have a big, huge pimple on my face. And it's not going away soon. Yes, my only hope is to walk around today with my left hand covering as much of my face as possible for as long as possible.

I'm late. Dad doesn't say anything at breakfast, but I know that he knows. It would be like missing a Boeing 747 landing in your backyard. Lumpy is out front, waiting patiently. I grab my books and head for the car, left hand firmly in place on my left cheek.

"Hey, Wally."

"Yo, Lump."

We drive almost all the way to the church. Lumpy says nothing. Maybe I'm overreacting. Maybe it's not as noticeable as I think. Maybe this will work out okay. Relax, Whipple.

We pull into the church parking lot.

"Rand McNally been in touch yet, Wally?"

"Who?"

"Rand McNally. The people who make maps. Thought they'd want to add your zit to their maps as a new landscape feature."

Arrrgh. "Real cute, Lump."

We start in toward class, which has already started. My fault that we're late.

"Lumpy. I, uh, don't think, um, I'll be going in today. I think I'll go, you know, study in the foyer. Yeah, study. I need to study."

"Okay with me, Wally. That's the biggest zit I've ever seen. Really. I wouldn't want to go into class, either."

What can I say? He knows. He knows. I slink down the hallway, flip off the light, and plop on the couch. I have this theory that pimples loosely operate on the same principle as plants, namely, photosynthesis, and the less light available, the sooner they will wither and die. The darkness makes me feel a little better.

I close my eyes and start to doze. Then, I hear two voices. I recognize them.

Julie Sloan and Amy Hassett!

Flashback! A year ago I overheard them talking about me, and it wasn't pleasant.

"Vesuvius, what do we do?" I frantically think. It is a defining moment, a place to exhibit my maturity, my confidence, the fact that I will not let one pimple dictate how I will act. They are closing in. Oh dear. Why of all days does Vesuvius appear now?

Be calm, Wally. Trust in yourself. Believe in yourself. You can handle this.

And I do. Just before they come into view, I make a manly decision.

I jump over the back of the couch, curl up my long legs and hide, praying that they will sit on the two chairs in the other corner of the foyer.

My prayers are answered. Julie comes dangerously close as I cower behind the crushed orange velour couch that the church must have made a great deal on 20 years ago. She flips on the lamp on the end table. Please! Don't let me be discovered! What can I say if Julie sees me? I can just imagine:

"Wally, is that you?"

"No."

"Wally, what are you doing down there?"

"Lost a contact."

"I didn't know you wear contacts."

"I don't."

I hug the carpet, afraid to move, afraid to breathe. So far, I am undetected. I can see their shoes from my vantage point under the couch.

"I feel bad that we're late," says Amy.

"Yeah. Sorry. I just couldn't get it together this morning," Julie answers.

"Are you going to the dance, Amy?"

Hmmm. This might be interesting, I decide. I may grasp something akin to pure intelligence. For the first time, I dare to breathe.

"Yeah. I asked Aaron Phillips on Friday."

"Aaron? He's cool. You'll have a good time."

"How about you?"

Behind the couch, my heart starts pumping hard. A good portion of my whole life passes by me. What if she says, "Yes, I'm going to ask Wally Whipple?" Shall I stand up, take them both by surprise, and utter something hugely romantic like, "Yo, Jules. We're on!" The whole building must be shaking by now from the thumping of my heart, which must be registering on the Richter scale. What will she say? Speak, Julie! I need to hear!

"I haven't asked anybody yet . . ."

Yes! I'm still in the running!

". . . but I'm thinking about asking someone who might surprise you."

Double yes! I humbly submit that Julie asking me would be a surprise of the Presley-Jackson marriage magnitude!

"Who is that?"

Tell me! Speak my name, O fair one, and I shall be yours! My mind races into Shakespeare-like prose.

"I think I'm going to ask . . ."

I can feel it. This is going to be good!

"Orville Burrell."

What? Orville? Julie and Orville? Together? Julie . . . Sloan . . . Burrell? Huh? Wow, does my face ever hurt.

"Orv is such a nice guy. I think he's great. You'll have a super time. He's so sensitive and so different from other guys."

What about me? I'm sensitive. I didn't want them to be horrified by my pimple, that's why I'm behind the couch right now. I'm oozing in sensitivity. And I'm different. Way different. But Orville? Yeah, Orville. My friend. And Julie. There *was* a charge in the air when they did Romeo and Juliet. I was right. Why couldn't I have stayed true to form and been wrong?

They chatter on for a few more minutes. I now know exactly what Julie has in mind for Orv that evening. It sounds fun. I'd like to go.

Class must be over. I hear footsteps. I peer under the couch and recognize Lumpy's brown wing-tip shoes, the only guy in school who wears them. "Anyone seen Wally?" he asks.

"No, no. We've been here awhile, Lumpy, and we haven't seen him," Amy says. "Didn't he go to class?"

"No. Wally is such a dedicated student that he came out here to study today. He wants to be a doctor or an astronaut or a talk show host, so he knows grades are important. It killed him to skip seminary, but it's the first time he's ever done it."

Sweet, sainted, devious Lumpy. I could almost kiss him. My eyes moisten.

He walks over to the couch that I'm hiding behind, plops down, and looks over the edge. I smile at him and give him a little wave.

Lumpy almost croaks.

"Are you okay, Lumpy?" Julie asks.

"Bah, er, uh, I think so . . ."

"Are you sure?"

"Dah, erg, yessth."

"Guess we'd better be going now."

"Yeth. Good idea," Lumpy mumbles. They stand, then leave. Lumpy's face hovers over mine.

"Wally, what are you doing down there?" he hisses.

I can only sigh. "A long, sad story, Lump. I'll tell you some other year."

TUESDAY, FEBRUARY 11

How do I handle this?

Julie *likes* Orville, I think. A little tiny part of me wants to go up to her and say, "Julie, Orville is a great guy, but do you really want to spend the rest of your life on a ranch? Do you want all the guys in your wedding photos to have toothpicks in their mouths? Do you want to be a midwife to cows at 3:00 A.M. on cold spring nights? Do you like cowboy boots, big belt buckles, and heavy denim shirts with tassels? Not on Orv. On you and your children? Are you ready to interpret phrases such as 'he bunched the remuda a bit, then I dropped the loop on my top paint hoss?'" I'm not even sure what he means sometimes!

But I can't. No way. Orville is too decent a guy. He wouldn't trash me in front of Julie or anybody for anything. So what I do is be happy for them. All smiles and good thoughts. Take the noble part and give it my best. It is the mature thing to do.

Being mature isn't all that fun sometimes.

WEDNESDAY, FEBRUARY 12

Julie asked Orville to the Anything Goes last night. I know because Orville told me outside the gym, before he went to wrestling practice.

"Wally, I got some dickerin' to do with you," he said. "Don't want you to think that I'm givin' you the glass-eyed snaky look."

"Go for it, Orv."

"Well, I know that you still got some feelin' for Julie, but she went and asked me to the dance next week," he said.

"Are you going?"

"I don't know. Said I'd tell her today. You see, I feel like I'm just about to get whupped off a bronc. You don't know if you want to land at the front end or the back end because both can be dangerous."

"What do you mean?"

"If I say yes, then I worry you might brood or think less of me. If I say no, then I might hurt her feelin's. Either way, someone might feel like they're kissin' cactus."

I drew in a deep breath. The old movie *Casablanca* came to mind, the scene at the airport where Humphrey Bogart tells Ingrid Bergman that despite their feelings for each other, she needs to get on the plane. I know what the right thing is.

"Orv, I'm not much good at being noble. Go out with Julie. You'll have a great time. She's cool." Then, in a lower voice, "Besides, we always had Paris."

"Huh?"

"Never mind. Thinking of an old movie. Don't worry, Orv. Julie and I aren't in the same league. You and Julie are. It's okay."

"Don't understand that talk about leagues. You sure about me goin' out with her?"

"Yeah. I'm sure."

"Okay. Guess I'll tell her it's fine, though I still feel like I just bit into a frozen biscuit."

"Honest, Orv. It's okay."

That was it. No whining. I'm going to again be the Man of Action. Edwina is still a possibility, and so is Vanessa. Whipple *will* go to the dance, *have* a good time, and on the small chance that Julie looks my way during the course of the evening, I want her to *know* that Wally Whipple can have a great time without her.

FRIDAY, FEBRUARY 14

Valentine's Day. When red hearts, candy, and Cupid set the tone of the day. I celebrated it in fine style: eating pizza with Orville, Mel, and Lumpy.

We are cruising. Three pizzas down, a little root beer left in the jug, and a pleasant sensation creeping over our corner of the restaurant. We are loose. Life is good.

Except for Lumpy. He's worried about his date next week. Being a rookie in the game of love and knowing that Nancy likes him and he likes her, he is nervous.

"If I do something dumb, then she might not want to go out again with me," moans Lumpy. "Puts more pressure on. I want everything to go great."

We recognize that while Lumpy is perfectly unflappable when it comes to some things (like eating a green hot dog or licking the cheese off a cardboard pizza box), he may need some help in other areas, such as the social graces. We are his brothers and we want him to succeed next week. We want Nancy to walk away a woman in deep, unfettered *like*. We want him to feel good about himself. As I've said before, you remember your first date for all eternity, and it's nice if it's a good memory. We decide to help Lumpy get centered before the big evening comes by offering our gentle guidance.

"Okay Lump, first thing. You go in to the Smisores' house, and Mr. Smisore comes out to greet you. What do you say to him?" I ask.

Lumpy thinks hard. He gulps root beer. He casts his eyes upward to the ceiling of the restaurant. This is work for him. Then a slight smile comes to his face and he relaxes.

"I know!" he says, pleased with himself. "I say, 'Brother Smisore, I find your daughter very attractive.'"

Orv and Mel give me a look that says, "We've got a bigger project here than we thought."

Which may be true, but one thing can be said for Lumpy: He's going out and I am not.

SUNDAY, FEBRUARY 16

The kid is rocked. Now that the long shot of being asked to the Anything Goes by Julie is in the buzzard kitchen (a phrase I picked up from Orville), my next move is to ask out Ed.

Ed. The sure thing. Dependable. There. Steady. And a fun date, too.

"Hiya, Ed. This is Wally," I began last night. "How are ya' doin'?"

"Good, Wally." (Note: In her voice I detected a hint of excitement. In her mind, I was sure she was saying, "Please, Wally. Ask me out. *Please.* I have hungered for your company. Ask me, merely ask me, and I will be yours!")

"Uh, Ed. I was wondering if, you know, you'd like to go to the dance next week with me. A date. That's what it is. A date with you. And me. I'll be there, too."

"Wally," she said, "nobody talks like you do. It's so cute."

Cute. Yes! Take this one to the bank. The social slump is over. Wally will be back on the board, joining millions of other hormone-plagued teenagers next weekend, enjoying an evening of socialization with a female-type person. Sweet.

"But . . ."

Uh-oh. *But* is not the word I wanted to hear at this point. It sounds negative. Shields up, Whipple. You may be getting ready for a female photon torpedo blast.

". . . I'm going to the dance with someone else. Dick Dickson. Do you know him?"

Dick Dickson! My male ego is crushed. Aced out by a worm. Not Dick!

"Oh. Uh, well, er. Dick. Bla, um goodsky you um Dick . . ." My brain turned to smashed bananas. Dick? He of the highwater pants and pocket protector going out with Ed? My Ed?

Salvation comes. Sort of. "Yes. Dick asked me a couple of weeks ago. I don't really know him, and I guess he's not who I would have asked out, but I didn't want to hurt his feelings. So I said yes."

Only someone of Edwina's high character and standards would even consider that Dick has any feelings. Only someone like Edwina would go out with Dick, the mealy-mouthed little twerp. Have to admit, though, he beat me on this one.

"Er, okay. Have a nice time with, with, Dick!"

Next up: Vanessa Peterson. The big gamble. What if she says no?

I am facing the very real prospect of sitting at home alone next weekend.

Again.

MONDAY, FEBRUARY 17

Okay, time to load 'em up and ride 'em out. I'm moving—to Wyoming, I think. I will be a cowboy, far away from civilization. Where a man and his horse and the dogies they watch are all that count. Where a guy can bond with nature and sing soft lonesome songs while picking at his guitar. (Note: I need to buy a guitar.) Far away from society, girls, rejection, girls, high school, dances, girls, and, once more, girls, if I didn't convey that thought before. As one might infer, I asked Vanessa and she said no.

How was I to know that she had been dating the same guy for almost a year?

Man, what a dork I felt like. Hoof in mouth disease strikes again. I think it's something genetic with me.

No hope. The dance is too close now. No one will ask

me and I will ask no one. I will spend the night studying the scriptures and figuring out what I need to repent for. I will begin memorizing the missionary discussions. I will dedicate my life to service.

"Wally, isn't the Anything Goes dance coming soon?" Natalie asked me tonight. "Aren't you going? Hasn't anyone asked you? Seriously? Like that's too bad, Wally. You'd think out of about a thousand girls at school, one of them would have asked you."

Yeah. You would. But no one did.

TUESDAY, FEBRUARY 18

Sitting around tonight, trying to do some homework, but my heart and head aren't into it. This nagging thought keeps buzzing through the gray matter. It goes something like this: "Whipple, can't you get anything right?" My thoughts are on the Anything Goes Dance and how I muffed it. Not once, but twice. First, I thought someone would ask me. Big assumption and, as it turned out, very wrong. Then I messed around so long that everyone has already been asked. And getting cut from the JV team is still a fresh, open wound. I stayed after school and did some homework last week, then walked by the gym on the way to the parking lot. The JV team was there . . . I peeked in, watched the guys warming up. I couldn't handle it. The emotions started churning. I should be out there. *I should be out there!* But I'm not. Instead, I'm lifting weights and playing church hoops, trying not to slip into the dark waters of being a nobody.

High school can do that to you. Make you feel like a nobody. Every day you have to face the fact that you're not going to graduate #1 in your class, not going to get the lead part in the play, not going to be student body president, not going to make a crummy JV basketball team. You want things to be simple, like back when the only decision you made was using more blue or more red in the picture you were coloring. Nobody ever told me that life gets more complicated as you get older.

Not that it would have helped much, anyway.

THURSDAY, FEBRUARY 20

We are gathered at the Whipple Family Forum tonight, otherwise known as the dinner table. The topic at hand is my social life, which, given its severe limitations, you'd think would take about 12 seconds to discuss from beginning to end.

"You're not going to the dance at school this weekend?" Dad asks.

"Uh, no, Dad. I didn't ask anyone—"

"And nobody asked him," Natalie jumps in. "It's one of those dances where girls do most of the asking. And although Wally is like this big huge social animal, and girls like really go psycho over him, no one asked him. They must like worship you from afar, Wally. The farther the better."

"Cute, Nat." I make a face at her.

"Now tell me about this girl Orville is going with," says Mom, who talked with Mr. Burrell earlier in the day about having dinner at our house again soon.

"You mean Julie Sloan?"

"I think that's her name. Julie."

At the other end of the table, I hear a thump. Natalie's head has fallen and whacked her plate. She raises her head an inch and in a sickly voice says, "Julie Sloan is going with Orville? Did she ask him?"

"Yep and yep." It is wonderful to see Natalie humbled.

"Oh no! Seriously disgusting!" Down goes her head again, barely missing the mashed potatoes.

It becomes obvious to me. As long as Orville was going out with someone like Viola Barkle, Natalie was okay. Viola is no threat to Nat. But Julie Sloan represents competition. Real competition. Someone who has obvious advantages, even over Nat. Like a brain in her head and the disinclination to say "Seriously" at the end of most sentences.

"It's okay, Natalie," I comfort. "It's not like they're going to end up their date at the Portland Temple. They probably won't even get serious for at least a month or two."

"Wally! You're so totally insensitive."

"Sorry, Natalie."

"No you're not!"

"You're right. I'm not. I repent."

"Mom, Dad, can I start dating soon? Seriously. I won't do anything bad. Please, you guys? Can I? It's a totally unfair advantage that she can go out with Orv and I can't."

"No way, Natalie. You know the rules," Mom says.

"Case closed, Nat," Dad adds.

She is stunned. She is defeated, at least for now. Yet I know my sister well enough to understand that already the brain cells are greased and ready to go, and it shouldn't be long before she launches a counterattack of some kind. Gosh, this could be really interesting. Nat's finest thinking and most entertaining moments come when she feels second best to anyone in any way.

At times like these, I can honestly say that I love being around my sister.

SATURDAY, FEBRUARY 22

The day of the big dance. All over southeast Portland, cars are being shined, hair is being done, clothes are being selected and laid out, teeth are being brushed, and mouthwash is being gargled in anticipation of the big show. A big show that I won't be a part of.

I went over to Lumpy's this morning to check out how he was doing.

"Not good," Lumpy said glumly. "I'm so nervous I can hardly eat."

True statement: I have never known Lumpy not to eat, other than the Scout trip four years ago at a place called Camp Inverness, which we fondly renamed "Camp Intestinal Virus." And even then, Lumpy was the holdout, still trudging down to the camp mess hall when all the rest of us were flat on our backs and moaning, getting in one last meal before returning the food whence it came, sort of a dust-to-dust concept.

But I digress. Point is, Lumpy was tense. Very tense. I knew that I had to say just the right thing in a sensitive and gentle way to turn around his attitude. I thought hard, then uttered a little prayer to help me in my first test as his Mentor of Love.

"You'll be okay. Trust me," I said soothingly. "I was like you last year. I actually hoped I would get sick so that I could skip the dance. But I went and had a great time. You will, too." He turned his hopeful eyes toward me. I had to think of something profound right then. Fortunately, the Kid came through. "Look at dating like anchovies."

"Anchovies?" he asked, a note of disbelief in his inexperienced voice.

"Yes. At first the thought of dating is like eating anchovies. You're unsure. You wonder if you should eat these small, salty, smelly little fish. But now—"

"I like anchovies!"

Move over, Solomon. "Exactly. Dating grows on you, like eating anchovies, Lumpy."

He sighed, relieved. He looked grateful. I could sense his appetite coming back. I must admit it was a good move for me to draw the analogy of dating and eating anchovies. It was something Lumpy could understand and relate to.

"Each time you have a moment of doubt, look at Nancy and think of an anchovy. Pull you right out of it, guaranteed."

"Thanks, Wally. Good advice, Wally. I'll try to remember it."

"Then have a good time tonight. Remember who you are, and who you aren't. Nothing good ever happens after midnight. Don't do anything you wouldn't do with a bishop there, although since it is Nancy you are dating, you probably are going to feel like a bishop before the night is over. And Lumpy, return with honor."

"You're sounding like my dad, Wally."

"Well, sorry. But it's like you're my proxy tonight at the dance. I'll be experiencing it through you. Wherever you are, I will be there . . . sort of."

I felt wise and wonderful after leaving Lumpy's. I came home and Natalie was sitting in a chair at the front window, staring at the big tree in our front yard. She's been sulky and pouty most of the week, no doubt because she fears Julie is stealing her man.

"Oh, it's you," she said in a wonderfully warm and heartfelt manner.

"Yeah. It's me, Nat. Still worried about Orv?"

"No. I am not worried about Orv. Not at all. Seriously. Only a little bit. But those guys can go to the dance tonight and have a great time, I don't care."

"Nat, think of it this way. You've still got a chance with Orville. He asks about you a lot. And so what if you're fifteen and he's seventeen? Remember, he's probably going to head out on a mission, and that sort of like retards your social life for two years. All the good ones are gone when you get back. Guys almost always marry someone younger. Brother Hansen always tells us to be nice to the Mia Maids because they're the ones we're going to marry. See what I mean? You're in the perfect position. You have time on your side."

She stood up and paced to the end of the room and came back, her chin cradled in her hand, her brows furrowed, her brown hair hanging straight down. "Are you serious?"

"Yeah. I'm serious."

The light dawned. "Cool, Wally. I never thought about missions letting Mia Maids catch up. I think you are really smart when it comes to, like, human being relationships."

"You shouldn't just wait around and see if it happens, though Nat. You should encourage Orville to serve a mission, if you see what I'm saying."

"Oh, yeah," she said, suddenly getting into the spirit of missionary work. "I should, like, tell him how totally cool missionaries are and stuff. You know, like they say, every guy should serve a mission and have their social life put on ice for two years."

"Sort of. You get what I mean, though."

"Maybe I'll make Orville and his dad some cookies and tell them when a guy goes on his mission, they get lots of cookies, unless they get sent somewhere kind of gross."

"Sure. Maybe it will help. He might think you're spiritual."

"I feel like I'm way spiritual now, Wally. I feel better, though."

"That's what I'm here for. Free advice during all my waking hours."

With that, she headed toward the kitchen. "Mom, we

need to make cookies. Do you, like, use flour and choco-late chips?"

The rest of the afternoon dawdled by. We had a week off from basketball, so I mostly made like a bear in hiber-nation and tried not to worry about the dance. Lumpy was going with Nancy. That was good. Orville was going with Julie, and that was, well, that was . . . that was good, too. Two nice people. With a lot in common. Kind of. I'm sure they'll have a great time and become better friends during the course of the evening. Friends. Yeah, that's it. Julie and Orv will be just friends. No need to worry, Wally. Chill out a little. Relax. Try not to think about it.

So, on this evening of romance and amour, excitement and high expectations, I trudged up to my room and did homework. Yes, homework.

Six o'clock came around, and I tried not to think that right now Orville, Lumpy, and even Dick Dickson were getting ready for their dates.

Seven o'clock rolled by, and I tried to avoid any thoughts about how the dinner tables now had the final touches on them and a great meal awaited so many of my friends.

Seven-thirty arrived, and I tried to push out of my mind the fact that Orville and Lumpy were now getting the final once-over in front of the mirror and in a matter of minutes would be leaving to meet Julie and Nancy.

Eight o'clock, and doorbells within the school bound-aries everywhere were ringing sweet chimes, while I strug-gled to memorize Spanish phrases such as, "The cheese looks moldy."

Eight-twenty, and my own doorbell rang, right after I had gone to the kitchen to graze a little. I walked to the door figuring it must be one of Natalie's friends. I opened the door with the well-practiced self-righteous look of an older brother who is slightly annoyed by his younger sis-ter's friends.

"Yo. Brother Wimp Pole!" Evan Trant greeted.

"Uh, hi, Evan. What are you doing here? Scouting out a new neighborhood to vandalize?"

"Huh-uh. Just cruising on the hog tonight and thought I'd make, you know, a social call to my skinny pal Wimp Pole. Mind if I come in?"

"No. Not at all," I said, wondering if that was the right decision.

Dad came around the corner and, cool as he is, almost dropped the book he was reading at the sight of Evan, elegantly dressed in his black motorcycle boots, black leather pants, black leather hat, and a black leather jacket with silver spikes, nobs, and doo-dads. "Friend of yours, Wally?"

"Yeah. This is Evan Trant. He plays basketball on our church team. We got to know each other when I was in metal shop."

"Hey. You must be Brother Wimp Pole, senior."

"Hey. You're right."

Next up was Natalie. She was wandering aimlessly through the house, having finished the cookies a couple of hours ago. She looked up at Evan and said, "Hmmmph. Who are you?"

Evan smiled. "Wimp Pole, you never said you had a babe for a sister."

Natalie gave him a pure, 100 percent plastic smile. "At least he's got good taste."

"That I do, Little Sister Wimp Pole."

"My name is Natalie."

"However you want to cook it, Little Sister Natalie Wimp Pole."

Mom heard the chatter and entered the room. "Hello, Evan. Wally's told us a lot about you," she said placidly. "Would you like something to eat?"

"Chow? You bet, Sister Wimp Pole."

"The kitchen is right over here. We can whip up something for you right away." Mom intuitively guessed that with Evan, you need to appeal to the baser instincts, such as food, water and shelter. He wandered off with her. "So, is that your Harley out front, Evan?"

"I am totally blown away, Sister Wimp Pole. You know hogs. We could go riding together some time. You'd rule on a hog."

Dad pulled me aside. "Who is that guy?" he asked. "And is he asking out your mother?"

"It's okay, Dad. That's just the way Evan is. He actually likes me. And I'm sure he left his knife, chains, and fellow gang members outside."

Well, that's the way I spent the bulk of my evening— explaining Evan to my family. While Lumpy looked fondly at Nancy and thought of anchovies, while Orville talked cowboy and swayed across the dance floor with Julie, and while Dick Dickson nerded out on poor Edwina, I ended up entertaining Evan Trant in the cozy comfort of my own home. He played on the rug with Chuck ("Little Brother Wimp Pole," of course), going head to head with the rest of us in a game of Scrabble ("Is *gonzo* a word?"), and just generally making himself a Whipple for a night. He finally left about 11:00 for destinations and activities unknown.

"Gotta go now. You know, appointments to keep," he said, pulling on his leather jacket and captain's hat. "Nice food. Nice house. And I might want to take out Natalie sometime," he announced as he left. "She's got sass. I like that in a woman."

Dad, as anyone would expect, almost choked at the thought of Natalie taking off on the back of Evan's motor-cycle. Mom just smiled and looked serene. "She's too young to date yet, Evan. But with Natalie, you might be biting off more than even you can chew."

Evan looked puzzled for a second. "Oh. Like that's a joke or something?"

"No. No joke," I said, while Natalie wickedly lurked in the living room.

"Whatever," Evan said amiably. With that, he disappeared into the blackness, the roar of his Harley fading. We all just stood there and watched for what must have been a full minute before anyone said anything. Finally, Dad spoke.

"Who is that guy?" he asked.

TUESDAY, FEBRUARY 25

Monday came and went in a blur. I was eager to talk with Lumpy and Orville about what happened on Saturday but didn't get the chance. It was at lunch before the Posse settled in at the cafeteria and chowed down. I was patient and diplomatic, waiting until Lumpy at least sat down before asking him about his date.

"Super. That's the only way to describe it," Lumpy said happily. "Nancy laid out a dinner that was like what you see on Thanksgiving. And dessert—oh my! Some sort of chocolate cake with pudding inside of it, with this raspberry sauce spread all over it. I wanted to propose right there. Then we went to a restaurant for a snack after the dance."

"But did you and Nancy have fun, I mean other than the food?"

"Oh yeah. She *is* nice. And she didn't pray or anything before we left, which I was worried about a little. We talked a lot and I danced a little, too. And every time I didn't know what to say or I started to get nervous about something, I just imagined Nancy as sort of this big pizza with anchovies. It really worked, Wally."

"Anchovies?" Mickey asked. "Your date reminded you of anchovies?"

"Not exactly. It was Wally's idea. He'll have to explain it to you."

"Another time," I said.

Orville was just pulling up his chair with his tray of food. I wanted to ask him about Saturday, but something told me to let the conversation go his way. It didn't take long. Lumpy, bless his round little head and round little waistline, asked him right away. "How did your Saturday night go, Orv?"

Orv took a bite out of his cheeseburger. "Pretty fair," he said after chewing. "Julie and me sort of doubled with her friend Amy and the guy she went with. They looked real nice and they cooked up some good grub, and we ended up back at Amy's watching a video for a bit. 'Bout all there was to it. Wasn't a big whup."

Pretty fair? Not a big whup? Orville had a date with Julie and he didn't think it was any big deal? Music to my ears! There is still hope! Orville is not in *like* with Julie! I can tell just by the way he's talking. He's more involved with his cheeseburger than he is with Julie. I looked at him closely. No clues in his face. Wait, he speaks again. Maybe this will tell me something.

"Actually, I think maybe I had me more yippin' and stompin' when I went out with Viola last year. We ended up singin' some cowboy songs back at the apartment. I don't know. Julie's nice and all that, but I think I got too much leather in me and she's got too many frills to ever get beyond jus' bein' friends. I like a girl with a might more grain to her."

Proof! Maybe I *do* have a chance with Julie. And now, I have to do something about it. The door is open. Julie is a free woman and I'm a free man. Time to plan. Time to make my move. Time to go for it!

I came home after lifting tonight and, once the homework was done, grabbed my CD player and put on some Torme.

Do I read too much into the simple things of life, or is there a Message from Mel here?

The song he sang was, "You Gotta Try."

I will! I will!

CHAPTER 7

March

SATURDAY, MARCH 1

Today I made a huge mistake in front of my parents. I whined.

Someday I am going to make buckets of money as a motivational speaker for teenagers. I will tell them how to get exactly what they want by engaging their parents in meaningful, purposeful conversation, speaking to them in cyberparent talk.

ME: "Mother, Father. How good it is to visit with you this evening! As you will note, I have printed out an agenda for our gathering tonight. The first item of business is to discuss my allowance. As you know, inflation has been creeping again, and the index of leading economic indicators does not look promising. Then, the bond market is soft, with no hope for a turnaround in the near future. T-bills are floating. Couple those less-than-hopeful economic harbingers with the fact that Hamburger Bob's has raised its prices by 8.9 percent in the last year, and you can see that my request for a larger allowance is not based on personal greed but rather is an offshoot of a volatile economic situation over which I have no control."

DAD: "Yes, son. I see your crystal-clear logic and realize that you only want your fair share and nothing else."

MOM: "I think an increase of approximately 13.6 percent per annum is totally justified. I'm sure your father will have no cause to debate that."

ME: "Thank you, Mother. Precisely the figure I had in mind."

What I whined about today was not my allowance but my social life. Mom and Dad were just getting back from the Burrells' store, packing in a bunch of garden seeds and a few plant starts. It was about 5:00 P.M., and the hormone flow must have been at high tide. I started to pace a little, then tried watching TV, then went out on the driveway and shot some hoops with Chuck. Nothing was working. I felt distracted, restless, uneasy. I couldn't concentrate. I couldn't think clearly. I knew what the problem was.

I needed a date.

Finally, I ended up in front of the mirror in the bathroom, staring at the guy in front of me. So maybe I'm not the best-looking guy in the world. I have . . . have . . . inner beauty. Yeah, that's it. Inner beauty. Except maybe in my case it should be called inner ruggedly handsomeness.

"Primping in the mirror, Wally?" It was Natalie, who has a radarlike ability to zero in on her older brother at the most embarrassing moments.

"No. I prefer to think of it as taking inventory of my physical being," I said. "Now, why don't you go play with some dolls or rock out to one of Mom's old Barry Manilow tapes?"

So much for my inner beauty.

"You ever going to date again? I mean, seriously, Wally, you haven't gone out in a long time and I know you're breaking hearts, like, all the time. I can almost hear them going kaboom at church every Sunday. Seriously."

I was about to launch yet another counterattack when Dad strolled by. "Are you two bickering again?"

"No. Natalie was only reminding me that it's been awhile since I've gone out, Dad."

Mom came up the stairs and starting listening. Man, a guy just wants to look at himself in the mirror for a few minutes in peace, and suddenly, the ward activities committee is at the door. Give me some space!

"It *has* been a long time since you've been out. Nat's right about that," Dad said.

Knowing I was outnumbered, I decided to go for some sympathy. Looking back, it was a huge tactical error. "You guys, I've tried really hard. (Sort of a lie.) I can't help it if (sigh, look of self-pity) I just don't have any luck with girls." (Slight groan, big whoosh of air.) There. I await my family's mercy.

"Wally. Don't feel sorry for yourself," Dad says, frowning. "You haven't tried very hard at all to go out with girls. You've got to work, son, work at everything. Work," Dad says, raising himself up a bit, getting ready to say something that he thinks is deep and profound, "will never be replaced by whining." He beams at Mom and Natalie, who nod approvingly. "I like that."

Oops. This is going to turn into a full-blown lecture, or FBL as I am wont to call them. Mom weighs in next.

"Your father is exactly right. Work. You need to work. You even need to work to have fun, and that means putting some effort into your relationships, Wally."

"Totally, Wally. You need to work," Natalie hisses.

"But look. I go to seminary and I go to school, then I lift heavy metal objects to build my muscles, then I do homework, then I do church stuff, then I finally go to bed after studying the scriptures (Note: does a verse a night count as studying?), then I get up and *start the whole thing over again the next day!*"

"You need more rest, Wally," says Mom, my emotional plea apparently zipping right over her head. Dad nods. "She's right. More rest, Wally."

"But how can I work harder and get more rest at the same time?" Ha! Got them! Irrefutable logic wins a round for Wally.

Dad gives us the "I'm-going-to-say-something-very-wise look" again. "Well, Wally . . ." Speak my Father! I await knowledge, light, truth, and direction regarding the American way of life! ". . . you can do both, Wally."

What? I can do both?

"Yes, Wally. You can do both."

Oh my. Dad is losing it. And so young, the best years still ahead of him.

I plot my next move. "I don't get it."

"Your father is right," Mom says. "You can do both. That's all there is to get."

"For sure, Wally. Like, our parents are right," Natalie snipes.

I think this is something parents are taught very early in marriage. Right along with the classes about having kids and giving birth with dignity and making funny little triangles so that the mom will breathe correctly and concentrate on something other than the fact that she feels pain roughly equivalent to that of someone pulling her ear lobes down to her toes and tying them in knots, taught by some old guy who never had any children who is telling them, "Whenever your kids whine or give you a hard time, the universal answers are these —"

At this point all the eager young parents lean forward on their chairs, awaiting pearls of wisdom from the guy who knows kids about as much as I know angioplasty. "You tell them that the answers to all of their problems are to work harder and get more rest."

The parents all smile at each other. They are happy. They are in on the secret. They are armed with the most irrefutable argument known to humankind: work harder and get more rest. Your whole life will instantly become better.

How can I argue with that? Countless generations before me have tried and failed.

My ship is taking on water and listing badly. I run up the white flag.

"Okay. You guys are right. I will work harder and get more rest. I can do that."

Mom and Dad look a little surprised at their quick and easy win. "That's the attitude, son," Dad says. "We know you can do anything you put your mind to," he adds, throwing in another parental cliche classic. Soon, Mom and Dad mosey on down the hall. The fun now over, her brother defeated, Natalie quickly disappears. And I am left to lick my wounds, having been lacerated by my parents and sister, all over a little ill-timed whining.

Back to the mirror. There's that face again. What was I saying about inner ruggedly handsomeness?

At this precise moment I notice a gargantuan new zit coming in, one worthy of a mountain name, forming on my chin. Wally Whipple, can you ever win?

TUESDAY, MARCH 4

A little lifting, a little work at the high jump, and then I decided to swing by the old junior high. It was the last basketball game of the season, and I hadn't seen Nat do any cheerleading. I thought it would be, well, nice, to go down and see how things were going at the old gym. It was just before halftime when I arrived and was surprised to see Nat and her gang slumped against the far wall of the gym, yelling and jumping around and doing all those other weird cheerleader things with all the enthusiasm of a bowl of wet, cold spaghetti. I mean, no rah-rahs, no splits, no swish and flash of pom-poms. It was a sorry sight to see.

When halftime came, I strolled up to Natalie and tapped her on the shoulder when no one else was looking. She doesn't like to be seen much in public with her older brother.

"Nat, what's wrong? You guys don't have anything going. You act like you're dead."

"Oh. I guess it's you," Natalie said with her customary warmth, her eyes darting around to see who might be watching us. "Well, if you were more sensitive, you'd know what is going on."

"Give me a break, Nat."

She scrunched up her nose and put her hands on her hips. She blew on the bangs hanging down on her forehead. "Wally. It's like this is really sad. Seriously."

"Sad?"

"Yeah. Totally."

"Did someone get hurt?"

"No."

"Then what's the problem?"

She sighed. "Okay, Wally, but I guess it's like I have to spell everything out for you all the time. I wish you were more sensitive, but not many guys are, except for Orville."

"I know. It's tough to live in Orv's shadow."

"Well, it's the last game of the season. That's what is so sad. Like, after today, we'll never see each other again. This is really emotional."

"Wait. What do you mean you'll never see each other again? Don't you go to school with these guys?"

"Yeah."

"So it's not like they're headed for Mongolia. And next year, you can be a cheerleader in high school, which is even cooler, plus you'll get to meet guys from different schools, Nat. Think of this as not the end of the book," I said, with what felt like an incredible amount of wisdom. "Think of it as one chapter closing and the next opening."

"Huh?"

"Does that make sense, Nat? Do you even know the names of the players on your team? Do you even know how many games your team has won?"

"Yes, I do. There's a guy named Jim and another one named Spencer. And the coach is Mr. Flannery. He's a science teacher and sort of a hunk. The other guys on the team all have names, too. And we've won four games this year. I think. Well, I'm pretty sure. So do you think I'll meet a lot of new guys next year?"

"Yeah. You will."

"Okay. I won't be depressed. But I might cry a little at the end of the game."

"That's fine, Nat. Have yourself a good cry, then pull yourself together and remember that the sun will come out tomorrow."

"Well, duh, Wally."

Some of her pals were walking our way, which meant that my audience with Her Highness was over. So I ambled back up into the stands and watched the rest of the game. With about four minutes to go, Natalie, accompanied by the other cheerleaders, all began to cry. The guys on the team just looked at them, probably wondering what was going on.

I don't know how to say this without risking another huge, "Well, duh, Wally," but I'll write it for posterity's sake anyway: Girls and guys are different, way different.

THURSDAY, MARCH 6

After our junior class government meeting today, Alex pulled me aside. Alex looked just as he always did, every hair moussed into place, not a cloth pill anywhere to be found on his perfectly pressed clothing, his complexion wonderfully clear.

In some ways, I can't stand Alex.

"Wally. Great job on the pledge today. I always feel so patriotic when I hear you lead us. I want to do great things for my country, become a part of it, involved."

"You could join the Marines," I offered.

"Marines? Well, yes. Hey, a joke. I get it. Great sense of humor, Wally."

"Thanks. Humor comes naturally to me."

"Good. What I wanted to talk about with you is this," he said, motioning me to come closer. "It's no secret that I have my eye on student body president next year. I'm putting together what you might call an exploratory committee, consisting of representatives of every segment of the school. I figure that my committee should be structured so that every person, no matter their social standing, grades, or whatever, feels that he or she has someone working on my behalf, to make them feel as though they are represented. Get it?"

"Yeah, I think so." I sort of regretted making the comment about joining the Marines. Maybe Alex wanted me to help deliver the jock vote or be his liaison with the Honor Society.

"So you're with me?"

"Count me in."

"Great, Whipple. I knew you'd come through," he said, lightly punching me on the shoulder. Now for the pitch. I could help with the athletes. Cross-country and track, for sure. And I knew most of the basketball players. This might be kind of fun.

"Wally, although you are not, and I repeat *are not*, like this particular part of the student body, they represent a sizable portion of the voters. And I have reason to believe they do vote, so I think the work you'll be doing is critical. You relate well with this group. You speak their language, although you are not—and I mean this—you are not like them much. Hardly at all, in fact, although I guess all of us do have certain traits. I remember once, a few years ago, when I was much younger, that I actually wore a striped shirt and checked pants to school. Can you believe it? Me! It must have been very dark that morning when I dressed, but you get the drift of the kind of people that I need you to communicate with for the benefit of the Coles election team. Are we on the same wavelength here, Wally?"

Yes, we were. Alex wanted me to deliver the Nerd Vote.

"I'll be getting in touch with you again. In the meantime, thanks for your support."

"It's okay, Alex."

Tonight, I was thinking about it: Wally Whipple, head nerdmeister. That's what Alex thinks of me. That's why he's been so nice to me all year long. Is it okay to be nice to someone, hoping they'll do something for you? I don't think so. It's called "using someone."

Should I be offended? Maybe. But I've got to remember that maybe Alex's perception of me is accurate. Then who can blame him for treating me that way? I'm confused.

Voices. Too many voices.

SATURDAY, MARCH 8

At the end of lunch, if you're really cool, you hang out at the bottom of the main stairway near the principal's office. It is the best place to see and be seen. Usually the ultra-insiders, seniors, student body officers, cheerleaders, and the most popular student drug dealers hang out there. The stairway about 20 feet away is where all the wannabes hang out. That's where the Posse ended up on Friday, just out of range of all the truly beautiful people of Benjamin Franklin High School.

I was comfortably slouched over one of the bannisters, trying to look cool, when Evan Trant came by. "Hey, Wimp Pole."

"Hi, Evan."

"You tryin' to be cool or what?"

"I guess it's 'or what,' Evan."

"How's the cowboy doin'?" Evan nodded toward Orville. I can tell he likes Orville, one reason being that he actually calls Orv by his real name most of the time.

"Doin' purtinear fine," Orv said amiably.

"You talk funny, cowboy."

"Yep. And durned proud of it, too. This here school needs a dab more of cowpunchin' talk. Too many folks around here got their cantle string comin' unwound."

Evan snorted. "So what are we talkin' about?"

"Not much," Mel said. "Wally's love life. Like I said, not much."

"You go out with girls?" Evan asked.

I stiffened my back. "Yeah. A lot."

"You lie, Wimp Pole."

"Hey, I am wounded and deeply offended—"

"You lie, Wimp Pole."

"He's right, Wally. You lie," Mickey joined in.

"You need a date? I can fix you up good," Evan offered. "I know some good women."

The thought of Evan as my social director was about as appealing as pouring warm brake fluid on my corn flakes in the morning. I wanted to head off this conversation—fast!

"Uh, no thanks, Evan," I said. "Ah, you know, I do pretty good on my own."

"Sure you do, Muscle Man. The girls just go nuts over you I bet. I'm gonna get you a date. Right now."

"It's okay, Evan. It's really okay."

"You know anyone around here? How about that one? She's good looking." Evan pointed to a skinny girl who was heavy into purple hair and black eyeliner. She had on a short leather skirt and looked like she hadn't slept in about four days and was living on a diet of highly caffeinated drinks.

"No, really. Honest, it's okay, Evan."

"You don't like her? She's cute. I know her. We call her Squeegee. You don't see anyone around here you want to go out with?"

The Posse—my friends, my comrades, the people I have shared many wonderful experiences with, such as misfiring a spit wad in sacrament meeting and beaning the bishop, the guys I could count on for anything, except for help at a moment like this—were all abandoning me squarely in Evan's corner. "Look. There's Edwina, Wally," Lumpy said.

"You want to go out with her?"

"No, well, yeah. But this isn't the way I operate. This isn't my style. Honest. I'm more of the sensitive and quiet type. I grow on girls."

"Yep. Just like mold on a good pony blanket," Orville piped up, with what I thought was incredibly bad timing.

"We need to help old Wimp Pole out here," Evan said with great conviction.

"Yeah, we do," Lumpy agreed, while everyone else nodded enthusiastically.

"Let's do it then, men," Evan said, and before I could get away, arms were all over me and I was being lifted up in the air.

"Guys, guys. I mean, well, guys. Hey, let me down. This is funny, right? But it's just a joke. Right? Ha ha. You got ol' Wally this time. Uh, guys, can you hear me? Would you mind putting me down?"

They ignored me. They carried me over to Ed, the innocent passerby. The ultra cool crowd was also looking on now. Ed noticed the general commotion and turned my way. For a split second, she looked surprised, but to her credit she smiled as the guys set me down on the floor in front of her.

"Wimp Pole here has something to ask you," said the ever-so-subtle and charming Trant. "He loves you. Don't you, Wimp Pole?"

At this point, I turned a deep shade of red and said something that will ever stand witness to my keen, steel-trap mind. "Ohwwwwggrrrhhh."

Ed looked around at the crew. "Wally, you have the most interesting friends!"

"I like her, Wimp Pole. She thinks I'm interesting. And she ain't even seen my tattoos. Should I show her my tattoos? I can take off my shirt."

"No, Evan. Not now," I said, still flustered.

"Go ahead and ask her," Evan urged. I hesitated, trying to find the right words. "Wimp Pole, you are messed up. I'll tell her." Evan gave me a look of disgust. "Okay. What Wimp Pole wants to tell you is that he wants to marry you and have you be the mother of his children." I fell back on the floor and put my hands over my face.

"Better say something, Wally," Lumpy whispered.

The only way out was to ask Ed for a date. By now, a crowd of about 30 kids were around. I spread my fingers so I could see Ed and croaked, "Can we go out?"

"Sure, Wally. I'd like that. And I've never been asked out by a committee. I like it," said Edwina, the gracious and poised one.

"I'll call you later," I promised, again sitting up on the floor.

"Great. Let's go out soon."

Mercifully, very mercifully, the bell rang. The crowd dispersed, except for Evan and Orville. "Way to go, Wimp Pole. You're a man," Evan congratulated.

"Yeah, guess so."

"Wally, you look like you been rode hard and put away wet," Orville said. "Better get your legs under you and try to walk."

"Yeah. Sure," I mumbled.

Evan slugged me in the back, delighted at playing Cupid. "Didn't think we'd do that, did you, Wimp Pole? Fooled you," he said, slugging me this time on the shoulder as I wandered off. Then he turned around. "You need me, Wimp Pole. I'm gettin' you buff. I beat up any of the brothers who get in your face on the basketball court. And now you're gonna marry that girl. You need me," he repeated.

As he wandered off and I staggered ahead, I decided that in his own little way, Evan was right: I need him.

MONDAY, MARCH 9

Yesterday at church, Brother Hansen mentioned that we needed a priest to give a talk in a few weeks. He looked around at us and we all went into our no-eyes-making-contact mode. "C'mon, men. Someone step up," he pleaded.

"Shucks, I can do that. Talkin' ain't hard," said Orville. "When did you say?"

"Two weeks from today. Thanks, Orville," he said, giving the rest of us a look that said, "You guys are not exactly foot soldiers in the army of Helaman."

A couple of other notes: we start our regional basketball tournament on Friday, but Orv will be tied up in the state wrestling match. With Orv, we've got a good chance to take the whole pie. Without him, we're just another good team. We'll see what happens.

Natalie got a note from the school today, requesting that Mom or Dad or both of them come and see her counselor tomorrow. This could be fun. What kind of trouble is Nat in this time? Has she been feeling "ill" again? Mom agreed to go, since Dad can't get away from work. Nat seems cool about the whole thing. "Honest, Mom. I don't think I'm in trouble at all. Like I've not messed up anywhere," she said tonight. "Totally. I think I'm okay on this. Maybe like Mr. Kenniston has me confused with someone else."

We'll see. In the meantime, Nat was pretty quiet around the house tonight and I noticed she really hit the books hard, which by her standards, means at least 20 minutes. Stay tuned, film at eleven of Mom vs. the School Counselor.

TUESDAY, MARCH 10

I am stunned. And humbled. Maybe I need to repent.

The school conference today wasn't at all what I thought it was. I was totally blown away. So was Mom. And Dad's surprise could probably be felt on the other side of the ocean.

This is the news. Natalie, my sister, air head supreme, whose idea of an intellectual experience is listening to a Billy Joel CD; she of the somewhere between a C and B grade point, the young woman who once watched a rerun of "Leave It to Beaver," then looked up and said, "I didn't get it"; the young person who I once overheard ask a friend, "How does chewing gum know when to get sticky," is, I hate to admit, a genius.

A math genius.

That's what the conference was about. To tell Mr. and Mrs. Whipple that Natalie scored in the 99.7th percentile on a standard math test given six weeks ago.

True, I knew that Nat was good with numbers. I'd seen her throw three purchases down on the counter, calculate the prices of each, minus the discount, and tell the clerk the exact figure even before it was added up, but this is still a surprise. I always figured it was just a surge of adrenalin at the counter, allowing Nat to do something extraordinary, sort of like when you hear about someone who weighs 97 pounds and carries an injured friend twice his size off a mountain after an accident, or someone who is found alive under the rubble of a collapsed building ten days after the earthquake.

Natalie, a math genius?

"Like, neener, neener, Wally. You always thought I was dumb. Well, I'm not dumb. I'm smart. In fact, I'm smarter than you, Mr. Smarty Pants," Natalie brilliantly stated tonight after Mom and Dad broke the news to her. "I am not so D-U-M after all, Wally. Is that how you spell *dumb* anyway?"

Good news for Wallace F. Whipple, Jr.: maybe Nat can help me with my math homework. Maybe Nat can *do* my math homework.

"And if you think I'm gonna help you with your math, I have just two words to say: No way," Natalie taunted, as if reading my mind. "Were those two or three words?"

"Nat, I don't need your help. I don't want your help."

"You're lying, Wally. I can always tell because you bite your lower lip after you're done. You're a crummy liar, Wally."

Anyway, she is going into some kind of citywide accelerated math program right away. The counselor said she could be taking college math courses in a year.

Who would've figured? Natalie, a math wizard.

It just doesn't add up.

Friday, March 13

How fitting and proper—the day of no luck and we play our first game in the regional basketball tournament. And we lose by three points.

Season's over.

Orv was in Eugene at the state wrestling tournament. With him, we would have won. No doubt we would be playing again tomorrow. Lumpy wasn't there either. The flu.

It was a good game. Back and forth, back and forth. Evan was a rebounding monster, but the other team, from Beaverton, had a guy who was 6'7" and tough. He scored almost every time he got his hands on the ball. They had quick little guards who handled the ball well and got it inside to him. Brother Owens even had me guard their big guy for a while, but I couldn't slow him down either. Evan was overmatched, not to mention six inches shorter. If Orv had played, we could have double-teamed their animal and pulled it out.

I ended up with 22 points, but missed some easy shots early on. When you lose by a few, those easy shots that you missed flash into your mind all night long. When the buzzer sounded and I looked at the scoreboard, it was almost as if it were a bad dream. But there were the numbers: Guest 62, Home 59.

"Nice season, great job, guys," Brother Owens said as we filed off the court. "We did better than anyone thought we would. You all played with a lot of heart this year."

Evan caught up with me in the parking lot. "Adios city, Wimp Pole. It was fun to play hoops with you. All the brothers were nice dudes. Too nice, but I figure maybe I loosened everyone up some."

"Yeah, you did."

"See you in the weight room, Wimp Pole."

He turned and walked toward his Harley.

"Hey, Evan!" He climbed on his bike and looked back at me. "Evan. Thanks. It was cool of you to come out and play with a bunch of church guys."

He started up his Harley, revved, and came gliding over to me.

"Yeah. It was cool of me," he said, then screamed out of the church parking lot as a couple of the old high priest types shook their heads and commented about the younger generation.

MONDAY, MARCH 16

Caught up with Orville yesterday at church, and he said he finished fifth in the state tournament. "Not bad, but I can't imagine you losing to anyone."

He grinned slowly. "Well, I can now. They had some big ol' boy from Medford, and he was a tough critter. Got some pretty fancy moves. Didn't pin me, but he roughed me up a bit. Keeps me humble, Wallace. I guess he showed me what Coach Waymon's been tellin' me all along. Get a little technique and I may turn out to be a durned fair wrassler yet. Next season, I'm gonna try harder and we'll see which way the bull spins."

"Should be fun to watch you."

"You gone out with Edwina yet?" Orv asked, deftly changing subjects.

"Uh, not exactly. But I will. My honor is on the line."

"Think it's her honor, Wally."

"Yeah. You're right."

"Would you like to saddle up and accompany me and a lady of my choosin'?"

"You mean double?"

"Yup."

Instant moral dilemma. Point: Yes, I'd like to double. Orv is a hoot to be around. He talks funny, but girls think it's cute. Plus, he is a hunk and it never hurts the old image to be seen socially in the company of someone whom the opposite sex finds attractive. It's like you hope the magic rubs off on you. Counterpoint: Don't want to double with

Orv because he might be asking out Julie. She took him to Anything Goes, and there is this sort of unwritten code of teenagerhood that says, "Never go out just once with a person, because it is a total rejection if you never go out with them again, and if anything bad in life happens later on, like they go berserk or fall into a life of crime, it is probably a delayed reaction to having gone out with you only once and their whole nasty miserable life is your fault." Well, that's sort of the gist of the code. And it's even more of a face job if the girl asks the guy, and then he never takes her out again. Orv, being your all-around gentleman, knows the code and understands he needs to take Julie out. But I don't want to be in the same car as Julie, Orville, and Edwina, even though I love them all, but each in slightly different ways.

"Wally, don't go and get all puckered up about it," said Orville. "I'm thinkin' of askin' Viola Barkle," he added, exactly guessing my thoughts.

"Viola? You're thinking of asking Viola? Cool, Orv! I like Viola! I mean, not *like* her, but just like her! I respect strong women, and Viola is sure strong. She could take me if I ever got in a fight with her! Not that I would, because I like her, although I don't *like* her, even though I think I said that!"

I was thrilled that Orv was going to ask Viola, the state shot put champion last year, a woman with bulging biceps and broad shoulders, who is nice but not my type. Orv, on the other hand, might actually give her something of a challenge if they decided to arm wrestle.

"Uh, aren't you going to, you know, ask Julie out again sometime?"

Orv smiled slyly. "Already did. As you city folks would say, been there, done that."

My eyes widened and my jaw went limp. In fact, my whole body pretty much went limp. I was shocked. "You mean you took her out? Again? I mean, this soon?"

"Yup. I figured that since she took me out, I needed to do likewise."

I wanted to ask a big question. Not to put too fine a point on it, but I believed it might have a direct influence on the rest of my life, start me on the path to either eternal bliss and celestial marriage or a life in a faraway foreign nation, serving fourteen consecutive missions and entering the twilight years on my own, alone. "Uh, well, Orv . . . I mean, you know. Orv, you know." Not exactly a textbook example of communication, but Orv figured out what I was trying to ask.

"Nope, Wally. I like Julie, but I don't believe I *like* Julie." He made a face. "Now I'm startin' to sound like you city fellas. I talked jes' fine 'til I come to Portland."

Joy! Another rival for Julie is cast by the wayside, even if it was Orville and I would have wished him and Julie a long and happy life together. "I'll call you tomorrow and we'll figure out what we'll do and when. This is going to be a super date, Orv."

He put a hand on my shoulder. "No doubt, pardner. No doubt."

WEDNESDAY, MARCH 18

Natalie came home from school today sporting eyeglasses. This took me by surprise, since I didn't know she needed glasses. Apparently, it took everyone else in our family by surprise, too. "Natalie, are those your glasses?" Dad asked.

"Well, yeah. You know, since I'm, like, this super brain in math now, I, like, wanted to sort of look intelligent, and I was talking to Lindy and she goes, 'Since you're so smart, you need to wear glasses because that's what everyone who is smart does. Like, Einstein wore glasses, and so does Oprah Winfrey, although hers are contacts.'

"So I go, 'Okay.' Then we stopped by Aisles of Value and got these reading glasses. Do you think they're cute?"

"They don't look smart. They look kind of dumb on you, Natalie," said Chuck, the wise and truthful one, although he occasionally lacks diplomacy.

"Hmmphf. I think they make me look smart so I'm going to keep wearing them whenever I want to. Seriously. You're only in first grade, Chuck," Natalie huffed.

So I guess Natalie has a new look, until she figures out how dumb they really do make her appear.

Friday, March 20

Yes! Spring break all next week, and nothing much is planned. I love spring break. In Portland, it usually rains the whole time, so about all that is left to do is eat, sleep, eat, and sleep. Next Wednesday is Chuck's birthday, so I'll slightly alter my pattern, more along the lines of sleep, eat, eat, sleep, but other than that, cruise city. Mr. Leonard is dropping some very big hints about coming in for an hour or two each afternoon to work on high jumping, and since my goal is to be city champ this year, I guess the sacrifice will be worth it.

Orville, the Lumpster, and I hung out together tonight. Haven't quite seen as much of Lumpy lately because he's been at the Smisores' house a lot.

"But Nancy is really understanding; she says it's okay for me to be out with the boys every once in a while," Lumpy says, sounding very domesticated. "Although next week, you guys are on your own. Nancy and I will be attending the Know Your Religion series. You guys should think about going with us."

Orv and I hatched a few plans for our date. After discarding the auto show, the horse exposition, and a sports card fair, we decided to pick up Viola and Ed, go to a grocery store, get the fixings for a picnic, head for a park, and have a meal. Rain or shine, it doesn't matter. If we have to sit in a park under a tarp, we'll do it. We both decided to adopt a basic "who cares?" attitude about our date, just sort of go for it and let the chips fall where they may. The key to spontaneity, I believe, is proper planning.

By the way, for Chuck's birthday present: a Portland Trail Blazer shirt and a stack of basketball cards. I may need a slight loan from the parents to pull off my date and Chuck's birthday, but Pop has always been good about floating me a few bucks whenever the kid needs it.

One of the great blessings of life is to have parents who understand the financial needs of their children and are willing to support them in their worthy pursuits, such as, in this case, women.

SUNDAY, MARCH 22

Parents who understand their children? Was that I, Wallace F. Whipple Jr., who penned those words only a short 48 hours ago? How life can change! How we are but tiny leaves upon the water, subject to the whimsy of life's currents!

I didn't make a big deal of it. The straight-on approach, I reasoned, would be best. Man to man. Son to father. No frills, no whining, no begging.

"Dad, I need money. For a date." My exact words. Honest. Straight up. Gritty.

"Wally, I'm glad you have a date. You're overdue. But if you expect me to pay for your social life, then you've got another thing coming. Better start collecting pop bottles and turning them in for refunds," he said, with an air of carelessness that I thought was uncalled for.

"But Dad, this is important to me. I haven't dated in months. Do you want me to be socially awkward?"

"Better socially awkward than taking handouts from your parents."

"Dad, think of it as a long-term investment in your son's eternal progression!"

"Good try, Wally. I think of it as a short-term investment in my son's fun."

I next stated something that I thought perfectly captured my heartfelt emotions at that juncture in my life. "But Dad!"

"Okay, okay, Wally," he seemed to relent, and I thought that he at last was seeing the light and my plight at the same time. "We have shipments coming in this week at the store. A lot of late spring stuff. I could use you for about 20 hours. That would put some money in your pocket."

"But Dad—"

"Take it or leave it. I saw a bunch of pop bottles in the garage. You can start there. At a nickel a bottle, you'd only need to collect about 400 to have enough money to take your date to Hamburger Bob's."

Useless. And I thought my Dad was a kind, caring, sensitive, '90s sort of guy. But he actually expected me to work! Extended times of vegetating on the couch were only but a fleeting and rapidly dimming hope at this point. I caved in. "Okay, Dad."

"Thanks, son. Knew you'd come around to see it my way."

That's not all. Mr. Leonard coaxed me into high jump practice every afternoon this week. The adults of the world, it seems, are out to get me.

So much for spring break. Farewell, chili dogs with cheese while lying on the couch watching the ESPN sports highlights videotapes. Farewell, sweet slumber, my eyes remaining closed and my dreams blissful until about 10:00 each morning. Farewell to the good life, before it even had the chance to begin!

TUESDAY, MARCH 24

Trouble.

Not with the job, the high jump, Natalie, or Dick Dickson.

With Evan Trant.

I saw him today in the weight room, before I began to work out on my high jump. Evan looked grungy, like he was in a bad mood, and would willingly break anyone's arm who dared to talk with him. In short, Evan looked like he did most days.

But I'm used to him. For some reason, he seems to let me in a little more than anyone else, other than perhaps his tattoo artist. So I ignored all the storm warnings and sailed right up to him.

"Yo, Evan. What's up?"

He clunked down about 300 pounds of weights and said, "Wimp Pole. Little church-going phony."

"Evan? Are you okay?"

He grunted and lifted the bar again. "Leave me alone," he snarled. And when Evan snarls, it is a major league snarl. He could stop a charging rhino dead in its track with that snarl.

"Okay. Sorry if I said something."

"You're always sorry, little Mormon boy. You and the brothers. Always sorry. You guys make me sick."

"Evan, I don't deserve that."

"Yeah, you bet. Anything outside of your little bubble, you don't deserve."

I was hurt. It was not pretty. My animal instincts told me to turn and get out of there and hope he was in a better mood next time I saw him.

"Bubble boy, that's what you are. You don't know nuthin'. What have you ever done in your prissy little life that was hard? What? Name sumpthin'. You can't."

I thought about telling him of the time I banged up my knee at Scout camp and had to have four stitches, but decided that might not work here. I didn't understand what was going on. I'd heard about big dogs that suddenly turn on their owners and wondered if humans could be that way, too. Evan kept right on charging.

"You got a perfect dad and a perfect mom and your house is always clean, and your mom cooks good, and your sister is a cheerleader. You live in a bubble, Wimp Pole. Get out of here. Now."

"Evan—"

"*Now!*" With that, he turned and started pumping furiously. I walked out of the weight room, trying to figure out what had gone wrong. I guess I don't have to say it bothered me a lot. Evan and I are friends. Yeah, the Odd Couple, for sure, but somehow we'd always managed to communicate. Now, it wasn't so. What went wrong?

And is he right about the bubble part? Is it true? What rough things have I gone through in my life? Nothing. Nothing at all. Look at Orv. He's lost his mom. Look at Evan. I don't know much about his life, but I'm sure he doesn't come from your basic nuclear family. What's going to happen to me when a real test comes along, and I'm not just talking about seven months without a date? Have I ever faced anything hard, and when I do how will I react? Have I had to fight for anything in my life yet?

What did Orville tell me a couple of months ago? "Two kinds of people," Orv said. "Rocks and dirt clods." Which am I? Will I crumble under a little pressure?

Why did Evan turn on me? Was it really me, or just the fact that I was in the wrong place at the wrong time?

I don't know.

And am I a rock or a dirt clod?

I don't know; I don't know.

WEDNESDAY, MARCH 25

Chuck's birthday. Awesome. Yeah, I had to work, and in the afternoon there was track practice, but we still spent some quality time together at Hamburger Bob's slurping milkshakes and talking about life. We shot hoops for almost an hour, even had a little one-on-one, in which Lil' Bro somehow miraculously took me, 21-16. At his family party tonight, Chuck was all smiles with the presents I gave him. Mom and Dad came up big, too, and bought him his own leather basketball. Natalie chipped in with a new net for our basketball hoop and, of course, a pair of nice athletic socks. All in all, a good day for the Chuckster.

In the evening, Chuck put his earphone in his little transistor radio and sat contentedly in the middle of the living room. He has a map of North America, and when he hears a radio station from another town, he marks it on his map. It was a clear, cool night, and Chuck was really enjoying himself. He had on his new hat, a shirt that he got from Grandma and Grandpa, cradled his new ball under one arm, and slowly turned the dial on his radio. Late in the evening, he let out a little yelp of joy and then announced he had just pulled in a station in Omaha, Nebraska, a new eastern record for him. For Chuck, it was the perfect way to end a perfect day.

As I said before, Chuck is totally cool.

Wonder if he'd give me lessons someday.

THURSDAY, MARCH 26

Because it was Chuck's birthday yesterday, I sort of put aside my thoughts and feelings about Evan. Couldn't let anything get in the way of enjoying my day with the little brother.

Today, though, was different. I figure there are two ways of approaching this. One, try to ignore it. Cut a wide circle around Evan. See how he treats me, then react to it. If he ignores me, I ignore him. If he's friendly, then be friendly back.

Approach #2. Talk it out with him. Go one-on-one with the guy. Find out if it really was something I did or if he took out a bad experience on me. I told Orv about what had taken place.

"Seems to me that when you get ready to ride a bull, you better not let him know that you're afraid. He knows that and he owns you. You'll get whupped every time."

"So you think I should talk it through with him?"

"Yup. You want me to go along?"

"No. Like they say, 'A man's gotta do what a man's gotta do.'"

Tonight I made a flimsy excuse to get out of the house and headed for the place where Evan lived. It was an apartment building, off 63rd and Powell. When I got there it was dark, though I could see that Evan's front door was open a little.

Slowly, I made my way up the stairs to the second floor. I walked in front of apartment 213 and peeked inside. The place was a wreck. Bottles all over the floor. Cans of food open, sitting on the kitchen table. Filled ash trays, the smell of smoke heavy in the room. I couldn't see anyone. Maybe I could just glide on back to the car, say I tried, and leave it at that.

"Wimp Pole."

Evan's husky voice startled me. Actually, *startle* isn't quite an accurate description. I almost wet my pants.

"What you doin' here?"

The tone was slightly more friendly than two days ago in the weight room.

"I came to see you."

"Yeah?"

"Yeah. I did."

"You want to come in and sit down in the penthouse suite? Don't think my roommates are here right now. Viper and Weasel. Good guys. You'd like them Wimp Pole, except they drink a lot and put things into their bodies that you wouldn't."

"Let's stay out here, Evan."

"Okay. You called this meeting, you talk."

"What you said to me a couple of days ago—"

"Oh, that—"

"It wasn't just an 'oh, that.' What you said wasn't fair, Evan. I've tried to be friends with you all year long. And you turned on me." I was surprised at my tone of voice.

"Didn't mean to hurt your little feelings, Wimp Pole. But you are a bubble boy."

"So what? I've made choices to live this way. And I like it. Guys like you are always putting guys like me down, but there's nothing wrong with the way we are. There's a lot right with it. At least I don't have to live in a grungy apartment with guys who do drugs and are named after members of the animal kingdom."

Evan, tough guy that he is, whose personal motto may have been something like, "Die before showing weakness," actually winced and mumbled, "They ain't their real names."

He looked around a moment. "I've got a home, Wimp Pole. Just don't live there. Me and the old man don't get along too good. Mom don't get between us."

He turned his head away. Yes, there is the heart of a human being ticking away deep inside Evan's chest cavity. This sounds very crazy, makes no sense whatsoever, but I almost felt a little sorry for him. He seemed vulnerable. Then something just fell out of my mouth before I even thought about saying it.

"Did you and your dad have a fight or something the other day?"

Evan half smiled. "You're good, Wimp Pole. You're really good. How'd you know that?"

"A hunch. The brothers are good at them." There was a quiet moment, other than the sound of traffic coming from Powell and the thumping of someone's stereo downstairs. Evan turned and leaned over the railing in front of his apartment. "I think, Evan," I began cautiously, "that your dad would like you to move back. And maybe you'd like to move back too, but you think he'll look at you like you're a wimp or something if you do."

"Yeah. Maybe. Sure we had a fight Tuesday. Again. So I was in a bad mood. Then here you come, little Mormon guy with no muscles and a bunch of neckties in your closet. And you bing right up to me and give me that 'yo, how-ya'-doin'-babe' stuff. Didn't like it. Wanted to punch you, but your mom makes good cupcakes and I want to go out with your sister."

I said a quick prayer of thanks for Mom, adding a line about protecting Natalie from harm and evil.

Silence, again.

"Sorry, Wimp Pole. You have been okay to me."

I was feeling lucky.

"Didn't hear you, Trant."

He frowned. "Okay, I said I'm sorry. I won't yell at you again, even if you deserve it. Won't slug you, either. That okay, Wimp Pole?"

"Yeah, that's fine, Evan. And you really should think about moving back home. This place isn't going to do you any good."

"Yeah, but Viper and Weasel are cool. They both work at the hog shop. They're teachin' me a lot about bikes. Start work there Saturday."

"Good. But you know what I'm saying."

Another few seconds of quiet. "Yeah. I know what you're sayin'. I ain't dumb."

"I know, Evan. Trust me, I know."

"You wanna come in? We got some leftover Spam. Good stuff. We could pour beans over and have ourselves a little party. Like Trant and Wimp Pole make up."

"Not tonight. Got to get home. Back to my bubble, Evan."

He smiled slightly. "It's really okay in the bubble, Wimp Pole?"

"Yeah. It's where I want to be. When I have to, I can come out and get along just fine. Give me some credit, too."

"Come out like tonight?"

"Like tonight."

"See you doin' weights tomorrow."

"You got it."

I walked back to the car and drove home, trying to make sense out of the evening. I'm not sure I said everything just right, but I felt really good about taking something head on. Maybe I am more rock than dirt clod.

"Where've you been, Wally?" Mom asked when I got home.

And because I couldn't think of anything better to say, I just told her, "Doing a little missionary work, Mom." Which may not have been stretching things at all.

SATURDAY, MARCH 29

Spring break came and went too fast. This morning I went to Sister Lawson's house with Dad, and we put fertilizer on her lawn and cut back her rosebushes. She thanked us and invited us in near the end for a small lunch. The day started out with high clouds, then the big jumbo grays moved in. As we were putting away our tools, the rain started. It had all the makings of a typical Oregon storm, rain coming down in a steady flow.

Which posed a slight problem. Today is the day Orville and I were supposed to go out with Ed and Viola.

"You think we should cancel?" I asked him on the phone, the sound of rain pattering against the window.

"No way. Little rain mixed in will only make it a little more memorable. Ain't that what we want to do? Create a few memories?"

So at 3:00 P.M., I threw my dad's fishing rain gear in the back of the station wagon. I was dressed in Dad's big rubber boots, with his long rubber pants and poncho over me. For insurance, I took an umbrella. No need to check in the mirror before I left—I knew I looked like a dork, a latex-coated dork at that, but at least I wanted to be a dry dork.

Natalie had a field day with me. "Don't run into anything, Wally. You'll bounce a mile. Do you think Chuck will let you borrow his Big Bird raincoat? Seriously, Wally. You could make a fashion statement, you know, like, this is not how to dress for a date. And don't curl up, either, because someone will take out one of those you know what things—golf clubs—and try to put you on a tee. Seriously."

My only consolation was that I was going out with Ed, who would think it all fun; with Orville, who would make it fun; and with Viola, who would punch out the lights of anyone who made fun of us.

Orv came by, dressed in his cowboy rain gear, which

he actually looked good in, much the way he did when he showed up at our front door last October. He reminded me a little bit of Clint Eastwood in his better days, kind of lean and raw. Nat, naturally, showed up as soon as he did, telling him how good he looked, scoring high on the hypocrisy scale. We got out of my house and picked up Viola, who had on a raincoat. "You're gonna be wet as a worm on a driveway in a cloudburst, Viola," Orv told her. "Here. I brought some extra duds for you." He handed her a bundle, which contained more rain gear.

"Thanks, Orville. You watch out for me," Viola said. It was nice to see Viola smile. Sometimes, I forget that big strong people need attention, care, and rain clothing too.

"Yep. I try," Orville shrugged. "Wouldn't be much of a cowboy if I let a friend get cold and wet. That ain't the way we are."

Next was the Purvis home. I trudged up to the front door hoping that her father wouldn't answer: I had met Dr. Purvis on my very first date ever in eternity last year, and I'm sure he thought there wasn't much water in my well, if you catch my meaning. But no luck—when the door creaked open to the huge Purvis home, there he was.

"Hello, Will," I blurted. Oops. Bad move. *Never* call the dad by his first name, unless he insists about five hundred times, or you've proposed to his daughter, neither of which events were in my near future. Especially don't call a dad who is a doctor by his first name. "Uh, I'm Wally Whipple. Hope you remember me. I took Ed out last year."

"Yes, yes, Wally. Come in. Edwina should be ready in a moment. And I do remember you," he said with the air of a man recalling what he ate before getting the stomach flu.

I walked in and sat down, desperately wanting to be left alone, but Dr. Purvis sat down on the opposite side of the room from me. Ed once told me he had a great sense of humor, I reminded myself. Let's hope he trots it out soon.

He looked at me and sort of smiled and nodded. I looked back at him and sort of smiled and nodded. This was not going well. It reminded me exactly of what happened last year at Ed's house. I needed to say something, so I figured the manly thing to talk about was his work. "Been busy at the office?"

"Well, yes. Yes, it's been very busy, Wally. I have an incredible patient load right now. People always seem to become ill."

"Yes, they do. I myself have been ill several times. Have you seen anything unusual? You know, like flesh-eating bacteria or stuff like that?"

"No, Wally. Pretty routine, with the exception of a few unusual viruses."

"Good. Seen one virus, seen 'em all, I bet. Hope nothing too gross. Do you ever get grossed out?"

He sat back a moment and looked as though he wished he had escaped when the opportunity was there. "No, Wally. Some cases are sad, but one relies on professional detachment, so I rarely, if ever, get, as you say, grossed out."

"Good. I'd not like a job where I got grossed out a lot. You know, like working in a sewer plant or a place where they slaughter animals. I wouldn't want chicken blood all over me when I got home from work. The wife and kids might not handle it so well."

He nodded. "Indeed." About 20 seconds went by, and it seemed like 20 years. I shifted in my chair and looked up the Purvis's long, curving stairway, hoping to see Edwina. No luck. I was forced to make more intellectually stimulating conversation, something I've decided I could use some work on. In the great tape recorder of life, why do I always hit the ejection button?

"So, I hear Ed went out with Dick Dickson. Did you meet him?"

"Yes, I did."

Was it my imagination or did Dr. Purvis frown slightly at the mention of Dick's name. I decided to gamble.

"Dick and I sit by each other in math. In my opinion, although Dick has many fine points, such as he is good in math, he is kind of a dork and far beneath your daughter, Ed."

Dr. Purvis did smile this time. "Yes, Dick is a very different young man, I noticed. He is, as your generation would say, a real 'dufus.'"

I couldn't believe my ears! It was the last thing I expected to hear from the good doctor! I tried not to laugh but couldn't help it. Out came a giggle, then a genuine guffaw. Dr. Purvis began to laugh too. There we were, doing some instant male bonding, courtesy of Dick Dickson. Yes!

Ed came down and gazed at the sight of her father and me laughing. "What's going on here? Wally, are you and Daddy talking about Dick Dickson?"

"No, dear, we're not. Well, just a bit," Dr. Purvis managed to say.

"Time to go then," Ed affirmed. "Am I dressed okay, Wally?"

"Yeah. We've got some extra rain stuff in the car."

Well, the date turned out great. We went to the store and bought all the fixings for a picnic, drawing a few long stares as we traipsed up and down the aisles encased in plastic. Then we all drove across town to Washington Park and sat in the rose gardens. We were the only people there, which wasn't surprising, since by now the weather had turned into a near monsoon. Orville lugged two huge tarps out of the car, one for our ground cloth and the other to throw over a rope he had strung between two trees. And that's how we spent the next hour and a half, until it was almost dark, eating our picnic lunch under the tarp in the middle of a driving rainstorm. And I can't remember when I've had so much fun, not even when a bunch of us pooled our money one night and bought 32 rolls of you-know-what and paid a visit to an unsuspecting bishop's home late one evening, a deed that I have not quite fully repented of but plan to before my mission interview.

Oh yeah. There was the small matter of the police officer.

About an hour into the picnic, we heard some rustling outside the tarp. Then a cop stuck his head under.

"You kids don't know when to come in out of the rain or what?" he asked, his eyes darting around the makeshift shelter, looking for signs of crime.

"Guess we don't, sir," Orville said. "My daddy always wondered if I was smart enough to pour water out of a boot, and I guess I'll have the chance to show him that I am."

"Would you like some dessert?" Ed offered. "Graham crackers and marshmallows, with a little chocolate syrup on top. They're good."

"But a little soggy," Viola warned.

"No, thanks. You have a good time, drive home safely. And next time you go on a picnic, you might want to check the weather forecast first." With that, he let the tarp flap down and walked away.

Next time I will check the forecast before going on a picnic, and if it shows that the weather is going to be clear and warm, I don't think we'll go.

What a great day! Teenagers can have fun, although it sometimes requires an extraordinary amount of work and luck.

Tonight, I salute you, Orville Burrell, for being a true friend and one not deterred by the storm raging about.

And I salute Edwina Purvis and Viola Barkle, damsels with a sense of humor matched only by their sense of adventure.

And also to Dick Dickson, with whose unknowing assistance I successfully bridged the generation gap between Dr. Purvis and myself.

To all friends everywhere: good night and may a little rain always fall on your picnic of life!

CHAPTER 8

April

Tuesday, April 1

Although I am 17 years old, I freely admit to not quite knowing everything. It amazes me, for example, how quickly life's fortunes can turn. A month ago, Wally Whipple was a sorry dog, with little to look forward to, still not recovered from getting cut from the basketball team and sitting idly by, dateless for the Anything Goes Dance.

Now, I feel a cautious air of optimism slowly enveloping me. I feel good, almost as if things are going my way. High jumping is just around the bend, our first meet this week, and I'm clearing 6'2" with hardly trying. My once-dismal social life has picked up, having proved to myself that I can go out with an intelligent, attractive female person such as Ed and have a good time in the rain. I can impress the father of my date, and no one, but no one, leads the pledge of allegiance as well as I do.

In the great Zoo of Life, I am feeling like a young and masterful lion, surveying my domain—proud, powerful, and semiregal.

I am even thinking about asking Julie out. It's been almost a year, so she's probably had enough time to recover from our first date.

"You *should* ask her out," advises Lumpy, he of the romantic bend. "I mean, like my life is a lot better since Nancy and I started going out. It's just sort of cool to know you don't have to worry about who you're going to take out."

"Lumpy, you never did worry about that," I reminded him as school ended and he and I headed to the gym.

"Well, I did. I just didn't show it much. I was just hiding my inner feelings. By the way, did I tell you that Nancy and I are reading the Old Testament together? We're in Leviticus. Not much plot, but I guess it gets better."

I winced. Lumpy too was becoming a spiritual giant. Before his time, I think. I wanted to change the subject quickly. "So you think I should let Julie have another chance? I mean, do you think she's ready?"

"Yeah. People recover from broken legs in less time than since you guys went out."

"Well, I don't know . . ." I mumbled, trying to look doubtful but searching for any sign of encouragement.

"Go for it, Wally. Look, I know she's been hanging out in the library before school. You know, we get here about 20 minutes before class and she heads straight up there. She always goes way over to the left-hand side and studies."

"How do you know?"

"Nancy and I go there, too. We review our homework for the day."

I gave him a long, pitiful look. Lumpy wasn't quite Lumpy anymore. Next thing you know, he'll be eating salads and sprouts three times a day. "Do you think I should?"

"All she can say is no, which puts you exactly where you are now."

"But what can we do? Last year, you guys told me to

take her to the opera, and it was a disaster." Actually, *disaster* hardly describes my date with Julie. The shifting of the San Andreas Fault to somewhere in New Mexico would pale in comparison with that evening.

"Well, maybe you should do something more in your element. Why don't you take her on a hike? Up in the Columbia Gorge. Show her your strong, outdoors side. A guy who is more comfortable in the wild than in civilization. I think she'll go nuts. And my brother got some new aftershave called Sagebrush. I can get some for you. It'll be cool. Wear a plaid shirt and hiking boots and wrap a bandanna around your head."

I was getting this new vision of Wally Whipple: Eco-warrior. A man comfortable with nature. A guy who could catch fish with his bare hands and eat them uncooked. A guy who conjured up the smell of burning wood and wet brush.

I could see Julie in jeans and hiking boots, decked out in a canvas shirt, her brow sweaty from chopping wood, her hair pulled back in tight braids. A man and woman in their element: the environment.

I could see us as a wilderness family—hewing trees, building our own log cabin, delivering our own babies ("Boil some water!" I'd command as Julie smiled contentedly; "Put this between your teeth," I'd say, giving her a thick aspen twig), chasing off grizzly bears, mountain lions, and California land speculators. Yes, it would be a good life, shared with my brother the eagle, my friend the wolf, and my companions the fox, wolverine, and wild chicken.

"Maybe I will ask her out. The library, you say?"

"Yeah, the library. Maybe you and Julie and Nancy and I could double."

I turned to sweet, unadventuresome, fairly boring Lumpy and said, "Not where we're going. You won't find home-delivery pizza in the wilderness where Julie and I will live."

"Wally, you are getting ahead of yourself."

"Maybe," I said, smiling recklessly. "And maybe not."

THURSDAY, APRIL 3

The early-morning hour found me in seminary, as usual, feeling fairly fuzzy-brained and trying to stay awake, even though Sister Habben was doing a good job of keeping Hebrews alive and well and a semi-important part of my life.

"Let's take a look at Hebrews 11," she instructed. "'Now faith is the substance of things hoped for, the evidence of things not seen,'" she read, which sums up my renewed and intense desire to take out Julie again, if for no other reason than that I'd like to prove to her (not to mention myself) that I can go out with someone I am in *like* with and not make a complete fool of myself. Tall order, I know. You gotta have faith, Whipple.

Anyway, today is the day that Lumpy and I were on red alert. I mean, the amen was said and we were out of the church like arrows on fire.

Julie wasn't even out of the doorway when Lumpy and I left. We quickly drove to school and I headed to the library, a place that I visited about once a year anyway. Following Lumpy's direction, I arrived at the place that he all but guaranteed me she would be within a few short minutes. My heart was thumping, and I worried that the cold steel of a razor had not touched my face since Sunday. I was ready to mumble and berate, but then I remembered a little stubble is sort of a guy thing and would fit in perfectly with my new motif of Wally-as-a-mountain-man kind of guy.

I spread my books around and grabbed a couple off the shelf to make it look like I was really into studying. Papers and a pen were arranged to give just the right air of what I hoped would be the combination of unrestrained intellect and, for lack of better words, the aura of eagles, buffalos, and grizzly bears.

Second tall order of the day, I realized.

Lumpy and Nancy came in, and I gave him the quick thumbs up.

Footsteps clicked across the linoleum floor. I grabbed the one book nearest to me, opened it, and then took a pen from behind my ear and started furiously scribbling on a piece of notebook paper. The footsteps were near. I buried my nose deeper into the book and tried to imitate the most earnest look of deep thought I'd ever seen, namely, when Lumpy once actually didn't finish a triple-cheese, double-beef hamburger at Bob's and could only say by explanation, "I'm full. I don't get it."

"Wally? Is that you?"

Yes! It was Julie's voice, soft as the May wind, fragrant as wet fir needles. Uh, can a voice be fragrant? Well, you get the point.

"Yes, it is I," I answered, mentally congratulating myself on my use of proper grammar, although it did sound a little funny. I ran my hand over my stubbly chin, winced, and hoped she noticed.

"I didn't expect to see you here. Do you come to the library often?"

Time for quick thinking. I gave a small laugh and cocked my head slightly. "Can anyone ever come to a place of learning, such as the school library, too often?"

She gave me a funny look. "I guess not."

"And I agree. I look at the mind as an empty bucket and at libraries as deep wells." Nice, Whipple. No way would Julie ever think she was dealing with your basic, run-of-the-mill dummy. I was proving that my bucket was at least moist at the bottom.

"What are you reading?"

I recklessly pushed the book in front of her. Problem. It was titled *Immanuel Kant and the Critique of Pure Reason*. Hmm. Who was Immanuel Kant? I thought he was a rock group singer in the 1960s, but wasn't sure.

"This here is a book about Immanuel Kant," I said, pronouncing his name "Can't."

"Oh. You mean 'Kant,'" she said, pronouncing it "Cahnt."

"Yes. That is what I mean. You can confuse con't with can't, con't you."

"Wally, you're funny. I didn't know you were interested in philosophy."

"Oh, I am. My own philosophy is to be interested in philosophy," I said, bagging the theory about Kant on the keyboard or strumming bass. "I find Kant most challenging but also very rewarding."

"I'm impressed, Wally. I don't know much about Kant, but I do think his views regarding deity were remarkable," Julie said.

"Me, too. I mean, I also find it remarkable that he even thought about deity, instead of like sports or lowering one's cholesterol count or any of the other numerous distractions. It sets my mind at ease. Oftentimes, I think about Kant, and just knowing what he knew gives me great comfort." Teeny white lie, I suppose, but I don't think I'm the first person to tell one in the name of intellectualism.

"We should get together and read some philosophy," I suggested. "I like to read of Dr. Joyce Brothers, and I think that Billy Joel sings songs of great meaning. Sometimes."

She gave me a long gaze before answering. "Maybe. Wally, you do make me laugh."

"Part of my philosophy of life is to laugh, make others happy, and also enjoy the wilderness," I replied. Not exactly smooth, but I did work in the plaid shirt angle. Hope she picked up on it.

"I need to get in a little studying now. Two tests today."

"Go right ahead. I 'kant' keep you from your work any longer."

She giggled. "No, you 'kant.' Wally, you've brightened up my day."

"It's okay, Julie. Like I said, it's part of my personal philosophy of life, along with chopping wood and being one with nature. We must talk about nature sometime."

"Okay, Wally. See you."

She sat down at the table next to mine and started to study. I fidgeted with my books for a few more minutes, then quietly got up and left. All morning long I thought about how good it felt to possibly be reaching Julie's heart through her mind.

Is that a great idea or what?

FRIDAY, APRIL 4

The sweet taste of victory. Like sugar upon the tongue or root beer down the esophagus, it is wonderful to win. Given the choice, I will eagerly take being a winner rather than being a loser, a statement of noble wisdom and simplicity.

Today was our first track meet. And I won the high jump. Six feet three, and then Coach Leonard stopped me. "No need to let it all go just yet, Wally. We want to build you a block at a time, so that you'll peak right at the city meet. You can do it this year, Wally. You can take city. At the varsity level."

Music to my ears. May I make Coach Leonard a prophet this season.

"Nice jumpin'," Orv congratulated me. "Them other guys looked downright docile compared to you."

"How'd it go in the shot?"

"Second. But the coach told me I was goin' up against a good one. He's a senior, so he's a year older than me, but I'll git 'im by the end of the year."

Back home, Dad beamed with fatherly pride when I told him about the track meet. Mom, too, was pleased. "I'm glad that you can jump so high. It's much better than those other sports, where everyone tries to break you into little pieces," she said.

"Yeah. Like nice work, seriously," Natalie complimented, for absolutely no reason whatever, other than maybe she also wanted to be affiliated with a winner.

So life is good now. I believe I am taking large, swift steps toward adulthood, and it doesn't even bother me one bit, other than someday my parents will want me to pay more of my car insurance.

SUNDAY, APRIL 6

General conference day, the one occasion every six months where you can wear your sweats to church, sort of. I love it.

Natalie used the break between sessions for a quick presidency meeting to plan for the mother and daughter dinner next week.

"So, like, should we have macaroni?" asked Janna Cowles, one of her counselors.

"No. Let's have something nicer," said Eryn Magee, who sounded like the one voice of reason in the Mia Maid presidency.

"Like, I agree totally," Natalie said, trying to sound, shall I say, presidential.

"It's for our moms, and they're the greatest. We want to show them, like, we appreciate all they do for us, especially when they buy stuff for us. We need something really special."

"Yeah, but like what?" Janna raised the question aloud. "We can't, you know, like, have roast duck and cheese balls."

At this critical point, I peeked into the living room, where the Mia Maid brain trust was deep in thought. Nat, feeling the burden of the call and the mantle of leadership, suddenly said, "I've got it. This is cool."

"What? Tell us, Natalie," begged the class secretary, Brittany Bledsoe.

"Pizza. We order out for pizza. Then, like, we don't have to cook and cleanup is really easy. And if there's any left over, we take it home and have it for lunch."

"Great, totally cool," said Janna, as Heather nodded.

"No, wait!" Eryn protested. "That's not special at all!"

"Pizza not special? Like, everyone likes it, and it really is sort of us, and we're special because all our leaders are always telling us that, and I think it's cool," Natalie counterpunched. "So let's vote. All in favor?" Three hands went up. "Guess that's it. Pizza it is, with some pop, and we can get some of that bagged salad stuff, too."

"But what about, you know, dishes?"

"Let me guess. You'll want paper plates," mumbled Eryn.

"Good idea!" gushed Natalie. "No cleanup. We wouldn't want our moms to have to clean up. For real, we'd go, 'We'll clean up,' but since they're our moms, they'd go, 'No way! We're the moms, we'll clean up.' And then there might be, like, a fight, even though it wouldn't be serious because we'd probably give in and let them bop into the kitchen. So if we have paper plates and stuff, there won't be any cleaning at all for the moms to do and no fights either. Okay, I'll make assignments."

Eryn started to say something but then seemed re-signed to defeat. I decided to step away before being de-tected.

I have to give credit to my sister for one thing: al-though her methods are a little crude, she gets the work done.

Someday, she's going to make a fine Relief Society president.

TUESDAY, APRIL 8

Confidence is a funny thing. It's not something tan-gible that you can pick up and carry around, but you know when you have it and when you don't. I'm the same basic guy every day. I look the same, act the same, have the same likes and dislikes. But when I feel confident, it makes all the difference. I look better. I act smarter. The things I like and dislike seem more important. I feel better about myself, what I can do, and what I am going to do with my life. Does this make sense?

If I could only figure out the way to feel confidence all the time. Look at Natalie. Same parents. Same home. Same basic genetics. She's confident all the time, and I'm confident hardly any of the time. How do I figure that? Sometime, I'd like to ask Nat why she is so confident.

She'd probably say something about clothes, looks, friends, and being smart in math. But I think it goes be-yond that. I think confidence is about knowing who you are and deciding that you really are okay, no matter what all the other signs in the world are telling you. I think it has something to do with knowing what really counts in life and what doesn't. I think it's about looking in the mir-ror and saying, "I like the guy who is staring back at me." I think it is about being a rock, not a dirt clod.

Wouldn't it be great to be confident every hour of every day? But how do I get there from here? I don't know.

It's not that my confidence is bad right now. In fact, by Wally Whipple standards, it's just about off the chart. I am an accepted and respected member of the track team. I've been meeting Julie each morning in the library and having some fairly normal conversations with her, and I might even ask her out again. Grades are due out at the end of the week and I think I'm going to do okay. And Bishop Winegar called me in and asked if I would serve as the second assistant in the priests quorum presidency. So life is looking up.

Someday, I'm going to figure out the formula. "Confidence for Kids" is what I'll call it. Put it in a bottle, record it on a video, and write a best-selling book or two on the topic. I'll make a bazillion dollars. At least.

On the other hand, if it helps others to feel better about themselves, maybe I'll just give it away.

THURSDAY, APRIL 10

I didn't see Orv until track practice. Finally caught up with him at the shot put area, where he and the other slabs of beef were practicing putting the shot.

"Howdy, Orv. How's it goin'?"

"Purty fair. Flangin' the old iron ball pretty good today. Feel like I got some real heft into it. How 'bout you?"

"Great day. Dick Dickson has the flu. Didn't see his mug once."

Orv turned away and picked up another shot put and balanced it in his hand. "You really don't like him much, do you, Wally?"

"Well, I guess he's not my favorite guy. I mean, he's been rude to the max to me. He's like a little bitty dog that is always nipping at your heel. And he thinks he is so superior to me. It's his, you know, attitude." For some reason I could not stand there and tell Orv that I don't like Dick. I was confused.

"Hmmmph!" Orv grunted, putting the shot. He rubbed his hands on his sweat pants, then wandered over to me. "I once had a bitty dog that was always yappin' and yippin'. Didn't like him much, neither. Then one day we was out in the corral, and I was workin' with one of our new horses, gettin' the halter on. Here comes this biddy ol' dog, kind of squeakin' and bein' ornery, and the horse was actin' spooky and I was just about to kick that little hound out of the way. But I reckoned, 'You could kick him around, 'cause that's about all anybody ever done to him his whole life, or you could toss him a little piece of meat and have a friend for life."

Orv picked up a shot again. "You're up, Burrell," one of the coaches barked at him. "Get a little lower at the back of the ring."

"Sure thing, coach."

He started to walk away. Something inside didn't feel right, like he hadn't finished the story. "But, Orv, what did you do?" I asked anxiously.

He stopped and turned toward me. "Threw him a bit of steak. Turned out to be the best durned dog I ever had." He walked back to the ring, squatted, twirled, and threw the shot about five feet farther than his last attempt.

"Nice, Burrell. You put something extra into that," the coach praised.

"Yep. I did. Like to do a little more sometimes," Orv said to the coach, while looking right at me.

Okay. Got it, Orv.

After practice tonight, I drove by Dick Dickson's home. I got out of the car and walked to his front door. It wasn't much of a house. Small, in need of paint, with an overgrown lawn. I knocked twice and shivered in the suddenly chilly spring air. A short, thin woman answered, someone about my mom's age. "Can I help you?" she asked. She looked tired but had a nice smile. I could see a lot of Dick's features in her face.

"Uh, yeah. I'm a friend of Dick's." A near untruth, Whipple, for sure. "We're in math class together, Mrs. Dickson. I heard he was sick. I wanted to drop off the homework assignment to him. I know how Dick likes to keep up on his studies. He's a really smart guy. Sometimes, he gives me pointers in class."

She nodded, pleased by what I told her. "Thank you very much. That's so sweet of you. And he helps you in class. Good for Dick. I'm glad that Dick has a friend like you," she said, almost in a whisper. "I worry about him sometimes."

"Yeah. I guess I do, too." I started back to the car.

"I forgot to ask. What's your name?" she called to me.

"Wally Whipple, Mrs. Dickson. Tell him Wally Whipple stopped by."

I got in the car and drove away, wondering what Dick was thinking at that moment.

SUNDAY, APRIL 13

Great track meet on Friday. Our team won big time, and I jumped 6′3″. Wanted to go a little higher, but Coach Leonard still has this thing about peaking too early, so I quit, put my warm-ups on, and hung out, trying to look very cool.

It is easier to look cool after you have just done something highly athletic, I've decided.

While at my most ultra cool moment, when I was squirting a sports drink carelessly in the general direction of my mouth, my head tilted at a definite rakish angle, light green liquid sort of gushing down my cheeks, I looked for Julie or Ed in the stands, just in case one of them had decided to watch the track meet. There, way back near the top railing, *both of them stood.*

Yes! It was worth squirting the gator juice into my left eye! It didn't sting that much.

But the real news of the day is Orville. He gave his talk in church today. Now, I've been in the position more than once of wondering what Orv was going to say or do, like the day he recited a poem in English class last year. The thing is, every time I worry or wonder about Orv, he always comes through. Today was no exception.

He was dressed in his Montana tuxedo—cowboy boots, western sport coat, string tie, and a pair of sand-colored slacks. When his turn came, he smiled and confidently stepped up to the podium. He didn't have a single note in front of him.

Natalie was sitting next to me, all eyes and ears. "Does he, like, have his talk memorized?" she whispered.

"I guess, like, he does, Nat."

"Orv is so cool. Do you think he'll go on a mission? You know, like I believe all guys should do that, and it will give me a chance to catch up with him in age. You see what I'm saying?"

I didn't have time to answer. Orv smiled and looked at the congregation.

"Mornin', brothers and sisters. My name is Orville Burrell, and I'm one happy guy to be a Mormon. Wouldn't have happened if it weren't for my best saddle pal, Wally Whipple, who is a good hand and a durned good missionary."

I sort of ducked my head down because I could feel my face turning red and my sweat glands going on full alert.

Nat poked me in the ribs. "Does Orv know about temple marriage?"

"Anyhow, I wanted to talk to you all 'bout a time me and my Dad and my older brother Will went huntin' high up in the Blues. They're mountains, just to the east of Pendleton. I figure you know where they are.

"Well, we was huntin' elk, and it was late October and colder than a dog's bone left in the snow. We could see some tracks, and we knew there was a big ol' buck somewhere close. I told my dad that I wanted to take my horse around to the top of a wash and flush that big ol' elk down, where he and Will could get a clean shot off.

"My dad, he looks a little worried. He says to me that he don't like the look of the weather. We've been seein' clouds waller on in for a couple of hours, and they're lookin' like slate, which means they're full of snow. So I tell my dad, if it starts snowin' hard, I'll follow my tracks back down to him and Will.

"Well, I get up on top of the ridge and it flattens out in a hurry. The snow starts comin' down hard, but I keep pushin' ahead, figurin' I'm gonna see that gulch and follow it right on down and end up in my dad's lap. But the clouds sink low, and the snow is blowing in at me sideways, and I can't see too much. It's 'bout as dark as the inside of a cow's stomach, and I'm startin' to get a tad worried, not to mention cold. I try to get my horse turned around, but it's snowin' so hard that I can't make track. It's about along then that I realize, 'Orville, you've dug yourself into a mighty deep hole.'"

I sneak a quick glance around the chapel. Everyone, and I mean everyone, is listening, from young to old, and even the Evans's five-year-old boy, who has never known a quiet moment in church from the day he first showed up to be blessed, is suddenly still.

"I decide to head for a clear spot, figurin' that's the

best place I could be. I knew my Dad would come and git me. I knew he would be there.

"So I hunker down a bit on my horse and call out every minute or so. I shoot a round in the air every so often. It seems like I been out there about half the night, but it's only been a couple of hours. Now, I'm gettin' right cold and thinkin' about how the paper back home in Heppner is gonna run a story about how I got lost and stupid at the same time and didn't make it outta the mountains.

"I think, 'I hate to end it this way. Everyone I know would think, 'Orville got a little too cocky and it cost him.'

"Then I heard a couple of horses and seen my dad's big flashlight. I whoop and holler at him, and he and Will come ridin' up to me kind of slow. My dad gets close to me and says, 'Glad you found us, Orville. Me and Will was lost, but I think we kin find our way out now. Let's git home, son.' And all of a sudden, I don't feel cold no more.

"Now, what I think is that Wally here was like my dad. He's the one who found me, showed me the light, and then said let's go home."

Orville stopped a moment and looked right at me. "Thank you, Wally."

Then he raised himself up a little taller. "And I wanna tell my dad thanks too, and that I love him. Cowboys don't often talk that way much, but we're gettin' better at it. He's a great man. We've been through some tough times the last few years, with my mama passin' away, but I want to tell you that I know we're gonna make it."

I turned around and looked to the back of the chapel. Mr. Burrell sitting on the last row, and nodded toward his son.

At the end of our row, Mom was wet around the eyes. Even Dad looked a little floody. And Nat looked about as serious as I've ever seen her. Orville finished by bearing his testimony, then sat down.

I could write a lot more about today, but I think we'll leave it here. Twenty years from now, when I'm middle-aged and losing my hair, and either Julie or Ed or some other lucky woman and I sit and read this journal entry, I'm still going to get chills and remember the feeling I now have. When the Spirit touches, you remember it. Always.

At the end of Orville's talk, Natalie let out a sigh. "Orville's cool. Way cool. And spiritual, too."

Let the record show that for once I think Natalie is 100 percent right.

MONDAY, APRIL 14

Grades. Yuck.

For the third quarter in a row, I got exactly the same grades! Two Cs, two Bs, and the three As. I can't believe that Mrs. Garrison gave me a B after my sterling performance as Romeo the Comedian. The laugh factor alone should have endeared me to her forever. "Hmmm," she should have said to herself. "Wally is right on the edge between a B and an A, but he is so good for class morale, well, you've gotta love the kid. He deserves an A. By cracky, I'll give him one!"

But no luck. Mr. Flagg once again only gave one "A," and I'm sure it went to Mel Pyne. Somehow, he managed to again link his very weird grading system to the Constitution, bellowing out at one point, "Do you think the Founding Fathers were dummies? No! They were intelligent, resourceful men, who understood biology!" Anyway, a C for Wally in there again. Social studies, another B, and math, another C. Thank Heaven for Spanish, journalism (where I am the class star, no doubt), and choir, all As.

My next chore was to sort of finesse this one with my parents. Most of the time we get along okay, which is to say they don't embarrass me too much. But when Dad saw the old 3.1, especially after nailing a 3.8 my last quarter as a sophomore, he had one of those very fatherly reactions: "Wally, we'll need to look at some of your outside activities if your grades don't improve next quarter. You're not going to get into Harvard with a B average."

Tonight after family home evening, Dad was waxing the station wagon and I thought it might be a good time to approach him.

"Mind if I help?" I asked, risking sending him into a coronary, since he knows that waxing the car is up there with a career in compost management as things I want to do.

"No, not at all, Wally."

We applied wax and buffed for about ten minutes. My personal tension level was rising, so I decided to go for it and bring up the subject of grades. "Dad, you've always said that being dependable and consistent is very important."

"Yes. People need to be the same. 'Steady' is the way Orville puts it."

"Dad, I agree with you. Steady. The same today, yesterday, tomorrow, and forever." Good move, throwing a scriptural reference into it.

"Right, Wally. Did you get that spot under the taillight?"

"Yeah. I did. Well, Dad, I want you to know that I am steady. Dependable. Not much changes in my life or the way I look at things. Steady as a rock, that's me. Most of the time, anyway, and especially at school."

Dad put his rag down. "Wally, is this about grades?"

"Sort of."

"Sort of?"

"Well, yes. Sort of. Uh, I got my grades today and they are exactly the same as last time. You know, steady. Consistent. Like no surprises."

"Wally. You can't get those kinds of grades—"

"I know, Dad. And get into the school I want to. They aren't that bad. I mean, I'm not going to end up at Tire Changing U. And at least I didn't go down."

"Steady is fine, but there's still the law of eternal progression," Dad said, niftily outscripturing me. "If you're standing still, you're falling behind."

"I'll do better, Dad."

"I know. If you don't you'll be grounded in June."

I tried to look shocked and hurt and determined all at the same time. Actually, since I don't have much of a social life, and I spend almost all my hours at home in the summer anyway, grounding doesn't mean much.

I did the guy-to-guy thing. "I'll do better, Dad. I promise."

"Good, son. Now can you use those long arms of yours and buff the top?"

"Sure, Dad."

It all went better than expected. A valuable lesson may have been ingrained on my puny mind today: when you have bad news to tell a parent, wait until said parent is busy, and they may be distracted enough to not yell at you.

Call it Whipple's First Rule for the Art of Handling Parents.

TUESDAY, APRIL 15

Dick Dickson came back to school today. I barely got into class before the bell rang, and the whole time during class I felt his beady little gaze on me. When math was over, he tugged on my shirt sleeve.

"Wally. Thanks for bringing my homework to me. I didn't expect you to do that."

"Neither did I, in a way. But it seemed like the right thing to do. So I did."

"Well, thanks."

"It's okay. I know you'd do the same for me." Big stretch, I realize. When I was sick, I'm sure helping me didn't even occur to Dick. But when you set expectations higher for someone, sometimes they might come through, and then you're both better off.

"If you ever miss class," Dick said slowly, "I'll make sure you know what went on."

"Good deal, Dick."

Then he sort of slithered away. The funny thing is, though, I could sort of tell his attitude toward me was different. He slithered in a nice way.

Dick may turn out to be the best durn dog around yet.

Thursday, April 17

We didn't work out much at track today—we have a meet tomorrow. Track coaches have a tendency to treat you like a mollusk for six days of the week, and then on the seventh—the day before meets—they rest. All of a sudden they become nice.

"Okay men, take it easy today. Don't strain yourselves. Big meet tomorrow; we want you healthy and ready. And above all, don't pull a muscle!" They must figure that if they treat us okay the day before a meet, we will all go home and say, "Wow, are they great coaches or what? I can hardly wait to go out and bust the gut for them tomorrow!"

But we see through them. We know that late Friday afternoon, when the meet is drawing to an end, they will be over us like ants on a smooshy candy bar, dropping huge reminders about working out over the weekend. "Just remember this, boys (editorial comment: notice how fast we went from men to boys), if you're not out there training on the weekend, your opponent is. And he will take you."

Oh, well. When I am a parent, I will never engage in psychological warfare with teenagers and children. This is a true statement.

Tonight we were sitting around—Chuck listening to his radio, Natalie on the phone, and me trying to get into some biology (next week: frog dissection, which Mr. Flagg promises "will be the highlight of our biology class, if not your entire academic experience this year")—when the doorbell rang. Mom was at a school meeting, and Dad was splitting with one of the elders. Being the man of the house at this moment, at least in theory, I opened the door. It was Evan Trant, resplendent in his basic black leather wardrobe and his baseball hat worn backwards, the one with the words "Harleys Are Life" written on it.

"Food," grunted Evan.

"Let's see, Evan. This means you're hungry, right?"

"Right. Food, Wimp Pole."

"Come on in. Mom isn't here, but we have leftovers we can nuke for you."

"Food," Evan repeated for the third time, reverting to his one-cell mentality.

We walked into the kitchen, where Evan sat down at the table and drummed his fingers nervously. I warmed up some chicken-and-cheese casserole and a couple of dinner rolls. I tossed on some broccoli, figuring what Evan ate I might not have to. In this respect, Evan is becoming very much like our family pet. Evan cast greedy eyes on the plate.

"So how's it goin', Evan? Don't see you much at the weight room anymore."

"Naw. Don't go there much. Got to work now more. Rent and utilities and that stuff. Never even knew what a utility bill was until I moved out."

"Evan, wouldn't it be smarter to move home and have a life again?"

"I am smart, Wimp Pole. Most people don't think so, but I am."

"I know. That's why I can't figure why you don't move home again."

"You know why. My old man and me don't get along."

"Don't be stupid, Evan."

"Wimp Pole, sometimes I wonder why I don't pick you up and break your scrawny little body in two. You are a pest."

"I know. And you don't cream me because, number one, you like my Mom's cupcakes and food—"

"Except broccoli. Don't like veggies."

"Okay. Number two, I saved your rear end in Scleavege's class. Number three, I got you to play on our basketball team and you enjoyed that. And number four, you're sitting in *my* house eating *my* food that *I* cooked for you in *our* microwave, and this is probably the only place you're going to get fed a decent meal."

"You sound like my big brother."

"You know what we call each other at church."

Evan sneered, something he is all-world at. "Yeah. Brother Wimp Pole."

"You got it."

"Brother Wimp Pole and Brother Trant. Maybe I will go back home so that you and all the other brothers don't gang up on me."

"Evan, we're going to get you. You know it. You're gonna be one of us someday."

"No way, Wimp Pole."

"Yes, way. Big way, Evan."

He left a half hour later, after asking out Natalie (who quickly invoked the no-dating-until-I'm-sixteen-or-maybe-it's-21 rule) and telling Chuck that he needed to save all his money to buy a Harley-Davidson. "Bikes are cool," Evan told him.

"I know. I like bikes," said Chuck, thinking of the kind with ten speeds, pedals, and spokes.

Dad came home an hour later. "How'd it go here, kids?"

"Pretty good, Dad," I said, feeling fairly awesome about Evan's visit. "We've been your basic superstars, you know, feeding the hungry and spreading the gospel."

Dad pulled off his coat. "Huh?"

FRIDAY, APRIL 18

I drove home with Lumpy today after the track meet, another ho-hum, run-of-the-mill, routine event in my life.

(Ha! I won the high jump at 6'4" today. I love being in the spotlight! I love being a contributing member of the team! I love it when Coach Leonard smiles warmly and tells me I'm a champion! I look forward to my name being boomed over the loudspeaker, the dozens of track scholarships awaiting me, the chance to participate in the Olympics, to endorse tennis shoes, to have my name and picture on boxes of cereal, and to cut my own rap album!) Hey, if you can't dream at 17, when can you?

Anyway, Lumpy started to quiz me about my social life. "Going out with Ed again?"

"Yeah. But I don't want to ask her out too soon, because she might think I *like* her more than I do, even though I do like her."

"I think you should ask out Julie."

"Why?" I said, my interest surging. Did Lumpy have secret information? Did Nancy by chance talk with Julie, who happened to say something like, "I wish Wally Whipple would ask me out? If he only knew how much I want to be with him. Nancy, can you talk with Larry, and perhaps he could at the right time drop a well-placed hint with Wally about my never-ending, burning desire to go out with him again?"

"Well, because as I've said before, Julie has had a year to recover from that bomb date you took her on. And you've still got the hots for her."

"No way. Well, maybe a little. About 98.7. That's all."

"*And* you've been talking with her every morning at the library, *and* you've read up on Kant enough to know he isn't a rock musician, *and* you're not speaking in tongues with her anymore, *and* you're only drooling a little bit now, so why not go for it."

"Do you think I should?"

"Wally, what have I been saying? Hello, anyone in there?"

"But what could we do? You know me, I can't do a normal date. Genetics, I think."

"Man, you are helpless! Remember Wally the Macho Outdoorsman? You and Julie as the Wilderness Couple? Take a hike, Wally."

"What?"

"I said, take a hike. With Julie. Get it?"

"Oh. Like hiking outdoors, with a little stream rushing by and enjoying nature and maybe putting some pizza in the backpack? Stuff like that?"

"Yeah. A lot like that. Take her up to the Columbia Gorge. You know some trails up there and there's a ton of waterfalls. She's from California, remember? She doesn't know what water looks like outside of a swimming pool."

This most superb vision again began to blow into the windmills of my mind. California Babe meets Oregon Wilderness Stud. Yes! I can see it again. "See these here things? They're called 'streams' or 'creeks.' They are caused by snow melting and running downhill. When they go over the edge of a cliff, we have a waterfall. See the green stuff here? They are called plants. The tall ones with bark are called trees. As you can tell, I feel very strongly about the earth. Although I am equally comfortable in an opera as I am in the outdoors, I am more comfortable outdoors, Julie. Oh. And watch out for that little slimy thing. We call them 'slugs' here in Oregon."

"Lump, you may be onto something. A date in the wilderness. I like it."

"Then are you going to ask her out?" Lumpy has great instincts when it comes to closing a sale. He could make a zillion selling insurance, only he needs to hone up on being more obnoxious.

"Yeah."

"When?"

I drew a deep breath. The sweet vision of Julie and me, walking along a rushing mountain stream, with towering fir trees overhead, smiling, laughing, and softly singing "Kumbaya" was almost overpowering.

"The next time I see her, Lumpy. Promise."

SUNDAY, APRIL 20

So I think a lot about Julie and sometimes in my mind and journal refer to her as "Sister Whipple." Yes, I *like* Julie. I've had a crush on her for more than a year and a half, which almost represents eternity when you're my age.

Recognizing my feelings for Julie, and sort of giving my word of honor to Lumpy that I'd ask her out again the next time I saw her, you'd think I'd put a plan of action together. Well, I did. My plan of action was something like this: whatever you do, don't run into Julie for a while. Avoid her. Pretend she doesn't exist.

This is all so confusing. This is the woman I may sort of (probably do) want to spend the rest of my life and then some with, and I'm desperately hoping that I don't see her for a few weeks at least. *Like* turns your world upside down. No wonder Sinatra sings so much about fools in love. You have to be a little foolish to fall in love.

How bad did it get this weekend? My imagination went into warp drive. I mean, the phone would ring and I'd start to get jittery. Not that Julie has ever called me before, but when the old phone chimed, I'd jump up and say, "I'm not here."

"You expecting a phone call from, you know, like, a girl, Wally? You're acting psycho," Natalie said, using her highly developed instinct for torturing her older brother to the max. "I bet you think, like, Julie Sloan or someone is going to call you. You're such a dork, Wally."

"Ha! Not true! Julie? Ha again!" I sputtered. "Julie? I hardly even know Julie! You amuse me, Nat. But you are wrong," I said, figuring repentance would soon figure into my life in a major way.

Orv and Lumpy wanted to go to the stake dance last night, but I told them I had a sore throat and didn't want to risk spreading germs and contaminating the stake's entire population of 16- to 18-year-old young women. Naturally, what I really wanted was to avoid Julie. I did have a tiny sore throat, probably because of all the heavy swallowing I've been doing thinking about Julie this weekend. Nevertheless, I might have to repent of using that as an excuse not to go. Maybe I should just roll up both of my white lies into one and repent of two things at the same time, if that's possible. (Note: Ask Bishop Winegar if you can do two-for-one repentance.)

I did manage to ask Lumpy to put in a good line or two for me if he happened to see Julie.

"You don't want me to say you have a sore throat?"

"No, Lumpy. Tell her something else, like I'm doing research or helping Chuck with a science project or organizing a canned food drive. Something that will, you know, elevate me in her eyes."

"You can count on me, Wally."

That's about where I stand right now. I am making a concentrated effort to avoid being around the person I would want to be around the most. Does that make sense? Does anything make sense when it comes to falling in like?

MONDAY, APRIL 21

We did the truck pool to seminary and school today, meaning that Orville and Lumpy picked me up.

I climbed into Orv's pickup, a rolling tribute to the staying power of rust. My two dear, close friends immediately zeroed in on my pledge to ask out Julie. Obviously, Lumpy had filled Orv in the second he climbed into the truck.

"Hear yer goin' to break new sod in your social life," Orv asked, toothpick dangling from his mouth.

"Can I have no secrets? Do I have no privacy?" I mildly protested, tossing Lumpy a look of disapproval. "Why not just have the bishop announce it from the pulpit?"

"Well, are you or aren't you? Don't get bowed up on us, Wallace. We jes' want to make sure you got a well-rounded life, like Brother Hansen was talkin' about yesterday."

"Orv's right. It's your long-term welfare we're concerned about. You know, can't make it to the celestial kingdom without a wife," Lumpy said. "Wally, it's because we love you. That's all."

"Lumpy, save it for Nancy. I'll let you guys know when I ask her out. I am a man of honor. You will be the first to know, as two of my closest friends. I promise."

"Okay, Wally. We wanna be roped in as soon as you hatch the question."

"You will."

But nothing happened today. True, I saw Julie in English class, but it's not exactly like you can raise your hand, stand up, and say, "Mrs. Garrison, I need to conduct a little class business now. Julie, would you like to go out with me?"

So maybe tomorrow, or the next day, or the day after. What's that word Miss Richardson taught us? *Mañana*. Yeah, that's it. *Mañana*.

THURSDAY, APRIL 24

I have had many bad days in my life before. They're sort of a specialty with me. I could write a book about the disasters I've experienced. Witness: the time when I flunked my driver's test; my first (and heretofore only) date with Julie, which certainly will be remembered as the worst date in history; diving into the swimming pool at a combined activity when I was a deacon and feeling my trunks slide down to my knees as the Beehive class presidency stood next to the pool, giggling. Today will take its place right beside any of them.

It is a dark, dark day for Wallace Whipple.

For the second time in my somewhat brief high school career, I have an appointment with Mr. Otis McCloud, the vice-principal for discipline at Benjamin Franklin High School, a man who is taller than I am and about 100 pounds heavier, someone who is not known for his sunny disposition, especially toward students who have been accused of "subversive acts, insubordination, and contributing to the delinquency of an entire class," which is exactly what Mr. Flagg wrote on the note to Mr. McCloud. Even the drug dealers and the gang members steer way clear of Mr. McCloud. I wish I could too. But too late.

I need to go over the details again. I need to have them

down cold in my feeble attempt to prepare my defense, shortly before Mr. McCloud creams me from school.

It began with a frog—my frog, the guy I named "Chester" for the cute little way he puffed out his chest. Chester came into my life on Tuesday. Mr. Flagg handed out frogs to all of us in class, and while he droned on about the habits and anatomy of frogs I sort of started to play with Chester. Chester and I hit it off. He was a natural entertainer. Jumped all over my desk. I knew I had the next Kermit right there. I don't know how to say this, *but Chester and I bonded.*

Yes, I became emotionally attached to my frog.

But I knew what was in store for him: death. That's what. A long, slow trip to the great pond in the sky. A quick dose of chloroform in a heartless plastic bag. Chester's eyes would bulge out. He'd kick, he'd thrash, the one question tumbling from his tiny green lips, "Why? Why me? Wally, help me! I thought we were friends!" There I'd stand, my hands tied, nothing I could do. And then Chester the Frog would have croaked, while Mr. Flagg stood at the front of the class and laughed maniacally.

Today in class, Mr. Flagg started the grim business. "Kellen, bring your frog up!" Kellen Taylor slowly walked to Mr. Flagg, who, I thought, was a little too eager to wrap his fingers around the frog and plunk him in the plastic bag. "Won't feel a thing, Slimy!" Mr. Flagg chuckled.

"Wally! You're next!" He looked at me with his dark, deep-set eyes, his short gray hair sprouting at odd angles from his head above his long beakish nose. "Well, Wally?"

I picked Chester up. He winked at me. Honest. I walked slowly. "This is going to hurt me more than it is you." I looked at Kellen's frog, now on his back, his little webbed feet up in the air. Chester croaked. It sounded like my name! "Whipple! Whipple! Whipple!" How could I do this? A poor, sweet innocent creature.

Mr. Flagg was running out of patience. "We're waiting, Wally!" I stood up.

I ran my finger over his little green body. Get a grip, Whipple! This is a frog, that's all! He's a good frog. He'll go to the highest kingdom there is for frogs! Someday, you'll see him again!

And the question he'll croak is "Whipple? Why, Whipple?" In fact, he seemed to be asking that very question now as he gently croaked. I noticed that the windows were open along the west side of the room. There is a marshy area in the park that adjoins the school. Suddenly, I found myself plotting, of all things, a jailbreak.

I mumbled to Chester, "Be cool and nobody will get hurt. When I make the move, you run like crazy. Uh, jump like crazy. Got it? I'll give you the signal." I smiled at Mr. Flagg, then turned abruptly toward the wall, cut in front of Terrah Johnson's desk and pushed Chester out of the window!

"Go, Chester! Get out of here! Go for it!" I yelled.

Chester turned and looked at me, blinked once, and I think, although I'm not 100 percent sure, croaked, "Thanks, Whipple!" Then he bounded for the trees and bushes.

I turned. Mr. Flagg was taking on a bright red hue, and out of his mouth was coming an interesting though unintelligible mixture of saliva and the spoken word.

"Grrsh, what, urrr, be done, grrph, plunk . . . frog . . . AARGHH!!!"

I sensed movement around the class. Terrah stood up and pushed her frog out of the window. Mel Pyne put his perfect 4.0 on the line and dropped his frog out. A half-dozen other students did, too. I heard applause. I heard my name. "Wally, way to go!" A chant started, "Wall-eee! Wall-eee! Wall-eee!" Someone shouted, "Free the frogs!"

The class was out of control. I don't really know how

many other frogs got their freedom. Mr. Flagg was getting closer. He fumed, he stuttered, but the basic message was, "You have doomed your frog to death! He cannot survive in that environment!"

"As if he would have survived in here, Mr. Flagg," I shot back. "At least this way, he's got a chance." I turned to the class and raised my fist in the air.

"Freedom to the frogs!"

"Yeah, freedom! Freedom! FREEDOM!" Most of the class was standing and chanting, pounding each other on the back. A few simply got up and left. I knew the sweet feeling of liberation. I felt like a revolutionary, but a righteous one, like Moses or Joshua. Apparently, I was not the only one who had less-than-great feelings about Mr. Flagg this year.

Everyone started out through the door, even though the class had just begun. Mr. Flagg didn't even try to get them back in. "Whipple," he snarled. "You'll be seeing Mr. McCloud in the morning. I guarantee it." Then he stomped out of the room, no doubt headed to see the Intimidator and schedule an appointment.

I kept it quiet at home tonight, figuring I'd rather break the news to my parents when I have all the facts. (Read that when I find out how long I will be suspended.) My guess now is about three days, although I may get a week. Around the school, though, it was a different story. Bunches of kids came up to me, most of them people I don't even know, and congratulated me. "That was so cool. Wish I had your guts," was the general theme of their comments. So I'm a folk hero, for now. Funny thing is, I didn't mean to be. All I was trying to do is what I thought was right. That's all. Maybe it was dumb, but it seemed right at the moment. Freedom to the frogs? It sounds silly now.

And now to you, Chester. It is midnight and I am so wired that I may not get any sleep, all because of a frog.

Somehow, I hope you found your way to the marshy area and have a nice little lily pad to sit on. I hope you have a few juicy bugs to chew, and you and some of your pals are enjoying the full moon, all singing in deep bass voices the praises of your liberator and friend.

"Whipple. Whipple. Whipple!"

FRIDAY, APRIL 24

The silver lining to the sordid Chester Affair is that the members of the Posse are no longer on my back about asking out Julie. They recognize my new, higher calling as Representative of the Oppressed (Frogs) Everywhere. Nary a word was spoken to me about Julie today.

Doesn't mean advice wasn't to be had, though. Everyone seemed to have an opinion, from "get yourself a good lawyer" to "let's call the news media" to the one offered by Evan, which basically was, "Don't take no guff. Don't say nuthin'. I'm proud of you, Wimp Pole. Frogs are cool."

Probably the best counsel came from the level-headed Orville. "You're gonna see McCloud? Don't do no fancy talkin'. When you dance with a grizzly, let the grizzly lead. Be a rock, Wally."

First period, sure enough, here comes the note from the office. My math teacher stops talking to us about binomial equations, looks at the note, and says, "Wally, guess you have a date with the front office. Better get down there now."

Dick Dickson, my new ally, looks at me sympathetically. "I heard about the frog. McCloud is going to kill you, Wally. You're dead meat. I'll bring you your homework in jail. Good luck."

I rise slowly, thinking it would be nice to hear my name chanted once more. No luck. My hope was to not meet with Mr. McCloud until near the end of the day, giving me time to think up some kind of strategy and also enjoy being a hero for a few more hours. Guess it will be different. Be a rock, Wally. Be a rock.

I turned the corner in the hallway and was surprised to see Miss Richardson, my Spanish teacher, there. "Hola, Wallace," she said.

"Hola, Señorita Richardson."

"Are we a little glum this morning, Wally?"

"Yeah. We are. On my way to see Mr. McCloud about freeing the frogs in biology class yesterday."

"Hmmm. You were the talk of the teachers' lounge this morning. Frankly, what you did was admirable, I think. Maybe there was a better way of approaching it, but you got your point across. Don't quote me to any other teachers, though." She smiled and winked. It was a wink I'd long remember if I ended up rotting in jail somewhere.

"Uh, thanks, Señorita Richardson. If I'm not in Spanish class, you'll know why."

"Buena suerte, Wally."

"Gracias. I'll need muy bunches of buena suerte."

The head office is painted mostly in grays, which matched my somber mood. The secretary knew all about me. "Wally Whipple? Mr. McCloud is waiting for you." I walked in, my eyes down. I was being humbled by the second.

Then it got worse. Mom was sitting at the corner of the desk.

"Mom?" I said weakly.

"Hello, Wally. I got a call right after you left for seminary this morning."

Mr. McCloud was behind his desk, his chin resting in his hand. "Back again, Whipple. You have a penchant for getting into trouble, it seems." He didn't look happy with me. Of course, he hardly ever looks happy.

"Yes, sir. I'm back."

"Frogs this time?"

"Yes, Mr. McCloud. Frogs. I didn't want to, you know, see my frog killed."

"*Your* frog?" he demanded.

"Well, he seemed like my frog. I mean, you get to play with him for a couple of days and then you sort of get attached to him, like he's a pet or something; then the next thing you know, the teacher is telling you to march up and hand him over."

"Wally, there are better ways to handle it. You could have talked it over with the teacher and maybe worked something out," Mom said, joining forces with Mr. McCloud.

"Listen to your mother, Whipple. She's right. We don't force anyone to do something that violates their conscience in this school. You need to give us a chance to let our system work, Whipple."

"I know that now, Mr. McCloud."

"You sure you weren't being smart? You sure you didn't think it was fun or cute? You sure you weren't trying to do a face job on Mr. Flagg? Be a big man on campus for showing up a teacher who isn't well liked? Are you a little too smart for the faculty members around here, Whipple? Why did you do it? Why?"

I felt like I'd been put in a vise and now Mr. McCloud was tightening it, so much that it was beginning to hurt. No, I wasn't trying to be cute or smart or show anyone up. I liked my frog, Chester. That was it. I didn't want to see Chester put in the bag. So what if I didn't think everything through all the way? Mr. Flagg isn't the kind of teacher who would listen anyway. There are a few around like that. I could feel the eyes of Mr. McCloud drilling through me. Mom was staring too.

"Well, why did you do it, Whipple?" he repeated.

"Because I thought it was the right thing to do," I said, clearly, boldly, and without shame.

Mr. McCloud put his arm down at his side and leaned back in his chair.

"You thought it was the right thing to do," he said. "Hmmmph."

I shot a quick look at Mom. She seemed a little less tense, as she focused on Mr. McCloud.

"Whipple, you amaze me. You've been in here twice, and both times I was ready to toss you out for a few days. But you thought you were doing the right thing."

"Yes, sir."

"Can't get too upset over that, I guess. Isn't that the whole point of an education? Wish we could get every student to try to stand up for what they think is right. You frustrate me, Wally. That's the only answer I guess I would have accepted from you."

He swiveled around in his chair. "Thanks for coming in, Mrs. Whipple. Turns out Wally won't be needing a ride home after all."

Mom stood up. I wasn't sure what to expect.

"Wally. Get out of here. Walk your mother to the car. Then get back to class. Got that?"

"Yes. Sure. You mean, nothing is going to happen to me?"

"Not anything more. Next time you want to do what is right, though, use a little more common sense. Okay?"

"Okay."

"And good luck at the meet today. You're one of the best high jumpers in the state, I hear. Keep up the good work."

"I will."

I'll cut it short here. The rest of the day was pretty darn good. I won the high jump again, although I only cleared 6′2″. Maybe the stress took a little bit out of my legs. Orville, Lumpy, and the other Posse members were pumped by the news that I wasn't suspended, folded, bent, or mutilated.

"Come out without a scratch on your back. Nice work, Wally," Orv congratulated.

So now, let me say only one thing: let my life return to normal, let it return to its normal broadcast, let it be so normal that it will be sweetly boring. Yes, normal is what I want, if I can only figure out exactly what normal is.

Tuesday, April 28

From the Whipple Files:

A. I want to run for another class or student body office. Good for the old college application. Which office, I'm not sure, but I have to decide soon.

B. Mom is making big-time noises about me going to the prom, which is at the end of May. If I have a good date with Julie in early May, it may set the stage for taking her to the prom. In *like*, you've got to set the table just right. Strategy counts.

C. Natalie is pumped because we had a day where it actually reached 69 degrees and was sunny. She got out the baby oil and laid out in the sunshine for an hour after school. "No way, I repeat, *no way* will I ever be under-tanned again," she vowed.

D. Dad and Mom have been having some long talks late at night. Don't quite have the gist of them, because they're being pretty secretive. Maybe they're planning to buy a new car or adopt out Natalie. Ah, there's always hope.

E. Alex Coles asked me again to work on his campaign, the next step on his way to conquering the world before his 34th birthday. I gave him a vague, fluffy answer like, "Yeah, sure, maybe, sort of, Alex."

F. Dick Dickson said he's thinking about running for office. I figure what he really was doing was asking me if I planned to run for sergeant-at-arms for the senior class.

Don't think he wants to run against me, which is good, because just when we're starting to get along, I don't want to end up rivals.

G. Mr. Flagg has not looked at me since the Great Frog Escape last week. I may be lucky to hold a C in there. Will Mr. Scleavege take me back?

H. Evan Trant thinks I am a genius. "Hey, tell me how you got out of McCloud's office without a suspension. Need a few tips for next time I'm in there. Me and him don't get along so good."

I. And last, Chuck and I just happened to drive up to the park near the school to listen to the sounds of nature. In the distance, there was the clear, steady sound of a frog solo, "Whipple . . . Whipple . . . Whipple."

Yes! Chester lives!

CHAPTER 9

May

Life is good. Life is sweet. Life is beautiful. I feel like breaking into song, handing out ten-dollar bills, patting little runny-nosed children on the head. I feel great and good, noble and wise. I may clear seven feet in the high jump tomorrow on the strength of good feelings alone.

And to what do I owe this wonderful, adultlike mood? This euphoria, this state of pleasure, this feeling that my life is one long lick of creamy chocolate ice cream?

To Chester. My frog, my buddy. Because of him, Julie and I are going out a week from Saturday.

The weather was great today. Since it was the day before a track meet, the coaches went into their nice guy mode and we only worked out about an hour. On the spur of the moment, I went over to the park to the miniswamp where I hoped to hear Chester. I understand that it is a little weird to show continued interest in a frog, but Chester has become a symbol. Not just of freedom and doing the right thing, but because I sort of relate to Chester. Believe me, there are times I feel a lot like a little green warty frog.

But I digress. I stood at the edge of the little marshy area, hoping to hear Chester croak my name. Instead, I heard someone else call my name.

I turned, facing back toward the school. It was Julie.

"Oh. Hi, Julie."

"I didn't expect to meet you here," she said. "But I saw you after we got done at tennis practice. What are you doing?"

Problem: How do you tell the person that you may possibly want to spend eternity with that you were stopping by to check up on a frog?

Just then, Chester repaid me for saving his life. "WWWWhhhiiipppplllllee!" he croaked.

I must have looked a little red in the face.

"Wally, are you here to see the frog?"

"Um, uh-huh."

"I think it's wonderful. I think what you did was great. I've heard all about it and the way you stood up to the teacher," she said, with a smile, a real smile, one that had admiration, respect, and perhaps a tinch of *like* in it.

"Well, I don't think it was all *that* wonderful," I mumbled. "A man's got to do what a man's got to do. A woman, too. They've got to do what they've got to do. In fact, we all have to do what we have to do, except some people don't do what they have to do. I guess those are the ones we call slackers and fools."

I thought it almost sounded poetic.

"Wally, nobody makes me laugh the way you do. Slackers and fools! I haven't seen you in the library much lately and I miss that. My morning got off to a better start whenever I talked with you there."

Well, there it was. Almost a rock-solid declaration of everlasting love. I get her mornings off to a good start. Right then, I almost fell on one knee and popped the old question, being careful to make sure that I worked in a mission and college first. I wanted to say, "Just think, Julie, I could get your mornings off to a good start every day if . . ."

Wait though, Wally. You're skipping over the preliminaries, like getting her to go out with you. Marriages based on the love of frogs tend not to last, I think.

"I really like nature, you know, natural things like waterfalls, trees, bananas and other fruits, and also many forms of insect life, except for mosquitoes and flies."

"I love nature, too. I've really enjoyed living in Oregon because it's so beautiful here, even though it rains a lot."

"Yeah. It does rain a lot. But that's why it is so pretty here, too." I felt deep and profound.

I remembered Lumpy's advice about asking Julie out for a nature adventure. Rats! I wasn't wearing a plaid flannel shirt. In fact, I was wearing baggy pants and a tee shirt that advertised a line of hand tools sold where Dad works. But I'd never have a better chance to ask her to take a hike than right now. I felt something close to inspiration well up deep in my soul.

"Julie! Do you want to take a hike?"

She turned and looked at me, not quite sure what I was asking and which galaxy I really came from. "Right now, Wally?"

"Well, no. I mean like later. We could go up to the Columbia Gorge and hike around at some of the waterfalls. They're great at this time of the year."

Julie studied me carefully. At first, I could almost tell what she was thinking, reliving the horror of our first and only date. She looked as though her stomach was mildly upset. She looked as though she'd just been asked to kiss, well, a frog.

And then Chester—dear, sweet, sainted Chester— came to my rescue again. "WWWWHHHHIIIPPPPLLLEEE" he crooned, sending forth a note as sweet and perfectly pitched as Tony Bennett ever did on his best night. (Note: Clean up all the dead flies in your windowsill and scatter them in the marsh tomorrow as a payoff to Chester.)

Julie looked over her shoulder at the little marshy area. "Sounds fine to me, Wally. How can I say no when even nature is calling your name?"

After that, it was just the details. A week from Saturday. We'll go in the morning, have a bit of a picnic, and then I'll send off for plans that tell how to build a log home because Julie will know that it is destiny that we be together.

Do I leap to a conclusion? Of course, but that's the fun of being in *like*.

Tonight, Chuck asked me to read him a story before he turned in. I thumbed quickly through the stack of books on his side of our room and found just the right one.

The Frog Prince.

It seemed to fit.

MONDAY, MAY 5

It's been a few days since I've taken pen in hand and written in the journal. It has been a time of intense reflection and contemplation, as I think about getting my Big Second Chance with Julie, running for school office, thinking about my semigood chance at winning the high jump at the city meet, improving my grades, seeing nuclear disarmament, observing the peril of endangered species, and wondering just exactly when an over-the-counter cure for zits will come on the market.

For the last week, I've been dropping hints here and there to the Posse about my possible candidacy for an as-of-yet-unnamed office, hoping to get some encouragement from my friends. For example, on Friday as we merrily munched on cuisine ranging from creamed beef over toast (hot lunch of the day—Orville actually bought it) to the more traditional double cheeseburger, double order of fries, with about 24 ounces of ketchup dumped on both (my choice), I innocently said, "Guys, I'm thinking about running for office. Anybody want to help on my campaign?" Their reaction was dead silence and complete avoidance of eye contact, which I took as a very good sign, roughly translating their response as one of such overwhelming support that they were rendered inarticulate.

After thinking long and hard, I mean at least ten or twelve minutes, I decided to run for senior class vice president. It is the perfect choice: a step up from sergeant at arms, looks good on the college application, and yet requires very little responsibility, as has been proven by no other than a host of U.S. vice presidents. Also, I checked with the office today and found out that nobody else has decided to run for V.P., which will make my campaign much easier.

Anyway, I made my announcement today at the cafeteria, that well-known gathering spot of rising political stars. "Uh, guys. I have something to tell you. I think I'm going to run for vice president of the senior class. I know I can count on you to help with my campaign and push me over the top."

The only sound was that of food being masticated. "Uh, guys. I said I'm running for vice president. Remember last year? 'Don't be a pickle, vote for Whipple?'"

Orville looked up from his chili dog. "Yep. That's mighty special, Wally."

"So can you help?"

I got a few murmurs, all along the general theme of "Well, yeah, even though I'm sort of busy," but I took them all as ironclad guarantees of loyalty, hard work, and dedication.

So the Whipple Campaign Machine is again greased, oiled, and ready to go.

Vice President Whipple. I can live with that. Totally.

TUESDAY, MAY 6

When I got home from school today, Mom was in the yard, planting some flowers. "Hi, Wally? How did it go today?"

"Great, Mom. Coach Leonard says I'm looking good in the high jump and should peak in about two weeks, just in time for the city meet. Had a test in Spanish and did okay."

"Good. You've got so much to offer, Wally. I was talking to Dorothy Cage and she said the same thing, that you have so many talents."

Uh oh. The bells started ringing in my head. Dorothy Cage is the mother of Bernice Cage, better known as B.C. among her contemporaries. My mom might be taking a run at one of her favorite pastimes: trying to improve her oldest son's slumbering social life.

"I think Bernice is such a nice girl, and the prom is coming up."

My instincts served me well. Bernice *is* a nice girl, as nice as a budding nuclear physicist can be. You see, Bernice is a genius. She is the smartest human being I've ever known. Not that I'm afraid of intelligent women, but remember that I'm the one who thought Kant was a rock musician and have brought home a steady stream of Cs in math this year.

I would bore Bernice. She'd think I was dumb. For kicks, I guess we could figure out baseball batting averages on a date. I'd use a handheld calculator; she would do it all in her head. It would be no contest. Bernice would win. I needed to derail this conversation before the train of my Mother's thought got too far down the tracks.

"Mom, do you think I'm handsome?"

Mom looked up from her gardening. She took off her gloves and looked at me with her large, understanding eyes. "Why, yes. You are a very handsome young man, Wally. Whatever made you ask?"

"I just wanted to know, I guess. I look at myself in the mirror and I can't really tell. Sometimes I think I am, but most of the time I don't."

"Never worry about that, Wally. Never. It's not important anyway."

"Well, I'm going to get something to eat now, Mom."

"Sure, Wally. Help yourself to anything you can find."

I quickly walked into the house, relieved that I'd pulled a rabbit out of the hat and avoided another attempt by Mom to set me up.

I wonder how much longer my luck will hold out.

THURSDAY, MAY 8

Julie was at seminary this morning; when I walked in, she smiled at me. It was not an ordinary smile, but one that fairly shouted, "Wally, you ruggedly handsome man of nature, I am seeing a new and very appealing side of you. I thought you were just a geek, but now realize that the city is not your element. Nature is. I find a man very attractive who is at home among cougars, bears, slugs, and wildebeests." (Note: Check to see if there are any wildebeests in Oregon.)

I still can't believe I have a second chance with Julie. That never happens in dating. One strike and you're out. But here I am, only nine days away from our second date, one that cannot fail. Could it be that there is dating repentance? Sometimes, just maybe, do you get another try? Even though the girl you took out had a miserable time, can all be forgiven so that she remembers it no more? Based on my experience with Julie, the answer, I'd say, is yes. Ah, the wonder of it all: the feeling of controlling your own destiny, sitting on the top of the heap—it feels great. Absolutely great. Except . . .

Except for the tiny part of me that says something isn't quite right. How do I explain this? Let's see. I have everything I need right now. I have a good life. Great parents. Great family. Super friends. A bed to call my own, a roof over my head, food in the cupboard, all the good things of church. Plus, I can dunk a basketball with two hands, and Hamburger Bob's has extended me my own credit line.

Does it get better than that? Maybe not. So why do I not quite feel there unless I think Julie is in *like* with me? Here it comes, in big, bold letters. *Am I being selfish?*

I don't know. On the other hand, though, I don't want to go through life taking whatever is thrown at me. Is it okay to want to be in control, to set high goals, and then go after them? Is Julie a goal?

In the great ocean of life, I do not want to be a bottom feeder. I want to rise to the top, yet at the same time stay nice and be humble. Is that a tough combination or what? I mean, tens of thousands of people in the Book of Mormon couldn't handle it. What makes me think I can?

And how much am I willing to compromise to get what I want to achieve? Where are the lines drawn?

I guess you follow your instincts. Don't get me wrong, I'm in no way thinking that I'll call up Julie and say, "Can we cancel our date? I think I've been too blessed and am worried about getting cocky."

Maybe when I'm older and wiser, I'll have the answers down cold. Twenty-one. Yeah, that sounds about right. When I'm twenty-one, I'll certainly have it all under control.

FRIDAY, MAY 9

After school and before the track meet (our second to the last one of the year, except for the City Meet next week, where I hope to become king of the Portland high school high jumpers), I called a meeting of my campaign committee. Displaying my new political awareness, I mentioned the word *treats* to ensure that my faithful following would show. I realize I might be following some ancient tribal rite about food, bonding, and the hunt, but if it works, so what?

"Ahem. Will the meeting please come to order?" I started off masterfully.

"Where's the food? You promised food," Lumpy immediately wanted to know.

"The food is here," I said, pointing to a large paper bag.

"Food. Now." I turned and saw Evan Trant walking into the room. "Evan. What a surprise," I mumbled. Well, I guess he could help deliver the criminal vote.

"Felton's right, Wimp Pole. Food. Now. Or we don't campaign."

There comes a time when an elected official has to realize that he needs to adjust his position on an issue, and my time was right then. I had hoped to hold the attention of my campaign committee plus Evan long enough to get some commitments from them, then hand out the food as sort of a reward. I read about anthropologists using the same strategies on chimps and it seemed to work pretty well, but these guys aren't chimps—they're less patient.

"Okay guys. Here's the food." I pulled out about three boxes of Twinkies, which Mom had picked up for me at the bakery thrift shop. No matter that they were a little out of date, the Twinkies produced the result I was hoping for.

"Wow. You got us Twinkies," said a reverential Lumpy.

"Nice goin', pard," Orville added.

"I want all of them," Evan declared.

The boxes were passed around. Everyone took a handful of old Twinkies and began pigging out. It was quiet: time to make my pitch.

"Okay, I need at least 200 campaign tags, a dozen posters, a slogan, and I want someone to check and make sure that I'm still the only person running for this office, which will make our job somewhat easier. Now, do I have any volunteers?"

Silence. "Okay. Not everyone at once. Let's see, Orv and Mel, can you do the campaign tags?"

"Sure, Wally. But we have to know the slogan first," the ever-logical Mel said.

"I knew that. I really did. The slogan. As you know, last year we did the highly successful, 'Don't be a pickle, vote for Whipple.' Any ideas for this year?"

"Vote Wimp Pole or Die," Evan answered.

"Nice. Real nice. You know, sort of basic. But we need a little more finesse, Evan."

"How about, 'It's Simple. Vote Whipple,'" suggested Lumpy.

"Don't rhyme," Orv pointed out.

"So?" pouted Lumpy. "Doesn't have to. We didn't rhyme last year and won."

"But it should," I said.

"Why?" asked Evan. "Rhymes are prissy. 'Whipple or We'll Break Your Face.' I like that one a bunch."

"Rhymes are easier to remember," Mel said.

"Maybe we can compromise," I tossed in, hoping to sound wise and insightful, the way politicians try to.

"No way!" Lumpy bristled. "It's like the principle of the thing."

And on it went until it was time for me to get down to the track. In the end, we decided, at least for now, that my campaign slogan would be, "It's Simple. Vote Whi(m)pple," although I did reserve the right to change it over the weekend. My last duty was to assign Lumpy to find out if I had any competition. Then it was off to the locker room.

An hour later, I had won another high jump, going 6'5"

and feeling like I could have done another inch, maybe two. I was sitting on the infield of the track, glorying in my victory, watching some guys warm up for the 800 meters and thinking how good it felt to be done for the day with hardly breaking a sweat.

Then Lumpy walked up to me and broke the sweet feeling of calm with one devastating sentence. "Yo, Lumpster. You look a little torqued. What's up, bud?"

"You've got competition," Lumpy told me. "Julie Sloan is running for vice president, too."

SUNDAY, MAY 11

Finding out that my opponent this year is Julie and not someone like Dick Dickson blew me out of the water. Lumpy almost had to lead me back to the locker room.

"What do I do, Lump? What do I do?"

"Well, you could drop out, which might pick you up a few points for chivalry, but you also might look like a wimp to her. I don't know. You decide."

Upon hearing the news, Orville ambled over to where I was slowly taking off my track shoes. "Sometimes you draw a tough bronc, but you got to go with it. No choice, Wally," he advised. "And Lumpy here's got the right idea about maybe lookin' like a wimp."

I was not convinced. Yesterday I even talked with my mom about it while I was tilling our garden spot and she was getting the seeds ready for planting.

"Mom, let's just suppose that you were running for an office—you know, like mayor or something—and then you found out a friend, someone you really liked was running too, and you know that she, or he, would be good. What should you do?"

"Which of your friends is running against you, Wally?"

Mom asked, removing several layers of fluff with one quick stroke of the knife.

"Uh, it's Julie. You remember Julie?"

"Of course. She's the one who went out with you last year when you had that terrible date. I never did get that enchilada stain out of your shirt."

"Yeah. It's that Julie," I said, feeling a little limp at her recollection of the world's worst date, for which I was totally responsible.

"You kind of like Julie, don't you?" asked Mom.

What could I say? "No, Mom, I don't. She's just another pretty face in the sea of dazzling women in my life"? On the other side of the coin, should I tell Mom that Julie, I hoped, would someday be the one who bore her grandchildren?

It's not pleasant talking to your mother about your love life. Reason seemed to dictate a course somewhere toward the middle.

"Yeah, Mom. I sort of like Julie, although there isn't much between us right now."

"So you're worried that you'll offend Julie if you run against her? And you think enough of her that you don't want to take any chances on harming your relationship?"

Can't fool moms. Trust me on this one, *they know everything.*

"I guess. That's the long and short of it. What should I do?"

Mom didn't hesitate. "Run, Wally. Run for the office. Give it your best. Don't run a negative campaign, don't make it a personal thing, but focus on what you have to offer. If Julie is the kind of girl that I think my son would like, then she won't be offended."

"You make it sound easy," I said, ignoring the fact that Mom used the words *Julie, son,* and *like* in the same sentence.

"It is. Don't let your life be one of could haves and should haves. Go for it, Wally. And take out Julie again. You can't bomb twice in a row with her."

"Well, we are going for a little hike next Saturday—"

"Super. Have a good time. Don't take any enchiladas with you."

"Got it, Mom."

So I guess that's my answer. *Go for it, Wally.* And if Julie and I ever do sort of get together and hit it off, we'll undoubtedly have many other huge challenges in our lives that will make this one look trivial, you know, like who controls the TV remote, whether we drink skim milk or not, and how many children we should have.

Life. I grow philosophical, like Immanuel Kant or Oprah Winfrey, but it seems to me to be a series of challenges. How well you deal with those challenges determines who you are, what you are, where you are, and who controls the TV clicker.

MONDAY, MAY 12

Mom had a lot more on her mind, it turned out, than helping her firstborn child through another of his emotional semicrises. Tonight, after family home evening, Dad dropped the bomb on us.

"I want to tell you kids about something that Mom and I have been talking about for a long time," Dad started. "We've felt a change was needed for a few months now, and we think the time is right to tell you about our plans."

"Are you guys getting divorced or something?" Nat jumped in.

"No, nothing like that. But it will mean some changes in our family."

"Like what?" Chuck wanted to know. "I like our family now."

"So do we. But I think this is going to be best for all of us in the long run," Mom said thoughtfully.

"Here's the situation. I've worked at Aisles of Value for 15 years. I'm 41 years old, and after I wasn't selected for the manager's position last December, I began to think that maybe I need to look for a new profession. I've got about 18 months to go before I could finish my coursework in accounting. That's what I wanted to do when I was in college, but I didn't quite finish my degree." Dad paused for a moment. "Mom and I got married and soon we had a baby on the way. College just didn't work out for me, although Mom got her degree just before you were born, Wally."

As Dad was explaining all this, I was beginning to get the drift. Looked like Dad was headed back to school. He and I might even be college classmates in a couple of years, a thought that didn't exactly send me into cartwheels.

"So I'm going to continue working at Aisles of Value, but as an assistant manager, so that I can go back to school and have enough time for homework."

"Dad, that's totally gross," Natalie spouted. "Like, will we have enough money for, you know, food and clothes?"

"We will, but Mom is also going to start looking for a job. She has a degree in economics and hasn't been able to use it much. We'll be a two-income family for a few years to get us over the hump."

"Is this, like, a midlife crisis, Dad? Wouldn't it be easier to go buy a sports car and let your hair grow out a little?" fussed Natalie.

My thoughts were not much different than Natalie's, which gave me cause for concern. What are you supposed to do when your father may be about to jump into water way over his head? I mean, this guy is our rock. Dependable. Steady. So what if his favorite clothes are made of pure, foreign-made polyester. He's always been there for us and there's nothing he wouldn't do for us. I looked at him. He was a little nervous, which I suppose any good father would be when telling his family about big changes.

And for the first time in my life, he didn't look young to me anymore.

Not that he looked old and grizzly, but a few wrinkles had taken up permanent residence on his face. His hairline was in full retreat too, and he seemed a little bit tired. Suddenly I felt protective. I didn't want him to go back to school with people 20 years younger than he. What if, what if they made fun of him? What if it didn't work out for him? What if he failed? What if he got hurt in some way? He's my dad, and I couldn't let that happen. My whole life he's been there to protect me.

Another first-in-my-life then happened. I felt the son becoming the father.

But, he also had a look in his eyes, a look that told me he was excited, that he really wanted to do this, although he was anxious about it. He didn't say anything for a few seconds, just sat there, a funny expression on his face.

There he was, the guy who wrestled with me on the floor and always let me win. There he was, the guy who sat through a thousand of my Little League games, and no matter how I'd done, always told me I'd played well. There he was, the guy who coached my nine-year-old soccer team to a perfect record, even though he knew nothing about soccer and became the coach only because no other parent would. There he was, the guy who had helped me build Pinewood Derby cars, read bedtime stories to me until I was thirteen, and still came up every night and gave me a kiss before I fell asleep. There he was, the guy who let me borrow his socks and best neckties and pretended not to notice whenever I used some of his aftershave. There he was, the guy who served three stake missions and never grumbled, gave us blessings every September before the school year started, and hardly ever missed a school talent show or a parent-teacher conference. There he was, the guy who got up and went to work at a job he didn't particularly like, just so he could keep a roof over our heads, clothes on our backs, food on our table. There he was, the guy who still got the car door for Mom and walked on the outside of the sidewalk with her.

And I knew he loved us more than anything else on the earth.

I looked at him and knew that my biggest hero wasn't someone who ever hit a three-point shot in the NBA, played in a good band, or even presided over a meeting at church. I knew then that my hero was the guy who sat across the dinner table every night, asked us about our day, and seemed happiest when we were all there together.

"Dad . . ." I said, and my eyes stung and my throat felt thick, and I knew that I would never want to disappoint him in any way. "Dad . . ." He looked up at me, the same kind expression that I'd seen before a million times and yet never understood until that very moment. "I think it's great. I know you'll do super. I'm with you, Dad, all the way."

He smiled, his shoulders sagged a little, in relief.

"Thank you, son. Thank you."

"Go for it, Dad. Seriously. We'll get the sports car later," Nat said, coming through in the pinch.

"You'll get good grades in school, Dad," said Chuck. "I can help you with homework."

That's the news out of the brown house on Craig Street tonight. Dad is about to begin a new career. Mom too.

I want them both to succeed.

TUESDAY, MAY 14

Wiped out tonight. I'll jot a few lines and then nose dive into bed.

Dick Dickson is going to run for senior class sergeant at arms. He told me in math class today. "I've got to fatten up the college application. I need the scholarship money, Wally. Grades and the computer club aren't enough."

"Can I wear one of your tags, Dick?"

"Yeah. I'd like that."

So I'm on the campaign team of my archrival from last year. Life can bend you 180 degrees before you know it.

Call it a reckless impulse, but I walked down the shop wing today. Evan was hanging out, which I sort of expected. After exchanging slugs on the shoulder, which is Evan's quaint method of saying hello, he looked at me and said, "I like my apartment, Wimp Pole. You were wrong about getting back with my dad. You were wrong, so don't think you and the other brothers got all the answers all the time."

"Never said we did, Evan. I guess whatever works for you."

Then there was Nat. I saw her gathering up some of her clothes and putting them in a large shopping bag, then she slipped out of the house. They were nice clothes, too. I couldn't figure it out, until I asked Mom about it.

"Well, I don't think she wanted anyone to know, but she is giving some of her clothes away to one of the other Mia Maids. Clarissa Staples. Brother Staples has been out of work for almost a year. You know Wally, Natalie does have a soft heart."

I guess she does.

Chuck and I talked a little tonight. He told me how much he misses seeing Dale Murphy's name in the sports page anymore. Chuck and I both agree that Dale Murphy was about the best guy ever to play baseball, and we miss seeing how he did in the box scores.

"But he lived in Portland for a long time, so maybe he'll do a fireside or something on a visit," I reassured Chuck. "If he does, I'll sneak you in."

"Okay, Wally."

Mom and Dad are pumped about him going back to school. I even heard Dad mention something about getting some new clothes for school. He'd better not take Nat shopping with him, or he'll blow all his tuition money before he knows it, although he would look good.

Big date with Julie on Saturday; last regular track meet on Friday. This is going to be some week for Wally Whipple.

I wish I could know now what I'll be writing in my journal in another seven days.

THURSDAY, MAY 16

Julie missed seminary on Monday and Tuesday, and I missed yesterday, although I must say with some pride that it was my first unexcused absence (i.e., I slept in) this year. Both of us were in class today and I wondered what exactly would happen. The possibilities in my mind were:

1. She would say, "Our date is off, Wally. I don't go out with political rivals. I think you are an insensitive lout and hope you grow a pimple the size of a daffodil on the day you have to give your campaign speech."

This option, I think, is not likely.

2. She doesn't mention anything. I am not even worth a blip on her radar screen.

A more likely scenario. She knows that she will probably trounce me, and to avoid embarrassment decides to pretend the whole situation doesn't exist. "Oh, Wally

Whipple? Is he the only person running against me? I was actually hoping for more competition," she might yawn to her knot of friends. If this is the case, I would rather that option #1 occur.

3. She'll smile and say something like, "Well, Wally, looks like we're rivals! Next time, we'll have to check with each other first."

That's the way it turned out. When I dragged into seminary in the middle of the night (okay, at 6:30 A.M. and the sun was up), Julie was already there, wearing one of her campaign tags, which were not in the shape of a pickle. She looked at me and said, "I guess I can't vote for you Wally, but there is only one reason why I wouldn't. We need to promise not to talk politics on Saturday, okay?"

I agreed, much relieved. In fact, I took it as a very good sign that she made sure to reconfirm our date when she first saw me.

But why should I be surprised? People in *like* overcome much more than mere politics to make successful lives with one another, obstacles such as hectic travel and work schedules, in-laws, dual careers, and major church callings.

Julie and I can overcome.

FRIDAY, MAY 17

Yes, I won the high jump, clearing 6'5 ¾", my personal record and second best in the city this year. Coach Leonard is as happy as a frog in mud. (No offense, Chester.) "You will be the champion this year. You can take that guy from Grant High, Wally. If you keep it up, you're a shoo-in for a track scholarship next year."

It felt so good to hear him say that that I hummed Sinatra and Bennett all the way home.

Yet this is not the big news in my life. Tomorrow is Saturday, the time in history when I reverse my previous heretofore disastrous relationship with Julie, when I show her the man I am, one of true grit, rolled oats, weathered leather, a regular wilderness warrior. I have checked with my Scout book and feel comfortable that I can identify most of the major trees and plants, with special notice paid to poison oak. "Stop! Don't touch that! It's poisonous!" I'll shout to Julie, who will look up to me with eyes brimming in gratitude for saving her from an outbreak of red, itchy skin.

On the advice of Lumpy, I dressed for the part today. Wore my wool shirt, wool pants and yuppie hiking boots to school, even though it was clear and in the upper 70s. "You want to have an aura about you. One that shouts to Julie, 'I am a man of sweat and dirt, at ease with the elements because so many of them are on me,'" Lumpy said. I spent part of last night at Aisles of Value at the fragrance counter, searching for a new scent to splash on. I found it—Pine Breeze Aftershave—and then, joy of joys, I got really lucky and found some deodorant with a scent named Rain Forest. Blew five bucks on both of them, but then, my aura alone might set the stage. She'll think she's somewhere deep in the woods as soon as I get her into the car.

This time, no mistakes. It's *going to work*. I can hardly wait for tomorrow. And every time I think about it and the intricate details that I've planned for our outing—right down to the aluminum foil dinner and sharing the same water canteen—I can feel a turning point in my life coming right at me. Let it all begin!

SATURDAY, MAY 14

I am in pain, anguish, sorrow, and deep humility. My social life is a mess, my life may be over, and Julie will never talk to me again.

My day didn't exactly unfold the way I had envisioned. In fact, it didn't even come close. Remember all that confidence I had about never having a date with Julie as bad as last year's? Remember how I figured it couldn't get any worse?

Well, I was wrong. Today was worse, proving that everything is possible with Wally Whipple. I am a walking, talking, living, breathing example of Murphy's Law.

What went wrong? Oh, just about everything, that's what. Start with the weather.

Somewhere over the Pacific Ocean about a month ago, a bunch of clouds were hanging out and getting bored and said, "Hey, let's form a pack, swirl around in a counter-clockwise rotation, make a little rain, then smash ashore in Oregon just in time to wreck Wally's date. Great idea, huh?"

It was raining hard this morning. The tapping—no, make that the pelting—began about six, and I laid on my bed getting extremely tense. Rain. Yesterday was so beautiful. Why did it have to rain today? Do I call off the date?

No. I had waited a year for my chance at redemption with Julie. I'd had a good date in the rain a few short weeks ago with Ed. This is Oregon, where it doesn't come as a big surprise when it rains. Wilderness guys aren't supposed to let a little wet get in their way. The date had to go on.

I got up, showered and shaved, and threw about a half pint of my pine aftershave on. Then I dressed in wools and plaid, and for special effect strapped my Boy Scout knife on my belt. I started preparing for the hike, taking a break about every three minutes to check for a shaft of sunlight breaking through the clouds. No luck. I put together the aluminum foil dinner—cut the carrots, sliced up the potatoes, stuck a hunk of meat in, and doused it all liberally with salt and pepper. As a backup, I stuck some cold pizza in a plastic bag and tossed it into my backpack, along with two cans of root beer. A true wilderness gourmet, that's Wally Whipple.

It was about 9:30, and Natalie groggily made her way downstairs and into the kitchen. "What are you doing, Wally?"

"I'm getting ready for the hike with Julie. It's sort of a date."

Nat's eyes snapped wide open. "Wally, I don't mean to, like, crush your feeble plans, but did anyone tell you it's raining outside? It's, like, a total hurricane. Seriously."

"Gee, thanks, Nat, I never would have noticed," I said sarcastically. "But we're still going out. It's a guy thing. You wouldn't understand."

She looked at me for about ten seconds and didn't say anything. Then she spoke very slowly. "You're right. I wouldn't understand. Wally, you're really stupid."

I turned to the backpack, making sure to throw in some matches. The phone rang and Natalie picked it up.

"Yeah, he's here. All dressed up in plaid. Something about a guy thing that I wouldn't understand. Wally, it's Julie."

I shot her a look that was not exactly charity filled as I took the phone.

"Wally, this is Julie. It's raining pretty hard outside."

I admit that when Natalie said almost the same thing, my reaction was firm, harsh, and masculine, but hearing it from Julie was different. Wilderness guys can be sensitive.

"No problem, Julie. Think I've got everything covered. Just dress warm and wear some rain gear," I advised, peering at Natalie, who sat across the kitchen from me with a blank stare. "We'll still have a great time. I am at home in rain or shine, in the forest or out of the forest. The elements do not phase me, and I do not want you to worry," I rambled. "Besides, I am an Eagle Scout and can take care of myself and yourself, too."

"Well, okay, Wally. See you in an hour."

I hung up. "See, Julie is a woman of true grit, Nat. She is looking forward to our hike in the rain. She is the kind who could give birth in a log cabin, with little more than a twig in her mouth, and still cook a nice rabbit stew for dinner that night. You need to be more like Julie."

Nat again stared at me. "Wally, you're really nuts. Not even Grizzly Adams would go outside on a day like today. I'm going back to bed."

"Ha! You prove my point exactly. You are soft, Natalie. Very soft. If you were asked to walk back to Missouri, you wouldn't make it three blocks."

She shrugged. "Yeah, sure. You're right, Wally. Let me know how it goes. And you smell like a tree. Seriously." Then she left. I felt that for once I had actually triumphed in an encounter with my sister.

Mom and Dad weren't around. They had left for the temple early in the morning. Chuck was in the family room watching the Saturday morning lineup. I got out my raincoat and started piling stuff into the station wagon.

"It's raining, Wally. Really hard." Chuck stood behind me.

"I know, Chuck. But you can't let a little rain stop you."

"Wally, that's not a little rain. That's a lot of rain."

"It'll be okay, bud. I can handle myself out of doors."

"Well, okay, but it seems kind of dumb to me to go outside when it's raining. You'll get wet and then catch a cold. That's what Mom says. She always says you should come out of the rain, so why should you go out into it? And you smell like a tree."

"Chuck, go watch Bugs Bunny. I know what I'm doing."

My last interrogation completed, I headed toward the car, beginning to feel free at last. I started the engine, my jaw set in grim determination. I was going to have my date with Julie no matter what. I'll show them all!

I drove slowly to Julie's, the windshield wipers on high, squinting. Chuck and Natalie, I had to admit, were right. Noah would have felt smug in this weather.

I got to Julie's house—okay, time to pull it all together, Whipple. I plastered a cheerful look on my face, and, if it can be described in such a way, optimistically walked up to her front door, my stride confident and bouncy.

It is also important to note that I got soaked between the car and her front door.

I knocked and Julie answered. At least I thought it was Julie. She was encased in some kind of light green tarp, it appeared, with a plastic hat on that looked like it could have come straight from the head of the Ancient Mariner. "I know I don't look very good, Wally, but this is some of my Dad's gear for when he fishes in the rain. He told me I should wear it. Are you sure you want to go?"

My confidence fluttered. Then I thought of how silly I'd look in front of Nat and Chuck if I came back and had to admit that they were right, it was raining too hard for a hike. Fierce pride welled up inside of me, something like that which led to the downfall of several dozen Nephite societies, I suppose.

"Let's go for it, Julie. We can always turn around if we're not having much fun." Or if we're drowning, I thought. "And you look great."

She hesitated. "Okay, Wally." And we both waddled to the car, our rain gear rustling and scraping.

We drove out to the freeway, splashing through standing water. I really had to concentrate, and so probably

wasn't exactly the best conversationalist. I did bring up
school, my ex-frog Chester, seminary, even Joe Vermeer
and Orville, in an attempt to get our minds off the monsoon raging outside. But Julie didn't seem to want to talk
much. She just stared at the low, jumbo clouds that
seemed to smother the earth as we got closer to the Columbia Gorge. Nothing was working.

I took the exit that led to the old highway that winds
around a bunch of really beautiful waterfalls. In my plan,
this was the mood setter. Julie was supposed to be gasping
with delight and wonder. "Oh, my, Wally. How beautiful!
How gorgeous! I feel so in tune with nature—and with
you. What a great idea for a date!"

Instead, grim silence. Dead air space. We couldn't even
see the waterfalls because it was so cloudy and dark. I
should have turned around.

"We're here Julie. You've got to trust me on this, but
there are some really cool waterfalls about a half-mile up
from here. We need to, uh, get out now and start hiking."

She looked outside and sighed. "Okay . . ." and the way
she said it was probably about the way some people said
okay when they were told it was time to leave Nauvoo and
head west.

I hopped out and got my backpack with all the food in
it. Julie edged out slowly, shivered, and pulled her Ancient
Mariner hat down over her ears.

"Trail's up this way," I said, and we started up through
the ferns, trees, and moss. Not ten steps into what was
supposed to be Our Hike of Magic, Our Trail to Eternity,
Our Blissful Path to the Temple, Julie suddenly drew in
her breath and squeaked, "Oh, yuck!" There on the trail
was the biggest, slimiest, ugliest slug I'd ever seen, ten
inches long at least, lying in its own trail of ooze.

"It's a slug, Julie. Very common to Oregon. The pioneers, I understand, used them as a source of food and en-

tertainment, since if you put salt on them, they tend to dry up."

"Oh. How nice to know, Wally," she murmured.

The wind howled, the rain bashed into us, stinging. The footing was slippery. "At least we're the only ones up here today," I called out over the squall.

"I'm sure we are," she said grimly, gazing straight ahead.

We tromped ahead for about ten minutes, then came to the first waterfall, called Pony Tail Falls. Julie looked at it and shuddered. "Very nice, Wally."

Very nice? A marvel of nature and all she could say was "very nice"? That's what you say when your Aunt Ginger sends pajamas for the tenth straight year on your birthday. This was when I had planned to take her hand and lead her close to the waterfall, and there, if everything worked out, and she looked at me and I looked at her, and as the scriptures put it, she drew her lips unto mine, that I was going to relent and plant a smacker right on her mouth. But no way. She was shivering again.

Great! My big romantic moment and Julie was showing the first signs of hypothermia.

"Maybe we should get something to eat," I suggested. "Let's go over underneath those large Douglas fir trees, named for the Scottish botanist David Douglas, who sort of discovered them, and we can start a fire and cook our meal."

Julie nodded, the water cascading off her rain slicker and hat. My rain gear wasn't up to the day either, and I was beginning to feel damp from head to toes. We walked over to the spot underneath the trees, but everything was soaked there, too. I tried to find some twigs or fir needles to start a fire, but it was useless. I might as well have been trying to light wet paper towels on fire.

"Guess this isn't going to work, Julie. But never fear, Whipple is always prepared. It's sort of a law of the wilderness, never go unprepared. It's a Boy Scout deal, too, you know, always being prepared." I gave her my most ruggedly handsome grin, hoping that it would, at least symbolically, melt the clouds away. Didn't work. Julie only sniffled. It began to rain even harder. She sneezed. I pulled out the cold pizza and root beer. "Tah-dah! A gourmet meal, right here in the great outdoors, prepared by Chef Wallace!"

She looked at the cold pizza and smiled slightly. "Wally, I'm not really that hungry. Is it okay if I don't eat right now?"

Oh, man! I'd struck out on hiking, now I'd whiffed on the food. There wasn't much else left to do. The wilderness warrior in me turned to wilderness wimp.

"In fact, Wally, I'm really not feeling that well. Maybe we could go back to the car and go home? Maybe we could come back here some other time, when it isn't raining so hard."

"Uh, right. Yeah. I was just thinking the same thing. Honest."

I felt relieved and disappointed at the same time, but packed up the food and stood. We began the miserable march down the hill, barely speaking a word to each other. The trail was muddy, and we had to watch our footing each step. Our friend the slug was still in place, and he seemed to be smiling at us. Curses! I wish I had some salt to throw on him. The only sound was the squishing of water in our boots and the rain splashing on our coats.

This can't get worse. This is the pits. This at least ties my own personal world record for the world's biggest social flop—and with Julie. Again! Face it, Whipple, you aren't the man of her dreams. Nightmares, possibly. Dreams, no way.

We got to the car and I threw my backpack in. I opened the door for Julie.

"Wally?"

Well, at least she still was calling me by name and acknowledging my existence.

"I think we have a flat tire."

Oh, no! A flat tire! The old family station wagon had done it to me again!

I glanced at the tire. "Hmm. Yes. Right you are, Julie, a flat tire. That happens when all the air goes out of it. I guess that means I need to change it."

"Yes, Wally. You can't drive on a flat tire."

"Okay. No problem. Flat tires are a specialty of mine."

Big lie. Truth of it is—and this is hard for me to admit, because it is a guy thing—but I don't know how to change a flat tire. Never have tried. Never had the chance. Never wanted the chance.

"Well, let's see. You start with the other tire, first."

"You mean the spare?"

"Right. The spare. Which is what you use to replace the tire with no air in it."

"The flat," said Julie, as she shivered.

"Yes, the flat. I already said that. Now I need to get the doohickey that you lift the car up with."

"The jack."

"Yes. The jack. It's in the back."

I went around to the back end of the station wagon and found the spare and the jack. The jack may as well have been an object discarded from a rocket booster, because I didn't have a clue how or where it fit, how it worked, or even which end was up.

The last realization proved to be my near-fatal mistake.

I mustered up the best job of faking confidence that I've ever done in my life and pulled the pieces of the jack toward the right front wheel. I smiled at Julie and gave her a thumbs up, the wind howling and the rain pounding my back. Julie climbed out of the car, with a look on her face that seemed to say, "I'd rather be slurping a household cleansing product than standing here," and stood close by me.

"I can't stay in the car while you're using the jack. It's unsafe," Julie sighed.

"Okay here . . . let's see . . ." I mumbled. There is something about all men everywhere that causes them to instantly mumble when they are confounded by a mechanical problem. How many times have I heard my father, for instance, say something like "Meresd mmm glllllbbbb er dddweeellbe" when he was trying to figure out a home or car repair? Maybe it is on the x chromosome and we just can't get around it, because I definitely went into full mumble mode. "Mmmirrtt em mmemm numble," I mumbled.

"Wally?"

"Rrttteeerr wheeellll—"

"I think you have—"

"Unnnn llliffff up en errr—"

". . . the jack on upside-down."

I looked at the jack. What could I say? She was right.

"Oh."

I turned the jack over and then disaster reared its ugly head. The arm of the jack, or whatever you call it, slid off the stick part of the jack and came rumbling down and crashed into my left foot with a sickening thud.

A flash of white-hot pain shot through my entire left leg. It hurt as nothing else hurt before; I thought I heard a crack and felt a pop. Color drained out of my face, I began to feel woozy and crumpled in a heap on the edge of the pavement.

"Oh, Wally! Are you hurt?" Julie sounded alarmed.

"No, I mean, yeah. I think my foot is broken."

The city meet! I was going to be the city high jump

champ! How could I compete now? I couldn't even jump over the curb!

But I had more immediate challenges, like how do I get the tire changed and get to the emergency room.

"Let me have the jack," Julie demanded.

"Yeah, sure. Be careful. It's a killer." I leaned back, closed my eyes and just let the rain splash on my face. I wanted to be anywhere besides where I was, be with anyone but Julie. Why? Why me? Why now?

I glanced at Julie. She was reaching for the gizmo to take off the tire lug nuts. Like an expert grease monkey, she grunted and twirled off the lug nuts, then placed the jack under the front fender and hoisted up the car. She ripped off the flat and with a mighty heave put on the spare tire.

I was amazed. What a woman!

"Daddy taught me how to do this. He said I might need to know how to change a tire sometime. I guess he was right."

I put my head back down on the pavement, feeling slightly better since at least I knew how I'd be getting back to town.

"Okay, Wally. Into the car. Do you need anything else?"

"Well, could you reach into my backpack and get some cold pizza? And . . . could you get me a twig to chew on?" I winced.

"I'll need a knife, Wally. Do you have one?"

"Yeah." I fumbled around and got my Boy Scout knife off my belt. Julie disappeared for a couple of minutes and then came back with a freshly whittled piece of wood.

"Here, put this in your mouth. You'd better get back into the car now. I'll get you the pizza in a minute."

I lifted myself up slowly. My foot was throbbing. It felt like someone had plunged a knife into it. "Can I just sort of lie down in the back?"

"Go ahead, Wally. I need the keys."

"Sure." I gladly surrendered my keys. The trip was a blur. I spent much of it with my eyes closed. Occasionally I opened my eyes only to see the flat gray clouds through the car windows. I felt hurt, dumb, humbled, and empty all at the same time.

Our arrival at my driveway reminded me of an old Western movie in which a woman in calico sees a wounded cowboy coming in all hunched over his horse. "He's hurt!" the heroine always yells, just before tearing up petticoats for bandages and boiling water.

Julie went to the front door as I hobbled up. "Oh, hi, Sister Whipple. Wally's had an accident, and I think he needs to go to the doctor." Mom, Nat, and Chuck came running out to the car.

"Oh, Wally," Mom said sympathetically.

"It's broken, Mom. I'm sure of it," I glumly told her.

"You biffed it again, seriously," Natalie keenly observed. She was right—I had biffed it big time.

I don't really feel like going into the rest of the details. Let's just say we got home okay, Mom ran me to the clinic, and Dr. Pratt, who happened to be on duty that day, read the X rays and solemnly said, "Your foot is broken. That bone right there. Too early to say if you need surgery, Wally. We should know in a few days."

Somewhere along the way, Julie slipped away quietly, after wishing me a quick recovery. I think she went into our house and called her dad and he came to get her. But I was in so much pain that I really didn't worry much.

"Sorry, Julie. Really sorry that we had such a rotten time," I groaned.

"It's okay, Wally. We'll go out again, I promise. Just get to feeling better, okay?"

"Yeah, I will."

But right now, recovery seems like a long way off. I

can't believe that I messed up again with Julie. Will I ever get it right?

At this point in my life, I have some major doubts.

SUNDAY, MAY 15

I slept. I slept so long that my family all got up and went to church without me, except for loyal Chuck, who volunteered to stay behind and keep an eye on his older brother. About 10:00, I arose for a few minutes, checked in with Chuck, then immediately fell back into bed—the victim of heavy pain medication, rotten luck, and a life gone sour.

It was a little after lunch when I woke again, the curtains pulled. Outside, it was still dark and gray, so there was little light in my room. Downstairs, Mom and Nat were in the kitchen, and I got the impression that Sunday dinner was being prepared.

I let out a long sigh and for the thousandth time asked myself the one-word question with no answer: Why?

Maybe I said it aloud, because I noticed for the first time someone was in the room.

"Howdy, Wallace. You look mighty rough."

It was Orville. "Came by to see you, and your mom talked me into stayin' for supper."

"Yeah. I suppose I do look bad. Can you believe how I blew it, Orv? Have you heard what went on yesterday? Man, my foot is sore."

"Sure did, pard. Mighty sorry. Must feel like the grasshopper that jumps into the ant pile. You do have a way of puttin' honey on your feet in the middle of bear camp."

"It's a talent, Orv." I sat up and made a face because of the pain in my left foot.

"Sorry, Wally. Really and truly. I feel sorry. I know how much you was lookin' forward to the city meet, and I know that you wanted to have a good time with Julie."

"I even thought of asking her to the prom, if everything went great yesterday. Now it seems really stupid. Maybe Julie's not my kind of girl, and this is the way I'm being told about it. This could be a message from heaven."

"She's nice and purty and all," Orv said. "But I wouldn't go writin' her off yet."

"Man, how could I top this disaster though? She won't get within a mile of me again."

"Maybe she's got more gravel than you give her credit for."

"Yeah, she's probably got more gravel than I ever will."

Orville frowned. "Wally, you keep underestimatin' yourself. You got a lot going for you. And you're tough. Tough as wet leather that's been in the sun for too long."

Wally Whipple, tough? Normally, Orv has great judgment, but . . . "Orv, I just made a fool of myself trying to be some kind of outdoors guy. It was, you know, immature. I'm all marshmallow—"

"Wally, you *ain't!*" Orv was more firm than I'd ever heard him.

"Like how?"

"You hung in there with me and got me baptized. That's steady. You poke along with Evan, and he scares half the guys on the wrasslin' team. You treat everyone good. You never really liked that little feller Dick Dickson, but you turned him into a friend. And you're tough enough to sing a Christmas carol to an old lady in a nursin' home. You think anyone else would do that? Anyone?"

Suddenly, I knew I had to ask Orv a question. It was a question that only he could answer. It meant so much. I couldn't believe how I was feeling inside: call it a moment of truth, like when you hold up a mirror and see not only someone looking back at you, but you also see who you are. My stomach churned; I seemed a little dizzy. I propped myself up in bed, looking into Orv's serious face. I thought of all the ups and downs I'd had the last two years—the times that I'd been on top of the world, the times when I felt like dust. I thought of the thousand things each day that seemed to tell me that I wasn't good enough in some way, didn't meet someone's silent expectations, didn't measure up. I thought of how I felt battling back those feelings, how I was happiest when I was with my friends, at church, and, most of all, in my home. I thought of how much I wanted to simply be someone who people liked and maybe even respected. And I also felt so very tired and drained of all the energy it took to go out and fight the everyday battles of confidence and worth. Now, I needed to know the answer to just one simple question.

"Orv, am I a rock or am I dirt clod?"

A grin flashed across his cowboy face as he rubbed his hands across the front of his Montana tuxedo. He twitched his bolo tie, let out a big whoosh of air, and said, "Wally, you're a rock. All the way. All the time. Ain't no doubt, pardner."

And me, Wally Whipple, the Rock, got embarrassed when my eyes watered. I didn't want to be a dirt clod. Maybe I'm not a dirt clod. Maybe I never have and never will be.

It felt so good to be a rock.

MONDAY, MAY 15

My alarm went off this morning and I dragged myself downstairs. Dad was there, fixing me breakfast.

"How do you feel, Wally?"

"Tired. Not very good. Dad, can I stay at home today?"

Normally when I ask either of my parents if I can stay home from school, they react as if I'd asked to get a nose ring. But Dad only asked one question. "Any tests that you'll miss?"

"None."

"Sounds okay to me, then. You've been through a lot, and we still have to get you fitted with some crutches. Why don't you head upstairs after breakfast?"

That's what I did. A couple of hours later, Mr. Leonard was on the phone with me.

"Wally. Are the rumors true? Did you break your foot?"

"Yeah, coach. I did. Sorry. It was really bad timing."

"Yes, it was. I wish we had you for the city meet this week, but the most important thing for you is to get better. Listen to your doctor and follow his advice."

"I will, coach."

"Good. You have the heart of a champion, Wally."

"Thanks. And I have one year left of track. Mr. Leonard, I'm going to give it my best next year. I'll be back. No one will outwork me."

"I know you will, Wally. I believe in you. Can you come to the city meet? It might give the team a boost."

"I'll be there," I said, which is what you would expect of a rock.

Other good things happened. Dick Dickson was at our door with my math homework as soon as school was over. Chuck brought me some drawings from school today, cool pictures showing me jumping over the moon. Sister Lawson dropped off brownies, which lasted about three minutes. Brother Hansen called, Bishop Winegar called, and Lumpy, Mel, Mickey, and Orv stopped by. Nancy Smisore, Vanessa Peterson, and Amy Hassett stopped by with more goodies. I may put on ten pounds before all this is over.

And the funny thing is, every one of them had the same message: We're sorry, Wally; you're a great guy,

Wally; get better soon, and you're a rock, Wally. Orv obviously had been doing some talking around school.

It's strange to think that breaking my foot might have been the best thing possible for my confidence, but that's the way it's working out.

Natalie got in the act too. She paid a visit just before dinner.

"As you know, Wally, I am like a genius at math; like, I'm never wrong and will probably go to MTI or MIT or TIM or whatever that place is because I'm so smart in math, and so you can tell, seriously, when I say that I did some totally awesome calculations and figured that you would have, seriously, high jumped 11 feet 7 inches at the city meet, and you would have blown away everyone and been on the front pages of major magazines," Natalie told me. "Oh, yeah. And you're a rock, Wally. A real rock. And I'm not going to tell you who told me to say that to you other than he's a hunk and rides a horse and do you still know if Orville has any girl friends? Hope you feel better soon. Have your people get in touch with my people if you need anything and we'll do lunch. I have to go call Lindy now. Tah-tah, Wally."

"Nat," I spoke slowly. "I love you, very much. Seriously."

"Gross, Wally!" she squealed, fleeing the room.

It felt great to laugh.

For now, the pain in my foot is subsiding. Dad picked up some crutches at Aisles of Value today, and I've practiced with them a little; should be gimping around the halls at Benjamin Franklin tomorrow.

The pain is less in other ways too. Tonight, I'm ready to fall asleep, and I'll do so not feeling the agony of having blown my date with Julie or being quite so miserable not to compete in the city meet this week. Instead, I'll lie down, close my eyes, and feel the sweet sensations of knowing that I have friends, lots of friends, who are with me no matter what.

What more can I ask?

TUESDAY, MAY 17

I made my triumphant return to school today. At least 50 times, I had to explain how I broke my foot. I wanted to say something like it happened while rappelling down a cliff, or that I broke it bodysurfing over a waterfall, but stuck with the truth. "A car jack fell on it." Nothing romantic or heroic about that.

My teachers took it easy on me, proving that they do have hearts. Mr. Flagg even showed some sympathy, telling me to keep up on my homework as best I could. "You can show me how tough you are, what you are really made of, Whipple. There's more to you than having a soft spot for frogs, I hope."

And weird old Mr. Scleavege, my ex-metal shop teacher, rambled his way down the hallway, stopped, and looked at me: "Whiffle! Broke your foot? Skip the doctor. Just stop by the shop wing, and we'll weld it all together for you! Lot cheaper and the guys will sure get a charge out of it!" Then he bounced on down the hallway, giggling.

Miss Richardson looked at me with her big brown eyes and murmured something very thoughtful in Spanish, the rough translation of which I think is, "Poor Señor Whipple! Your pain is my pain, and I wish you a fast recovery aided by the consumption of many tacos!"

Mr. Ashbury, the choir teacher, made sure that a broken foot wouldn't keep me out of the year-end concert in a couple of weeks. "You're one of the best tenors we have. And contrary to popular belief, tenors are not expendable!"

So it went. Dick helped me in math, my journalism teacher mentioned something about maybe getting an editor's position next fall, Lumpy hoped to cash in on the sympathy vote in the elections next week ("Face it, Wally, we need all the help we can get; I think we'll be creamed by Julie"), and when we had our school assembly to name the Man of the Year and Woman of the Year, I got a reserved seat right up front. I was answering so many questions about my foot that I hardly noticed that Craig Connor and Karen Nally got the awards, which is good, because they're both nice and super talented, and they're off to Stanford or Harvard or Duke or Yale to become neurosurgeons or nuclear physicists, I'm sure.

Pleasantly the day glided by, although I had a hard time navigating some of the hallways. When my last class was over, I sat awhile, letting the traffic clear. I grabbed my crutches and hobbled away toward where Mom said she would pick me up. She wasn't there, so I stood in front of the school by myself, until I heard the by-now-familiar roar of Evan's Harley headed in my direction. He pulled up fast, then jammed on his brakes, stopping right in front of me, leaving rubber on the road.

"Wimp Pole. Heard you busted up your foot. Smooth, pal."

"Yeah, I specialize in smooth, Evan."

"Got some news for you, Wimp Pole."

"What's that?"

"I been thinkin' a lot about what you said about me and my old man and goin' home to live. First thing, I thought, Wimp Pole's a fool. He don't know what it's like, because he lives with Ozzie and Harriet and his little brother and his babe sister."

"Maybe you're right. I do have it pretty lucky."

Evan scowled. "Naw. Don't talk yourself down. I told you that all the brothers were wrong, and I could do just fine on my own. Maybe I can, Wimp Pole, but I decided that maybe I missed my old man and my mom more than I was lettin' on. And I didn't like workin' all the time and eating chili out of cans and paying utility bills. Never knew what a utility bill was, Wimp Pole, until I got one. It's like electricity. You got to pay for electricity. See what I'm sayin'?"

"I think so, Evan."

"So I ain't sayin' I'm wrong, just that I changed my mind. You told me I was smart, Wimp Pole. I liked that. Most people think I'm dumb."

"You aren't. You know that."

Evan rested on his Harley and smiled happily. The wind kicked up and blew his Raiders cap off. The sun felt so good, the air sweet with the new springtime flowers.

"Anyway, Wimp Pole, I moved back in Sunday. With my family. Think this time we'll be okay. Think we're all more, you know, wiser. Thought you'd want to know."

"Yeah, that's something I'd want to know. You made a good choice, Evan."

He started up his Harley. He grinned wickedly as he gunned it, drowning out every other earthly sound. Then he throttled back a little.

A crazy thought entered my head, but I was sort of on a streak anyway, so why not? "Evan," I shouted over the engine. "You want to take the missionary lessons? You know, then you could become a brother too."

He looked at me for a good ten seconds, turning over what I'd said. He moved his head sideways a little. "Naw. Not now, Wally." And with that, he revved it up and roared away, leaving behind 30 feet of tire marks, a cloud of dust, and a couple of guys down the street covering their ears with their hands.

I watched him disappear over the little hill, the sound of his engine dimming. Well, it was worth a try, I thought. He didn't rule everything out. Maybe later he'd listen. I looked into the street and slowly bent over to pick up his cap.

Wait! He called me Wally. HE CALLED ME WALLY. I'd known Evan for nine months, and for the first time he didn't call me Wimp Pole. He called me Wally!

And although he was long gone, I shot my fist in the air, tossed his cap high, and yelled at the top of my lungs, "THANK YOU, EVAN TRANT!"

WEDNESDAY, MAY 18

Second day back at school, and it was a repeat of yesterday, except that I only answered the question about how I broke my foot about 45 times. Mom had a dental appointment and told me that she couldn't pick me up until a little after four. Lumpy offered me a ride home, but I told him the extra hour would be put to good use at the library, with finals coming in a couple of weeks.

When my last class was over, though, and the hallways empty, I didn't feel like heading for the library. Nor did I want to go down to the track and watch the team practice. On a whim, I headed to the west side of the building, near the park, where the marshy area was. Hadn't checked in with Chester for a while, and I wondered if he would still be there and if he'd remember me, although I realize it may sound weird to hope that a frog remembers you.

I limped over to the park and there was no sign of Chester. But I did see someone else, standing near the green, lush grass and shrubs near the marsh.

"Hello, Julie."

She was startled at the sound of my voice and quickly turned around.

"Wally! I didn't know you were here. How is your foot? I feel so bad about it. I feel like it was my fault. I couldn't even talk with you in English class. I've wanted to come to your house and see how you were doing, but I couldn't do it for some reason. I promise I would have been over soon, though."

"It's okay. It wasn't your fault. You know that I'm a klutz, especially when I'm around you. Maybe it's because I like you so much. It's like I try too hard or something."

I couldn't believe what was coming out of my mouth. Every little brain cell stopped working and looked at each other and started giving each other high fives and elbow bashes. "The kid finally said it," they all cheered. "Seventeen years with this guy, and he finally just blurts out what he's really feeling. *The man is in touch.* Maybe there is some hope."

I'd said it. After almost two years, I'd finally told Julie that I *liked* her.

She stared at me. She said nothing. I tried to read her face but couldn't. At least she wasn't laughing. She pushed her long brown hair back and then slightly rubbed her cheek. "I guess I knew that, Wally."

My foot hurt, my heart pounded, and my breath came in short, rapid bursts. My mouth went dry. I was feeling miserable and euphoric at the same time. Something seemed right and good, and at the same time it made me feel nauseous, which is what *like* does to you.

And I'm not making this up, it really happened at that very moment: from the marsh came a low, deep croak, "Whipple . . . Whipple . . . Whipple."

I could have kissed Chester. Boldness surged through my toothpick-like body.

"So, Julie, is there any chance, you know, that you could, well, ever like me? I guess I need to know."

There it was: my soul on the line. My life. My future. Children in the pre-existence were watching this moment on the big screen monitor.

"What she says will determine if they are our mom and dad," they say, all huddled around, dressed in white, their beautiful faces shining. "Oh, please, Sister Sloan, say the right thing! We want to be little Whipple babies! We want you for our mother and Brother Whipple for our father! We'll be great kids and always do our chores!"

Julie looked up, searching for the right words. It was a deep and profound moment for her too, I could tell. Her answer would be wise and wonderful, and I would remember it for all eternity. Yes, Julie. Say yes and I will be the happiest guy alive! I am ready to hear your answer. Speak!

She took a breath and looked at me, eye to eye. She hunched up her shoulders and held her hands out from her side a little. Then she opened her mouth, and I knew the next few words she spoke would be etched in my mind forever:

"I'm not sure, Wally. I don't really know."

Thud. Clunk. Sppffffttttt.

I didn't say anything for a full minute. I couldn't think of anything to say.

"You're not sure? You don't know?" I repeated, my voice hoarse and heavy.

"Yes. I don't know."

A revelation: when you are a guy, you expect girls *to know*. The way they hang around together, they way they talk, the way they walk, everything about them almost shouts, "We know, and you don't!" And they never give guys the answers because it is so much fun to watch us make fools of ourselves in front of them, trying to find out what they know. We are the primary source of entertainment in their lives. We are the mice, they are the cats. They toy with us. They tease us. They mess with our minds. They are in control. That's the way it is.

Or is it?

Julie had said, "I don't know." Twice. And if girls don't

know, and it's a cinch that guys don't know (I speak from firsthand experience), then who does know anything? Maybe adults don't know, either. What is this? My world is collapsing in front of me. Absurdity reigns!

"I don't know." The most powerful and cutting words ever spoken.

"Is that okay, Wally?"

"Yeah. Sure. Fine. I guess I hoped for, you know, a more definite answer."

"Sorry," she said.

"No problem," I said, trying hard to conceal the fact that my whole value system had been shaken to the core.

"Do you need a ride home?" she asked.

"No. My mom is coming for me."

"See you around then, Wally."

"Right. See you around, Julie."

And with that, me a more humble and wise man, I gimped, limped, and stumbled back in front of the school, where Mom was just pulling up in the Whipplemobile.

THURSDAY, MAY 19

I don't know. The words are haunting me. All the time, sweat, emotion, blood, and guts I put into my relationship with Julie, and she doesn't know if she likes me. I wish she'd just said no.

After dinner tonight, I hobbled out to the garage, where Dad was fiddling around at his workbench, dressed in slacks and a tie, working on a picture framing project before he split with the missionaries.

"How's it going, son? Back to Dr. Pratt tomorrow?"

"Yeah. Two o'clock. Then Mom is going to drop me off at the city meet. Guess I can still cheer on Orville and the other guys."

"You're handling all this with a lot of class, Wally."

"Trying to, Dad."

He pushed one corner of a frame into another, and they fit perfectly.

"Dad, how do you know?"

"You mean putting together the frame?"

"No. Not really. I mean, how do you know stuff? The important stuff. Like who you are, who you should marry, what's real, what isn't real, how to be a dad?"

He nudged another corner of the frame into place and put the picture in.

"Philosophical tonight, aren't we?"

"Guess so. Just tell me that parents know all that stuff."

"Well, Wally, that wouldn't be true. We don't. All we have is more experience."

"Then how do you get by? How do you figure things out?"

"Wally, I guess it's like this. Kids don't come with a set of instructions. Nobody can really prepare you for parenthood. All of life can be confusing and difficult."

"I was hoping for something a little more positive, Dad."

"There is a positive part. You know the difference between right and wrong. When you make decisions, make the right choice. Stick with the program, do the best you can, stay close to the Church, and be around good people who care for you, people you can learn from, and everything will work out fine."

"That's it, Dad? Stick with the program, do your best, and everything will work out?"

"Yes, Wally. It sounds simple. It *is* simple, in theory. You've got to keep doing it, though, and endure to the end. You've gotta believe, Wally."

He pushed the last side of the frame together and

turned the picture around. It was a photo we had taken of our family at Christmastime.

Chuck was in the front, dressed in his blue blazer and white shirt, a little red necktie draped from his collar. Mom was in a new white dress, sitting with Chuck in front of her. She looked so pretty. Natalie was in a cream-colored outfit, and she looked great—Evan's right, she is a babe. Dad stood next to Mom, wearing his old gray suit and a dark blue necktie, smiling, looking dignified and proud. And there I was in the back, in my camel-colored sport coat, white shirt, red and gold tie, towering over Dad and Mom. And you know what? I really did look ruggedly handsome.

"It's a nice picture, Dad."

"Yes, it is, Wally. It's our family."

And it felt great to realize that as I made my way through life, trying to stick with the program, that I'd have a family to help me every step of the way. That much I did know.

FRIDAY, MAY 20

I went to the city meet today. Orville, true-blue cowboy friend that he is, won the varsity shot put. Coach Leonard was elated. I was on top of the world, too, even though all I could do was hobble around the infield. The guy who won the high jump is a senior, and he cleared 6′8″. Don't know if I could have done better. Orville came over to me with his blue ribbon and pinned it on my shirt.

"You would've had one too if you hadn't busted up your foot. Next year, we'll both be struttin' around the barnyard like a couple of roosters."

"Count on it, Orv. It'll be way cool."

I got home a little after seven and was settling in with

an old Jimmy Stewart video when the doorbell rang. Mom came in and told me Edwina Purvis was at the door.

I limped into the living room where Ed was sitting on the couch. She looked different—must have been her hair. It was pulled back and off to the side.

"Your hair looks good, Ed," I said after we greeted each other.

"Thanks, Wally. I tried something different with it. How's the foot?"

"Better. Dr. Pratt said I don't need surgery, which is super-good news. A few more weeks and I should be back to doing anything I want to, except for cutting the lawn, I hope. Right now, I can't do too much, though."

"Can you dance?"

"I can't even dance when I have two good feet. You know that. Why are you asking?"

"Oh, I don't know." There was that phrase again. But she was smiling in a way that told me otherwise. "Guess that means you won't be going to the prom."

"Guess not. Never asked anyone, though."

"That's funny. I never asked anyone, either. And I never got asked. For the record."

"Yeah. For the record." We didn't say anything for a few seconds. Chuck came in, saw Ed, and immediately went over and started talking with her. Chuck thinks Ed is cool.

Come to think of it, so do I.

"Let's just say, for purposes of discussion," I began slowly after Chuck left, "that you knew someone with a cast on his left foot, and he didn't dance very well anyway, and the prom is only a week away, but suppose this guy asked you to the prom. And let's also just say that this guy didn't have lots of money, but he was willing to take you to a nice restaurant, nothing fancy, but better than Hamburger Bob's or Walt's Mexican World Buffet, to a place where the food is good and you need to leave a tip of more than a buck. If, let's say, you were personally aware of these circumstances, then I'd like to know what you'd think of this guy, and if you'd like to go with him or if you'd think he was too much of a dork to wait around so long before asking a pretty girl like you to the prom. What would you say?"

Ed pointed her chin up and giggled. "You know what I'd say? If by some strange coincidence all of that happened, I'd say I was pretty lucky. I'd say, 'Yes, I'd be honored to go to the prom under those circumstances.' Of course, I'm not sure I know anyone anything like the person you described."

"I think I know such a person, Ed. That would be me, Wally Whipple. Do you want to go to the prom with me?"

"I think it could be arranged. Wally, you are an original. We'll have a super time."

Just then, I heard the sound of high fives being exchanged from behind the kitchen door, and my Mom hissing, "Yes! He did it! Ed and Wally are going to the prom!"

Ah, my family. There is no other like it. And I'd have it no other way.

SATURDAY, MAY 21

I'm out of journal space again. Two years have gone by. Have I changed much since I started writing in my journal?

I think so. I hope so.

Will I change some more?

No doubt.

It's not always easy being Wally Whipple, just as I'm sure it's not always easy for anyone to be 17 years old. Slowly, I'm getting used to it, though. Maybe I'll have it down by the time I'm 18.

Eighteen! Let the adventure begin! My senior year. My life will be over. My life will be just beginning. How will my last year in high school turn out? I don't know.

But after talking with Dad, I guess it's okay not to know. I'll do what he told me to. Stick with the program, try to choose the right, stay close to the people who care about me. How can I fail?

Even Wally Whipple knows the answer to that.

I can't.